To Valerie

Merry _____, _____

All the best

Anita

FEEDERS

Anita E. Viljoen

Eloquent Books

Eloquent Books
An imprint of Strategic Book Group
P.O. Box 333
Durham CT 06422
www.StrategicBookGroup.com

ISBN 978-1-60911-754-2

Printed in the United States of America

Book Design: Linda W. Rigsbee

DEDICATION

I would like to dedicate this novel to my family and friends especially:

Martin, my loving husband; Brandon and Nicole my beautiful children – thank you for your patience and support.

To Marley and Joe, my parents being so far away – miss you.

Denise, my good friend that persuaded me to have this story published.

Love you all.

ONE

THE RAIN BEAT down onto the windscreen with such force; the wipers were working frantically to keep it clear enough for Anne to see where the road was. Pushing the speed limit a little to get home, she sat leaning forward into the steering wheel of her car with such intense concentration that every muscle in her body started to ache.

"I should have left earlier," she told herself through gritted teeth.

Just then, what she thought was a dog ran with incredible speed over the road. To avoid hitting it, Anne swerved and slammed on the brakes realizing too late, this was a mistake. The car spun out. Correcting the direction the car was taking and with pristine steering, Anne directed the car over branches of a fallen tree that lay on the side of the road. It was either over the tree and its branches or into a bog filled with muddy water. The tree would mean not getting stuck and having to get out into the rain, but unfortunately as the car sped over the branches, she heard one of the back tires burst — this meant she had to get out into the rain anyway.

"Shit, ahhhhhh shit," she shouted hitting the steering wheel with her fist. "Can't people look after their animals?" Grabbing her purse, she started muttering to herself looking for her cell phone. "Here I am on a dark deserted road" — finding her phone she flipped it open — "with no freaking cell coverage" she said throwing the phone back into the purse and back onto the passenger seat. Getting the flashlight out of the storage compartment between the seats, she realized she had to take a look at the damage and fix it herself.

Anne got out of the car, tucked up the hood of her rain jacket over her head as she slammed the car door closed and walked to take a look. She found the car's wheels made it over some branches but the left tire was flat. At least she knew where everything was to repair it, but she had never actually done this before, so it was going to be a challenge.

As she turned and walked toward the trunk of the car to get out the tire spanner, jack, and spare, she heard something moving in the forest, where the stupid dog had disappeared. Anne shone the flashlight toward the trees, squinting through the rain to see if she could find it, and whistled a calling sound hoping the dog might come out, but no such luck.

"Well, I hope you're as cold and miserable as I am, you stupid dog."

Putting the flashlight in her mouth to free both hands, she took out the spare tire and tools she needed. She walked back and knelt down inspecting the tire. As she started to put the jack in place, she felt an ice-cold hand grip her neck and an arm grab her around her waist, squeezing her so tight the air in her lungs was forced out. Then she heard the scariest growl in her left ear. It lifted her up and held her at least a foot off the ground, taking her into the forest.

Anne's body froze; she could not move, scream or think. Everything seized as she felt its cold breath against her skin. Anne closed her eyes as a sharp pain jabbed her in the side of her throat. She had no air left in her lungs to gasp. All she could feel was her heart beating erratically in her chest and her blood leaving her body. Yet she was conscious; everything was happening in slow motion. She felt her warm blood run down from her throat over her cold skin down her breast and stomach, feeling her shirt sticking to her. It kept making a sucking noise that made her skin crawl, the hair on her head rise and her body quiver. Why was she not dying — why was she feeling all this? The pain was not unbearable; it was like someone taking blood from her but the needle was thicker and the draw was stronger. She could feel every ounce of blood leaving her from the wounds this thing had made. Then it stopped; it started licking her. It smelled sweet, a unique sweet smell that she knew she would never forget. It still held her but less tightly and the air finally was allowed to re-enter the lungs. With a deep breath, Anne tilted her head very slightly to take a look at what attacked her – it was not a dog.

It was human, but all she could see was its eyes glowing red, its face gaunt; it looked starved with its cheekbones white against its grey skin. Anne could not make out its features. All she could see was blood dripping from its mouth, her blood. It tilted its head and looked back at Anne with a satisfied but confusing look in its grey face. It suddenly looked around as if something startled it. It threw Anne backwards through the air, arms and legs folded forward like a rag doll. She slammed into the side of her car, the door crushing it like a pop tin under a fist. Her head snapped back and the pain ricocheted through her skull; she heard things in her crack and snap. She was not sure how but landed face up in between the tree branches. Anne lay there still, unable to move, sensing the creature was gone.

The rain stopped. The air around her seemed warm; then again she was ice cold, realizing she had no blood to warm her up. Her breathing was shallow; her ribs hurt terribly as she did. With her head throbbing, she tried to assess the damages to her body. For one, she knew her leg and a few ribs must be broken. Anne thought she must be running on pure adrenalin, keeping her alive, instead of blood running through her veins.

All was quiet around her, and then she heard it — a car. Closing her eyes she prayed someone would see her car and come and investigate. She had not put her hazard lights on, so the chances that the driver of the other vehicle would stop were doubtful. They would think it's just an abandoned vehicle on the side of the road. Anne then realized she was behind the car away from the road and it was unlikely for someone to actually see her lying there. Panic set in.

Slowly everything started to fade; the cold, the pain and the car drifted into the distance. It must have driven past.

COMING DOWN THE dark road, they spotted a white on red, Shelby GT 500. It had driven over a large tree lying on the side of the road and was tangled up in its branches.

"Nice wheels. Do you think the driver got some help?" Roman speculated with a worried look on his face.

"Well, I hope so, with that bloody rogue running around killing whatever it lays its hands on." Luc leaned forward. "Stop the car; we should take a look."

"What? We're hot on its trail. If we stop now, it may get further ahead of us." Roman was not going to jeopardize a week's work getting closer to that monster just to investigate a car abandoned on the side of the road.

"Stop the car!! Something's not quite right here," Luc insisted.

Roman looked over to his friend, shaking his head in disapproval. "Your curiosity is getting in the way of our tracking," Roman said sarcastically.

"Roman, it's been here," said Luc, noticing a fresh trail into the forest.

"What?"

"Look closely behind the car. I'm sure you'll smell it once you stop and get out."

Slamming on the brakes, their car skidded to a stop just behind the Shelby. Doors opening simultaneously, both men climbed out. Roman, closing his eyes, sniffed the air and true enough, he smelled the scent; the rogue was here. Luc walked toward the Shelby. Spotting the flat tire, he knelt down to inspect the damage. He found the jack put in place but not raised and a flashlight lying next to a wheel spanner. Looking down the side of the vehicle, he noticed a large dent in the front door. Standing up again changing his attention to the forest behind him, he moved to where he noticed some of the bushes leading into the trees were damaged and disturbed. Roman, walking toward Luc, spotted a human lying awkwardly in some tree branches; the body was facing up and with its leg twisted the wrong way indicating it was broken. He walked closer and noticed it was a woman dressed in a black raincoat and black leather pants, so it would have been very difficult for Luc to have seen her. Roman, who had night and thermal vision, could see very little heat coming from her body, which meant the rogue must have fed on her very recently.

Roman leaped over some large branches and debris to take a closer look at the rogue's latest victim. Damn, she was beautiful, he thought. She was petite, about five feet tall, with fine features. He could not make out her hairstyle or color, as her raincoat hooded it. Her body temperature was showing a violet glow, but as Roman got closer to her, he noticed her heart and inner core of her body had a yellow to orange glow. "Impossible." Just as his words were spoken, Anne opened her eyes.

With a growl, Roman leapt a few feet back, landing in a crouching position hissing in the direction of the woman, startling Luc.

"What the hell?" Luc tried to focus on what Roman was staring at. "What is it?" Luc cautiously walked toward the black thing lying in between the branches. The closer he got, the better he could make it out. It was a body — a young man — no, a woman. Hastening his pace, breaking branches trying to get to her, he heard Roman say: "She's alive." Luc stopped and turned to face Roman. "What?"

"She's alive. I don't know how — she lost a lot of blood — but she opened her eyes," Roman said stunned.

Luc bent down over the broken body of the woman and looked into her eyes. Sure enough, there was life there, not focusing, but alive.

"Roman, phone Doc and let him know what we have here. Shit, I can't see as well as you; get back here."

"No," Roman said nervously, "too much blood."

"Roman, damn it, then get Doc on the phone and get that flashlight, the one by the back tire of the vehicle," Luc pointed.

Roman, with one hand phoning Dr. Ian Anderson, picked up the flashlight with the other and threw it toward Luc, hitting him in the gut. "Thanks," Luc grunted sarcastically.

Turning it on and shining it over the woman's body, he noticed she had a broken leg. He moved her raincoat aside and found her formerly white shirt was soaked in blood. Lifting her shirt to see where the blood was coming from, he noticed a broken rib jutting out of her skin, which only explained some of the blood. He gently put his hand over her heart and her blood soaked bra. He sensed she was trying her best to stay alive.

Anne, feeling the heat under her left breast, tried to focus. Seeing a large man leaning over her, she tried to say something or move, but nothing happened. All she could do was look at him and hear him shout something to someone.

God, Anne's mind was racing, *he was handsome.* She also smelled a strong scent of leather and spice on him. He was close, very close to her; she felt safe with him there. Why did she? She didn't know this man and what was he doing with his hand so close to her breast? She felt her skin tingle where he touched. "Goodness, have I died and gone to heaven," she managed to whisper.

Luc's face was inches from hers and he was able to hear her try to say something. "Roman, get over here now." Luc jerked back a little to focus on the woman's face. She was fragile and in a very unstable condition. He hadn't seen so much blood coming from one person before, yet she was looking at him and trying to say something. "Ro-maaaaaan." Luc was now getting anxious.

"What?" Roman grunted standing right next to Luc now.

"We need to get her help and fast. What does the doc suggest?" He looked up at Roman. "What do you see?"

Roman took a few seconds to study her. Talking into the cell phone and to Luc, Roman started doing a full scan of the woman's body injuries.

"Broken leg, cracked pelvis, two broken, five cracked ribs, a bite or what's left of a bite in the carotid artery and lacerations all over her body"

"What do you mean, what's left of a bite?" Luc asked, moving the raincoat hood off the woman's head to check with the flashlight.

As he did so, he saw the raw bite marks in her neck "It looks like it's healing, but how?" he asked, looking up at Roman.

"It must have licked her clean to seal it," Roman said staring down at Luc as if he was in pain. Luc knew how much power it was taking Roman not to feed on her, too.

"Focus, Roman, what does Doc recommend we do?" Roman nodded and hearing Ian say something to Roman that must have been upsetting to him, Luc took the cell phone from him and asked, "Doc, what did you suggest we do?"

"Well, you can't move her, not until Roman gives her some of his blood to heal some or all of those injuries, and because of the circumstances being attacked by one of us. We can't take her to the hospital; it won't be safe and too many unanswered questions. Once her ribs are healed, get her to my place, quickly. She will be anemic and will go into shock, and due to no blood in her limbs, she may lose them, not to mention she may be hypothermic. Do you understand what I have just said?" Dr. Ian Anderson asked. Slowly Luc looked up to Roman and replied, "Yes, we understand," snapping the phone shut and handed it back to Roman.

Roman shook his head. "This is not good," he said bending down.

"I know, but we need to do this. I think she may be a *feeder*," Luc said putting his other hand on Roman's shoulder.

"Why do you think she's a feeder?" Roman looked surprised.

"Because look at what she's been through and she's still alive." Luc, looking back down, saw the woman looking right back at them in complete surrender, with no fear in her eyes. Luc noticed his hand was still on her heart and could feel a tingle under it.

"Roman, you need to do this before it's too late. She will die here if we don't get Doc to help her."

Roman looked back at Luc and then to the woman, shaking his head. "I know."

Anne, not comprehending the conversation completely, knew she was in trouble. Unless this Roman character was going to feed her something or she was a feeder — it made no damn sense — she would die.

Then all of a sudden Roman's facial features changed and with a gnarl, his eye teeth grew longer — like fangs — glistening white against his lower lip; he bit into his own wrist.

Anne's eyes grew larger and out of focus. She could not breathe; she was choking. *No, no what was going on, was she going mad?*

Roman bent over her and let a few drops of blood drip from his wrist into her mouth. Anne tried not to swallow. The taste of the blood was surprisingly good; it had a hint of metal but yet it had a little bit of sweetness to it. It also smelled like that thing that bit her, but not as strong and deadly.

The aroma of the blood filled her mouth; it nauseated her and she wanted to gag. She heard one of them say, "It will help you; swallow it. Come on, lady, it's not that bad." Luc gave her a reassuring smile.

Anne was not too sure of this — *it's blood for God sake*. Suddenly, she realized she'd gone to hell not heaven; Angels wouldn't have her drink blood, would they?

She tried to focus on the men bending over her. They both looked like angels, with their dark hair, one long and straight and the other wavy to his shoulders; one with light eyes and the other dark, though she could not make out the colors. The man feeding her blood had a beautiful voice. The man with his hand on her heart was rough and deep, similar to his features. He was a well built man, with a seductive smile.

Anne melted into his smile and swallowed. As she did so, she closed her eyes. With every swallow, Anne felt her ribs begin the painful process of knitting themselves back together. She started to shudder as her bones straightened and fused and torn flesh mended. The man who held her heart moved over her to hold her down. It was agony. It was a miracle, and after a minute, she drifted off into darkness again.

"Well, is it working?" Luc asked holding the woman down as she shook and jolted.

"Yes," Roman said licking his wound closed.

"We've got to get her out of here; can we move her yet?" Luc asked looking at the woman's leg.

Checking the woman's vitals, Roman said, "Yes, let me carry her."

"No, I've got her."

Looking at each other for awhile, Roman nodded and led the

way back to Luc's car. Roman opened the back door for Luc, then slipped into the driver's side, started the car, and waited for Luc to get the woman settled on his lap and took off as fast as he could to the Doc's house.

Back in the woods, the rogue watched them speed off and started running a safe distance behind them to see where they were taking its sustenance.

TWO

DR. IAN ANDERSON was a well-built man with blond hair, a square face, and cleft in his chin that made him look very distinguished. He waited for them on his front porch, pacing up and down like a caged animal, hearing his wife open the door behind him. "Damn it, Florence, where are they? If they don't get here soon, she may not make it."

Florence was a tall beautiful woman with shoulder-length dark brown hair and strong features. She came up to her husband, taking his hand. "Ian, have faith. Luc and Roman are very good at what they do and I'm sure if what you told me is true, she should be replenishing her own blood by now."

"Do you have everything ready?"

"Yes, everything is ready upstairs, as well as the tub. I left the jets running to keep the water warm."

"Thanks, great, here they come." Ian was down the stairs, before the car made its appearance in the driveway.

The house, with two-door garages on both sides of it, was at the end of a long U-shaped driveway on the end of a ten-acre property backing up to the Fraser River on the outskirts of Maple Ridge. Just as Luc's black Dodge Charger stopped, Ian had already opened the back door to help Luc get the woman out. "Oh my God, Florence, it's Anne," he said, recognizing her from the hospital. She was there earlier that evening helping out like she always did on Fridays.

Florence, not believing what her husband just said, came down to look for herself. Florence and Anne became acquainted while volunteering at the hospital a few days a week. They didn't become friends as much as Florence would have liked since Anne always kept to herself and didn't communicate with anyone except the patients in need of her services.

"Ian, she looks awful." Seeing the concern in his wife's face, he carried Anne up to the top floor bathroom where Florence had set up an operating table and medical supplies.

Florence looked at Luc and Roman. "Come in, we need to talk," she said. Nodding, they followed her into the house. It was a two-story dwelling with a large wrap-around deck. The first floor consisted of a large entrance hall accommodating a large staircase with wrought iron railings. To the right was a study and den and on the left a living room, dining room and kitchen to the back with a main floor powder room. Upstairs consisted of five bed-rooms, all with bathrooms, overlooking the river.

Walking into the den, both men took a seat on opposite sofas looking at each other. Florence came in with a bottle of whiskey for Luc and a metal canister for Roman and two glasses. "Help your-selves. I will be down in a few minutes. I need to see if Ian needs my help and then we will discuss what happened here," she said. Both men nodded again and within seconds, Florence was in the bathroom, finding Ian bending over Anne's leg; her pants had been cut off and lying on the floor. "What's her condition?" Florence asked.

"Not good. We need to work fast and get her warmed up. Help me get the rest of her clothes off."

"Sure." Florence grabbed the scissors and started cutting off her shirt, then her bra, all soaked with blood. Florence worked with blood many times but the smell still got her worked up. Looking at Ian, she hoped she would be strong enough. Ian looked up at Florence and asked: "Are you all right; can you do this?"

"Yes, I'm fine. I can't believe she's a feeder and has been under our noses all this time."

"Well, our history indicates only one or two feeders at a time, so having three is very unusual," Ian said taking a syringe and injected the contents directly into Anne's leg. "We need to get her warmed up; help me get her into the tub." Slowly, Ian picked Anne up under her arms and Florence supported her already healing leg; they slowly eased her into the warm water. "Rub her legs and I'll rub her arms to try to get the circulation through." Slowly they rubbed and slowly Anne starting feeling the warmth running through her body. She noticed the hand on her heart was gone. *Where did the hand go?* Anne opened her eyes and saw Dr. Anderson. *What was he doing here?* "Dr Anderson, is that you?" Anne asked as she tried to focus on his face.

"Yes, Anne, you are going to be all right now; we're here to help you."

"We?"

"Yes, Anne." Ian moved over to show her that Florence was there, too.

"Florence?" Anne started to cry. Then suddenly she screamed as the blood entered her constricted veins; it felt as if her legs were on fire. Florence came closer and bent over the tub and held Anne tightly. "Shhhh, it's over, you're safe now." As she tried to soothe Anne, the bathroom door burst open and Luc skidded in.

"Luc, get the hell out. She's not decent; get out," Florence shouted. Ian nudged Luc out but not before he saw Anne looking at him with tears in her eyes lying in blood-stained bathwater.

"Luc, she'll be fine. She's healing and a little emotional right now. Florence will take care of her. Go back downstairs and when we're ready, we'll join you and discuss what needs to be done." Ian closed the door.

Turning back to Anne, Ian explained, "That was Luc; he was one of the men who found you."

"I know — I recognize him; the other man, what's his name?"

"Roman," Florence replied.

"Oh. What is he?"

"Why?" Florence asked looking at her husband, knowing what was to come.

"He has fangs; he bit himself and fed me his blood. Do you think I may have hallucinated?"

"No. Anne, we have a lot of explaining to do, but not tonight. You need to rest and get some of your strength back." Ian started walking over with a towel. "Florence, help Anne get out of the bath and take a hot shower to wash the rest of the blood and mud off her skin and hair."

With help and shaky legs, Anne got out of the bath. Then Florence wrapped the towel around her.

"Ian, I think you can leave us now and get Luc something to eat. It's getting late and I'm sure they're anxious to find out how Anne is doing."

Understanding Florence's reason for him to leave, he passed the table picking up the bloody clothes and sheets and left the bathroom closing the door behind him.

Florence then helped Anne get into the shower, pointing out the shampoo, conditioner and body soap. She gave Anne some space. She emptied the bathtub, cleaned up the medical supplies and left the room to get Anne a bathrobe and one of her T-shirts. She gave Anne's panties a rinse and threw them in the upstairs drier, ready to wear once she was done showering.

Anne started to scream. Florence was back in the bathroom so fast, Anne's breath had not even returned to her lungs. "What's wrong?" Florence asked.

"There, it was that monster; it was watching me through that window," Anne pointed to the tall window across the room. Shaking, Anne could no longer stand. She sank down and sat naked on the cold floor. Florence took a clean towel, wrapped it around Anne helping her up and then led her out of the bathroom. "The men will take care of it," she said hearing the front door slam shut and lock.

IAN, ROMAN AND LUC heard the scream and heard what Anne told Florence she had seen. Roman was up and out before Luc could even register what was going on. "Luc — stay in the house and make sure the ladies are safe. Roman should be on the rogue's trail. I'll be outside checking the perimeter."

"Fine," Luc answered, still amazed how fast these guys could move and hear. He stood in the center of the entrance hall obeying his orders.

Meanwhile, Florence had Anne in the bedroom putting on the bathrobe and wrapped her up in a blanket to keep her warm.

"Are you ladies all right up there?" Luc asked leaning on the banister at the bottom of the stairs.

"Yes, Luc, thanks — just getting Anne dressed and settled in. Is everything taken care of down there?" Florence asked from the bedroom door.

"Roman and Ian should be back soon with news."

Luc knew Anne would be safe with Florence, so he didn't bother going up to check. Florence would not like Luc barging in on them again, like he did earlier. Florence gave him such a glaring look then, it was worse than being scolded. *If looks could kill,* he thought to himself with a shudder.

Ian was first to return, then Roman minutes later. Both nodded to each other to say all's clear. "*It's* getting better at this," Roman said.

"Better at what?" Luc asked.

"Not getting caught. I lost its scent a few miles from here; it used the river to do so." Roman looked disgusted with himself.

"It must have followed us here, but why?" just as Luc said that, they all realized why.

"It wants Anne, doesn't it?" Florence said as she came down the stairs. They all turned back to look at her. Ian walked toward his wife with concern in his eyes, "Yes, we think so; where's she now?"

"Sleeping, I gave her something to calm her down and rest," said Florence, feeling drained herself.

"You need nourishment, my love," Ian said.

Walking back into the den, Florence took the metal container she served to Roman earlier and pored some of the contents into a glass and took a large swallow. Luc, accustomed to their ways, still shivered with the fact that his friends needed blood to stay alive and he was their supplier. But now he may not be the only one. With that thought he asked, "Do you think Anne is a feeder, too?"

Ian, helping himself to a glass of nourishment, nodded. "We need to run some tests and as you know, we can't do them here."

"Additional to that, we'll have to explain this to Anne first and see if she is willing," Florence said, giving her opinion.

Roman and Luc sat back down on the opposite sofas looking at each other again, while Ian and Florence sat in their favorite chairs next to the fireplace, which was rarely used except when they had company — human company that is. "Wow, what a night," Luc sighed, rubbing his hands over his face.

"Would you like to stay the night, Luc? I have your favorite room ready for you if you want," Florence suggested with a twinkle in her eye. "That way you are here when Anne wakens tomorrow morning."

"Yeah, that would be fine. We have nothing to do until then anyway." With a stretch, Luc got up, said goodnight to his friends and started up the stairs.

"Oh, Luc," Florence whispered. "She may not be sleeping."

"How do you know that?"

Florence just touched her ear and smiled. "Get her to sleep; she needs it."

Luc quietly walked into his favorite bedroom and found Anne in "his" bed. He stopped as he heard her mumbling something. *Was she awake or talking in her sleep?* he wondered. Walking up to her, he put his hand on her forehead; it tingled again. It was hot and wet with perspiration, quite opposite to what she was earlier that evening. After a feeding, he, too, gets feverish and weak so he knew what it felt like.

Anne felt something on her forehead. It must be *his* hand. It had to be, as she felt the same tingle she felt on her heart earlier but it was cool this time. "Luc?" she whispered.

"Yes," he said, leaving his hand on her head. "You're burning up."

"Mmmm, your hand feels good," she said, leaning against it.

"Let me get a cold cloth to cool you down a bit more," Luc said as he left to find a cloth in the en-suite bathroom. When he ran it under the cold water squeezing out the extra water, he heard her moan. Returning to the bedroom, he noticed she kicked off the bedding, leaving her body open to cool down; all she had on was a tight T-shirt stretching over her breasts and silk underwear. Luc stood at the doorway feeling his heart pound faster against his chest, his emotions on a roller coaster and his manhood stirring. He had not felt like this for a long time, especially by just looking at a woman. This was not a good time to get close to her.

"Luc?" Anne moaned and turned onto her side with her back facing him. Luc, letting out a sigh of relief, walked toward her, sat down next to her and put the cold cloth on her forehead.

"What's going on with me? One minute I'm cold as ice, the next I'm burning up" she said sounding sleepy.

"You get some sleep and we'll explain everything to you in the morning. You've been through a lot this evening." Getting up, Luc felt her hand grab his arm. "Don't leave me — please." Anne looked at him from the corner of her eye, just seeing his silhouette. She started to turn over and reach for the bedside lamp. "Don't," Luc stopped her. "Turn over this way and I'll lie down next to you."

As she moved over, she rearranged the cloth on her head and felt Luc move onto the bed and lay behind her. She could tell he was facing up, ridged and tense.

"Relax," she said with a smile on her lips. "I'm not as scary as the thing outside."

Luc looked over to her. "You have no idea." He tried to relax his tense muscles. She started to turn around. "Don't," Luc said again quickly. "Don't turn around. I don't think that would be a good thing right now."

"Okay," Anne said too tired to argue. Now that he was there, she felt safe. It didn't take long for her to fall asleep again.

Luc felt her relax and her breathing became even. Listening to her got him to relax and drift off to sleep himself.

THREE

AS THE LIGHT filtered through the window, Luc woke up first and found Anne's head on his shoulder, her arm draped over his waist and her knee on his. It felt like it belonged there. She was a good fit and so comfortable, which was probably why he didn't wake up when she moved onto him. He wanted to lie there and feel the warmth of her body against him for a while longer. Feelings crept up that were stored deep inside and forgotten for centuries. "Damn, why now, why her?" He needed to create distance between them before it took hold of his heart. He could not risk getting hurt like that again, but his body had other ideas. He started to get painfully aroused and it got uncomfortable. He felt it best to take a cool shower before he compromised the situation.

Regretfully, Luc moved out from under her. Anne woke up and moaned but didn't open her eyes. The stress and strain from the night before left her muscles sore. So she just lay there, listening to Luc move around the room into the bathroom and get into the shower.

He was in for quite a while when Anne started to feel nauseous and wanted to throw up. She crunched into a fetal position hoping the feeling would pass, but now something was coming up and she needed to get into the bathroom quickly.

Just as Luc stepped out of the shower, Anne burst in aiming for the toilet and by the sound of things just made it.

"Oh, God," Anne said hoarsely, "that was yesterday's lunch." Leaning over the toilet bowl, she heaved again but nothing came up. Luc, tucking a towel around his waist, walked over to her and put one hand on her back and the other lifted her hair off her face.

"Thanks," she said. "Sorry to intrude." She was wondering if she could do without him touching her; it felt so good.

"No problem," he replied. "Do you think you'll need to throw up again?" Anne just managed to shake her head. Before she could move, Luc picked her up into his arms and carried her back to the bedroom. She leaned her head against his shoulder and wrapped her arms around his neck, not letting go when he gently put her down onto the bed. Looking into Luc's eyes, it was the first time Anne could see him in full daylight. *God, he was an angel!* He had a handsome but hard face, sea blue-to-green eyes, black wavy hair just touching his shoulders and golden skin covering pure muscle. He was a tall man, over six feet she guessed, with wide shoulders and a large muscular chest with fine hair trailing down to — *oh goodness*. Luc watched Anne study him and took his time doing the same. She had a pixy-shaped face with short auburn hair and he noticed red filtering through it as the sun hit it; her bangs were quite long, which she tucked behind her ear. Her eyes were emerald green in the center and gold on the edges, her skin pale, but he understood why. It seemed they were staring at each other for only a second when Florence knocked on the door and asked if everything was all right.

Clearing his throat, Luc took Anne's arms away from his neck, straightened up and moved over to open the door. "Morning,

Florence," he said, letting Florence enter. Luc moved to the bathroom to get a glass of water.

Florence had a duffle bag in her hands and put it down in front of the bed as she went to the far side and sat down next to Anne. "How're you feeling?"

"A bit shaky," she replied, not knowing if it was because she just got sick or wanting Luc so badly it scared her. Florence started to rub her back, which eased the nausea building up again.

Luc handed Florence the glass of water. "I better get dressed and maybe make some toast. It always helps to have something in the stomach."

"Thanks, Luc," Florence said giving the glass to Anne to rinse her mouth out.

"I wish I had my toothbrush."

"Well actually, Roman and I did a couple of things last night while you slept. Roman repaired the car tire and took it back to your place, while I packed a few things for you in your duffle bag. I felt you may need them while you're here."

"Oh — um — thanks, I guess," Anne said embarrassed. She knew her apartment was a mess; it was clean — thank goodness for her cleaning lady that comes in once a week to clean the apartment and the office she lived over. However, the bed was not made, dishes not washed and she knew the laundry was not done for weeks. "Sorry about the mess; you probably took forever to find things."

"Anne, it's all right. I got a few things done for you, while getting your stuff together. We were hoping you might stay with us for a few more days until you feel stronger. I'll get you some tea to go with that toast and have Luc bring it up to you."

Anne just nodded and closed her eyes, too weak to argue. Also, the fact that a stranger went through her stuff made her very uncomfortable.

She must have dozed off again, as she didn't hear the tray with tea and toast being laid down next to her on the bedside table.

Slowly, she propped some pillows behind her head and pulled herself up to be able to sit up a little. Once she smelled the toast, she knew she was hungry but taking it slowly, she took small bites and small sips of tea to avoid unsettling her stomach again.

As Anne was going through everything that had happened to her these last twelve hours, she started to feel the anger build up in her. She was bitten, blood drained, thrown away like used garbage, body broken and left for dead, fed blood, violated, mended again, nauseous, weak and dizzy.

To top it all, she now needed to pee. Gritting her teeth, she got up, steadied herself and slowly made her way to the bathroom. She saw her duffel bag that she used to go to the gym lying in front of the bed. She realized strangers had gone through her personal space; that was especially embarrassing and angered her even more. She kicked it a few times, which made her feel a little better but left her weaker. She dropped to the floor.

Sitting next to the bag with tears rolling down her cheeks, she started to go through the contents and noticed clothing had been washed and neatly packed. Finding her toiletry bag, she grabbed it and made her way to the bathroom to pee, shower and brush her teeth, twice, just to get the sour taste out of her mouth. She avoided looking at herself in the mirror — being close to death, she didn't want to see what she looked like — not yet anyway. She already had a weak stomach. Avoiding the mirror meant avoiding applying makeup and putting her hair in place; she just pulled her brush through it and hoped for the best.

She then got dressed into the first thing she found in the bag, which was clean underwear, a pair of jeans, a white T-shirt, socks and sneakers.

Feeling refreshed and a little steadier, she decided to find someone who would explain the last twenty-four hours to her.

Slowly making her way downstairs one step at a time, she heard

voices and smelled something cooking in the kitchen. She let her
nose lead the way. As she walked in, she found Luc at the stove
leaning over a stew; Florence, Ian and Roman were sitting at the
kitchen table with mugs in their hands. They all turned toward
her as she walked in.

"Good evening," they said together.

"How are you feeling?" Luc asked her warily, noticing the look
on her face.

"I've been better. I've never felt so scared and vulnerable in my
life. I wouldn't wish this on anyone," Anne replied weakly.

"Come, sit; would you like a cup of tea?" Florence asked getting
up and moving a chair out for her.

"Thanks." Anne sat down across from a man she thought must
be Roman. He had long black hair, dark skin and dark to golden
eyes. He had strong cheekbones in a rectangular face and his jaw
muscles flexed as he studied her. She had never seen such beauty
in a man before; his features drew her in. As Florence put the cup
of tea down in front of her, Anne realized she was staring and
blushed.

"Anne, this is Roman, and don't worry, most women — even
some men — have the same reaction," Ian laughed.

"Sorry, didn't mean to stare." Anne then looked down to his
wrist where he bit himself the night before. "Your wrist — may I
see it?"

Roman looked back at Anne, surprised. "Sure," he said, giving
her the wrong arm to inspect.

"No, the one you bit into," Anne asked nervously, hoping she
wouldn't find anything, that what she saw was her imagination
and everything that happened had been a bad nightmare.

Roman looked straight into her eyes, chilling her and gave her
the other arm. Anne took his arm, which felt cool and moved his
sweater up finding a healing bite mark. "Oh, no," she said as she
stood up to leave the room.

"Anne, sit!" Ian said sternly enough to stop Anne in her tracks. "We need to explain a few things to you. This is very important and you need to understand what's going on here."

Anne just stood there swaying a little. Luc came up to her and put his hand on the small of her back, supporting her. "Don't touch me," she snarled at him. Luc looked at her surprised; her words hit him harder than what he liked.

"I don't know if I want to know. I have a very bad feeling the more I know the less I have my freedom," she said glaring at them one at a time ending with Luc, seeing hurt in his eyes.

The rest of them were all expressionless, which scared her. "God, I'm right, but I have a feeling it's too late. I don't have a choice now, do I?" Anne started to tremble.

Ian shook his head and pushed the chair back for her to take a seat. "You will have to keep our secret but what we will be asking from you, we would appreciate your sincere consideration."

Anne looked toward the door and wondered if she'd make it out the front door. Then she looked back and saw Roman with a smile on his lips and eye's saying *no, you won't*. So with a sigh, she walked back to the chair, sat down with her hands on her lap and looked at Ian with apprehension.

"I think we should eat before we start," Luc suggested returning to stirring the stew he was making.

"I agree. Ian, let Luc and Anne eat first, and then we'll talk, back in the den, where we can relax a little," Florence said sensing the tension in the room.

"Fine," Ian replied and got up leaving them to it, followed by Roman and Florence.

"Aren't they eating?" Anne looked up noticing everyone gone except for Luc.

"No, they don't need to eat human food," Luc replied.

"What? What about Dr. Anderson and Florence?"

"No!"

"Aren't they human?"

"No!"

Surprised, Anne's mouth just hung open for a bit, and then she whispered, "What are they then?"

"You don't know?"

"Shhhh, no," she whispered again, looking out the doorway toward the den.

"Seriously, you have no clue what they are?" Luc asked in surprise.

"Seriously — no."

Luc looked at Anne not realizing that not everyone knew or believed there were such things as vampires. "They're vampires and you don't have to whisper — they can hear you."

Anne, putting her elbows on the table and her head in her hands, sat in silence. Summing up all she had seen that was strange about them, nothing came to mind except Roman feeding her his blood and not eating.

Luc dished out their stew, placed Anne's bowl in front of her and handed her a fork. Anne looked up at him, taking it. "Thanks. So you're not a vampire then?"

"No."

"Then what are you?"

"Human, like you."

"All right that part I get, but what is your role in all this?"

"Now that is something we need to explain to you as soon as we are done here."

Anne was really nervous about what she was going to find out about her new friends. Luc and Anne ate in silence, looking at each other every now and again, wondering what the other was thinking. Once they were done, Luc took the empty bowls and forks to rinse, then returned to the table and offered his hand to Anne. Taking it, he led her to the den.

Holding Luc's hand made it a little easier to confront what was coming next and touching him again made her heart race, too. She didn't let go when they sat down on the sofa across from Roman and beside them Ian and Florence sat on their chairs.

"All right, then," Ian said as he got up and crossed over to where Anne was sitting and sat on the coffee table to be level, eye to eye, with their knees touching slightly.

Anne's hand started to sweat and her heart started pounding against her chest.

Luc leaned over and whispered in her ear, "It's all right; nothing is going to happen to you."

"It's all right, Anne. Luc's right. Nothing is going to happen to you. We are not your enemy. We're the same people who helped you yesterday and we'll be the same people tomorrow, but the only difference is you now know what we are. Luc told you we are vampires and as you know, vampires need blood to survive."

Anne nodded and also realized Luc was right about their hearing.

Ian carried on, explaining, "We have been vampires for many centuries. In fact, Roman has been a vamp for one hundred and twenty-five years. Florence and I were turned three hundred and fifty years ago on a ship that brought us to Canada from England."

"When you say blood, will that be animal blood?" Anne asked nervously.

"Rarely, it's usually human blood," Ian answered with a smile. "But don't worry, we have a supplier," Ian looked at Luc. Anne followed his gaze and noticed Luc looking uncomfortable.

"Oh my God, you bite Luc for blood?" Anne said, startled.

"No, Anne it's not like that. Let's explain." Ian put his cool hand on hers, trying to reassure her.

"I'll start with what happened to you first before we get into what Luc does for us."

Anne leaned back on the sofa taking Luc's hand into both of

hers; he smiled at her, feeling the anxiety in her grip, but not seeing it in her face. Ian got up and started to pace the room as he prepared mental notes of all the information he received from Luc and Roman the night before in order to be correct in the details of what happened to Anne.

Clearing his throat, he said, "Roman and Luc have been after a rogue these last few days and were getting closer to finding it when they found your vehicle. When they stopped to investigate, Roman smelled the presence of the rogue and finding you made it evident it attacked to feed. It would have tried to drain you because newly turned vampires are normally very hungry. Who- ever turned this person didn't stick around to help it feed or adapt to its new circumstance. It would have appeared cold, with red eyes and grey skin, the skin and eyes change once it's fed and sated. The concern we have is that the rogue followed you here because it fed on you and knows you're not dead and seeing you in the bathroom confirmed it." Ian paused and looked at Anne.

She nodded at him confirming the details.

Ian continued, "Now this leads to me explaining our theory why you did *not* die." He paused again to see Anne's reaction.

"Carry on," Anne said calmly.

"Well as you know, Luc is our supplier. By supplier, we mean he provides us with his blood. There are very few of his kind around. Through the centuries, vampires that come upon them kept them locked up feeding directly from them at will. We have come a long way since then as many of these *Feeders* as we call them didn't live long; they would die either by becoming sick due to their living conditions, malnutrition or from anemia. Today our Feeders are given the choice and live — under the circumstances — a normal life."

Ian then returned to sit in front of Anne and looked into her eyes. "Now, under the circumstances of what you have been through, we think you are a Feeder, too."

Anne's eyes widened. "How did you come to that conclusion?" she asked.

"Well, as your body makes its own blood from bone marrow all the time replacing the old with new, yours does something even more miraculous and that is it makes more as you lose it. That way, your body will never drain completely. In most adults, only the marrow from certain bones produces blood — the spine, ribs, pelvis and some others — but your body produces from all your bones. Now what the rogue did was what they normally do, they drain their victims till they die, but in your case the rogue filled up before it could drain you."

"Oh!" was all Anne could say, her mind trying to process all the information Ian was giving her and dreading what was to come next.

Ian got up from the coffee table and sat next to Florence taking her hand in his.

"In order to confirm our suspicions of you being a Feeder, we need to run some tests but they cannot be done here," Ian said.

"Tests, what kind of tests?" Anne asked, concerned if there would be needles involved. She shivered; she hated needles.

"Under a controlled environment, we need to see how much blood we can drain from you without harming you," Ian replied.

"No way, you're draining me. Not again," Anne cried out. Panicking, she jumped up from the sofa and started for the stairs when Roman with one leap was over her and stopped her in her tracks. He was crouching as if to attack and snarling at her like an angry animal, and the same snarl came from behind her; she froze.

Luc shouted "Anne, do not move a muscle, please trust me; don't move."

Anne listened. Roman came up to her, his beautiful features disappeared, and all she could see was this creature's fangs as he leaned toward her. She felt nauseous again and swallowed hard to keep from getting sick.

Roman's face was inches from hers, his eyes pitch black, and he smelled like lavender. This she could handle but what he said next made her go cold as ice.

"I gave you my blood, so you are mine," he hissed through his teeth. He held her against him; his body was cold and hard.

"No, please," she whispered and clenched her fists as if this would ward him off.

"Let me talk to her alone and explain the procedures," Luc said.

"I just needed some time to think," Anne whispered, breathlessly. She could feel Roman relax his grip, and slowly, trying not to alarm Roman, Anne breathed in some air. She turned her head to look at Luc still sitting on the sofa but with Ian and Florence holding him down.

FOUR

SITTING IN THE passenger side of Luc's Charger, driving much too fast, one neighborhood melted into the next as Luc worked the engine, shifting gears through the stop-and-go traffic of the city. Once past the outskirts of Maple Ridge, Luc drove without taking his eyes off the road, for which Anne was grateful, with speeds reaching one hundred fifty kilometers an hour. Anne was as good as or even a better driver than a passenger. "Are you okay?" Luc asked.

"I seem to hear that question a lot lately," Anne looked over at him, "and you're always there one way or another making me feel safe."

They drove in silence on the open highway, Anne looking around and seeing nothing in the darkness asked "Where're we going?"

"To my cabin. It's going to take a while so you may as well sleep. You can do so in the back if you like," Luc said still not looking at her. She noticed his knuckles were white as he gripped the steering wheel, his face stern.

"No, I need to know what happened back there, so start explaining," Anne said.

"Anne, you are under no obligation to be a Feeder, but you will be held responsible for keeping what they are a secret or there will be serious consequences," Luc glanced over at her.

"Who will believe me anyway?" Anne asked, thinking her world as she knew it was now lost forever.

"Anne, not a word to anyone, anytime, anywhere — please — they will know."

"Okay, okay, but say that I will help, what will happen to me then?"

"You will be taken care of."

"How?"

"With anything you may need, especially your personal security."

"Like bodyguards?"

"Yes and no; they won't be seen around you but they will be watching."

"Is someone watching you right now?"

"Yes."

Anna looked out her window then swung around to look out the back window and saw no one following them.

Luc smiled, "Anne, not physically; they will be using GPS and tracking."

Obviously, this is the twenty first century she thought to herself.

"Why would you need security?" Anne asked.

"You could say I'm very precious to them; after all, I keep them from feeding off other humans," Luc answered.

"How many feeders are there?" Anne asked.

"At the moment just one — me."

"Just you — and how many vampires do you feed?"

"Many."

"How do you manage that?"

"The older the vampire, the less blood they need. I donate my blood every month; they use that plus blood from blood banks."

"That makes sense," Anne leaned back closing her eyes going through what Luc had just said.

Luc looked over to see why it had gone so quiet all of a sudden and noticed Anne's eyes closed as she relaxed against the leather seat. It didn't take her long to fall asleep.

As soon as Anne fell asleep, her nightmare began: She saw herself running. It was dark and raining, just like the evening she was attacked. The same creature was chasing her. She knew she could not out-run it. She was carrying something heavy; it started to cry. It was a child. Her heart pumped faster; she had to protect it. Then she saw Luc standing on the ridge, wind blowing through his hair. She had to get to him before the vampire got to her. She pushed herself to go faster but its hand grabbed her throat. She heard herself say it could feed on her but leave the child alone. The vampire let her go and before it could grab her again, Luc stepped in-between her and it. Then with brute force, he punched the vampire in its face, and with his hunting knife, which he carried with him all the time, slashed at its neck, decapitating it. Anne screamed.

"Anne, you're safe; you're dreaming. Anne wake up," she heard Luc's voice in the distance. She opened her eyes and found herself still in the passenger seat of the car, her door open and Luc standing over her, one hand on the door the other holding her duffel bag.

Her face was wet with perspiration her heart racing a hundred miles per hour.

"I had a nightmare," she said more to herself.

"Come on, we've arrived," was all Luc said as he started toward an A-frame cabin. She could not see much as it was very dark. The light from the moon and stars were blocked out by the trees that surrounded the area. Luc was already in the cabin putting lights on when Anne climbed out of the car, still a bit shaky.

Walking in, her jaw dropped when she saw the all-wood interior with its large windows on the one side reaching from the ground floor to the second level. The stone fireplace on the main floor was surrounded by a couple of leather sofas and chairs with window seats on either side of the fireplace; the view must be spectacular. On the opposite side of the cabin was the kitchen, dining room, a wooden staircase and two doors leading to what looked like an office and a washroom.

"This way," Luc interrupted Anne.

Luc walked up the staircase with Anne's bag and she followed, taking in every detail. The staircase reached a landing with two bedrooms and a bathroom in the middle. Luc lead her into the first bedroom just off the stairs and put her bag on a large four poster bed covered with a cream handmade quilt. "There's a bathroom next door. When you are settled, come down for something to eat." Turning, Luc left her and went back down.

Anne took out some toiletries and fresh clothes then walked into the bathroom. It had a vanity with a basin on the one side, a ball and claw bathtub at the end, a large shower and toilet on the other side of the room. It looked spacious and comfortable. She took one look at herself in the mirror. That was something she had not done since Friday morning before she left for work, which now felt like a decade ago. Her eyes had sunk leaving blue rings underneath them; she was pale as a ghost. What frightened her most was the two puncture marks on her neck. The scar was bruised and still a bit swollen. She wondered why her bones mended but the puncture marks where still visible.

She opened the tap to splash some cold water on her face; it refreshed her slightly. Eyeing the tub, she then decided to take a relaxing bath before the night of interrogation began.

She must have been in the bathroom forever. She dressed in a red, soft woolen sweater and black sweatpants. She put her worn clothes and toiletries back in her room and made her way down, smelling fresh roasted coffee and freshly baked muffins.

Luc had just taken the tray of muffins out of the oven. "No way, you cook and bake?" Anne asked, surprised.

"Yep," was all Luc said as he took the muffins out of the baking tray and laid them out to cool. "Go make yourself comfortable in front of the fire. I'll be out with the coffee."

Anne chose a sofa across from the fireplace, curled up on it and draped a throw, with a deer pattern on it, over her legs. She noted it started to rain again. Winter didn't seem to let go this year. It was May and should be warming up by now, she thought. It was not long when Luc arrived with a tray containing their coffee, a jug of milk, sugar and a plate of warm buttered muffins. He lay it down on the table between her sofa and the chair, which he now occupied.

Stretching over, Anne helped herself to the coffee and a muffin; she savored every sip and bite. Once she was done with her second muffin, Luc cleared his throat, getting her attention.

"It's getting late and before we retire for the night we need to clear up a few things."

Anne nodded. "Tell me more about Dr. Anderson, Florence and . . ." she paused and shivered, "Roman."

"They're my friends and part of a team trying to find more Feeders that may be out there," Luc started to explain, noticing the pause before Anne said Roman's name. "As you know, Ian is a doctor who has been working in different hospitals, doing research on various patients."

"Yes, I know he's doing a thesis on various human blood disorders," Anne acknowledged and now knew why.

Luc nodded. "Florence is the head of security. She enforces the vampire laws and makes sure they stick to them. She's also very good in martial arts and has taught me a lot. Roman is a tracker. He can track down anything and anyone. He works with Florence in keeping law and order."

"That is why you and Roman were out tracking the rogue, because it's threatening the vampire's secrecy, so to speak," Anne said.

"That's right. With the rogue's killing spree, the cops will start closing in on it and if it gets caught, the secret will no longer exist and a large vampire hunt will begin," Luc confirmed.

"I see, but what's your part in this team?" she asked.

"Well, once we suspect we have a Feeder, my part is to convince them to help out with donations," Luc answered.

"Blood donations?" Anne asked.

"Yes," Luc confirmed. "Blood has a very large role in their existence. I cannot feed all of them so many feed on humans but in small doses for them not to notice. It's like leaving them with a *love bite.* Some have suppliers in blood banks, black market and other organizations. That can get expensive and it's illegal."

"So how does it work? Is it like donating blood at a blood bank?"

"Yes, something very similar, but my deposit is much larger and leaves me weak for a couple of hours. It feels similar to what you went through these last twenty-four hours, but less severe." Luc looked over at Anne but as soon as she looked back he diverted his eyes to the fire. Something had not been the same since they were able to leave the Anderson's house. There was a very important question Anne wanted to ask but thought it best to hold back, until the subject came up. He had been tense and standoffish, which bothered Anne so much it surprisingly angered her.

"How does it get less severe?" Anne asked, doubting that it could.

"They supply me with their blood. It has many advantages to it."

"Like?"

"For one thing, it slows my aging down."

"What do you mean by that?" Anne looked surprised.

"Like a dog to human is seven to one, I age one year every nine, give or take."

"Oh my, now that's a dream come true. How old are you, really?"

"I look and feel thirty but I'm actually around eighty years old."

Anne gasped, looking at Luc more intensely and not seeing evidence of his true age asked, "That's major; what else does it do?"

"Well, it gives you strength, alerts your senses, and, as you know, it heals"

Bingo — the subject had arrived. "Like what Roman did for me. Now I'm his — what did he mean by that anyway?" Anne asked cautiously not to show the anger that was building up in her.

Luc didn't want to answer this question but for her to understand what was to happen to her, he had no choice. "Like I said, blood plays a large role in a vampire's life. If it is given to someone, that person is theirs; if it's given in return, they're united forever. Blood makes and brakes deals and it seals contracts."

Anne, shifting in her seat and feeling very hot all of a sudden, asked, "Let me get this straight. Although I didn't ask for it, Roman, by saving my life, gave me blood to heal and now he owns me?"

"Yes, you are his," Luc answered feeling uncomfortable, started to shift in his chair, too.

"Is there any way I can get out of this mess?" Anne asked hopefully.

Luc, seeing where she was going with this, answered truthfully. "Yes, but you need to plea your case to the vampire council. Like any contract or deal one makes even if it's one-sided, only the council can rule for or against it."

"You said all deals that are made and broken are in blood. To break this deal, will someone need to spill blood?" Anne realized the complication of the matter.

"I don't know. I've never been in this situation before." Luc looked worried. Anne was bright; even with his answer, she knew that would be probable.

Anne didn't like this one bit, which led to the last question. Deep down she knew the answer but wanted to hear it from him directly.

"Is that why you're avoiding me?"

"What do you mean avoiding you? I'm here with you now, aren't I?" Luc knew what she meant.

Getting very angry, Anne stood up. "You know exactly what I mean. You're ignoring me. Is it because I'm Roman's property now?"

Seeing the pain in her eyes, Luc had to say it. Although it tore into his soul, looking into the fire again, he answered regretfully, "Yes."

Anne turned and ran up the stairs two at a time into her room, slammed the door and threw herself onto the bed. Shaking with anger and tears running down her cheeks, she had lost control over her emotions; she sobbed until her tears ran out. It seemed like hours when she finally sat up and listened to the quietness of the cabin. Luc must have gone to bed. The asshole won't fight for her. Roman may be his friend but he's a vampire for God's sake. Trying to put everything into perspective, if he was not going to fight for her, she would have to do so herself. She didn't know how or why it happened so quickly, but she knew she was completely in love with Luc. She didn't even know his last name for goodness sake but that was the least of her concerns.

She got up and walked out of her room. Everything was dark, so she had to feel her way to his bedroom door.

Knocking lightly, she asked "Luc, may I come in?"

Sitting on the side of his bed staring into the darkness deep in thought, he heard Anne at his door. "No, I think it best not to. Go back to bed; we have a lot to do tomorrow," he replied.

"Luc, please, I need you," Anne whispered, as if Roman could hear her.

Luc's heart felt heavy. He felt himself sinking deeper with regret. "Anne, please leave; you don't know what you're saying."

"Yes, I do. I have never been with a man before, Luc, and I don't want a vampire to be my first kiss or my first … you know." She started to panic. She leaned her hands and forehead against the door, praying that he would surrender to her.

Luc got up and walked to the door, but instead of opening it, he leaned his hands and forehead against the other side of the closed door and said "Roman will know you have been taken by me; he will smell and taste me on you." Anne cringed at his words, instantly regretting her situation. Luc had to convince her to back away from him for her own good. "I don't think what you are asking is appropriate, Anne, and it's out of respect for you and him that I ask you to go back to bed." Luc heard Anne sigh and walk back to her room, closing her door. Luc turned and leaned his body against the door. With disappointment, he closed his eyes. It worked. Anne was back on her bed alone.

Anne could not sleep. She tossed and turned all night, and as soon as she saw the dawn break, she decided to get up and have a shower. Taking her toiletry bag and fresh clothes, she walked out of her bedroom and bumped into Luc at the bathroom door. It looked as though he didn't sleep much either. She went cold and felt the hollow pain run through her veins. Her eyes started tearing again as she looked into his cold and empty eyes. Luc was stunned to see her up so early and saw the pain in her eyes. Her tears started to well up in them and her chin was dimpling as she tried not to cry. "Anne I —" Luc started to apologize.

"Don't," Anne interrupted him, then turned into the bathroom and closed the door. All the blood started to drain from his face at the realization of the pain he caused her. It gripped tight around his chest making it hard to breathe, leaving him feeling numb. Is it too late, could he get rid of her? Maybe hurting her was the best. Was it selfish of him to do this to her? His own feelings on this surprised him. He decided he needed to put distance between them. Putting a plan together, he went downstairs to his office and phoned Ian.

When Anne came out of the bathroom, she found Luc had left. She knew that as soon as she saw his car was gone. Hoping he would soon return, she curled up in the sun on one of the window seats and out of complete exhaustion fell fast asleep.

FIVE

ANNE WOKE UP hearing a car's wheels ride over the gravel in front of the cabin. "He's back," she sighed with relief. She stretched out like a lazy cat; the sun had turned and was no longer shining through the tall windows, and she realized she was cold. Taking the throw with her, she draped it over her shoulders as she walked to the front door and opened it. Instead of Luc standing at the door, she looked straight into Roman's cold eyes.

She screamed and slammed the door back into Roman's face. She could hear him laugh as she ran up the stairs to her room. She ran to the furthest corner and curled up by tucking in her knees against her chest and rested her head on them. She then wrapped the throw over her and waited. Where was he — why did Luc leave her alone to fend for herself? It's not that she couldn't try, but he was the one who made her feel safe. She started to shiver. Just then the door opened. She heard someone walk toward her and she let out a sob.

"Anne?" Florence whispered.

"Florence," Anne gasped and threw the throw off her and ran

into Florence's arms.

"Come, Anne, we need to go." Florence's voice was warm and concerned. "Get your things together; I'll be downstairs," she said, letting go of Anne.

"I have everything in the bag ready to go," Anne murmured. "Where's Luc?" she asked as she lifted her duffle bag off the bed.

"Can't say; he phoned Ian asking us to come and get you. He had things to take care of and didn't want you to be left out here alone," Florence said gently.

"I need your help to undo this, Florence. I can't be Roman's!" Anne pleaded.

"Be Roman's — what do you mean by that?" Florence asked confused.

Just then, Roman came into the room. "Anne, I didn't mean any of this to happen."

"But —" Anne started, when Roman interrupted her.

"Let me finish. When I said you're mine, I mean you're mine to protect. I will never violate you in any way and I hope you will forgive me frightening you like I did back at the house. I didn't want you to go out there alone with the rogue still on the loose."

Realizing this was all a misunderstanding, Anne moved over to Roman looked into his now golden eyes, saw his sincerity in them. With relief, she wrapped her arms around his waist. "Thank you," she whispered, leaning her head against his chest.

Roman bent down and kissed the top of her head. "No problem," he replied smiling, taking Anne's duffel bag from her and left the room.

"Anne, wait. Before you go, I need you to tell me something," Florence said.

"What?"

"Tell me honestly; are you in love with Luc?"

Blushing, Anne looked down at her feet knowing she won't be able to hide the truth from Florence. "Yes, I think so. I know it's sudden but before you say anything, let me sort this out between us first."

"Sure," was all Florence said with a smile and walked out of the room.

In the car driving back into the city, Anne realized, sitting in the back of their black BMW SUV, how long the drive was. Florence was in the passenger seat and Roman driving, not as fast as Luc had. Anne's mind drifted back to the present and she asked, "What will happen to me now?"

Roman looked using the rear-view mirror and Florence turned slightly to look at Anne. "Well, that depends on what you have decided to do — help us or not."

Anne, looking down at her hands on her lap, murmured, "I'm not sure yet. I still have concerns about needles."

Florence laughed. "Is that the only reason you have doubts?"

"Pretty much," Anne replied sheepishly.

"You can't be serious," Roman laughed. "The fact that we will be draining you does not scare you, but the needle we may be using, does?"

Anne felt a little embarrassed at that. "Well, I was drained unprofessionally and survived, so that part I know I can handle. It was not pleasant but it's the unknown I'm afraid of, like the sticking and probing that will be done. I'm concerned about the long-term effect it will have on my body and so on."

"Did you not discuss this with Luc? Florence asked.

"Well, I didn't have my mind made up yet, so we covered other concerns I had, until *being Roman's* came up." Then Anne realized that Luc didn't know. "Roman, Luc doesn't know what you meant when you said I'm yours; he thought like I did, that you meant I was yours in every way — your property."

"Well, he is not wrong in thinking that, because that is generally the custom, but I was forced to give you my blood to save your life and nothing else," Roman replied.

Florence then muttered, "Luc has been given our blood on many occasions to heal and strengthen him."

"You failed to mention, to keep him around a bit longer, too," Anne murmured.

"Ah, he told you about that?" Florence asked.

Anne just nodded and was silent for the rest of the way to the Anderson's house, hoping to see Luc's car there, but when they finally arrived, the only vehicle on the drive was Roman's black BMW coupe. She sighed and wondered what was up with all the black vehicles and tinted windows. Did vampires not like color? Even the house was decorated in dark woods and dark rich fabrics.

Walking into the house, Anne could smell last night's stew hanging in the air and realized how hungry she was. Making her way into the kitchen, she headed straight to the fridge and found the leftover stew in a Tupperware container. Taking it out, she popped it into the microwave for a couple of minutes. Once ready, she dug into it as if it were her last meal. *Maybe it was,* she thought.

🦉

THE NEXT MORNING, Monday, Anne called her office and told Jen her receptionist that she would be taking a couple of weeks off and to reschedule her clients to a later date or with another therapist. "What's wrong — are you okay?" Jen asked worryingly as she knew Anne never took time off, not even when she was sick.

"I'm fine, just finally taking your advice and taking some time off. My work load has quieted down so it's best I do it now." Anne tried to sound reassuring. "If you need me urgently, you can phone me on my cell."

"So explain what happened to your car," Jen asked, referring to Anne's Shelby that Roman parked at the back of her office/apartment.

"Deer ran into it on Friday night, which reminds me, could you have Joe pick it up and have it repaired?"

"Sure." Jen didn't sound convinced but let it go and warned Anne if she didn't call in every now and again, she would send out a search party.

Putting down the phone, she blew out some air. Looking up, she saw Roman leaning against the office door frame. "All set and ready to go?" he asked in his smooth voice. He had the kind of voice that made you listen, whereas Luc's was deep but soothing.

"Yes, I think so," Anne said nervously.

They were on the go again, this time only Florence and Anne were to fly over to a private island in the Gulf, south of Vancouver Island. This was where Anne was to undergo some tests and have her blood drained for the second time in seventy-two hours. She was a bundle of nerves and prayed for Luc to resurface. Florence knew where Luc was but he asked her not to disclose this information to Anne.

A couple of hours later, they were in a private helicopter flying over to the island. The pilot was African, his dark skin on a large frame with large black eyes, looked friendly — for a vampire. The place they were going to was on one of many private islands in the Gulf. As they approached, Anne saw what looked like a castle; it was majestic and looked old and worn. It had a large rectangular pool between it and the cliffs that sparkled as it reflected the sun.

The helicopter circled round one of the towers and leveled out to land on a beautiful manicured lawn. Stepping out onto the green grass, a wave of panic hit Anne. She started to hyperventilate, and her knees wanted to buckle. Florence grabbed her. "Breathe deep, slow breaths, Anne. Don't be scared. Ian and I will be with you all the way."

"I don't know if I can do this. Where's Luc?" Anne gasped. She desperately wanted him to hold her; even touching her would do the trick. She wanted to feel safe. The pain of being abandoned by him ran through her body; her muscles cramped. She passed out.

HEARING VOICES AND a rhythmic beep woke Anne. She was not sure where she was for one blissful second, but as she remembered, her heart started to beat faster and so did the beeping. She realized what it was when she opened her eyes: a heart monitor. She was lying in what looked like a hospital, with white drapes hanging on runners from the ceiling. She looked around; on her left was a heart monitor with wires running to her chest and a finger clip and an IV filled with liquid but not hooked up. *Oh shit, could they not have done that while I was unconscious?* she thought. Then to her right, she saw a blood filtering machine and to her relief an IV line was connected to her arm and her blood was being tapped into it. They had already started the procedure, so why was she not feeling queasy or dizzy? *Well that's a good sign,* she thought. The voices she heard were coming from behind one of the white drapes.

"Dr. Anderson, is that you?" Anne murmured.

Coming out from behind the curtain, Ian walked toward the heart monitor and started checking her blood pressure and other vitals..

"I see you're awake. I thought I would start the procedure while you where unconscious so that you wouldn't feel the needles. Was that okay?" Ian asked with an understanding smile.

"Yes, thanks for doing that; it made it easier," Anne said trying to reassure herself.

"You gave us quite a scare, passing out like that. How do you feel now?"

"Surprisingly well, I think," Anne smiled weakly.

Just as Anne was going to close her eyes again, Florence walked around the curtain with a man at her side; he was tall, dark to grey hair, gold eyes with an older yet perfect lean face.

"Anne, this is Sir Robert McKay, head of the council and owner of this establishment," Florence announced.

"I'm pleased to meet you," Anne acknowledged.

Standing next to Florence with his hands behind his back, he looked at Anne. "You have come a far way these last few days, from not knowing anything about us to helping us by becoming a Feeder," Sir Robert said approvingly. "Once the procedures are done and you are feeling well enough, we will need to talk and have a contract drawn up and signed. I trust you understand what you're doing here is very important to us and to show our appreciation, you will be rewarded by various means," he stated.

"As long as I don't have to sign in blood, I'm okay," Anne replied nervously.

"No, Miss Patterson, that won't be necessary." Sir Robert laughed.

Nodding to Florence and Ian, he said, "Carry on," Anne noticed how he seemed to drift out of the room. Also, the way he used her last name made her feel respected. He seemed more distinguished in his manner. She liked him, she decided.

Anne started to feel weak and tired. She felt Florence touching her hand. "You rest; we're nearly done," she said as Anne drifted off again.

ANNE WOKE UP feeling very warm, not ice-cold like she thought she would be, counting on the experience she had a few days ago. She was lying on something hard. She was naked and there was something over her eyes. She tried to open them but by doing so, all she saw was something bright surrounding her. Had she died and was now being transported toward the bright lights of heaven? No, it can't be. She moved her hand toward the object covering her eyes, knocking something hard a few inches above her. She traced it with her hand toward her face and took what felt like goggles off her eyes. What the hell — she was in a coffin of lights. She started to panic. Just then, the lid opened and Florence smiled down at her.

"Ah, you awake, feeling toasty?" Florence asked.

"Where am I?" Anne gasped.

"You're in a sun bed. The lights help you get warm and produce vitamin D to help you feel better. Luc found it helped him get over the cold feeling you have when you're replacing blood. It also speeds things up. Here, have some juice; it contains much-needed vitamins and minerals," Florence advised.

Anne sat up, taking the glass. She took deep swallows to drown the thirst; the juice tasted a bit funny – but she didn't think too much of it as everything good generally tasted bad. Anne noticed she was no longer in a hospital room but what looked like a spa on the one side and a gym on the other, with large windows looking over a pool and the sea, with automatic blinds now drawn down low. Looking around, she noticed a girl standing next to Florence.

"Anne, this is Meghan; she has been assigned to you," Florence stated.

"Assigned?" Anne asked, looking at the girl and noting she was maybe a few years younger than herself, same height but a little more filled out, black hair with purple highlights, brown eyes, piercings nearly all over her face and dressed in black, Goth-style clothing, holding a terrycloth robe for her.

"Yes, she is here to help you with anything you need and be at your service twenty-four hours, while you're here at the facility," Florence replied.

"I don't need a babysitter, Florence. I'm old enough to look after myself," Anne said angrily. The feeling came from nowhere. Maybe she was just in a bad mood, hormonal, or maybe she realized it was not Meghan she wanted to look after her but Luc.

As Florence wanted to say something, she saw the changes in Anne face. A look of anger melted into pain then moved over to a look of surprise and wonder.

Anne felt all sorts of feelings rushing over her. It started in the pit of her stomach; the tightening feeling disappeared. As her stomach relaxed, the muscles in her body started to relax, but she felt them getting stronger. She felt her senses were more in tune to her surroundings; her ears were picking up sounds she didn't notice before, like Meghan's heartbeat, breathing and Florence's airy silence. The room became brighter, and she saw dust particles dancing in the air, which she also felt against her skin. She smelled blood, berry juice, lavender, spices, and leather.

"Luc — he's here," Anne said surprisingly.

"How did she know that?" Meghan asked Florence.

Ignoring Meghan's question for a moment, Florence studied Anne's reaction to her new skills.

"He was here yesterday for his monthly feeding; he and Roman had to go back to the mainland immediately afterwards — a situation had come up," Florence explained.

"Yesterday, but I smell him close by." Anne stood up, looking around the room.

"He used the sun bed before he left," Florence said.

"Then why do I smell him so clearly all of a sudden? Did you not say you didn't know where he was?" Anne asked.

"Your senses are heightened because you have digested some vamp blood," Florence answered both Meghan's and part of Anne's question.

"Oh, how, when?" Anne asked with disgust on her face.

"The juice," Florence explained.

Anne got up, grabbed the robe from Meghan, put it on and walked over to the door.

"Where do you're think you're going?" Florence asked.

"To find my clothes and go home," Anne said, wondering where she would start looking for her clothing or how she was getting home — swim. Then she remembered: "Meghan, take me to where my clothes are, please," Anne demanded, turning around at the door and ignoring Florence.

Meghan looked up to Florence for approval.

"Take her to her room," she said to Meghan. "But Anne, unfortunately you will not be able to leave until Sir Robert has seen you and approves of it."

"So here it starts. I *am* a prisoner. Where is the 'normal life' you told me about?"

"Anne, you are being unreasonable and you know it." Florence started to get angry at Anne for the first time but probably not the last.

"Unreasonable. Florence, what I find unreasonable is the fact you go to my home and help yourself to my stuff, feed me blood — twice — without my knowledge or consent. Then there's Luc making me feel so safe, getting attached to him, then he disappears, not having the guts to look in on me or find out how I reacted to the tests," Anne shouted.

"Firstly, you were out of it both times, so I won't apologize for not getting your permission or doing what's best for you. Secondly, Luc doesn't know you're here," Florence yelled back.

"Hey, stop, that's enough," Meghan shouted to the two of them.

Just then, Ian walked in nearly bumping Anne off her feet.

"What the hell is going on in here?" Ian roared.

"Just a little misunderstanding, that's all," Meghan tried to explain.

Everyone stood in silence for a few minutes. Ian, assessing the situation, saw Anne flushed and panting with anger, Florence's jaw muscles tense, her fists clenched and Meghan just standing there chewing her gum.

"*You* take her to her room," he said to Meghan and Anne. "*You* come with me," he said looking angrily at Florence.

Ian stepped aside to let Meghan, taking Anne's hand, pass into the hallway.

SIX

MEGHAN LED ANNE through hallways, stairs and more hallways
to her room. Anne was grateful Meghan knew where she was
going.

Maybe it was a good thing Meghan was assigned to her twenty-
four hours as she may not find the bathroom or maybe a kitchen
when she got hungry.

They finally entered a room, which was known as her bedroom.
It was larger than her whole apartment. Against the left wall stood
a large king-size bed, surrounded by burgundy, heavy velvet
curtains tied back with gold cords; the side table, dressers, writing
desk and chair were mahogany as was the bed. There was a
fireplace on the far side of the room. Across from it stood a leather
sofa, and two gold and red embroidered wingback chairs were on
either side. On this side of the room, on the right wall was a large
window where the writing desk and chair were placed and just off
the same side were French doors leading out to what looked like
a small balcony, overlooking a cliff to the sea, all draped with the
same velvet curtaining. The doors were open and with Anne's new

senses, she could hear not only the crashing waves below, but the thousands of gulls that made the cliffs their home. She knew she would have to close the doors in order to sleep at night. Behind her were double doors and a single door a few meters down the same wall.

"I hope you don't mind but I unpacked your clothing into the dressers," Meghan said nervously remembering what Anne had said to Florence about her getting into her stuff.

"That's fine. I didn't realize I was going to stay long enough to have my clothing unpacked. Where is the bathroom?"

Meghan turned around and opened the double doors that led to what was the most wonderful bathroom Anne had ever seen. It was large with pure white tiles, gold trim and glass. It had a jet soaker tub large enough for two, an enormous shower with rain shower heads, not just one but two (according to Meghan also used as a steam shower), a double vanity with cascading water into large glass bowl basins. That's where Anne saw her toiletries all laid out neatly to use.

"Sir Robert also took the liberty to arrange a few evening gowns and accessories for you. He likes everyone dressed for dinner, which is at seven-thirty this evening," Meghan advised.

Anne turned looking at Meghan surprised and wondered why, since it was just herself and Meghan who ate food.

"Dinner, in evening gowns, where, why?" Anne asked confused.

"Okay, let me try to explain all this for you — one step at a time," Meghan concentrated, gaining a frown on her brow.

"There's dinner because we have to eat, and why is because Sir Robert is a stickler to tradition. Evening gowns are in the closet, as to where, they are over here," Meghan said as she walked to the single door next to the bathroom.

Opening the door, once again Anne's mouth hung open as if she had died and gone to heaven again. Not just one but a dozen or so gowns of silk, satin, and other fabrics she didn't recognize lined the one wall. On the opposite wall were shelves upon shelves of shoes, sandals, clutch bags, scarves and even hats. At the end of the closet was another dresser. Meghan walked toward it and punched a few numbers in a panel set on top of the dresser. It made a popping sound and then she opened the top drawer. It was lined with black velvet and on the velvet laid rows and rows of necklaces: diamonds, rubies, sapphires, emeralds, and the list went on, some solitaires, some not, some settings in gold, and others in white gold. They all looked beautiful, old, and very expensive.

"Are these real?" Anne asked.

"Are you kidding me — of course they're real," Meghan replied, shaking her head and smiling at her.

The second and third drawers had more necklaces, bracelets, rings and earrings, some as sets and some as individual pieces.

Meghan closed the drawers and the dresser made another popping sound; she then turned around and walked out of the dressing room. Anne was still in awe and could not move for a few more seconds.

Anne walked out of the room and closed the door behind her. "Would you like a tour of the place?" Meghan asked.

"Could we, I mean are we allowed to walk around?" Anne asked. They had been summoned to the room by Ian so the thought of leaving the room excited her.

"Why not? As long as we stay away from the council rooms, which are on the other side of the Manor," Megan indicated.

"Why call it a Manor if it looks like a castle?" Anne asked.

"Don't ask me; it's what everyone else calls it, so . . ." Meghan shrugged.

"Are there horses?" Anne asked excitedly feeling like a little girl. Anne had so much energy she didn't know how to release it. She could do a ten-mile run and not feel tired right now.

"Sure," Meghan replied opening the bedroom door and walking back into the hallway followed by Anne.

It took them all afternoon to tour their half of the Manor. Meghan showed Anne Luc's room, which was next door to hers. It looked similar to hers but different coloring and wood furnishings. It also still smelled like him, which surprisingly aroused her. Anne had to get out before she embarrassed herself. Back in the hallway, Meghan pointed out her room as they passed it. It was situated closest to the stairs.

Meghan showed her around the lower levels. On the level below theirs were bedrooms — ten in total on this side alone. On the main floor, she was shown a very large library, various sitting rooms, a ballroom, and the spa room where the tanning bed and gym were. A dining room and a den were also found on the main floor. Anne asked where the medical center was, but that was on the other side of the Manor where they were not allowed to be — on their own that is.

That side also had all the vampires' rooms, fully equipped with whatever vampires needed. The kitchen and staff quarters were at the back tucked away from the rest of the Manor.

They toured the gardens and then came to the pool. It was large and rectangular, filled with cool blue water. It looked beautiful just like the rest of the place. The stables, where the horses were kept, were quite a way from the Manor. The helicopter pad and rolling manicured lawns stretched between the two buildings. The horses were a combination of thoroughbreds, quarter horses and Arabians, all majestic and well looked after.

Anne turned to look back at the Manor; it was three stories high, with a stone face, tiled roof and two towers on either side, virtually built right on a cliff, set back by a magnificent infinity pool overlooking the ocean. Looking at the Manor from this angle, she understood why they called it a Manor because it didn't look like a castle at all.

This was going to be the place she would be returning to every month feeding her blood to vampires, keeping them from feeding on innocent men, women and children. This thought gave her the chills. While deep in thought, Meghan approached Anne and watched her studying the Manor.

"Beautiful, isn't it?" Meghan asked.

"Yes, it is," Anne replied looking at Meghan. "Why are you here?"

"I live here."

"Live here, as a human, but you're not a Feeder?"

"Oh, no. I'm not a Feeder. I'm family."

"Family to whom?"

"Sir Robert is my great-great-great- — you get the picture — grandfather. I'm Meghan Gabriella McKay."

"Well, pleased to meet you, Meghan Gabriella McKay." Anne smiled.

"We need to get back. Dinner will be in a couple of hours," Meghan advised.

"Great," Anne said feeling hungry and excited to get into one of those beautiful dresses.

Getting back to her room, Meghan asked if Anne wanted to shower or bathe. The bath looked like a real treat after a long day so Meghan ran her water and left Anne to bathe. After a long soak with the jets giving her muscles sheer delight, Anne regrettably climbed out when her skin started to prune. She toweled dry, put on some underwear and walked into the closet and looked through the dresses. Just then she heard Meghan walk into the room. "I'm in here, Meghan," Anne hollered.

SEVEN

"IT'S NOT MEGHAN," Luc called back.

Anne dropped the dress she decided to try on and her heart began to beat uncontrollably fast. With shaking knees, she slowly walked out of the dressing room and saw Luc standing just in the doorway. He wore black pants that accentuated his muscular thighs, a white silk shirt buttoned low enough to see his chest and black, silver toed boots. She could clearly see tension in the angles of his body and strain in the lines of his face, around the mouth and eyes. He looked mean and even seemed a little pale beneath the exotic golden skin. Luc, seeing Anne just wearing a black lace bra and panties, closed in on her. He didn't stop until Anne could feel the heat coming off his large frame. She had to tilt her head back to look up at him and when she did, she was taken aback by his glittering sea blue-green eyes and the sexy curve of his mouth, with that full lower lip, and the upper one that smacked of self control and perhaps a little bit of cruelty, making her wonder what it would be like to.—

"What you doing here?" he interrupted her thoughts.

"What do you mean, what am I doing here?" Anne asked stunned.

"The question is simple and I'm not repeating myself," Luc said angrily.

Anne swallowed hard not to say something she would regret later. She had already done that back at the cabin and didn't want to do it again.

"Well? Woman, answer me," he demanded.

"Firstly, don't ever call me woman — I have a name — and secondly, you know very well what I'm doing here," she glared back at him.

Luc took her by the shoulders and pushed her against the wall, looking down at her. "I thought you decided not to help them," he said.

"What made you get that idea?" she asked, looking straight into his eyes that had now turned pure green with anger.

"You gave me that idea," Luc answered.

"Well, don't assume. It makes an *ass* out of *u* and *me*," Anne said.

"Cute," he said, spelling *assume* in his head as he stared down at her.

"Why are you so angry to see me here? Isn't it what you wanted me to do?" Anne asked confused by this whole argument.

Luc leaned his forehead down against hers and closed his eyes. "No," he answered truthfully.

"What," she pushed him away from her, not realizing her own strength. He stumbled back.

"Jesus, they gave you blood," he said realizing her strength was not her own.

"Not by choice," she spat back.

"That's one of the reasons I didn't want you to do this," Luc admitted. "Did they get you to sign a contract yet?" he asked anxiously.

"No."

"Well don't, not without me," he advised.

"Who died and made you the boss of me," Anne scoffed.

"If you value your future," Luc sneered.

"It's too late for that now, isn't it?" Anne shouted. "You could have warned me back at the cabin but no. Instead, you leave me alone out there."

"It's not too late and you do as I say," Luc warned.

"Ohhhh, I hate you," Anne went for the desk chair but as she threw it toward him, he had gone and it hit the closed door instead.

Meghan, hearing the loud crash down the hall coming from Anne's room, ran out into the hallway passing Luc a few feet from Anne's door.

"Evening, Meghan," Luc greeted her as she passed him.

"Evening, Luc," she greeted back and hastened toward Anne's room.

"Oh, Meghan, you may want to knock first before you go in, or she may throw something at you," Luc smiled.

Meghan nodded seeing a look of satisfaction on his face.

Luc would rather have Anne hate him than want him. That way, they both were safe from getting hurt.

Hearing Meghan knock at Anne's room door, Luc entered his bedroom and got straight into a cool shower.

Meghan announced herself at the door and slowly entered, only to find Anne kneeling on the floor, her face in her hands, sobbing. Carefully stepping over the pieces of wood that were once a chair, she made her way to Anne. Meghan laid a hand on Anne's shoulder. "What happened?" she asked.

"I hate him, the son-of-a-bitch," Anne sobbed.

Meghan remembered the look on Luc's face in the hallway, which seemed to say he completed a mission. So to say that he didn't mean it would not be the correct statement. All Meghan could do was change the subject.

"Anne, you need to get ready for dinner. Sir Robert will not be pleased if his guest of honor is late," Meghan said.

Sniffing, Anne got up, walked to the bathroom and splashed cold water on her face. Looking in the mirror, she saw her faced glowed and her hair shone. She never looked so healthy in her life — even with red eyes due to crying. She straightened up, shoulders back and thought to herself, *I'll show him.*

A half hour later, she and Meghan walked into the den opposite the dining room where everyone gathered for a drink before dinner.

Sir Robert McKay, Dr. Ian Anderson and his wife, Florence, Roman, Luc and a few new faces all looked at the two ladies as they come into the room. The men dressed in tuxedos and Florence was dressed in a beautiful, long, royal blue, strapless gown that fit her body like a glove then flared out at the knees with soft lace reaching the floor. Meghan had on a black cocktail dress with sleeves down to her wrists; it was short, her black boots with silver buckles came to her knees and she wore a black and silver studded choker resembling a dog collar around her neck. Anne wore a long red, spaghetti strap, silk dress, with a very low back. She had to take off her black bra and swap it with a stick-on one. After looking through all the jewelry, Anne decided on a fine gold chain with an emerald pendant on it. She was nervous to wear anything else.

Luc noted the back was low cut; he used very little imagination to envision her black lace panties she wore earlier that evening. As Anne walked toward them, the dress had a slit that opened up to her thigh. *God help me,* he thought turning around facing the window, not taking in the view but getting his breath back.

"My, oh, my, look at the pair of you," Sir Robert said. "Black and red, my two favorite colors."

Anne noticed Luc turning away, so she greeted everyone by name, purposely ignoring him. Sir Robert took Anne's arm at the elbow and introduced her to the other men in the room. She learned they are part of McKay's vampire council.

"This is Sire Mark Aldridge from Halifax. He has a family of roughly twenty seven. This is Sire Jonathan Wright, Ottawa, twenty one; Sire Kevin Coupler, Calgary, thirty; and newest member, Sire Raymond Pitout, Yellowknife, with a family of twelve." She nodded at each one. Sire Raymond Pitout had dark beady eyes, framed with thick dark eyebrows and thick curly dark brown to black hair. He seemed to be about a head taller than her. He had a glare that sent chills down her spine and she didn't like him one bit. The other members were friendly and charming. Hoping to remember their names, Anne made mental notes starting with Mark Aldridge, who was a thin tall man with a brown moustache, long side burns and short brown hair. He reminded her of Sherlock Holmes. Jonathan Wright looked like a short aristocrat with light brown hair, long face and goatee. Kevin Coupler was as blond as Dr. Anderson but his hair was much longer and curly. His appearance was a lot more rugged; he must have been a true cowboy in his day. She also realized they were called sires not sirs and made a note to ask why.

"Are these the only vampire families in Canada?" Anne asked Sir Robert.

"No, these gentlemen are part of this coven; there are numerous other covens in Canada and worldwide."

"How large is your family, Sir Robert?"

"I have thirty-seven," Sir Robert said proudly, then turned his attention to the members. Anne excused herself.

She walked toward Ian and Florence and accepted a glass of red wine from Roman. As he smiled at her, Anne thought he looked like a Roman gladiator.

When supper was announced, he offered his elbow, which Anne accepted, and led the way to the dining room. He pulled out a chair for her, which she accepted with a seductive smile.

The smile didn't escape Luc's attention as he looked at her with a lifted brow. Ian and Florence looked at each other, noticing the tension between Anne and Luc, but didn't say anything. Sir Robert was in his own world and was enjoying the company.

While Meghan, Luc and Anne ate a three course meal — a soup, an entrée and a dessert — which was delicious, the vampires all had "red wine." Anne wondered if it was late Old Luc and early Young Anne vintage, smiling to herself at the thought.

After supper, everyone went back to a large sitting room situated left of the dining room through the large entrance hall. It was a cozy room with a couple of large fireplaces accompanied by a few sitting areas. Double doors opened out to a slate balcony that overlooked the rose garden, pool and ocean. The moon was full and its rays shimmered over the ocean. Anne made her way through the doors onto the balcony; it was breathtaking. Roman joined her and offered Anne another glass of wine. Anne knew after this glass she was going to get very tipsy, so she took small, slow sips. Luc noticed Anne nursing her wine. He smiled, thinking that she knew her limits and had better control then some, as he looked over at a tipsy, giggling Meghan. Anne also heard Meghan giggle, turned and watched Meghan hanging over a vampire known as Raymond. Anne shivered at the sight and moved over to Meghan and took her glass of wine away from her. "I think you've had enough," Anne whispered in her ear.

"Noooooo," Meghan said as she leaned over a bit too far and nearly fell onto the vamp's lap. "Oops," Meghan agreed, "maybe you're right."

"I'll escort her to her room and see to it she makes it," Sire Raymond suggested.

Anne was not too sure about that — she had a bad feeling about him — but Ian thought it was a good idea so she backed off, eyeing Raymond suspiciously as he held Megan up leaving the room.

Florence came up to Anne, a little tense since their argument. "I'm sorry about this morning," she said giving Anne a little hug.

"I'm sorry, too, so let's forget it happened," Anne murmured.

"Great." Flo seemed please.

"Why is Sir Robert a Sir and the rest are Sires?" Anne asked, changing the subject. She felt rather uncomfortable and wasn't big on apologies.

"Firstly, Sir Robert was knighted centuries ago and secondly, he no longer sires any new members. Whereas the other Council members are still siring, if you know what I mean – by request only that is," Florence replied. "What's going on with you and Luc?" she asked, still holding Anne's shoulders.

"Not much," Anne replied, feeling uncomfortable again.

Florence looked at her with concern. "Did something happen?"

"Just that he's an arrogant, male chauvinistic pig, who thinks he can order me around," Anne said angrily.

"You just had a fight." Florence looked slightly relieved as if to say: Oh, so that's all it was.

"Yes, just," Anne replied and walked back out to the balcony again for fresh air.

Florence let her go but nodded to Roman to keep her company. Florence noticed a couple of men in the council eyeing her all evening and didn't like it so she thought it best Anne had someone with her. She knew that Luc was not going to do it, so she decided to send Roman out.

Anne was standing facing the ocean with her arms straight on either side of her holding onto the railing, swaying back a forth a little. Luc watched as Roman was sent out to keep Anne company. He noticed Roman came up right behind Anne and stood barely touching her with his body. Putting one hand on her hip and passing her glass of wine with the other. Anne turned taking the glass of wine and feeling Roman's hand move across her stomach and ended on her other hip. He was very close to her and she could smell the lavender and feel his sweet breath on her skin. She closed her eyes and took it all in; the senses around her were magical. Opening her eyes, she looked at Roman, and then looked past him to Luc, then back to Roman again.

"You smell so good this evening, Roman," she murmured seductively.

"You smell good, too," Roman teased as he brought his nose to her throat.

She leaned her head back so that he could lean in a bit more. She felt his cold lips touch her skin, making it crawl. Tiny goose bumps appeared on her arms and her hairs stood up at the back of her neck.

"It's just a pity you're not the one I want," Anne whispered.

Who do you want?" Roman asked.

"Luc."

Stepping back, he sensed Luc behind him. "What you're doing is completely wrong," Roman said and disappeared.

Feeling the air move as Roman left, Anne smiled and looked straight into Luc's eyes. She turned around and looked back out to the ocean and the reflection of the full moon.

LATER THAT NIGHT, Luc was back in his room and for the second time that day took a cold shower. Leaning against the wall letting the water cascade over his tense body, he was thinking of a way to get Anne out of his head. "Good luck with that," he said to himself.

Stepping out, putting a towel around his hips, he walked onto the balcony to get some air. He stood there for a few minutes, taking in the sound of the waves below and the silence of the night. Anne also had a quick shower and getting into her T-shirt and panties that she always slept in, walked onto her balcony and leaning against the ledge, she watched the moonlight play on the ocean surface.

She suddenly sensed someone was looking at her. She straightened up and looked over toward Luc's balcony and sure enough, there he was with a towel wrapped around his waist staring back at her. They looked at each other for a long time, both with their own thoughts, neither of them wanted to move. Anne's nipples tightened and she felt her skin tingle. She would give anything to have him kiss her, touch her in places that were forbidden, take her into his arms, and make her his. She closed her eyes, holding that thought and when she opened them up again, he was gone and his light was off.

EIGHT

THE NEXT MORNING, Meghan made her way to Anne's room to see if she was awake and ready for breakfast. She knocked — no answer. Thinking she may be in the shower, she opened the door to find Anne still in bed.

"Wake up, you sleepy head," Meghan said walking to the side of the bed where Anne was lying and found her pillow wet with perspiration. She was dead pale. Touching Anne, she felt she was on fire.

"Oh my God," Meghan shouted, running out of Anne's room and down the hall, nearly bumping Luc off his feet.

"What's the hurry?" Luc asked.

"I've got to get Dr. Anderson. Anne's burning up," Meghan cried, dashing down the stairs two at a time, in such a panic she forgot she could have used the phone.

"Anne?" Luc ran to her room. He found her in bed; she was unconscious. He threw off the covers to find them soaking wet. Picking her up, one arm under her shoulders and the other under her knees, he took her to the bathroom. Leaning her weight against his chest, he opened the shower door and put both showers on cold. He took a deep breath. "This is going to be cold, Anne," he warned and stepped in under the running water. She moaned and held Luc close, trying to get away from the water that was cooling her down.

"Anne, stay with me — please — Anne, stay with me," he exclaimed with fear in his voice. He was starting to shake from the cold. His knees could not stand any longer and he sank down onto the floor, leaning against the shower's back wall. He sat cross-legged and placed Anne on his lap. Luc started rocking her and with his free hand, he touched her cheek, then her forehead, moving her hair to one side then back to her cheek. He could not stop looking and touching her face. She's so beautiful, young and innocent. He was nearly the same age of twenty-five when he became a Feeder.

Ian and Florence found Luc rocking Anne side to side in the cold shower. Luc looked as pale as Anne, even with the water running down his face. Florence could see his eyes were tearing up staring into Anne's face.

"Give her to me, Luc," Ian said, opening the shower doors and turning off the water. "Luc, come on; we need to take her to the medical center," Ian raised his voice a little.

"Luc!" Ian then shouted. Not having any more patience, he stepped into the shower, took Anne from Luc's grip and ran with vampire speed to the center.

Florence went over to Luc, touching his shoulder to get his attention. "Get into some dry clothes and meet me at the medical center," she said and turned to join her husband.

Luc, getting up very slowly, did what she asked.

A FEW MINUTES later, Luc knocked at the center's door. Florence came over to open it up for him. "Give me some answers," he said, not asking any questions but Florence knew what he wanted to know.

"The reason she has such a high fever is because we think the blood we gave her yesterday was tainted. Ian is working on getting the results as we speak," Florence explained.

"How the hell did the blood get infected, and with what?" Luc asked angrily.

"We don't know," Florence answered honestly, "but we will need to drain her again to rid her body of it," she said looking at Luc.

"No, that's too soon. This will be three times in five days; it will surely kill her," Luc yelled with concern.

"We have not been draining her completely, Luc. Monday, we only drew one-third of her blood for testing and to see how she would recover. Today, we'll need to draw more to clean her," Florence explained.

"How much will you need to take now?" Luc asked

"Just over two liters; the rest her body needs to take care of itself," Florence answered. "That way, she will create antibodies against the infected blood just like when you get vaccinated."

"May I see her?" Luc asked.

"We're still waiting for Ian to get back with the results, but when he does, you need to move out of here — do you understand?" Florence asked.

"Yes," Luc replied.

"Very well, then, follow me," Florence said leading the way to what looked like an ICU complete with a heart monitor, oxygen, IVs and other tubes and wires. They all were connected to Anne. It was overwhelming to see her like this.

Luc approached her bed with caution not to bump any machines. When he got to her side, he took her hot hand in his and kissed it. Leaving it close to his cheek, he closed his eyes.

"You get out of this, you hear me," Luc whispered in her ear. Just then, Ian came into the room. Luc nodded at Ian and walked out.

Ian could not identify what was in the vamp's blood so they decided to drain most of Anne's blood, which would be dangerous but necessary. They had little choice and in case they needed it, Ian asked Luc to stick around as he had the same blood type as Anne: AO negative.

Luc paced the halls while Anne lay in the medical center fighting for her life for a second time. This is why he didn't want to get involved with her; he could not stand losing someone he cared for — not again.

Florence monitored Anne with her infrared vision. She was white to red with heat and once the draining started, her body cooled down from red, to orange, to yellow, to green, to blue, to a dangerous indigo. When they reached that level, they stopped and for a while her level bordered indigo and purple. Slowly but surely, it came back up to orange and then red, where it stayed. It had been a terrifying experience for all of them but Anne was out of danger. Her heart beat was normal, her blood pressure started to rise and she started getting her color back.

Florence went out and found Luc in the hallway just outside the doors, sitting with his elbows on his knees and his face in his hands.

"Luc, Anne is out of danger but still unconscious. You can go see her now," Florence advised him.

"Thanks, Florence, but I don't think so," Luc murmured.

"Why not? What's going on with you and Anne?" Florence asked.

"Nothing, it's just like I want it," Luc replied.

"Luc, you're building that wall again and it's going to suffocate you." Florence paused looking at Luc with concern. "Luc, she cares for you just like I know how much you care for her," Florence stated.

"How do you know how much I care for her?" Luc asked angrily standing up, wanting to get away from this conversation.

"You cared for her the moment you found her a few nights ago. There was something in your eyes. Your behavior changed. You began protecting her," Florence said walking up to him. "You can't tell me that you are just going to walk away."

"It saves us from getting hurt. I have already lost someone I deeply cared about, Florence, and I don't want to go through that again," Luc murmured.

"I understand, Luc, but this is different and you know it."

"How's it different, Florence?"

"Well for one thing, she — I promised her I won't say anything, so you just have to trust me. She is worth every bit of pain you feel for her," Florence said and left him to think about what she said.

Luc didn't go see Anne, which disappointed Florence, so she made a point of being there for her when she regained consciousness.

It took a few days for Anne to feel 100 percent stronger. Ian didn't give her vamp blood to make her recover faster because he could not trust their stocks and needed to do more tests. When Anne regained consciousness, she found Florence holding her hand and Meghan was with her day and night, getting what she needed to help her get her strength back.

NINE

THAT SAME AFTERNOON, Anne was dismissed from the medical center and back in her own room. Sir Robert called a team meeting consisting of himself, Ian, Florence, Roman and Luc.

Sitting behind his large desk in his office, Sir Robert asked: "So what update do you have on Miss Patterson's situation, Ian?"

"She is out of danger and was released from the medical center this morning and in Meghan's care. We decided not to give her or Luc any more vamp blood until we have tested our stocks and suppliers," Ian replied.

"What was it that caused her to get sick so suddenly? She was fine at the dinner," Sir Robert asked.

"It's a bacterium, Sir, but I will need to send it out for identification. I have not come across this one before, but then again, it's not my expertise," Ian stated. "Another route we need to investigate is to find out if our blood has been intentionally tainted with this unknown bacterium."

Ian looked at Florence not believing someone would do that on purpose, but there was always a possibility.

"I'll investigate that possibility, Sir Robert," Florence said.

"To change my direction a bit, I noticed her blood type is the same as Luc's, which is rare. Do you think that AO negative blood groups may be Feeders?"

"That is a good point but, no, they just happened to be the same. Feeders in the past weren't AO negative," Ian replied.

Sir Robert nodded in acknowledgement. "Then third on my agenda is the rogue. What's the progress in apprehending it?" Sir Robert asked looking at Roman and Luc.

"Well, sir, we were hot on its trail until we came across Anne. It then followed us to the house, looking, we suspect, for her. I lost its scent as soon as it used the river and disappeared," Roman advised.

"And since then?" Sir Robert asked.

"It's been quiet as if it may have drowned that night. There have been no attacks or deaths of human or animals since then," Roman replied.

"May I also add that since it fed on Anne, it filled itself, so it will not need to feed for another day or two at the most," Luc added.

"Good point," Sir Robert stated. "Florence, I suggest you up the guard on Anne when she gets back to her daily routine, at least until this rogue has been caught."

"Yes, Sir." Florence looked at Luc. "I noted you said 'caught.' Does that mean you do not want us to destroy it?" Florence asked.

"No, I want to know who turned it. That vampire will need to be reminded of our laws. They are putting us all at risk and a serious consequence needs to be applied to this vampire," Robert said, annoyed with the past few days' run of events.

"As you know, the council is here because of this situation and they want answers," Sir Robert advised his team. "So get them."

"Yes, Sir," Florence replied.

"I just had a thought that may work. I want you to use Anne as bait to catch the rogue. As experience taught me, it knows how it felt when it fed on her so it may return for a second feeding," Sir Robert stated.

"Yes, Sir," Florence answered, watching Luc out the corner of her eye, hoping he would not react to this order. He didn't, to her relief, but she did see his fists curl and his jaw set.

Luc knew Sir Robert was a very powerful vampire and he does not like to be second-guessed. He had seen a vampire thrown across the room because he didn't agree with Sir Robert McKay. So Luc had to suck it up and shut up. He would talk to Florence later and find an alternative for Anne.

Then Sir Robert picked up the phone on the desk and asked Meghan to have Miss Patterson sent down to his office. Luc shifted uneasily in his chair. He knew what was to happen next for Anne. There was no turning back. Once she negotiated and signed the contract that was on his desk, she would belong to them.

"You're dismissed except for you, Luc. Miss Patterson may have some questions. She also asked you to be here with her when she signs, as her witness," Sir Robert advised. Luc nodded, realizing she wanted him there only to "witness" the contract.

A few minutes later, there was a knock at the door.

"Ah, Miss Patterson, I see you look a little better," Sir Robert said as he got up and walked around the desk to greet her. He took her hand and kissed it, and without letting go, he escorted her to the chair next to Luc. "Here, please sit," Sir Robert said.

Luc noticed she was getting a slight tan from the sun bed they used, but her eyes remained deep and had dark rings under them.

Anne's spine straightened when she saw Luc sitting there. She didn't look at him, as her heart was already racing and she realized her hands started to shake and sweat.

"Shall we get started?" Sir Robert asked going through some paperwork on his desk. "Firstly, do you have any questions or concerns to clear away before I go through these documents with you?"

Anne could not think of any at that moment and told him so.

"Great, here is your bank card; we set up an account for you so that our payments are directly deposited for you to draw at your leisure. After each donation, we will deposit the sum we agree upon into your account. No donation, no deposit understood?" Sir Robert asked.

"Of course, yes," Anne replied.

"Now the contract — I would like you to read it carefully. I will leave you to it. Should you have any questions, ask Luc here. I'll be back in a few minutes," Sir Robert said as he left the room.

Anne took the document and started reading, feeling Luc's eyes on her. She read the same sentence three times before she gave up and looked back at him. "What?" she asked angrily.

"What?" Luc asked back.

"Will you stop staring at me? You're making me nervous and I can't understand what I'm reading," Anne replied.

"It's very simple, really," Luc said.

"Really? Well, then explain it in layman's terms."

"It basically says once you start donating your blood to them, they dictate what is needed from you; in return you get financial support, security and vamp blood to keep you healthy and long lasting," Luc said sarcastically.

"Dictate what?" Anne asked.

"Ah, you caught that. You're not that naïve," Luc mocked.

"Fuck you," Anne growled and started reading the contact again. It took a lot of concentration but she got through it. It was basic and the dictation was understandable, for example, what foods not to eat, how to keep fit and make healthy choices, and what to do before and after donations. What stuck out the most was "don't do anything dangerous" but she figured she'll cross that path when she gets to it. The only part that still needed to be filled in was the deposit amount she would receive after donating her blood.

On cue, Sir Robert returned and asked if she understood the contract.

"Yes, just questioning the figure per blood donation," Anne stated.

"Ah, yes," Sir Robert agreed and wrote a figure on a piece of paper, folded it and gave it her.

Slowly Anne opened it and gasped, "Are you serious?"

She looked at Sir Robert then Luc; both just looked back at her.

"I trust that's sufficient?" Sir Robert asked, smiling at her.

"More than sufficient," Anne gleamed.

"So can I ask you to sign the bottom line and Luc, you to witness?" Sir Robert got up from his chair giving them a pen each.

Anne signed it, and then gave the document to Luc to sign. He paused to look at Anne; she looked back at him and urged him on with her eyes. With hesitation, he signed.

Sir Robert then took the document and neatly put it into a large white envelope, got up and walked to a door behind him. It was a large safe door He keyed in the code and opened the safe. It was as large as a walk-in closet, lined with drawers on either side. Putting the document in one drawer, he then opened another, taking out a shoebox size wooden box and brought it over to the desk.

Opening it, he took out two golden bracelets that looked rather heavy.

"I want you both to put these on and never — I mean never — take them off under any circumstances," Sir Robert said.

"What are they?" Anne asked putting hers on and realizing they weren't as heavy as she thought.

"They're there for your protection," was all Sir Robert said.

"Wh — ," Anne was going to ask what kind of protection, but Luc cleared his throat to say, don't ask. Taking the hint, Anne just smiled.

"And this." Sir Robert took out two little black boxes. They looked like electronic car immobilizers. "These are pagers. Should one of you need to get hold of the other, just click the button. They should work worlds apart," Sir Robert explained and demonstrated by pressing one of the buttons and the other vibrated and vice versa. He gave them each one.

"Well, now that's concluded, I think we can celebrate with a cocktail before dinner tonight," he winked at Anne. She smiled back at him as she got up and left the room with Luc close on her heels.

She moved across the hall as if she had a train to catch and was late. "What's your hurry?" Luc asked, taking two long strides to catch up to her and grabbed her wrist. Luc had strong hands and carried some kind of electrical charge because every time he touched her a tingle shot a thrill through her body. She stopped and stood there motionless for a while looking at his hand holding hers.

"I get it, Luc; I finally get it," Anne said shaking her arm loose from his grip.

"What do you get, Anne?" Luc asked scornfully.

"You don't want me here because you can't stand being near me anymore, not since I asked you to be my first," Anne replied.

"Yet, here we are, all signed and hooked up," looking at his wrist and lifting the pager. "Ready to go," Luc said angrily.

"People who feel things sometimes have weaknesses but you wouldn't know that, would you?" Anne said bitterly.

Luc stared down at her, his eyes cold. It made the hair on her arms and neck stand up. Not saying another word, he walked away.

TEN

THAT EVENING, ANNE chose a black dress. Its bodice had no back; the front consisted of two pieces of fabric that came from the waist, up, over her breasts and tied around her neck. It really accentuated her cleavage. The front of the dress flowed over her hips to her knees and the back to the floor. She wore it with high sexy sandals and the emerald pendent.

She walked into the same den as a few days before, where everyone stood with drinks in their hands. "Good evening, Miss Patterson," Sir Robert said pouring a wine for her, then walking over to hand it to her.

"Good evening, Sir Robert, but please call me Anne," she said quietly.

"Very well," he replied.

She looked around her and greeted everyone around the room. Meghan, again in a black creation, was with Raymond. Then there was Ian with Florence, like always. Roman with Luc discussing something quite serious and didn't take notice of Anne. Well, at least Luc made it appear that way, but he did see her come in and swallowed hard, trying to concentrate on what Roman was saying to him. Sir Robert went back to talking to the rest of the councilors.

They had supper, well at least the humans did, and the vampires again drank blood — this time Anne *did* ask whose. Luc nearly spat out his wine across the table when Anne asked.

"Yours of course, dear," Sir Robert answered with a smile.

"Oh, what's it like?" Anne asked with a smile and looked over to Luc who was going as white as a sheet.

"Anne, it's like a delicate wine, full of wholesomeness and good flavor," Sir Robert said and everyone except Luc started to laugh.

They returned to the large living room across the entrance hall. Anne made her way to the balcony to see the sunset; she noted that within a week the sun stayed up a little longer, the first sign of spring. She loved this time of day, when everything was settling down for the night to come. Birds sang their last song of the day and the air was warm and breezy. It was spectacular and she thought she would miss this when they returned to the mainland. She knew now that she will be back again next month and the month after that, till the end of her days, however long that may be. She held herself, not that she was getting cold just that she may be doing this on her own. She would never be able to fall in love, get married, or have children; a clause in the contract noted that, well at least the married and children part. It would be too complicated to try to explain her trips here and the risk of being drained and possible death. Not that Ian would let that happen, but accidents or errors can happen. She worked in hospitals, and care centers and knew mistakes are made.

Deep in thought, Anne didn't hear Meghan approach. She startled her and apologized. She gave Anne a refilled glass of lemon soda; she chose a clear drink to make sure no blood gets into it this time. Anne thanked her. Meghan then left Anne to go back to her thoughts. Instead, Anne drank her soda watching Luc standing with Roman again. They both had black pants on, Luc's was leather and Roman's looked like suede. Both men had white shirts not buttoned completely. Anne seriously thought of them as eye candy, looking good on the outside but a bit bitter on the inside. Finishing her soda, she decided to chat with Ian and Florence. They were in their little love's corner, and they abruptly stopped talking when Anne arrived. "I hope I didn't interrupt?" Anne asked.

"No, don't be silly," Florence said. "Sit, you look stunning again tonight, Anne."

"Thank you; so do you," Anne said touching the fabric to confirm Florence was wearing silk. As she sat down in a chair across from them, Anne asked, "So when do I get back home?"

"Well, Ian needs to get back tomorrow morning to run some tests on the blood that was tainted. The rest of us, probably the day after," Florence replied and said, "We'll need to discuss a couple of things, set up schedules and so on."

"Sure," Anne replied.

Anne started to feel rather strange. She knew she could not be drunk but felt a bit tipsy, which was very unlike her as she just had one glass of white wine before supper.

"Florence, I'm a little tired so I'm going up to bed, if you would excuse me?" Anne asked.

"You look a little pasty. Some rest will do you good," Florence noticed.

"Good Night," Anne murmured and nodded to Ian. She then stood up aiming for the door, not wanting anyone to notice as she slipped out of the room.

When she reached her room, her heart was pumping erratically as if she had run a marathon. It felt as if she had too much caffeine; her body started to tingle all over. Just wanting to go to bed and sleep, she threw her clutch bag onto the bed, slipped her dress off onto the floor where she stood, pulled off the stick-on bra and stepped out of the sandals. Shaking, she went to the bathroom to wash off her make-up and brush her teeth. She returned to the room and fell into bed with just her panties on, lying facing the ceiling and wishing this feeling would pass so that she could sleep. Her nipples started to harden; tiny electrical currents flowed down her back into her legs. It started to get hot and wet between her legs. Anne thought if she turned around the sensation would go away. She started to pulsate and had a strong need to touch herself. When she did, she came; her body climaxed violently without mercy. She bit hard onto her lip to prevent her from screaming out in ecstasy. As it eased, it started up again. This time it was getting worse. She needed more — she needed to be satisfied — but how? She needed Luc. She wanted him deep inside her now. "Luc, help me," Anne gasped to herself. Not getting up, she started to feel around the bed for her clutch bag. Finding it, she opened it and found the pager and pressed the button. Just as she did, she regretted it. The situation she found herself in was embarrassing to say the least, vulnerable again. Then lying as still as she possibly could, hoping the sensation would go away, she tried to breathe evenly, but nothing worked. It started to well up again as Luc ran into the room. "Luc, don't! Get out, lock the — Oh my God — door," Anne gasping for control and air.

"What's going on?" Luc asked in a panic. Moving over to the bed, he noticed she was perspiring and when he put his hand on her arm, he felt her skin cold and clammy. She gripped the comforter she was lying on in both fists; leaving her head on the bed, she arched her back. "Luc, help me!" she begged.

"What do you want me to do, what's wrong?" Luc asked.

"I need to come, help me come," she gasped.

"What?" Luc asked surprised backing away from her a little.

Anne had tears running down the side of her face and looked desperate, shaking and arching her back, needing release. There

wasn't time for pleasantries; she needed help now. "Shit, Luc —
help me?"

"You sure about this?" he asked as he leaned over her, putting
his one arm under her arched back. He hated seeing her like this,
the feeling of protecting her came to him once again.

"Now!" Anne shouted. Luc put his mouth on her neck, feeling
her pulse with his lips. Then slowly, he skimmed his hand over
her stomach, down under her panties to find her hot and very
wet. He gently separated the folds of her body to stroke her, and
then slipped his middle finger into her. On his way in, he found
a little barrier. "God, I'm sorry Anne," he said as he broke through
it. Her eyes flung open and she sucked her breath in sharply. Luc
held her tight against him but she didn't ease. She grabbed his
hand and pushed him deeper inside of her and flexed her hips to
get more of him.

"Luc – please I need you inside of me," Anne pleaded.

"No, not like this. Someone must have drugged you," Luc
concluded. His body strained, begging for him to take her but he
was better than that. He felt pain as his erection hardened against
his pants. He needed to release himself. He lay Anne down, taking
his arm out from under her and awkwardly unbuttoned and
unzipped his pants. He was wet with arousal, too; the pain
subsided a bit as soon as his pants were removed. "Anne, you need
to let go of my hand," Luc whispered in her ear. "I need to get you
into the shower."

As Anne opened her eyes to look at him, Luc noticed they were
dilated and pleading for relief. Why was this happening to her?
She let go. He then quickly and swiftly pulled off his shoes and
pants, ripped off his shirt and lifted her against him.

They once again were in the shower. She took his hand to her
again and as soon as his finger entered her, she came again. "God,
how was this possible?" Luc asked holding with the other arm.
"It's killing — me, Luc," Anne gasped and tried to suck air in

between convulsions. "I — need release. Aaaah," she cried. She was burning with desire and the need for him.

Luc took his finger out of her and put it in her mouth; it tasted salty and then she realized she needed to get this poison out of her stomach. Anne felt Luc's hardness against her stomach, so she slipped down him to kneel.

"What're you doing?" Luc asked not exactly stopping her as she put him into her mouth slowly, deeper and deeper, feeling him going down her throat, until he came.

Just then, on all fours, she got sick. All the liquid that was in her stomach washed down the drain. Luc knelt next to her and took her face in his hands and washed her mouth off. He then stood up lifting her back into his arms, turned off the shower, and grabbed a couple of towels on his way back to the bed. He lay her down and taking her panties off, he toweled her dry, then noticed she fell asleep; it was over. He then lay next to her, put her head on his shoulder and held her close.

"Anne, you certainly know how to get under my skin," Luc whispered against her head and kissed it. Lying naked next to her felt good, warm, and relaxed; he fell asleep, too.

ELEVEN

ANNE WOKE UP feeling Luc beside her. He was naked — very naked — and then found she was naked, too. Slowly the events of the night before started to come back to her. She felt her face glow hot and her heart beat faster the more embarrassed she got. She needed to get away from him, so she slowly got up and put a pillow where her body was. Not making any fast movements and trying hard not to make noise, Anne got off the bed, got some clothing out of the dresser, and went to the bathroom to wash up and change before Luc woke up.

Walking out of the bathroom, she realized he was still sleeping and stole a couple of minutes watching him. He looked so peaceful and vulnerable, which she knew he wasn't. The fine hairs did go all the way down to his goodness, and she remembered how big he was in her mouth. Glowing red again, she turned on her heels and left the room to find Meghan.

Meghan came to the door, answering Anne's knock, but only opened the door very slightly. "Why are you up so early? The friggin' birds aren't even up yet," Meghan asked trying to open her eyes.

"I need to get back home today," Anne whispered.

"Why? What's the rush?" Meghan asked.

"Don't ask; just get my stuff together and ready. I'm leaving with Dr Anderson," Anne said. About to leave, she remembered, "Oh and get hold of Florence and ask her to meet me in the den, please." Anne turned and walked down the stairs.

When Anne got to the den, Florence was already there talking to one of the staff.

"Ahh. Morning, Anne, what's your urgency in leaving with Ian this morning?" Florence asked suspiciously.

"Firstly, someone is trying to kill me, someone that's here and secondly, I need to get away from Luc," Anne said.

"What do you mean someone is trying to kill you? How did you come to that conclusion?" Florence asked.

"Well, first the blood contamination, then last night someone drugged my drink or food. Luc can explain that to you. I'm too embarrassed to even go there. Which leads to me getting away from Luc for a while," Anne said.

With a very confused look on her face, Florence crossed the room and took Anne by the hand and sat her down. "I ordered some coffee and toast for you," Florence said as the butler came in with a tray for Anne. "Who do you suspect drugged you?" Florence asked.

"I have no idea. All I had to drink last night was a glass of wine Sir Robert poured and the lemon soda, Meghan gave me. It could not have been in the food because Meghan and Luc ate the same thing," Anne noted.

"This is not sitting very well with me. I had news this morning of another rogue attack. This attack was vicious so we suspect another has been recently turned," Florence advised.

"There are two out there now?" Anne asked nervously.

"It looks that way," Florence replied.

"Anne, what kind of drug was given to you? I need to know from you," Florence pressed.

"A very potent sex drug. I was so aroused, I could not stop, you know," Anne blushed.

"So you got Luc to help you?" Florence asked surprised.

"Yes, what was I thinking, right?" Anne asked.

"Clearly you weren't," Florence said.

"Clearly," Anne agreed.

"Where is Luc now?" Florence asked.

"My room." Anne blushed again and asked, "Florence, tell me his story; how did you come across him to help and become a Feeder?"

"Just like you, by accident many decades ago," Florence said and settled into her chair looking at Anne sipping her coffee with a shaking hand.

"Luc was a Lieutenant in the U.S. Air Force in World War II. Lieutenant Luc Hastings was first stationed at Pearl Harbor until it was bombed by the Japanese. He lost his wife and son there, while he was saving his fellow comrades, for which he received a Purple Heart. Blaming himself for not being able to help his family, he requested he be sent to Europe — a kind of death wish. On one of his missions, he was shot down in France where he was brought to the hospital where Ian was stationed at the time. He had lost a lot of blood but could not bleed out completely; it kept regenerating, like yours. He had nothing to lose, so he and Ian started a team to find more Feeders. Over time he became immune — built this wall around his heart — so he didn't fall in love nor got serious with any woman. Don't get me wrong, he dated many, but nothing serious," Florence said sadly.

Meghan walked into the den as white as a sheet carrying Anne's bag.

"What's wrong?" Anne asked.

Meghan dropped the bag at the doorway. "Why the fuck did you not tell me there's a naked man in your room?"

"Oh, shit — yes, sorry," Anne said.

Florence burst out laughing, followed by Anne.

"It not fuckin' funny," Meghan said, turning on her heals as she left.

"I wonder what Luc will think about this?" Florence asked, still giggling.

"That's why I'm leaving. I don't want to find out," Anne said as she stood up.

"Wait, I need to discuss a few things with you first. Ian's not leaving for another few minutes yet."

"Oh," Anne said, sitting down again and looking at her watch.

"Now, there's possibly two out there, with one that had a taste of your blood. We need you to move in with us until such time we get a more secure place for you to stay. Living on top of your office is not secure for you or your staff," Florence advised.

Anne didn't like what she was hearing. What about her independence, her work, her life? She expressed her concerns.

"I understand this will be inconvenient but you're important to us now, Anne. Please consider it carefully," Florence pleaded.

Florence picked up a folder lying on the coffee table next to her and handed it over to Anne.

"This is your *Feeding* schedule. We matched it up with Luc's for convenience."

"Convenient for whom," Anne asked sarcastically.

"Sir Robert and Ian," Florence noted the tone.

"Great."

"You're a big girl; you'll handle it," Florence said as she got up to leave the room.

Just then, Luc walked in and the tension in the room rose and thickened; one could cut it with a knife.

He stopped in front of where Anne was sitting and stared down at her. His eyes cold with anger and jaw set.

"What?" Anne asked nervously, knowing very well what.

"After what we went through last night, you could have had the common decency to wake me up before you left and asked Meghan to pack up your stuff."

Luc was angry, and rightfully so, but Anne could not let him know how degraded she felt. It was the most exposed she had ever been in her life. The rogues attack was nothing in comparison. Getting up, she started walking out of the room when Luc grabbed her arm as she attempted to pass him. His grip was so powerful, it bruised her muscles; she looked up at him clenching her jaw not to show him she was in pain.

"Why?" he asked angrily, seeing her eyes flinch.

Ian came into the room. "Luc, drop it for later when you have cooled down," he said, feeling the tension between them. "Anne, it's time we get going," Ian told her sternly.

Relieved, Anne pulled her arm away from Luc's grip and followed Ian.

Once they were in the helicopter and flying over the Bay back to the mainland, Ian looked over to Anne finding her pale and shaking. "Are you okay?" he asked.

Anne shook her head and felt tears roll down her face. "This has been a tough week, a close second to when I had to bury my parents," Anne whispered.

"What happened to your parents?" Ian asked.

"My mother died due to an undetected brain tumor. Once they found it, it was too late. It took a couple of months to finally take her life. She fought every step of the way; she knew Dad was not strong enough to be alone. She was right. Three months later, Dad took his own life, overdosed. I sold all their assets, settled all the debts and started a new life for myself and a new business," Anne explained.

"And you volunteer as much as you can," Ian noted.

"Yes, keeps me busy, except for Friday nights. I indulge in some adrenaline," Anne said with a little mischievous smile. "Don't ask, Ian. I'd like to keep that to myself," she interrupted before he asked what the adrenaline indulgence was.

"Was that where you were going to or coming from that night," Ian asked instead.

"Yep, it was cancelled due to the rain, and I was on my way back to my apartment."

That reminds me, when we land, Roman will be going back with you to pick up some more of your personal items. I trust Florence asked you to stay with us until everything is sorted out."

"Roman? I thought he was still at the Manor," Anne asked surprisingly.

"No, he left last night. Luc was to go with him but you paged him," Ian said with a questioning look on his face.

TWELVE

AT THE AIRPORT, Roman was waiting for them with his black BMW coupe. He dropped Ian off at the hospital and then on the way to Anne's office/apartment, Anne thought this would be the best time to get to know Roman.

"Sorry about me leading you on the other night. The vamp blood got me a bit riled up and so I decided to try to make Luc jealous," Anne said a little shyly.

"I figured you were; it was still wrong."

"I know; forgive me."

"Sure, just don't use me to get to Luc," Roman said looking over at her.

"Roman how did you become a vampire?" she asked, changing the subject.

"Long story."

"Give me the footnotes then."

"As you guessed, I'm aboriginal, First Nations of Canada, and became a tracker for the white man many centuries ago. Ian found me about twenty years before he turned me into a vampire. I helping him track vampires to start Sir Robert's council. I was the best and had a *sense* for vamps. On one of my tracks, I was attacked and badly injured and was dying when Ian turned me. I'm now part of Sir Robert's team, still doing what I do best."

"What's your full name?"

"It's now Roman McKay." Roman smiled.

"You're serious?" Anne giggled.

"Yes, seriously, I don't know who my parents were," Roman said as he parked the car in front of Anne's office building.

Walking into the office, Jen looked up, raising her eyebrows seeing Anne with a very handsome man opening the door for her.

"Hi," Anne greeted her. "How's everything going?"

"Hi yourself, where have you been? No don't bother; I see you had some sun." Jen looking at Anne then gave Roman a thorough once over, from head to toe, returning to his face.

"Jen, has anything important come up?" Anne asked interrupting Jen's stare.

"Huh. Oh, your car's back from the shop," Jen stuttered.

"Humph, that's not just a car — that's serious muscle," Roman noted walking over to where Jen's desk was. He went around it, then half sat, half leaned against the corner closest to Jen. Roman did his own assessment of her. She was a tall, beautiful, young woman, maybe a couple of years younger than Anne, with long, straight, brown hair, and a pale, round face. She looked up at him with pure lust in her hazel eyes.

"Well, I'll leave you two at it, then. I'm just here to collect some more of my stuff," Anne said shaking her head.

"Okay, huh, what more stuff? Wait a minute, Anne, where are you going again?" Jen wanted to stand up but bumped into Roman and fell back into her chair.

Looking around Roman, she said, "Anne, answer me." But Anne was already upstairs.

As Anne opened her door, she sensed something was wrong.

Taking a step into the apartment, she could smell it; the bastard was or is still there. She slowly took a step back. As she did so, she stepped into something cold and recognized the sweet smell. Memories flooded her mind. She wanted to scream but nothing happened. Again, it was as if the rogue controlled her. She started to shake uncontrollably; her heart raced and she started to pant for air.

"Help me," the rogue said in a sweet voice.

It was as though those two words were a button that switched off Anne's fear. She turned around and found a woman, tall — at least a head taller than her — with red hair, pulled back into a pony tail. Her red eyes were now gold like Roman's and she had soft, creamy skin. She was stunning although she was dirty, smudged with mud and grime from being out in the forest.

"What did you just say?" Anne asked not quite believing she was having a conversation with the one that wanted to kill her.

"I don't know what happened to me and I need your help," the woman replied. "You gave me life. I don't know much until I fed on you. I don't even know why I wanted your blood."

"You're a vampire," Anne said carefully.

"A vampire — what — how did I become one?" The woman backed away from Anne, not believing what she just heard and shook her head.

"I didn't think they existed either until you came along and fed on me, unable to drain me. That's how we found out I'm a Feeder."

"A Feeder?"

"Yes. I'm able to feed vampires with my blood now," as Anne said that she realized the mistake. How stupid could she be, admitting that to a rogue? There was something about her that made Anne relaxed enough to tell her the truth.

The woman stepped toward Anne. "I'm hungry; feed me," she paused. "Please," she asked, her eyes pleading. "I don't want to become a monster and kill any more animals or start hunting or killing other people," the woman murmured.

"What's your name?" Anne asked changing the subject.

"Mia, my name is Mia O'Sullivan. Will you help me, please?"

"Mia, I can try but you need to trust me. There's another vampire downstairs. His name is Roman. He has been tracking you and will know what to do. Stay here and I'll go and get him. Do you trust me?" Anne asked again.

"I trust you but can I trust him?" Mia frowned.

"Yes," she replied, trying to sound reassuring. She didn't know how Roman would react finding the rogue in her apartment.

"All right, then. Please don't let me have to come after you."

"You won't have to."

Anne left the room leaving the door open. As she got down-stairs, she saw Roman and Jen chatting about what Anne does for people and the business.

"Roman," Anne said her voice broken up a bit. "I have a visitor you need to meet upstairs. Will you be kind enough to join me?"

Roman turned to see Anne's face looking pale. Jen gave a star-tling gasp. "There's someone in your apartment, but how did they get up there?" Jen asked surprised. "No one came through here."

"Jen, could you close up the office and take the afternoon off, please?" Anne asked hoping Jen would understand as the situation upstairs could go horribly wrong.

"Why?" Jen asked, surprised at the whole situation.

"Jen, now," Anne said sternly.

Understanding Anne's tone, she thought it wise to leave and leave quickly.

"Okay, call me," she said as she left.

Anne locked the office door and returned to Roman. "Before we go up there, promise me you will remain calm and not hurt my guest."

Roman raised his one eyebrow, "Why would I do that?"

"Roman, just promise me and trust me, please?"

"Fine," he said looking at Anne suspiciously.

Anne led Roman up the stairs. As they got halfway up, Roman started hissing. Anne turned to see he had changed into that scary vampire again. "Roman, please, you promised."

"It's the rogue, Anne," he snarled.

"I know — please trust me. She means no harm; she needs our help."

"She?"

"Yes, she."

He retracted his teeth and his eyes changed back to gold. They walked into Anne's apartment. The door led straight into an open-plan sitting room, dining area, and a nook separating the sitting room from the kitchen. It was a bright and cheerful place. They found Mia crouching in one of the corners to get out of the sunlight. This was Roman's second visit to the apartment and he found it a lot neater than his last visit when Florence had to do some hide-and-go-seeking to find clothes for Anne to wear. It was much brighter so he walked over to close the blinds.

"Mia, this is Roman; he's a vampire like you and here to help," Anne said as she walked toward her.

Mia looked up. Anne could feel the static in the air. Mia and Roman gazed at each other for a while, assessing each other. Even through the dirt and grime, Roman could see how stunning she was and realized she was much too thin, probably because she was starving. This realization was etched into his consciousness.

"Roman she's starving, tired and dirty. What do you suggest we do?" Anne asked.

Roman could not take his eyes off Mia.

"Roman?" Anne had to shove him, but he didn't move an inch, just stood there staring.

"Of course she is," he said, slowly coming out of a stupor.

Anne just looked at him, realizing he wasn't listening, and walked over to Mia, realizing she was in the same state.

"Will the two of you snap out of it please?" Anne started to get anxious not understanding the situation.

Mia snapped out first. "Anne is right. I need help," Mia said as she got up and walked up to Roman.

He didn't move, or rather, he could not move. He looked over her tall frame up to her fire red hair. He had never felt like this before. If he had a working heart it would be racing. As Mia put her hand on his arm, he felt an unexpected shock go through him. The voltage sent him hitting the wall so hard it dented.

"Roman!" Anne shouted.

Mia felt it, too, and held her hand with her other hand, close to her body as if in pain.

"What the hell?" Roman gasped. Mia just smiled back at him.

"Sorry," was all she said.

"Have you got any blood supply with you, Roman?" Anne asked.

"Yes, in the car," Roman replied clearing his head.

"Well get it. Mia needs some."

"Right, I'll be back," Roman said as he backed up to the door, not taking his eyes off Mia, then turned and was down and out the office in a split second.

"Goodness, he's stunning," Mia said in awe.

"Everyone has that reaction to Roman including me, but I've never seen *him* have that look before," Anne explained.

"Here," Roman said passing a silver container to Mia. "Drink this. It's Anne's blood; you'll recognize the taste." He passed the flask to Mia, careful not to touch her.

"Thanks." Uncertain, she opened it and sniffed it. Recognizing the smell, she turned around to take a sip. "Eew, it's cold." She swallowed turning back to Roman and Anne.

"Well, that part you'll need to get use to. We don't feed directly from our feeders, so to store the blood, we need to keep it cold," Roman explained.

Nodding Mia turned around again greedily finishing the rest of the flask's contents.

Anne shivered. She will never get used to this. "You need to wash up and get new clothes. Those are past being worn. I have some of Jen's clothes here you can use; she's about your size." Anne led Mia to the bathroom, handing her a fresh towel and clothing. Then she left her to do her thing. Returning to the living room, she noted Roman had not moved, but just stood there watching the bathroom door.

"Roman, we need a plan. What will Sir Robert do about her?" Anne asked.

"Anne, we have a problem," Roman said, realizing the rogue will need to be handed over to the council and not sure what they would do to her. He didn't like this one bit. "Sir Robert wants her alive to question who turned her. But it's her quality that will save her life."

"Quality — what do you mean?" Anne asked.

"She needs to prove herself useful to the council in order to stay a vampire. Otherwise she will be terminated," Roman replied.

Anne shivered. "So if you weren't good in tracking, you would be dead?"

"Yes, they would have never turned me," Roman acknowledged.

"My God, do you think Ian, Florence and Luc could help us and be on our side on this?"

"I don't know. Luc will, but Ian and Florence — well that's up in the air. Ian sired me, and Florence is the coven's watchdog."

"So let's contact Luc for some help then," Anne advised, not sure if she would want him involved because that means they would have to work together on this. She planned not to see him much except during their feeding schedules, but this was Mia's life.

Roman took out his cell phone and dialed. "Hey, where are you?" Roman asked Luc as he answered.

"Hey, at the Manor, where else would I be?" Luc replied.

"I need you to get here quick."

"Why?"

"I have a lead on the rogue and need your help fast."

"I can arrange for Florence and I to fly out in an hour."

"Great, I'll meet you at the airport." Slapping the cell phone shut, he looked at Anne. "You need to get your stuff together and I'll drop you off at the Andersons on my way to the airport."

"I'm not leaving Mia alone."

"She's a grown woman; besides, she will be safe here."

"Once I drop Florence off at the house, I need you to keep her busy until we get back." Roman started putting a plan together. Anne was in the dark and didn't like it one bit.

Mia came out of the bathroom looked refreshed and more stunning than before. Due to the nourishment and a wash, her skin glowed, but her eyes were strained.

Roman explained what they planned to do and told her that when he gets back with Luc, he would explain everything about being a vampire and what is expected of her. Anne finished packing the rest of her clothing and a few snacks. Roman dropped her off at the house. Mia was advised to rest. What that meant Anne didn't know, but she was sure she was not going to be able to do it.

ROMAN WAS AT the airport just as Florence and Luc arrived; he dropped Florence off at the house and then took Luc to Anne's apartment.

"What're we doing here?" Luc asked as Roman pulled up in front of Anne's office building. It was a corner unit of a newly built strip mall. The front was all glass with "Anne Patterson PhD, Therapeutic Message and Reflexology" written on it. After Roman took a flask marked "A" out of his cars cooler, they walked up to Anne's apartment.

"You'll see," was all Roman said as they walked up the stairs. They heard music playing, which surprised Luc.

"Who's up there?"

As Roman knocked on the door he said, "Mia are you decent?"

The door opened and a woman stood looking back at them. She had long, curly red hair, and was tall and slender with stunning features and vampire gold eyes.

Luc immediately knew this was the rogue they have been tracking and now she was in Anne's apartment.

"Roman, you have some serious explaining to do," Luc said as he passed him and the woman named Mia.

When they all were in Anne's tiny living room, Roman gave Mia the flask. She opened it and turned around before she took a few swallows. Wiping her mouth off with the back of her hand, she turned back to face them. "Thanks."

Luc grabbed the flask away from her. She hissed and was ready to pounce on Luc when Roman jumped between them. "Stop, Mia," Roman said being careful not to touch her.

"Hold on a minute, not so fast. We need some questions answered before you get this back," Luc said.

"You don't understand. I need that. I don't want to go out there and be a monster again," Mia cried.

Now that answer was a big plus in Luc's book, so he handed the flask back to her. Roman noticed Luc touched Mia briefly as he gave the flask back to her.

"Wait a minute. You didn't feel that?" Roman asked Luc.

"Feel what?" Luc asked, confused.

"Mia didn't shock you?"

"Shock me?"

"Yes, shock you."

"No!"

Roman then looked at Mia suspiciously, stepped closer and slowly touched her hand. He jumped back. "Stop doing that to me," Roman yelled.

"Sorry!" Mia said rubbing her hand that caused the static she felt, not understanding why her energy had increased and become so intense. She had to work that out herself, so she decided not to explain what was happening between Roman and her.

Luc, sitting on one of the stools at the nook, asked for the other two to sit down. "We need to talk."

"Mia, do you know who turned you?" Luc asked.

"Turned me?" Mia asked.

"Turned you into a vampire," Luc explained.

Mia shook her head. "No, not really. All I can remember was that I went out with a few girl friends to a bar. We met up with this guy; he was young and had a beautiful voice, the kind of voice that makes you melt." Trying to concentrate on his features, all she could remember was that he had a baseball cap on that was pulled over his eyes shadowing his face. He was not built like Roman or Luc but was a bit scrawny.

"What did you do for a living?" Luc asked.

"I'm a waitress by night and model by day," Mia said. "What do you mean *did*?"

"Well, you can't go back to what you did before because of what you've become," Luc advised.

"You're newly turned, so the sight or smell of blood can release that monster you don't want to become. It took me years to control myself, and I still feel the pull when I'm around blood. It takes a lot of discipline not to feed," Roman explained.

"We need you to stay away from people for a while," Luc suggested.

"But if I do that, how am I to practice self control?" Mia asked. She knew she could control herself in any situation that needed it. It was her personality.

"You can spend time with Anne," Luc replied. "She is the best human for the job."

"I don't think that's wise. Anne is Mia's feeder and the pull toward feeding on Anne again will be powerful," Roman said looking at Luc, surprised he even suggested it.

"We can't be here babysitting. We have another rogue to catch, remember?" Luc advised, noting Roman's concerns. "We can't leave Mia alone with Anne's staff working downstairs either."

"Right, maybe we should tell Ian and Florence about Mia," Roman said hesitantly.

"Let's just hold off on that for a couple of days until Mia is stronger and getting used to her new lifestyle," Luc suggested.

Mia watched the two men working the situation out but deep down wanted to be with Roman a little longer.

"Roman, will you teach me and explain things to me?" Mia asked.

"Um, I don't know," Roman looked at Luc. "We have a rogue to catch."

"On your off time, then?" Mia suggested.

"I think that's a great idea," Luc said getting up from the stool, "but it's getting late and we need to get back to the house before Florence gets worried."

"What about me?" Mia asked, not wanting to be alone.

"On second thought, maybe Roman should stay with you tonight so that you can ask him everything there is to know about being a vampire. That's not my department so I will be going," Luc said as he went for the door. "Roman you may want to get some more nourishment for the two of you."

"Yeah, right, I'll be right back," Roman said getting up and following Luc to the car. Luc noted Roman just taking "A" marked flasks. "I suppose "L" marked flasks are outdated now?" Luc said sarcastically.

"Sorry, Luc," Roman said sheepishly and took a couple of "L's" not to insult his friend. Luc just smiled getting into the car and drove off to the Anderson's house.

Roman taking the flasks back up to the apartment found Mia sitting on the couch with her feet on the coffee table and head leaned back looking up at the ceiling. "So!" he said getting her attention. Looking at him, she smiled. "So?"

"I'll put these away in the fridge for later; when it gets dark we'll go out for a little excursion and teach you what you are capable of. Uncertain of what he meant, Mia just nodded.

Walking into the kitchen, Roman put the flasks into the fridge and came back into the living room and sat where Luc was a few minutes earlier. He tried to stay far away from Mia as much as possible. Her beauty and the smell of her skin stirred him up and he didn't want to embarrass himself. She still smiled at him, unknowingly feeling the same way. She, too, was relieved that he sat away from her. Clearing his throat bringing her attention back to him, he said, "Well, what do you want to know?"

"I need to know how this is possible. How does one become a vampire?"

"Only a vampire can turn a human into a vampire, by draining their blood from them and replacing it with a lot of his own. The vampire's blood is rich in healing, immortality and intensifying powers, but requires human blood to sustain it."

"Break that down for me," Mia asked.

"It heals us fast because our body needs the blood stored in it to survive." Seeing the confusion on her face, he got up and got a knife from Anne's knife block on her kitchen counter, and demonstrated by cutting his hand open. Mia screamed at him and jumped up to stop him. As she got to him, the wound was already healing. "Stop — don't touch me — just watch," Roman jumped back. Mia stopped and watched the skin knit together. "Shit," she said in amazement.

"Then there's immortality. To live forever, we need human blood that is rich in oxygen, which vampire blood does not have but needs to survive. In humans, our blood extends their lifespan nine to one. "Wow," Mia said again. "But how does a vampire die?"

"By decapitation or fire."

"What about being staked in the heart like in the movies?"

"Staking only paralyzes but if the stake is left in our hearts, it can eventually kill us due to starvation, which will take years."

"God. That must be a shitty way to die."

"No kidding," Roman smiled.

"What about the sun? Why does it make me feel weak and hungry?" Mia asked.

"The sun damages the body and drains our energy, leaving us weak. The weakness is due to our blood trying to heal, so we become hungry for more blood to replenish the blood used to heal."

"Oh, I see. What else does that to us?"

"Silver burns our skin because of the purity of the metal; it's like a poison, which also weakens us. If that silver is shot into our hearts, it, too, can paralyze but eventually kill us much quicker than the stake but slower than decapitation and fire."

Mia nodded with acknowledgement, and then asked, "The intensity you mentioned, what do you mean by that?"

"As a vampire, all our senses are heightened, including our sixth sense. We are faster and stronger than any human or animal. In the past, the way we smell, speak and look helped us lure and feed on humans. Sir Robert McKay and his family of vampires no longer feed on humans directly. We seek Feeders like Luc and Anne to help supply us with blood without killing them or the risk of draining them. There are other cultures and families out there that still feed directly off humans or animals for survival.

"So we're not monsters like they are?" Mia sighed.

"I wouldn't call them monsters because they feed off humans. They don't kill them but do use mind control and other ways to have humans surrendering their blood to them. They have rules like we do to prevent having their secrecy revealed, so they are very careful in the way they get their blood."

Getting up Roman walked over to the window and opened the blinds. It was already dark outside, so he opened the window and climbed out onto the fire escape. "Come on, Mia, let me show you what we are capable of." Mia following him out. Instead of climbing down, he climbed up onto the roof of the building. Mia, keeping her questions to herself, followed him. That night, he showed her the speed, agility and strengths vampires had, which stunned and surprisingly pleased her. The only thing keeping her back in accepting her new situation was the fact she was in need of *human* blood, which she was a few days ago.

THIRTEEN

WALKING INTO THE house, Luc could hear Florence and Anne laughing. He found them in the den. Florence had her nourishment in hand and Anne had a mug of coffee. "Ah, you're back. Where is Roman?" Florence asked seeing Luc coming in alone.

"Roman had a few loose ends to tie up," Luc said looking at Anne.

"So what leads did he have on the rogues?" Florence asked.

"It turned out to be a cold trail, so he's making up for wasting my time and getting some fresh info," Luc lied. He hated lying to Florence because the consequences of her finding out the truth weren't pleasant.

"Had something to eat yet?" Luc changed the subject and looked at Anne for some help in getting out from Florence's stare.

"No, not yet, but I would like a pizza," Anne replied.

"Pizza?"

"Yes, pizza — those round, flat dough things with assorted toppings."

"Do you want to order in or go out?" Luc asked, ignoring Anne's sarcasm.

"Out, if that's all right with you?" she said looking at Florence.

"That will be fine; you'll be with Luc. Luc, you be careful and don't stay out too late," Florence warned, secretly hoping the two of them would work things out.

"Yes, Mom," Luc said sarcastically. "Are you coming, Anne?" he asked as he walked back out the door.

Anne ran after him, waving to Florence on the way.

They rode to the pizzeria in silence. Being a weekday evening, there weren't many customers. Luc asked for a table and was seated right away.

As Anne sat down across from him, Luc noticed the bruise on her arm.

"Where?" he was about to ask where she got the bruise, then he remembered: that was where he grabbed her that morning.

"Where, what?"

"Nothing, not important," Luc said shaking his head. He never hurt a woman before and felt sick to his stomach to see what he did to her.

Anne stared at him and wanted to press him into telling her what was on his mind but the waitress came over for their order.

Luc ordered beers and a large deluxe pizza for both of them to share. The waitress confirmed their order and left. A few minutes later, their pizza and beer arrived and they started to eat, still saying nothing to each other. Anne was staring out the window when she heard Joe's voice.

"Anne, is that you?" he asked realizing she was sitting with a man he had never seen before.

"Hi, Joe. This is Luc — Luc, Joe," she introduced them, still chewing on the last bit of pizza. The two men shook hands. Luc took the opportunity to sum the older man up. He was a large but not overweight man, with a friendly oval face. He had a goatee and dark hair. Luc noticed calluses on his hands.

"What did you do to your car, Anne?" Joe asked.

"Oh, a deer ran into it," Anne lied.

"Really?" Joe frowned, not believing that.

"Really," Anne said, trying to sound convincing. She did not like lying to Joe. He was her mentor and taught her a lot. She trusted him with her car and her life.

"When did this happen?"

"Two Friday nights ago. What's up with the twenty questions?" Anne started to get irritated.

"Just concerned that your performance hasn't been jeopardized by this incident. I have a lot riding on it."

"Really?" Anne asked.

"Yes. Really," Joe said worried.

"Well, I don't think I will be making it tomorrow," Anne said looking at Luc.

"Yes, she will," Luc said interrupting her with a smile.

Anne kicked him under the table.

"Ah, I'll make sure she's there," Luc grinned.

"Great," Joe said happily. "Well, it was nice meeting you." Joe turned to go back to his table.

"Same," Luc replied. Directing his attention to Anne, he asked "So where are we going on Friday?"

"You're going nowhere."

"If I don't go, you don't go."

"Great."

"So, where we going?" Luc repeated the question.

"Road race, for a selected few," Anne whispered. "It's very hush, hush; the race is by invitation only."

"Well, if you don't say anything, I won't," Luc said not believing she does this kind of thing. She's so tiny that to imagine her in that large car fascinated him.

"Seriously? That's the last thing I expected you to say."

"Well, don't get too happy. This will be your last race though, understand?" Luc said sternly.

"Why?" asked Anne.

"It's dangerous," Luc advised, "and you have a contract to uphold."

"I love dangerous," Anne smiled slyly.

"You're an adrenaline junkie getting your fix, you know that?" Luc said shaking his head and drinking the last of his beer.

"Well, I'd rather get my fix being in control of my destiny than not."

"Or being unaware that you're getting your fix," Luc reminded her.

"What do you mean?" Anne asked, confused.

"Making others so angry, you could get hurt or worse." Luc looked at her arm again. "You do it to me; do you like making me angry?" Luc asked.

"No," Anne replied, remembering that morning.

"Liar. Tell me when you weren't in control of your adrenalin rush, Anne."

"When Mia attacked me, I thought I was going to die. The fear of dying alone scares me the most." Anne looked into her empty beer glass.

Luc noticed Anne's eyes changed from anger to fear to sadness. Her eyes welled up with tears. Luc was about to say something.

"Leave me alone," Anne interrupted and got up from the table and made her way out of the restaurant.

Luc followed and requested the bill, keeping an eye on Anne standing at the car. He paid, then walked out and opened the car door for her.

She slipped into the passenger's side and stared ahead not saying a word.

"You don't like feeling vulnerable, do you? Like last night at the Manor?" Luc asked breaking the silence as he settled into the driver's side.

"You're stepping into dangerous waters," Anne replied.

"That may be but I want to understand you."

"Well back the hell off, Lieutenant Hastings," Anne yelled.

"What did you just call me?"

"You heard me."

"Don't *ever* use my rank again. That was my past and I want to leave it there, do you understand?" Luc yelled back.

Anne thought it wise to back off. "Fine, but what's good for the goose is good for the gander."

THE FOLLOWING EVENING, after an uneventful day, Luc advised Ian and Florence that he would be taking Anne out that evening and would be back late. They took Luc's Charger to Anne's apartment to get her car.

"I need to get a few things from upstairs first," Anne said.

"Fine," Luc replied getting out of the car. He walked around to open the door for Anne but she had already beaten him to it. They both made their way to her tiny apartment to find Roman and Mia chatting in the living room.

"Hi, you two," Mia greeted.

"What's up?" Roman said getting up from the sofa.

"How would you two like to join us in a bit of Anne's adrenalin fix?" Luc suggested.

"Oh, no, they can't come. This meeting is strictly members only," Anne said nervously.

"Aren't members able to bring guests?" Luc asked.

"Yes, I suppose so. I never did before and they may find it suspicious."

"More the merrier" Mia chipped in.

"Where are we going?" Roman asked.

"To a drag race," Luc said.

"It's not a drag race, you idiot," Anne said angrily and left the room before she lost it. She got into her backup leather pants, which were part of her leather armor; the first pants were cut off her by Ian. The rest of the armor consisted of a padded leather jacket, gloves and a helmet, which she kept in a large bag.

Returning to the living room, she found three eager "kids" looking back at her.

"Okay, let's go before I change my mind," Anne said locking her apartment door from the inside and then climbing out the living room window onto the back fire escape.

"This is so exciting," Mia said on her way out the window.

Roman jumped and landed gently onto his feet. Mia watched him as he did so and did the same. Then Luc climbed out and was followed by Anne. She closed her window and they made their way down the stairs, joining Roman and Mia in the alley behind her building. In a storage facility behind her office, they found her torch red and performance white striped Shelby Cobra GT 500 coupe, with all the extra trimmings needed to win races like these.

She unlocked the gate and climbed into the driver's side, throwing her bag onto the back seat.

"Luc you can come with me. Roman, you and Mia can follow," Anne said out of her window before she started the engine.

The engine roared with power and gave her a thrill to feel the energy beneath her again. Luc threw his car keys to Roman. He and Mia then followed Anne in the Charger, to his best ability, through the streets of Maple Ridge onto back roads where houses seemed to get fewer and further apart and then onto a stretch of gravel road, over a Texas gate which had "Hue Ranch" hanging over the entrance.

Riding past the ranch house and barns, they reached an old and dry corn field. They followed a narrow gravel road, which looked like a corn maze, until they reached a large, paved circuit and parking area. In front of them, they found a fully equipped race track.

"What's up with the corn field?" Luc asked amazed.

"It's to keep the track concealed and acts as a noise barrier," Anne explained.

"But it can be seen by air, can't it?" Luc asked.

"They have their ways of concealing it when it's not in use," Anne assumed.

Anne stopped and directed Roman to park his vehicle to one side and join them in the pits.

Once parked between a few other muscle cars of all shapes and sizes, Anne asked Luc to stay with her car and wait for Roman and Mia while she registered.

"Ah, I see you brought company," Joe nodded toward the three standing by her vehicle.

"Yeah, hope you don't mind, being my last race and all I thought I could bring some company," Anne said.

"What do you mean last race?" Joe asked anxiously.

"I mean what I said, last race. I'm under a new contract."

"Anne, you can't do this," Joe pleaded.

"Do what?" a very thin, middle-aged man asked as he approached them.

"Hi, Matt. Just letting Joe here know this will be my last race."

"Oh, what a pity," Matt said sarcastically.

"So, I'm going to make this one count."

"Is that a threat, missy?" Matt asked.

"I don't make threats. I state facts," Anne replied, curling her fingers into fists. She hated this man with every fiber of her being. They had been rivals on the track from day one. He raced dirty to win, but this race she wouldn't let him get the better of her. She had some new tricks up her sleeve, which she had been holding back on until it counted. Today counted.

Walking back to her vehicle, she saw Joe had already popped the hood to check the engine. Joe's, Roman's and Luc's heads were under the hood discussing what they saw and they asked Joe various questions about the engine capacity. Mia stood to one side, looking around eyeing the men and their vehicles.

"So, how you holding up?" Anne asked Mia as she came to stand next to her.

"Better now that I spent the last twenty-four hours with Roman explaining things and having a constant supply of nourishment," Mia replied.

"Good," Anne said as she went over to the car to get her stuff from the back seat.

"Anne, I'm sorry for what I did. I had no control over myself and —" Mia explained.

"Mia — don't — it was fate," Anne interrupted her.

"Fate? I didn't think of it that way."

"Well, I believe everything has a purpose and happens for a reason; either it's meant or not meant to be which results in our fate," Anne explained. As she looked up, she saw Luc looking at her with that seductive smile. She felt cold shivers down her spine.

"Wow, that's deep," Mia replied.

"Yeah, it's deep. I need to get going. Joe, is everything ship shape?" Anne called out.

"Yeah," Joe replied.

Anne zipped up her jacket, pulled on her gloves and as she was about to put on her helmet, Luc came up to her and took her hand.

"Good luck and be careful."

"Careful does not win the race."

"Then be safe."

"I'll try."

"Anne," Luc gave her a warning look.

"Look, I'm going out there to win this race, Luc. It will mean danger and a little carelessness, but I'm not going out there to be reckless and kill myself," Anne said. Looking into his eyes, she saw concern. Nobody had ever been concerned for her before, and that worried her.

"Okay," Luc said softly and kissed her forehead, then released her hand and joined the rest of the crowd.

Luc watched as Anne pulled up to the starting line. As the countdown began, he could feel his adrenalin pump through his veins. He then realized what Anne went through every Friday night. It can be addictive.

Then they took off with such power and speed it was deafening. Anne stayed a bit behind Matt pacing herself, shifting up and then backing off, just to tease him. She did so a couple of laps and on the final, Anne was on the outer lane when they approached the last turn. Matt then fell back enough for his front bumper to touch her rear and make her spin out. She had remarkable steering skills as she hit some corn. She geared down for more power and got back onto the speedway, gunning it toward Matt again, this time holding nothing back and she reached the finish line first by a bumper.

Everyone was jumping up and down. Luc, Roman, Mia and Joe, high-fiving each other, ran down to congratulate Anne on her victory.

As they reached her, Anne was already out of the car, heading for Matt, inspecting her rear bumper on her way. She was so pumped; she saw nothing but the asshole that nearly took her out. As Matt climbed out of his car and took off his helmet, she was in his face with her tiny fist.

"Bastard, you could have killed me."

"Ouch, that would be very unlikely. You can't kill a heartless bitch even if you tried," Matt growled, holding his jaw.

Anne was just about to leap at him again when Luc grabbed her around the waist.

"You're a bad loser, and dangerous when you do; that's why people are so fuckin' scared to beat you. You son-of-a-bitch, you play dirty. I hope there is someone other than myself willing to beat your sorry ass and take it down and while they do that teach you some respect — fuck — I hate you," Anne yelled struggling to get out of Luc's grip.

"You better hold her back because I'm the kind of guy that gets off hitting women — especially bitches like you," Matt yelled back.

Roman stepped in and with one easy swoop, grabbed Matt and threw him over his car, and then hit his hands together as if to dust them off.

They all stood there amazed for a second and then started to laugh. Luc took Anne's face in his hands and slowly bent his head down toward her; he was close enough to smell her. He heard her gasp for air and as she did, he took her mouth to his. It was surprisingly soft. He had to have more and slowly he opened her mouth and tasted her. She tasted sweet and warm. It made him want more; she wanted more. Anne closed her eyes and absorbed every second of the kiss. Goodness, she waited so long for this, she didn't want it to end, but it did — abruptly. She felt a cold hand on her shoulder and a familiar voice that startled her.

FOURTEEN

"WHAT THE HELL do you think you are doing?" Florence growled.

Anne jumped back and still holding onto Luc's arm quickly moved behind him, having him protect her.

"Let me explain," Luc said.

Anne looked around; there were six vampire *police* standing around them, all dressed in black with long black leather coats. Anne recognized one of them as being the pilot of the helicopter. Three stood next to Roman and Mia, and three stood behind Florence looking at Luc and Anne, their eyes black with anger and if it were not for the spectators, Anne was sure they would be vamp dust.

Florence's glare gave cold shivers down Anne's spine; she felt Luc shiver and his arm got cold, so she was sure he felt the same way.

"Who's this?" Florence looked at Mia. "No, don't tell me, let me guess — the rogue that fed on Anne? You found her and didn't bother bringing her in." Florence was getting madder by the second.

"I want you all in the council room for debriefing in half an hour. No detours and remember, if you're not there, we will find you and I don't have to explain the consequences," Florence snared and turned clicking her fingers. The rest followed her, leaving the four staring at her back. Their long coats swooped as they walked. They looked daunting, Anne thought.

"Shit, now what?" Roman said looking from Mia to Luc.

"We have no choice," Luc replied.

"Do you realize how much shit we're in?" Roman warned.

"Do you think I'm stupid?"

"How much?" Anne asked, terror welling up inside of her; the adrenalin she felt now had no comparison to when she was racing. Luc looked at her and seeing her fear, decided not to explain.

"Will it mean blood exiting our bodies involuntarily?" Anne asked.

"You have a strange way of saying punishment through bodily harm," Roman replied shaking his head.

"No, we'll probably be under personal surveillance or house arrest but the worst is what can happen to Mia," Luc explained.

"We need to go," Roman suggested.

Anne and Luc got into the Shelby and reached Roman and Mia on their way out.

"So what's going to happen to Mia?" Anne asked concerned.

"Do you really want to know?" Luc asked.

"Yes."

"She'll be sent to the island for interrogation by the council. Then worst case, as you know, she has no quality so that will mean —"

"No!" Anne cried out.

"I'm afraid so."

"Luc, there must be a way we can help her. After all, she attacked me and I have forgiven her for that. They can't—."

"Anne, these are their laws not ours," Luc interrupted her

knowing how upset she was getting. He put his hand on hers, which was resting on the gear shift.

She looked down at his hand and wished there was something they could do.

ARRIVING AT THE Anderson's house, Anne didn't realize the basement was set up for all kinds of dark and scary things. The council room was like a board room complete with a large table and chairs. Roman, Luc, Mia, and Anne sat on one side of the table, Florence at the head.

Anne looked at the six vamps. She decided the way to identify each one was to number them. They weren't introduced, but personally, she didn't want to know their names. They all had various stages of meanness to them. The second in charge, the alpha male — Florence being the alpha female — had the scariest eyes and the meanest look she had ever seen. He would be number one. Numbers two to five sat across from them at the table and joining number one was number six, standing on either side of Florence.

It was like a scene from a mobster movie and Florence was the *Don*. The air was tense and Anne, sitting next to Mia, held her hand under the table for reassurance — for Mia and for herself.

Anne was new at this so she didn't know what to expect.

"So who wants to start explaining to me why the rogue was not handed over straight away?" Florence demanded.

All four started to say something when Florence hit the table with her fist. "Enough, obviously you all have something to say," Florence yelled.

"May I?" Anne asked appearing calm.

"You may," Florence's voice settled.

"Firstly, this is Mia O'Sullivan. Yes, she is the rogue who

attacked me but she had no control of herself and for the record I forgave her for that."

Anne proceeded explaining to Florence where Roman and she found Mia and all that happened until they found them at the race.

"Ah the race, you do know you violated our contract, Anne?" Florence asked raising her eyebrows at her.

"Yes, and I'm sorry I had to do it. I had to finish what I started, you see I —" Anne started to babble.

"You can explain that to me later," Florence interrupted.

"So tell me, Miss O'Sullivan, what do you do for a living?" Florence redirected her questioning to Mia.

"I'm a waitress by night and a freelance model by day," Mia explained.

"So basically, you have no career or life ambitions," Florence said sarcastically.

Anne never saw this side of Florence before and didn't like it.

"Excuse me, I do have a modeling career, which is very important to me," Mia replied.

Roman shifted in his chair, which took Florence's attention away from Mia.

"And you, what do you have to say for yourself?" Florence asked Roman.

He just stared at Florence not having to say a word; he knew he did wrong. His jaw was clenched and eyes black with anger.

"I'm very disappointed in all of you. So that brings me to what we decided the consequences will be for breaking the rules. Luc and Anne, due to both of you participating in a dangerous activity, you will both provide the council with two free Feedings. Roman, you will be on scouting duty twenty-four/seven until that second rogue is apprehended and brought to council. Understood?" Florence glared at all of them. "Miss O'Sullivan, you will be taken into custody until the council meets and dictates your fate."

Anne gripped Mia's hand tightly, wishing everything would be all right until Mia asked her to let her go. Reluctantly, she did so.

Florence motioned to the two vampires behind her. "Take Miss O'Sullivan to the security quarters."

As they approached Mia, she stood up and stepped out from her chair. As the two vampires took hold of her arms, she let out an electrical charge that shocked and threw the two across the room. "Oh gosh, sorry," Mia said sarcastically.

Everyone in the room looked stunned. "Anyone else want to take me somewhere?"

"Well, well now, that's handy," Florence noted. "You may have a chance after all, Miss O'Sullivan."

"Roman, take her to a room, the one next to Anne's."

"Yes, ma'am," Roman replied and smiled with relief.

"Miss O'Sullivan, you may stay in these quarters as long as you promise not to try to leave this property and agree to meet with the council at the end of the month," Florence stated.

"I agree and promise to do so, ma'am," Mia replied.

Anne sighed with relief. "May I join her?" Anne asked.

"Yes, you're all dismissed," Florence said quietly.

Anne took Mia's hand again; she still felt a slight tingle coming from her hand. Florence noticed this and asked: "Why didn't Anne get shocked?"

"It's because she comforts me; she either absorbs it or is a bad conductor to my charge. When I was human, my body generated static and I shocked a lot of people especially when I'm stressed, upset or hum—." She looked over to Roman. "I'm finding it much stronger as a vampire for some reason," Mia explained.

"Interesting. This is definitely an attribute playing in your favor, Miss O'Sullivan," Florence advised.

As Anne and Mia, followed by Luc and Roman, walked up to Mia's room, Anne told her that the "attribute," as Florence called it, saved her life.

"We got off quite lightly," Roman said with relief.

"Wonder why," Luc agreed.

"You mean to say working for nothing or continuously is light?" Anne asked.

"Well, we could have had a finger forcefully removed," Luc teased.

"You said they wouldn't cause bodily harm as punishment," Anne panicked.

"We weren't given house arrest either," Luc smirked.

"You're full of it," Anne said throwing a pillow at him. "I am truly sorry for getting you into this mess, though," Anne apologized.

"Well, I did force this on you," Luc added.

"Oh, that's right, you did," Anne giggled. This time it was Luc who threw the pillow back at Anne.

"I just want to know how Florence found us," Mia commented.

Luc lifted his arm. "The bracelets Anne and I are wearing — they're sensors and track our every move. It senses when we're in danger and sends out a signal to the command post downstairs," Luc explained.

"Oh, very clever. Why didn't you say anything to me before we pushed our adrenalin level up?" Anne asked.

"Because I realized it too late," Luc replied.

"I wonder what else they have to keep tabs on us," Anne said.

"You'd be surprised," Luc replied.

"No, don't tell me."

"I wasn't going to."

Just then, there was a knock on the door. It was one of Florence's vampires. He came to advise Roman and Luc that a report came in; the rogue had attacked a homeless man. He described his attacker having red eyes, so they left to investigate.

Anne felt tired, excused herself and went to bed. Sleep didn't come easily as a lot had happened since Luc's kiss. It was only after Anne analyzed the evening that she remembered how wonderful it felt and was saddened by how short lived it had been. She vowed that she would kiss him again before the end of this weekend.

FIFTEEN

TAKING ROMAN'S BMW, they made their way to where the homeless man was attacked. While Roman scanned the surrounding area for clues, Luc asked various homeless people in the area questions. He was advised that a man in his late twenties, looking pale as death with red eyes, had attacked one of them using his teeth.

The others tried to pry him off the old man, and eventually they scared him off. He ran into the wooded area close to where they were camping for the night. The old man was then taken to the hospital. The police had already come and gone.

It was at the hospital where Ian was working that evening and he contacted Florence with the information and asked Roman to investigate. Luc, feeling the need to help him out, decided to join Roman on the hunt. The sooner they find this guy, they may find out who the vampire is that's turning people and having them fend for themselves. Luc didn't know why but he had a feeling this vampire was doing this on purpose, and he needed to find out why.

Roman followed the direction the witnesses pointed him toward, and started to search for any signs left by the rogue making his way into the woods.

"Luc, you take the car and meet me a couple of miles down the road. I'll give you a call if I find anything. I'm following the trail by foot." Roman indicated where he was going and Luc, getting into the car again, drove down to where the wooded area met the river. Taking out a flashlight, he scanned the river banks for any fresh footprints or indication that the rogue may have come this way. The night was dark and quiet with a slight mist rising from the river. All Luc could hear was the water splashing gently against the shore and the crunching sound his shoes made as he walked over the stones. It was peaceful.

A few minutes later, he heard a twig break behind him and saw Roman coming toward him shaking his head.

"I smell the bastard, but his trail ended a few clicks north leading into the river. It looked as if there was a boat waiting for him or he stole one," Roman advised.

"Well, this is it then," Luc said.

"No, not this time. I still smell him, so he's close by. I need Ian's boat to patrol the river until I find this son of a bitch."

"I'm coming with you." Luc headed back to the car with Roman following him.

The search carried on through the night into the next day — then the next and the next — every time just a few minutes too late in apprehending the rogue.

ANNE WAS KEEPING busy; she went back to work that Monday, accompanied by one of Florence's "vamp police." He was a very large, unfriendly vampire. He had a shaved head, square face, thick neck set on wide shoulders — Anne's number two. Jen just loved him. She tried desperately to get him to notice her, but *fortunately* for her, he ignored her. Anne explained that he was an auditor or something and was sent to keep an eye on how they operate their business and he would not be staying longer than a week or so. At least that is what Anne was hoping would be the case.

TWO WEEKS PASSED and Anne was beginning to think that Luc and Roman were abducted or killed by the rogue. No new reports of random attacks or strange deaths had occurred, but some people of a certain age group were being reported missing, which concerned Florence. Florence could not link that to the rogue but had reasonable belief that either the vampire was turning these people or it could be just another case of foul play. One thing was for certain and that was that they needed to stop this at all cost and fast.

To Anne's relief — after she cautiously questioned Florence as to the progress of the hunt — she was advised that Luc had been coming in some days to eat, shower and rest while she was at work. Anne desperately wanted to see Luc again, but also didn't want to distract or interfere with his well-needed sleep. Roman, on the other hand, not needing to sleep much was still on the rogue's trail, with slow progress. They needed a break in catching this guy, but he was clever and had experience in the forest. He may have been a hunter and knew the woods like the back of his hand, which made catching him so much more difficult.

Finally, Roman, after a long night tracking the rogue up the Golden Ears Mountain, followed his tracks to a hunter's cabin deep in the forest. He gave Florence the coordinates and was now waiting it out, either for the rogue to move on or Florence and her men to come up. At dawn, all was quiet and Roman sensed movement a few meters from where he was sitting. He was well hidden from the cabin, so he assumed it to be Florence; it was downwind so he couldn't catch the scent of what was making the noise.

Before he could adjust his stance, he was attacked by the rogue. He felt a knife penetrate between his shoulder blades. Not being able to reach it to take it out, it made him stagger a little before he realized what was going on. He looked straight into the rogue's eyes. They were black, so he must have gotten more blood from a human somewhere, somehow.

"Shit," Roman snapped.

The rogue noticed Roman was not phased by the knife in his back, so he backed off a little to see what was happening.

Roman took the chance and pounced at the rogue, hoping to overpower him. But he underestimated the rogue's power and intelligence; he was trained in combat fighting and swung Roman off him like a dog shakes water off its back. With a punch deep into his guts, Roman hit the ground hard and before he realized what was happening, the rogue was on top of him swinging good hard punches into his head and torso. The knife in Roman's back dislodged with his fall and was now lying a few inches away from his hand. Fighting hard, he rolled toward it. Roman grabbed the knife and stabbed it into the rogue's guts. Knowing it would not kill him, he stumbled back so that he could get up and kneel over the rogue, taking the knife out. The wound healed and the daze of being stabbed was quickly over. Both Roman and the rogue threw good punches, one having advantage, then the other, neither of them tiring.

Roman held the knife tightly; he needed information from this guy, if only he would give him a chance. The situation got worse; Roman had to temporarily incapacitate him, so he leaped and stabbed the rogue in the heart, paralyzing him.

The rogue fell directly on top of Roman, not moving a muscle. Roman rolled him off. "Now you don't move," he said and got up dusting himself off to take a better look at the rogue. He was a strongly built man, over six feet tall, with red, crew-cut hair and strong features that were very familiar to Roman. He could not place him; he knew for certain he had not met this man before.

Just then, Florence, four of her men, and Mia came running up the ridge, all ready for action. "So what do we have?" Florence yelled across to him before they got to see the rogue lying at his feet.

"I have him here; he's a big son of a bitch. I had to paralyze him though," Roman boasted.

As Mia come over the ridge to where Roman was standing, she saw a man lying on his back, looking up, with a large knife sticking out of his chest. She recognized him. "Oh my God, Michael," Mia cried running toward the body. His eyes widened as she ran toward him. She stopped just before she touched him; instead, she sat by his head and crouched over him putting her hands on the ground on either side of his head, tears rolling down her face. "Michael, you will be okay; you just have to listen to me," Mia sobbed.

"Michael? Do you know him Mia?" Florence asked.

"He's my twin brother," Mia explained. "The asshole turned my brother, the only family I've got," she sobbed.

"What's the coincidence in that?" Roman asked now realizing the resemblance. So that was what made him think he knew him. He was Mia's twin but a very large, masculine version of her.

"I don't think that was a coincidence; this was very deliberate but why?" Florence asked, partly to Roman, and partly to herself.

"I'm going to check out the cabin to see if there's anything." Roman left, hearing Mia explaining to her brother what he had told her in Anne's apartment when they first met.

The cabin was one large room with an overturned table, a single iron-frame bed and foam mattress, a wooden chair and shelves stacked with tin food covered in dust. The floor was layered with sawdust; Roman guessed it was to absorb the blood of the hunter's kills. Roman could also smell human blood. He recognized the very distinct flavor; it was Anne's. But how? He knew she was safe at the Anderson's house. So he started sifting through the sawdust when he came across a silver flask with the family's crest and a large "A" engraved on it. "How the hell did he get this?" Roman asked himself.

"Florence," Roman called as he walked out of the cabin to join her and the others. "Look what I found," he said handing her the flask.

"How the hell?" Amazed, Florence looked from the flask to Roman to the man still lying on the ground staring up at his sister's wet face. Florence walked over and knelt down next to Michael. "Where did you get this?" Florence asked.

Michael looked over at Florence. "I — found it — lying — bed in — cabin," Michael stammered.

"Florence, can't we release him from the dagger, please?" Mia pleaded.

Florence nodded but as she took hold of the knife, she indicated to her men to fall in behind Mia and herself.

Florence pulled the knife out of Michael's chest. He gasped for air, and he rolled onto his knees, he held his chest where the knife was and looking down he noticed no blood coming from the wound and the skin had started to knit together again.

"Fuck, what's going on here?" he asked in amazement. As he made the effort to stand up again, he towered over everyone except Roman, who seemed to be the same height. Roman came up to him giving him a hand. "No hard feelings, I hope?" Roman asked, eyeing Michael warily.

"None," Michael said as he took Roman's hand and shook it. "You fought well," he said smiling at him.

"Where did you learn to fight like that?" Roman asked.

"U.S. Marines, for six years," Michael replied.

"I didn't know you were back," Mia said with pain still in her eyes.

"I didn't have a chance to tell you; the evening I came home I went to your apartment. There was a man there going through your things. He told me that you had left and would not be back for a while," Michael explained.

"Did you see what he looked like?" Florence asked.

"No, not clearly. I couldn't see his face."

"Let me guess, he had a baseball cap pulled over his eyes, right?" Roman noted.

"Yes, that and it was dark. How did you know?" Michael asked.

"Mia had the same guy turn her," was all Roman said.

"But I can tell you he was thin, young and had a soothing voice, the kind that could put you to sleep just by listening to him. I'll definitely recognize it when I hear it. So anyway, as I stepped into the room where he was standing, he flew at me and bit into my throat. I went weak and fell to my knees. I never want to feel that helpless in my life again. I could feel myself dying. The next thing I knew, I was in the apartment alone and very disorientated and the hunger was unbearable. Everything was loud and bright, and my body was so sensitive, it hurt. I hid in the bathtub until that night. I had to find something to eat and drink; whatever I did, nothing satisfied me. So I came to the place I knew best and that was my cabin. I hunted and killed deer with my bare hands, and then graduated to bear and then cougar. It satisfied me — not completely, but it did strengthen me. I decided to go back down to the city where I found a few homeless men camping near a wooded area where I attacked a poor old man. His blood tasted so good. I hate what I've become," Michael said as he looked over to Mia.

She walked over to him and put her arms around his waist leaning against his hard chest. "You'll be taken care of now, Michael. With Roman and Florence on our side, we'll be okay," Mia said reassuring them both.

"We need to get back; Luc is down there wondering where we are," Florence interrupted, looking toward the trail that brought them up the mountain.

As they reached the base of the mountain trail, they found Luc pacing up and down between the two black vehicles.

"Looking for me?" Roman asked as he saw Luc.

"Hell, what took you guys so long?" Luc smiled back at them. He then saw a very large man, who looked very much like Mia, holding her hand walking toward him, surrounded by Florence's four vamps.

"Oh, I take it he gave you a run for your money," Luc stated in amazement.

"No kidding," Roman replied looking over at Michael. "Let me introduce you. This is Luc. He's human so don't attack him; he's on our side. Luc, this is Michael, Mia's twin brother," Roman teased.

"Are you shitting me?" Luc asked.

"No, and we found this," Roman gave him the flask with Anne's initial carved into it.

"Oh, this is getting better by the day," Luc shook his head.

When the two cars with their passengers arrived back at the house, Anne and Ian were attempting to play chess to pass the time. Ian heard them first and was at the door before Anne looked up from the chess board. When Anne joined him on the front porch, she noticed Mia and a large man who looked like her getting out the back of Roman's BMW, followed by Luc and Roman. Florence and the four climbed out of the SUV. "Finally they are back, safe and sound," she sighed.

As they all walked up the stairs, Florence ahead of the rest, Anne noticed the long affectionate hug Florence gave Ian.

Florence then stepped away and turned toward Anne; "Evening Anne. Thanks for keeping Ian entertained while we sorted out another mystery," Florence said winking at Anne. "Ian, Anne, this is Michael, Mia's twin brother. He happens to be the rogue terrorizing the city these last couple of weeks."

"Oh my," Anne said nodding in his direction.

"Well I'm glad you were apprehended safely, for Mia's sake," Ian said noting the resemblance and stepping toward Michael shaking his hand. "Welcome to our home — hope you've agreed to stay?" Ian asked.

"Yes, sir," Michael replied.

As he moved over to Anne, he recognized her scent; his eyes turned black and he gripped Mia's hand. "Michael this is Anne. She is the other Feeder that Luc and I told you about. Take it easy. The blood you had from the flask was hers, so that's why you are feeling a little edgy," Mia explained and held his chest with her other hand. Anne stepped back a little. "I'm pleased to meet you. What did you just say about a flask of my blood?" Anne asked weary and confused, looking over at Luc.

"Roman found a flask of your blood in his cabin," Luc said with a shrug.

As they all walked indoors, Florence and Roman took turns explaining the last few hours to Ian and Anne.

"Could I have the flask to send in for some tests?" Ian asked.

"Sure," Roman said, giving it to him.

Anne, getting tired and hungry, excused herself from the rest. They were still discussing a few things concerning Michael and Mia, preparing them for the council meeting.

Anne made her way to the kitchen to make herself a sandwich before bed and found Luc standing over the center island doing the same thing.

"Oh, here you are," Anne said as she walked in.

"Hi, want something to eat?" Luc asked.

"That's the plan; can I help you with anything to increase that order you're busy with?" Anne replied, eyeing the different ingredients for what would be an excellent Dagwood sandwich.

"Sure, I'm missing a fresh tomato."

Anne bent down in front of the open fridge looking for one when she heard Luc swear, and throw down the knife he was using.

Surprised, Anne turned around and saw Luc had cut into the palm of his hand; it bled badly. By the time Anne ran over with a dish towel to wrap around his hand, it started to heal.

"Give me your hand!" she demanded, grabbing his hand and wanting to look at it.

"I'm fine," Luc said and pulled away from her.

"Luc, give me your hand," she said, snatching it back.

"It's healing already," he said and watched her take his hand and put his palm, where the cut was, to her lips and kiss it. She looked up to him, seeing him looking back at her in astonishment. She then took the same hand and put it to her cheek stepping closer to him. He took his other hand and did the same as his first, holding her face in his hands. He bent down and kissed her lightly on the lips. They were soft and warm. He felt her put her arms around his waist, drawing him closer so that their bodies touched. Their kiss deepened and Anne was breathless as she felt her knees buckle under her and held Luc tighter not to lose balance. Luc pulled away first and looking at her. "You need to eat before you fall over," he suggested smiling at her.

They ate, watching each other doing so. *Well, I got that kiss but two weeks later,* Anne thought.

SIXTEEN

THE LAST FRIDAY in July came upon everyone at the Anderson house much too soon. Anne was very nervous for Mia and Michael because of their first encounter with Sir Robert and the council meeting, and for Luc and herself, because of the first of two "free feedings." They flew over to the island mostly in silence, commenting either on the weather or scenery below. When they arrived, Luc and Anne were escorted to their rooms. They looked at each other as they reached their doors before entering.

As Anne entered her bedroom, she was greeted enthusiastically by Meghan. She was so excited to see Anne again, she could not stop talking. She asked thousands of questions about the rogues and their apprehension and what was she up to the last four weeks. Anne sat on her bed with Meghan, answering her to the best of her capabilities, making Meghan even more excited.

"Meghan, I realize now that the family is growing with more vamps and not more feeders," Anne said as she lay back against her soft pillows looking up at the ceiling.

"Yeah that sucks, excuse the pun," Meghan said giggling.

Just as Anne threw a pillow at Meghan, someone knocked at the door. Laughing Meghan got up and answered it; her face went serious immediately and she turned to face Anne. "They want you for your feeding, Anne," Meghan said with stress in her voice.

"Already — we just arrived," Anne said as she got up to join Meghan at the door. As she opened the door wider to see who was there to claim her, she stared up at a tall, thin man with mouse brown hair, number six of Florence's vamp police, who stood looking down at them. He stepped aside for Anne to enter the hallway. As she did, she met up with Luc and vamp number four. He had blond hair and a scar that ran down from his right eye to the corner of his upper lip.

Luc didn't say a word to Anne but just took her hand in his as they were escorted to the medical center. As they passed through the double doors, Anne started hyperventilating. Luc stopped, wanting to help her, but his escort pressed him on, while Anne's escort picked her up before she fell.

Anne was getting dizzy and felt herself being carried and laid down on the bed. Looking over, she saw Luc lying on his bed being strapped in and looking back at her with concern. "It's going to be okay," he mouthed. She wanted to ask why he was being strapped in, when they started to do the same with her.

This was a first. Her anxiety started to increase and she found it difficult to breathe. An oxygen mask was then placed over her mouth.

She turned her head to look over at Luc again. Watching them work on him, she could feel the same thing happening to her, except for the oxygen mask. They connected him to the heart monitor by placing wires with round pads onto his chest and a metal peg clamped to his finger. They then took his blood pressure and indicated the results on a chart.

Ian then walked in, talking to the staff. "Is everything set up and ready to go?" he asked.

"Yes, Doctor," one of them replied.

Ian then walked over to Luc. He picked his arm up and tapped the soft area on the inside of the elbow and taking a long needle, inserted it into his vein. Anne filled with fear as she watched Luc's reaction to the procedure. He had his eyes closed and stiffened up a bit as the needle was inserted; once it was done he opened his eyes and looked over to Anne again.

He wanted to make sure she knew he was all right; he nodded to her with a smile, which didn't reassure her at all.

As Ian made his way over to her, she could feel herself start to breathe faster, the heart monitor started to beep erratically and her muscles stiffened up. The last two times they drained her, she was unconscious so she was unaware of the procedure. Did they always strap her down? She could not remember.

In the back of her mind, she thought that this was her punishment for taking part in the race and putting herself in danger, which resulted in her breaching the contract. Would they do that, therefore, strapping her down?

"Anne?" Ian touched her arm. His voice calm and brought her back to reality — this was it.

"You'll be fine; look over at Luc," Ian suggested. Anne did and noticed Luc watching her and noticed how calm he looked.

"Breathe," Ian said.

Anne realized she was holding her breath and took in a deep breath. It smelled a little strange. Slowly, things started to go hazy and with her third breath she was asleep.

Anne woke up in the sun bed and to her relief, she realized it was over. Knowing where she was this time, she enjoyed the warmth of it. As she was lying absorbing the heat, she heard a squeak next to her. It was the same noise that her bed made when she moved, but further away.

"Luc, is that you?" Anne asked.

"Hmm," Luc replied. He was just waking up himself.

Still weak, Anne had a pressing urge to be with him, so she slowly opened her sun bed's lid, took off her goggles and slid out of it. Not able to stand yet, she crawled toward his sun bed a few feet away from her, noting the bed's weight capacity. "How much do you weigh?" Anne asked.

"Eh? Why?"

"Roughly, how much do you weigh?"

"Eh, one-eighty."

The bed should be able to handle both of us, she thought, and she opened the lid of his bed.

"Move over," she said, becoming aware of his attractive and desirable naked body.

"What the hell are you doing?" Luc asked taking off his goggles and cupping his private parts with the other hand.

"I want you to hold me; move over."

"You're crazy; go back to your own bed."

"Luc, shut up and move over before I fall on you," Anne said getting weaker.

"Shit," Luc said as he moved over as much as he could.

Slowly, Anne climbed in and as she settled into his arms, closed the bed's lid and the lights came on, warming them both up again.

"You're going to give me tanning lines," Luc noted.

"Shut up and hold me," Anne replied and nestled into his side, her head on his shoulder, arm over his stomach and knee on his, breathing in his scent of leather and spice.

"Hmm, we should do this more often," Anne said.

"You're killing me here," Luc informed Anne as he felt himself getting hard.

"Now, that is not my intention," Anne replied, taking her hand from his stomach, caressing him as she made her way up and over his chest to his face. Tilting his face sideways with her hand, she felt for his lips and moved up to kiss him. His lips where warm and inviting; she wanted to absorb him into her mouth. With her tongue, she teased his lips until he parted them, taking her in. Slowly their hearts beat as one, lost in the moment, when they heard Meghan come into the room, gasping to find Anne's bed empty.

"Florence!" Meghan yelled as she left the room.

"Do we tell her, I'm with you," Anne giggled.

"No, let them stew in it for a few minutes," Luc smiled.

"Well, her monitor indicates she's still in this room," Florence was advising Meghan a moment later as they walked back into the room.

"See her bed's empty, so where do you—" Meghan stopped as Florence opened Luc's bed finding two naked bodies entangled in each other. Anne strategically placed her leg over Luc's manhood, feeling him pulsate against her.

"Oh my God," Meghan gasped and turned around grabbing Anne's robe and throwing it to her.

Florence shook her head and laughed as she left the room.

"Your bath's ready, Anne," Meghan said in a shaky voice.

"Thanks, Meghan," Anne replied and lifting herself onto one elbow looked at Luc and kissed him gently on the cheek. "I'll see you at dinner."

Holding her hip with his hand, he drew her closer. "Hmm, now that was not a 'see you later' kiss," he teased.

"Oh please, would you two stop. I liked it better when you hated each other's guts," Meghan said with annoyance as she left the room.

"Wait up," Anne called after her. She reluctantly got up and out of Luc's arms and ran after Meghan putting her robe on as she went.

THE COUNCIL ROOM was situated in the basement on the vampire side of the Manor. A large double door made of solid wood lead into a large rectangular room. Bordering the left and right rock walls were three rows of tiered wooden seating, now empty, and high above were small square windows allowing a little light into the room. A large candle chandelier illuminated the large room. Along the back wall was a large solid wooden table with high back chairs, two on either side of one large center chair. They all had red velvet upholstery surrounded by carved wooden frames. In the center of the room were six chairs behind two smaller wooden tables, where Ian, Florence and Roman sat.

A side door opened and the council stepped in; Sir Robert McKay walked in first taking the center chair, followed by Sire Mark Aldridge and Sire Jonathan Wright taking the chairs on the left. Sire Kevin Coupler and Sire Raymond Pitout took the chairs on the right.

"Before we send for the newly turned, are there any new developments on Anne's case that the council needs to know about?" Sir Robert addressed his team.

Ian stood up and bowed to the council. "If I may?" he asked.

"Go ahead," Sir Robert replied.

"Firstly, the vamp blood stocks from which we give Luc and Anne are all safe. However, the vile we fed Anne with was tainted with the septicemia plague. It's one of three, and the least common, associated with the Black Death that peaked in Europe in 1347 and 1351. Draining her when we did saved her life. Secondly as to Anne's second episode . . ."

"What second episode? I wasn't aware of another attempt on her life," Sir Robert asked.

"There wasn't any attempt on her life, Sir. I can only suspect she was given an aphrodisiac and with her desire for Luc, brought on an episode of orgasmic proportions, you could say," Ian said with a smile on his face. Florence looked up at Ian with disgust and anger.

"Sir, if I may, this is not relevant to the council; it's of a private nature. I apologize for my husband," Florence interrupted.

"True it may be, but it does impact their contracts, which we'll discuss privately," Sir Robert indicated.

"Very well, sir, that concludes my report," Ian said and sat down. Florence then got up and bowed to the council.

"So that brings me to our largest concern: the mysterious vampire turning people and leaving them to fend for themselves. Both Mia and Michael O'Sullivan were turned by the same vampire. What concerns me is that Anne may be a link to this," Florence said.

"Reason?" Sir Robert asked.

"Well, Mia attacked Anne, bringing Anne to our attention as a Feeder. While in our care and at this very establishment, she was fed tainted blood that may have been fatal if it were not for Ian's decision to drain her again. Then we found this flask containing Anne's blood at Michael O'Sullivan's cabin," Florence said as she took out the flask and put it on her table for the council to see.

"What!!" Sir Robert yelled in surprise and anger.

"This brings us to suspect the vampire is one of us, one that has access to Anne's blood and able to poison her while staying here," Florence said.

"I don't care how long this takes but I want you to interrogate every single vampire and human that was at the Manor when Anne was poisoned," Sir Robert said with concern.

"That will include you and the council, too," Florence said warningly.

"I don't care; this must end," Sir Robert roared. He took in an unnecessary breath to calm down. "Bring in the O'Sullivan's so we can hear their account," he said finally.

Florence pushed a button on the table and the double doors opened. Mia and Michael walked in, escorted by two of Florence's security men.

Mia took a seat next to Florence and Michael sat next to Roman. Both gave the council the rundown of how they were turned and what they remembered of the vampire that turned them. Florence and Roman advised the council of their account on how they found the two and what their contributions are.

"So Florence, what do you suggest you want to do with these two?" Sir Robert asked.

"Both Mia and Michael have proven themselves to me as being an asset to our family."

"Explain how."

"Michael is a U.S. Marine, tracker and hunter, which may come in handy. Mia, on the other hand, has a very unusual attribute."

"What may that be?" Sir Robert asked skeptically.

"May I demonstrate?" Florence asked as she stood up and directed Mia to join her in standing in front of the council's table. Florence clicked her fingers and one of her men, a large tattooed man, stood next to Florence opposite Mia.

"Attack!" she said to her man. He looked at her and crouched into position. Mia started to back up with eyes wide.

"Florence, are you sure you want to do this?" Sir Robert asked as he sensed a charge of tension coming from Mia.

"Yes, sir," Florence replied, clicking her fingers. Just then, her man pounced. Mia, building up enough energy, shocked the vampire with enough force that he flew back hitting one of the walls landing into one of the benches below, unconscious.

"Well done, Mia." Sir Robert stood up laughing and clapping his hands, joined by all the councilors, except one who was in complete shock.

Mia returned to her chair. Sitting down, she looked over to Michael; he returned her look with a shake of his head. Florence noticed the exchange as she came back to her chair.

"Well under these circumstances, Florence, I think you're right. They will definitely be an asset," Sir Robert said.

"Thank you, Sir," Florence said with a sigh of relief.

SEVENTEEN

ANNE FINALLY CAUGHT up with Meghan. "So — what's going on with the two of you now?" Meghan asked Anne as soon as she reached her.

"Now, I'm not too sure," Anne replied. "It's like a yoyo; one minute he allows me in, the next he shuts me out," Anne explained.

"And what are you going to do about it?"

"I don't know."

"How do you feel about him?"

"Hum — Goodness, well, I know when I'm around him, he makes me feel safe," Anne replied, not being totally honest.

"Just safe — nothing else?" Meghan stopped and grabbed Anne's arm to stop her, too.

"What do you want to know?" Anne asked getting a little angry.

"Do you love him?" Meghan asked.

"I — I don't know," Anne said with tears welling up.

"Anne, look at your reaction when I asked you that, and all you can say is *I don't know*," Meghan said softly. "Well I do know. I can see it. I feel the energy the two of you have when you're together."

"You do?"

"Admit it."

"No." Anne started to walk a bit faster this time.

"Why not?" Meghan asked, trying to catch up.

"Because he doesn't feel the same way about me, Meghan," Anne said, standing there for a bit. "Have you ever heard the saying: 'If you love someone, set them free'? Well I'm setting him free from knowing how I feel," Anne said.

"That's bullshit!" Meghan replied.

"Have you ever fallen in love, Meghan?" Anne asked.

"I don't think so; how do you know you're in love?" Meghan asked.

"It's different for many; for me it's better than an adrenalin rush. I should know because I'm an adrenalin junkie."

"Anne, is it like when Mia bit you, that feeling of nearly dying?" Meghan asked.

"No, that's extreme; that's total fear," Anne replied, surprised.

"Okay, a little less extreme — say you know you are not going to die. You get bitten out of pleasure?"

"Meghan, you're scaring me. Why — have you been bitten?" Anne asked wanting to grab her arm. Meghan now was the one walking away from the conversation.

"Meghan, answer me," Anne shouted after her.

"Let's take it outside where there are no eyes and ears," Meghan indicated a wall mounted camera in the hallway.

Meghan led Anne down to a small, white sand beach that was only available at low tide. They sat in the soft sand, Anne looking over to Meghan. "Well?" Anne asked.

Meghan sighed and took off a piece of leather strapping with silver studs she wore around her neck. When Anne saw the puncture marks, it reminded her of her scar where Mia bit into the side of her neck, but this bite was a bit fresher.

"You better explain this one to me Meghan, because my mind

is racing with who, when, why, what?" Anne asked fearfully.

"Who — not saying. When — while we were passionate. Why — because I thought I loved him. What am I going to do about it — have no idea yet — he used me." Meghan replied.

Anne just sat there, mouth gaping, completely stunned.

"Well, say something," Meghan demanded.

Anne didn't know what to say. She just shifted over to Meghan and put her arms around her. After a while Meghan started to cry, the kind of heartfelt cry that made Anne join her. They both sat there in each other's arms crying for a while, when they heard a big motorboat take off from the docks. The island's dock was located five hundred meters away, around a bend from where they sat. Anne could not make out who was on the boat as it was too far away, but she could make out three people all in black heading for Vancouver Island not the mainland.

"I wonder who that was," Meghan said. They both stood up to take a better look.

"I couldn't make them out either. I think we should be getting back," Anne said wiping her face. Then with her thumbs, she wiped Meghan's tears off from under her eyes. Seeing the sadness still in them, Anne gave her a little kiss on her forehead.

"It'll be okay; we'll get through this," Anne said.

"Yeah."

"When you need to talk, you know you can trust me, right?" Anne asked.

"I know," Meghan replied.

When they got back to Anne's room, she took that bath Meghan promised to have ready earlier. Resting in the warm water, she didn't realize how tired she was and fell asleep. A knock on her door startled her and she noticed she was still in the bath but the water had turned cold. With a shiver she climbed out, dried, put on her robe and answered the door.

"Hi," Mia said.

"Hi, Mia, how did it go?" Anne asked, surprised to see Mia and stepping aside for her to enter.

"We are part of Florence's — how do you put it? — *Vamp Police* and Sir Robert's elite team," Mia scoffed as she walked in.

"So you and Michael are numbers seven and eight" Anne giggled.

"Florence wants to see you so she sent me to get you," Mia turned serious.

"Oh, I'll get into something quickly." Anne ran into her closet and slipped into jeans and a T-shirt, with sneakers.

Mia led Anne to Sir Robert's office, where she joined Ian, Florence, and Meghan, who looked like she had been crying again.

"Come in and please take a seat Anne," Sir Robert said. Anne nodded and took the seat where he indicated.

"Anne, we called you in to inform you of what's going on," Sir Robert began.

"After our council meeting, we are happy to say both Mia and Michael O'Sullivan will be joining our family in Florence's security team, but with that being said, we also lost a few of our members. Mia and Michael suspected one of our council members as being the vampire that turned them. Being under suspicion, he and two of Florence's security men took off by boat this afternoon." Sir Robert explained.

"Let me guess: its Sire Raymond Pitout with numbers one and six, the alpha and the omega," Anne said.

"How did you possibly know that?" Florence asked.

"Firstly, one and six scared the hell out of me, especially the way they looked at my every move. Secondly, the first night I was here, Sire Pitout was all over Meghan and after our little chat this afternoon, I put things together," Anne said looking over at Florence. "Where are Roman and Luc?" Anne asked.

"They have gone with Christopher and Michael to find the three traitors," Sir Robert replied sternly.

"Christopher?"

"Your number two," Florence replied.

"You sure you have enough manpower to take them down?" Anne asked.

"They're only to find them, not apprehend," Florence replied.

"What then?"

"Once they've located the hole they are hiding in, we will go in full force and take them down as you indicated," Florence answered.

"There's another thing I would like to ask you, Anne," Sir Robert requested.

"Yes, sir."

"It's personal but it does concern your contract."

"Sir, I already understand the race was a mistake—" Anne started.

"It's not about the race, Anne," Sir Robert interrupted.

"Oh?"

"It's about your relationship with Luc."

"What relationship?"

"That's what I'm asking you."

"I don't think I follow."

"Do you or do you not love Lt. Hastings?" Sir Robert asked impatiently.

"Huh—I—" Anne hesitantly looked over at Meghan and then Florence who said what she wondered.

"It's all one-sided, Sir Robert. I am completely to blame for my own feelings here and I do understand I can't get involved with anyone seriously, but—" Anne stumbled through some kind of explanation.

"Anne, Miss Patterson, stop! It's all right," Sir Robert chuckled.

"What's all right, Sir Robert?" Anne asked nervously.

"You and Luc are both in the same boat, so to speak, so what-ever happens, we are here to support you in it; the contract only stipulates an outsider."

"Oh, I see. If only there was something going to happen," Anne said sadly.

"Well, I just wanted to make that clear," Sir Robert said smiling.

"Now, Meghan. You need to apologize to Anne about what you did," Sir Robert looked sternly at his great-great-granddaughter. Anne gave Meghan a questioning look.

"Anne, I'm so sorry I betrayed you. I was the one who gave Raymond, I mean Sire Pitout, all kinds of information about you. I was also the one that gave him a few flasks of your blood and the one who gave you the drink that had an aphrodisiac in it."

"Why, Meghan?" Anne looked stunned.

"He was very influential and I was charmed by him. When I overheard that he was the one who turned Mia and Michael, I knew he must have been the asshole that poisoned you," Meghan explained and started to tear up again.

"At least she was wise enough not to confront Sire Pitout directly as she may have been killed or turned and if anyone is going to turn Meghan it will be me," Sir Robert said thankfully.

"Turn Meghan?" Anne asked.

"Yes, but that will be a choice she'll have to make," Sir Robert replied looking at Meghan with loving eyes.

"Going back a bit, you said it was a poison that nearly killed me?"

"Well, it was a bacterium to be exact, known as the Black Plague," Ian said and explained the strand, the symptoms and diagnosis.

"So what happens to me now?" Anne asked.

"To be safe, Mia will accompany you wherever you go," Florence said.

"I will be able to carry on with my work and volunteer?" Anne asked hopefully.

"Yes, but again Mia will be escorting you," Florence replied.

"Very well." Anne was grateful as she had many patients booked for Monday and Jen wouldn't have been forgiving if she had to postpone them again.

EIGHTEEN

MONDAY CAME AROUND again. Anne, getting up early to get her day started, was on her way from the kitchen to the front door with a piece of toast in her mouth when she met up with Mia.

"Morning, Mia," Anne said half chewing.

"Morning," Mia said taking Anne's hand that had the toast in it and took a long sniff. "I miss toast," she said regretfully.

"Oh, I'm sorry. I forgot you must miss food; that was inconsiderate," Anne said turning back to the kitchen.

"No, don't worry about it, Anne. I love the smell. I can eat it but it doesn't taste the same anymore," Mia said cheerfully.

Shrugging at that, Anne took her keys of her Shelby and walked out to the garage with Mia close behind her. Seeing her red car amongst all the other black vehicles, she had to smile.

"What are you smiling at?" Mia asked.

"The symbolism of my red car amongst the black ones."

"What does it symbolize?" Mia looked questioning.

"Red, my blood amongst the black, the vampires," Anne giggled.

"You're weird."

"Maybe, but it's fun to make up stuff like that sometimes," Anne said climbing into her car.

On the way to the office, they discussed their strategy on why Mia would be joining Anne. They decided that Mia would be an intern and needed some work experience and so asked Anne if she could follow her footsteps for a while. When they got to the office, Anne introduced Jen to Mia and seemed to hit it off straight away. The first client was already waiting for his nine o'clock appointment so Anne set off to work, with Mia sitting in a corner of the room, *observing*.

By lunch, the three met in the office kitchen and had some Sushi Jen ordered earlier and Mia drank her *supplement* out of a flask.

Anne's cell phone rang. "Good day, Anne Patterson."

"Good day, Miss Patterson," a male said in a soothing voice.

"How can I help you?" she asked not recognizing it.

"Ah, good question. How would you like to save a life today?" the voice said.

"What?"

"Don't say another word; just listen and Lt. Luc Hastings won't get hurt, well not badly anyway." Anne shivered then got up and went to her office for privacy, but Mia followed. The voice continued: "You need to get rid of the vampire and your bracelet by the end of the day. When you come to the hospital to see Mr. Thompson, he's your last appointment. Go down to the morgue and I will have further instructions. Oh, another thing — we'll be watching you, so you better not tip your vampire off, just nod your head and I'll know you understand."

Anne nodded.

"Good." Click — the phone was dead.

Seeing and smelling pure fear coming from Anne, Mia asked: "What's wrong?"

"Call Michael and find out where Luc is," Anne said.

"Okay," Mia replied, sensing she should do as she was asked and nothing else — not yet.

"Hi Mike, where's Luc? — Where? — Really — Can't say but check it out — Bye," was all Anne could hear Mia say.

"Well, where's he?" Anne asked anxiously.

"According to Mike, he went to his cabin to freshen up, sleep and will meet up with them at midnight. I asked him to check it out," Mia replied.

"Good," she said. Walking out of the office, she asked Jen to see what her last appointment was. Jen, looking it up in the planner, said it was Mr. Thompson at the Ridge Meadow Hospital. Anne asked to clear the calendar for the next few days as she suspected she wouldn't be around to come back to the office for a while.

"Anne, Mrs. Rose is here for her two o'clock," Jen advised.

"Thanks, Jen. Send her in," Anne replied. She greeted Mrs. Rose and painstakingly got through her day in a trance not knowing what she did or said to anyone. By the end of her office appointments, which was around five, they closed the office. Anne and Mia made their way to the hospital for Anne's last appointment with Mr. Thompson.

"Is everything okay?" Mia asked Anne.

"Yes," Anne lied.

"Anne, the car is safe to talk. I checked it out early this morning," Mia advised.

"Checked it out for what?" Anne asked not trusting a thing.

"Bugs, tracking devices — not ours of course — and so on."

"So you think it's safe to tell you what's going on?"

"Yes."

Just then Anne's cell phone rang; Anne jumped swerving the car a bit.

"Hello," Anne answered the phone, feeling her heart beat

against her chest.

"No, it's not," was all the voice said.

"God!" Anne said throwing the phone back in her purse and taking out her IPod to listen to music. That way, she could ignore Mia's persisting questions. Immediately Mia knew there was something wrong. She took Anne's cell phone and checked the incoming calls, making note of the number. Getting to Mr. Thompson's room, Anne asked Mia to stand outside while she worked on her last client. Mia used this opportunity to phone Florence advising her in vampire undertones and codes what she suspected was going on.

"Good evening, Mr. Thompson; how are you feeling this evening?" Anne asked as she entered the room.

"Anne, darling, it's been over a week since I last saw you," Mr. Thompson said. He was an old man with grey hair and beard. He reminded Anne of Col. Sanders on the KFC bucket, but a lot thinner due to his cancer.

"How you feeling, Mr. Thompson?" she repeated.

"Much better now that you're here," he replied.

"Let's get started then."

"Anne, you have changed, you—" Mr. Thompson looked at Anne with great detail making her feel very edgy, as if she could be any more uncomfortable. "Come here, my child; let me take a look at you."

Anne came around the bed and stood next to him. He took her hands and one by one pulled back her sleeves of her medical jacket. "I knew it," he said seeing the puncture marks the IVs made.

"I'm not doing drugs if that's what you thinking, Mr. Thompson."

"I'm not; you're a Feeder, aren't you?"

Anne backed up and knocked over a tray. "Don't worry, Anne. I was one, too. That is why Dr. Ian Anderson is helping me get through this tough time. I've lived a very long life and don't regret a minute of it and meeting you was the icing on the cake." Mr. Thompson smiled at her.

"How did you know I'm a Feeder?" Anne asked, surprised.

"Well, I didn't at first, not until I saw the changes in the glow of your hair and skin, then the puncture marks, not to mention Ian came to me last week saying you're special," Mr. Thompson replied.

"Mr. Thompson, I need your help."

"Sure, my child."

Anne then whispered in his ear what had happened and asked him to distract Mia long enough for her to get down to the morgue. She then took off the bracelet and put it on Mr. Thompson and leaving the room, asked Mia to stay with him while she went to the front desk, which was only a few meters away. As soon as Mia went into the room, Anne dashed to the elevators and went down to the morgue. As the doors opened, she expected it to be dark and smelly but it was quite the opposite. She walked through the double doors marked "Morgue" and snapped off and dropped a button of her coat. She walked down the empty corridor, peeking into what seemed to be an office and then two autopsy rooms. At the end of the hall was another double door but before she got there, she felt a sharp pain coming from the back of her head and then nothing.

SHE FIRST FELT the cold, then the pain in her head. Lying very still and keeping her eyes closed she tried to get a sense of where she may be. She didn't want them to know she was conscious — not until she could assess the situation. She heard someone else in the room about two arm-lengths away from her. It felt like she was strapped to a table, a cold hard table. All she had on was her underwear and her short sleeve white blouse; her grey tailored pants were missing as she felt the cold air on her legs and feet. The air smelled damp, with disinfectant, copper and a hint of leather and spice.

"Luc?" Anne whispered and opened her eyes slowly. It was dark with enough light to just make out a few things in what looked like a bricked up cave.

The moonlight was coming from various grated holes in the curved ceiling. She looked around, finding Luc strapped to an iron table like hers a few meters from her. He was beaten up badly. Why was he not healing? The vamp blood would have healed him by now. Anne's mind was racing. Taking in a breath, she forced herself to assess the situation. She saw needles, IV tubes, and empty plastic donor bags on a tray by her feet. On Luc's side, it looked like he had his arm linked to a bag and blood was dripping slowly filling it. She shuddered; she then noticed a chair and table with a computer monitor and a desk lamp on it. The lamp was turned on, giving off additional light. Scanning the room, she saw an old wooden door at the end of the room. Anne could not see what was behind her, as her head was strapped down, so it limited her movement. No one else was in the room; it was quiet and airy. She concentrated to hear Luc breathe but it must be shallow as she heard nothing else.

"Luc?" she whispered a little louder but still no reaction from him. He only had his briefs on; his chest and arms were bare but crusted with dried blood that must have come from his face. She hardly recognized him. His lower lip and eyes were swollen. There was a cut on his right cheek, his ear was bleeding, and there were black and blue bruises all over his torso.

Suddenly the door swung open. Raymond came in with his two goons following close behind.

"Aah, you're awake, see your — what is he to you, exactly?" Raymond asked looking over to Luc.

"Fuck you," Anne said with disgust.

"Such an ugly word from a beautiful mouth; we should wash it out with soap," Raymond grinned.

"What do you want from us?" Anne asked.

"Ah, you get right to the point, don't you? Your blood, of course, what else?"

"You had our blood all along; the council would give you what you needed."

"No, they don't *give* anything away; everything has a price. We have to pay for it so now it's time to pay back," Raymond advised. "Although it's a small price to pay but having you is power and that is far more important; with power comes wealth."

"So this has to do with greed for money and power?"

"Absolutely, my dear."

"I'm not your dear, you son of a bitch; what did you do to Luc?"

Raymond just laughed and walked toward the tray at Anne's feet. Picking up a needle, he made his way to her arm. Anne started to wriggle and swear but nothing helped.

"It will only be more painful if you don't hold still, but that's your choice now, isn't it?" Raymond smirked.

"No, please, no," Anne started to cry. She could feel her airway constrict and her heart pound against her ribs.

Raymond took her arm and shoved the needle into her vein. It burned and Anne screamed. He then attached the IV line to the donor bag and watched as her blood slowly started dripping into it.

"This will take much longer to drain you but that way as we drain, you regenerate and we can be here for a very, very long time," Raymond laughed.

Anne felt her body tense up and breathing became difficult. She kept her eyes squeezed shut.

"Oh, if you die by either suffocation, hyperventilation or heart attack, I'll just make Luc suffer a lot longer. So smarten up and get yourself settled down," Raymond said as he turned around and left the room, leaving goon number one sitting at the desk. Anne tried desperately to calm down her breathing by taking in a breath, holding it, then releasing her breath every three counts. The counting helped her heart rate slow down and her breathing became stable. She must have passed out or fallen asleep because when she woke up, she noticed goon one was replaced by goon six. There was also sunlight coming from the grates in the ceiling.

"May I have some water please?" she asked him an hour later, coming up with a plan.

Getting up, he poured water into a plastic cup with a straw and came over to Anne, putting the straw into her mouth. She drank thirstily and when the cup was empty she whispered something. The vamp came up closer to her to hear what she was saying. "Come closer," she barely whispered. He did. As soon as his ear was a few inches from her mouth, she bit into him. He screamed as she held on with her teeth, taking in as much blood from him as she could before he pulled his ear from her mouth without ripping it off.

"Bitch," he said and slapped her hard across the face. Anne's face was numb with pain but didn't take long to start throbbing and then it dissipated as the vamp blood pumped through her veins. She could feel the strength build up in her muscles but she lay very still until she was 100 percent certain she could take goon six down without raising an alarm to the others.

It didn't take long for the vamp's ear to heal and another hour later, he was sitting in front of the monitor watching something that had females panting and other sexual sounds coming from the speakers. He seemed quite absorbed and didn't notice Anne break through the straps holding her ankles and wrists; the little metal rings holding the leather to the bed just snapped like twigs. She didn't have too much of a plan from there on, so she had to improvise as she went along. Removing the needle from her arm and keeping pressure on the punctured skin, she waited till it healed, which only took a couple of seconds. Slowly, she took a scalpel from the tray and as quietly as humanly possible crept up to the back of goon six. As he sensed her behind him, she slashed his throat with the small blade; blood squirted everywhere. She realized this didn't kill him only angered him a lot more. So as he turned around, he fisted her hitting her squarely in the face, but this time she had no time to recover. He was on top of her grabbing her shirt as he pulled her up toward him. She drove the knife into his heart.

Paralyzing him, he slumped down over her. Taking hold of him, she moved his body over to the chair where he sat earlier and positioned him so that he was watching the monitor again. She ran toward Luc and slowly removed the needle from his arm and undid the straps that held him down. She then took one of his arms, pulling him up into a sitting position, then positioned herself under him and pulled him across her shoulders. "Shit you're heavy, even with vamp strength." Not sure if she needed more but just in case, she replaced Luc on the table and returned to the goon. Closing her eyes, she put her mouth to the now nearly closed neck wound and licked and swallowed some more blood. With a dance of shear disgust going through her body, she made her way back to Luc and lay him over her shoulders. She passed the paralyzed vamp; she shuddered again at the thought of what she had just done. Feeling the strength going through her, she repositioned Luc and made it for the door.

As the door opened, she walked right into someone hard and cold.

She screamed.

NINETEEN

WITH ALL HER MIGHT, she swung Luc round to catch the vamp in the guts and knocked him off his feet. She was just about to run for it when she heard a familiar voice.

"Shit, Anne, it's me," Roman said.

Realizing who it was, Anne sank to her knees and with Luc still on her shoulders, she started to cry.

"Here, let me take him," he said, amazed at her stamina.

"Where's Raymond and his goon?" she asked trying to compose herself.

"They're not here but Michael and Christopher will be staking out the place to see if they come back." Roman carried Luc over his shoulder and hugged Anne under his arm till they got to his car. He laid Luc on the back seat, checking his vitals. Taking out his cell phone, he phoned Florence advising her that both Feeders have been found and Luc seems to be in bad shape. Anne got into the back seat, lifting Luc's head onto her lap. "I've got you; hang in there, will you?" Anne whispered into Luc's ear. Roman took off to the air strip where Ian, Florence and Mia were waiting at the helicopter. After what felt like hours, Anne was finally led to the medical center of the Manor and lay down next to Luc. Anne asked Ian to put their beds as close as possible. They needed Anne to give Luc a blood transfusion in order to build up his supply; otherwise he would die.

Ian wanted to put the oxygen mask on her. "No, I'm fine; just get on with it, please," Anne said not taking her eyes off Luc. She felt a slight prick; it was nothing compared to Raymond's jab. Anne made certain she breathed evenly and surprisingly, her heart rate was even. She could tell by the heart monitor they linked up to her. Luc's, however, was very irregular and his hand felt cold under hers.

As the blood left her into him, she watched him carefully. It took a while before she could see the vamp blood that was in hers start to take down the swelling in his face and the Luc she recognized was returning to her. Tears rolled down the side of her face as she drifted to sleep, feeling him warm up a little.

She woke up under the lights of the sun bed; it felt good, thinking back to how cold she felt when she came round the previous night. "Luc!" she said. She needed to get to Luc. As she opened the bed's lid, she found Meghan sitting in one of the lounger, waiting for Anne to wake up.

Meghan came rushing toward her with her robe. "Luc's fine," Meghan advised. "How're you feeling?"

"I'm fine; could you take me to him?" Anne asked.

"Sure, I think he's still in the medical center," Meghan replied. "But get dressed first."

"No! I need to see him." Anne was anxious to get to him. She put on her robe as she walked, with Meghan jogging to keep up.

"Hey, slow down. I'm not on vamp speed here."

"Then catch up later. I know where I'm going. You said the medical center, right?"

"Right," Meghan yelled after her and then stopped, taking a much needed breath.

As Anne got there, Ian had told her Luc was in a meeting with Sir Robert.

"What! He's up already?"

"You have very good blood, Anne, and having a bit of vamp in it sped up Luc's recovery time," Ian said approvingly.

"Thanks," Anne said and turned to leave.

"So where do you think you're going? You can't interrupt the meeting, Anne. You'll have to wait until he comes out."

"Well this is a special circumstance," she said as she ran down the hallway. Ian folded his arms and shook his head. "Two peas in a pod," he said as Florence joined him, looking at Anne run off.

LUC JUST TOOK a seat in Sir Robert's office when he took a seat himself. "I want to discuss Anne with you, Luc."

"Anne?" Luc asked confused, thinking Sir Robert wanted to discuss the abduction and what Sire Raymond Pitout was planning.

"Yes, Anne. What's your relationship with her?" Sir Robert asked.

"Relationship, Sir, I don't quite follow," Luc looked nervous.

"Deja vu. Do you or do you not love Anne?" Sir Robert asked.

"Well I do care for her, but I'm not —"

"Hold that thought; let me show you something," Sir Robert interrupted.

Sir Robert picked up a remote control and pressed play on one of the many screens he had on one of his walls. The first scene was Meghan and Anne talking to each other in one of the hallways.

"Do you love him?" Meghan asked.

"I — I don't know," Anne said with tears welling up.

"Anne, look at your reaction when I asked you that, and all you can say: "I don't know,"

Meghan said softly. "Well I do know. I can see it; I feel the energy the two of you have when you're together."

"You do?"

"Admit it?"

"No." Anne started to walk a bit faster this time.

"Why not?" Meghan said, trying to catch up.

"Because he doesn't feel the same way about me, Meghan," Anne said standing there for a bit. "Have you ever heard the saying, 'If you love someone, set them free'? Well I'm setting him free from knowing how I feel," Anne said.

"That's bullshit!" Meghan replied.

Luc's eyes widened and his mouth went dry and if he could get any paler he would.

"Here's another one we taped in my office and her answer to the same question I asked you."

"Do you or do you not love Luc?" Sir Robert asked impatiently.

"Huh — I —" Anne hesitantly looked over to Meghan and then Florence. "It's all one sided, Sir Robert. I am completely to blame for my own feelings here and I do understand I can't get involved with anyone seriously, but —" Anne said.

"Anne, Miss Patterson, stop! It's all right," Sir Robert chuckled.

"What's all right, Sir Robert?" Anne asked nervously.

"You and Luc are both in the same boat so whatever happens, we are here to support you in it. The contract only stipulates outsiders."

"Well, what do you say to that?" Sir Robert asked, but before Luc could answer, Anne knocked at the door and peeked in. "May I come in Sir Robert? Sorry to bother."

"Ah, Anne, no not at all; come in," Sir Robert said mischievously. "We're just talking about the two of you."

Anne stepped in and walked over to Luc and knelt at his chair looking up at him. She had tears in her eyes. "Are you okay?" she asked taking one of his hands and realizing it was warm and clammy.

"Yes, thank you," he said faintly.

"Luc, did you hear how Anne got you out of that forsaken place?" Sir Robert asked.

"No. I thought Roman got us out," Luc said, surprised.

"Quite the contrary."

"Sir Robert, it's not necessary," Anne objected.

"It's quite necessary, my dear Anne," Sir Robert replied and continued.

"Apparently she bit into Roy's ear by tricking him into putting his ear close enough to her mouth," Sir Robert laughed. "I should have been there to see this — but anyway, that is how she got some vamp blood into her to get enough strength to loosen herself from the straps tying her down. Then she took a scalpel and sneaked up to Roy and slit his throat. With a bit of a fight, she stabbed him in the heart, paralyzing him. It gets better; she unties you and swings you onto her shoulders. Finding you a bit heavy, she makes her way back to Roy and drinks more of his blood that was coming from his neck. She then moves out with you on her shoulders and bumps into Roman. Not knowing it was him, she tries to fight him with you still on her shoulders. Now tell me that wasn't love and dedication to save your life," Sir Robert stated.

"Anne, did I run it down correctly?" Sir Robert asked.

Anne didn't hear what Sir Robert had to say; she was concentrating on Luc so intently. It was only once Luc looked back down at her did she realize Sir Robert was asking her something.

"Oh, sorry Sir Robert; I wasn't listening," Anne replied.

As Luc got up, he pulled Anne up with him. "Sir Robert, would you excuse us? We have some matters to discuss," Luc said as he led Anne to the door and out. Not saying a word, he led her down the hallway up the stairs and down another hallway to her room.

All the way, Anne just looked at him and kept the silence.

Walking in and closing her door, he turned to her. "How would you treat something that had been locked away for a very long time?" Luc asked her.

"With care and respect," she answered looking back into his eyes.

"It will be very fragile."

"I'm very gentle."

"It's vulnerable."

"I know but you'll have to trust me like I trust you," Anne said lifting her hands to place on either side of his face. "I'm going to say something to you and I don't want you running off or getting angry with me," Anne said.

"Say it."

"I love you deeply," Anne whispered. Tears rolling down her face, she knew this was it. She was so scared that he would walk out on her.

But he just stood there looking back at her and taking his hands to her face, wiping her tears from her cheeks. "Don't cry for me, Anne," Luc whispered taking her into his arms. As he wrapped his arms around her shoulders, she took Luc around the waist holding as tight as she could, trying to absorb him into her. "Don't ever cry for me, and I will make sure you would never need to," Luc said softly.

"Luc, love me back, please?"

Taking her arms from his waist, he stepped back enough to be able to see her eyes. "I do love you back, Anne," he smiled.

Anne smiled back and closing the gap between them, she leaned into him and kissed him sweetly. Luc wanted her so badly, tasting her drove him crazy, like a drug that made him feel so good he had to have more and more, but he knew he would never get enough of her.

Untying the belt of her robe he slipped it off her shoulders.

Doing the same with his, he found them both naked underneath. He then picked her up and put her on her bed, gathering her into his arms. The sensation of her velvety shin rubbing against his aroused him. He took her lower lip between his teeth and nibbled until she surrendered into a kiss; as their lips met he inhaled the warm scent of her skin. He took her kiss in and danced with her tongue. Anne shivered with the feel of him on her and the touch of his hand brushing up and down the side of her body. His hand stopped, cupping her breast and then using his finger and thumb he teased her nipple. She found her body arch and her throat moaned with the pleasure it gave her running down her spine. He left her lips, kissing a hot trail down to her neck and ear. He didn't stop there; he moved over her body slowly, thoroughly kissing and licking each inch of her, from her throat to her breasts then lower to her hips down her legs to her feet and toes. Squealing in pleasure, she had to force herself not to kick as he sucked each toe.

But it was when he came up between her legs to taste the part of her that he craved the most that her real pleasure began. He lifted her hips from the bed as his tongue drove deep inside her. Anne couldn't breathe at the intensity of the heat that cut through her body until he sank his fingers deep inside her. She screamed out in release as her body burst into ribbons of ecstasy. Luc smiled at the sound of her orgasm.

She was still convulsing as he lay over her, even though he was so much larger than her, yet fit her perfectly. He saw her love for him burning hot in her eyes. She felt his hard erection pressed against her. Her hands skimmed over his skin teasing and delighting him.

"Now, Luc, I need you now," Anne whispered.

Slowly, watching her carefully for any signs of distress, he slid himself inside her. Anne gasped at the sudden fullness inside of her body. She never could imagine just how wonderful it felt. He slowly rocked against her. "Are you all right?" Luc asked. She wrapped her legs around his, drawing him in even deeper. "Absolutely," she replied.

He then reached down between their bodies to where they joined and with his fingers stroked her cleft. The moment he touched her, she shuddered in pleasure. "Oh my."

He smiled again. "Like that?"

Unable to speak, she nodded as he stroked her in time to his thrusts.

He clenched his teeth trying to hold off his climax, but as she found her own release while he was inside her, he was lost to it.

Throwing his head back, he roared with the ferocity of his own orgasm.

Damn, he thought as he drove himself as deep as he could when his body exploded with pleasure and he realized how much he did love her.

Rolling off her, both of them panting for air, he made sure to keep her close to him. He realized she wormed her way into his soul and he was lost to her now. All he could do was as she promised and that was to trust her.

TWENTY

The e-mail:

Good Day Sir Robert,

I see you have your Feeders back. I underestimated the Bitch, however if she is not returned to me, I will turn as many people as I can and build up a resistance to your little council and make sure I come up on top.

Your reign has ended.

Have her delivered to me by week's end, return to sender once you have a time and place.

Sire Raymond Pitout.

As soon as the e-mail arrived, Sir Robert McKay called the team in. They all sat in anticipation to find out what was going on. Sir Robert gave them all a copy of the e-mail to read. "This is war! Ladies and gentlemen, after you read this, we need to discuss a game plan," Sir Robert said. Taking his seat, with his elbows resting on the armrest of his chair and fingers touching, he waited for them all to finish reading.

Florence was the first to sum up the situation and looked up at Sir Robert with fear in her eyes, which was a first for her.

"We need to call the council and have them bring their security teams in."

"Get on that, Florence, please; we only have a couple of days to get everyone together," Sir Robert said anxiously.

Florence signaled to Roman to join her and they left to the command center situated on the same floor as the medical center.

Florence sent a priority red e-mail to all families and other Covens in Canada asking for their help in the situation they found themselves in. Sir Robert's Council responded immediately, but surprisingly found many Covens joined up with Sire Raymond's cause, which was a concern. This information was passed on to Sir Robert.

"So the bastard had already infiltrated other Covens to join him," Sir Robert concluded.

"It looks that way," Florence replied.

"When will the rest of the Council get here?" Sir Robert asked.

"They'll be here this evening, Sir Robert," Florence replied.

"Get everything ready for the meeting and all the additional guests we're expecting," Sir Robert said.

The manor started to feel very small with all the vampire families coming in from all over.

The council room was packed, every seat against the walls was filled, and the four chairs in the middle were taken up by all the security leaders, Florence being one of them.

Anne looked for Ian, Roman, Mia and Michael and found them sitting to her left, with Florence's remaining four security men. Luc and Anne were sitting nearest to the doors in two additional chairs that had been brought in for them. Anne was nervous just seeing a hundred or so vampires in one place at once. Being a human and a Feeder — other than Luc of course — didn't settle her stomach either.

She jumped when Sir Robert slammed his fist onto the table in front of him getting everyone's attention.

"Most of you know the situation we find ourselves in," he said, looking around the room. "Sire Raymond Pitout is responsible for kidnapping our Feeders and has been responsible for turning people in the lower mainland to increase his family. By doing this, he let a couple of rogues run around, taking our attention away from what he was really up to. He is after power and wealth and that greed has threatened our existence. Our secret will not be held for too much longer if he is not stopped. That is where we need your help, fellow members," Sir Robert roared.

The meeting took nearly two hours where the four security leaders put a plan together for them to overrule Sire Pitout and his Coven and bring them to justice. This would mean fighting them to the death or have them surrender leading to their demise anyway.

Later that night, they put the plan in motion. Sir Robert replied to the e-mail giving Raymond the coordinates to where they would leave Anne and have his men pick her up. Once they have done that, Florence's teams would follow them to where Sire Pitout had his lair. Then they would attack, killing or taking all that was left alive to be judged and sentenced.

Group one, Sire Mark Aldridge's four men, were the ones to stay out of sight and wait with Anne at the pick-up point. Group two, Sire Jonathan Wright's three men, were to help Florence at the command center. Group three, Sire Kevin Coupler's five men, were to follow on route with group one, once Anne was picked up. They were to follow in various stages and not have Raymond's crew know they were being followed. Anne suggested not using black vehicles — that was a dead giveaway to vamp cars. Florence then realized how ironic it was that all vampires had black, tinted window vehicles.

Roman, Luc, and Florence's team were to join the others by helicopter once the lair was located. Too many on the ground would prove fatal and having them in the air may prevent them from losing Anne to Raymond.

WHEN ANNE AND Luc were alone in her bed again that night, Luc expressed his concerns about the following day's events.

"Luc, I know this is not what I signed up for. I became a Feeder to save humanity against vampires feeding on innocent people; this is going way past that. Raymond is murdering for power and all he wants is me. It's one sacrifice to save many," Anne said.

"No! Anne, there will be two sacrifices to save many. If you die, I'll die with you, as simple as that."

"He's not going to kill me, Luc. He needs me alive to be his Feeder."

"How sure are you of that?"

"I'm not sure at all. I just have to believe in it."

"God, you're braver than I am."

"Well, at least one of us has to be." She gave him a teasing smile.

"I don't want you to do this, Anne. I don't want to lose you; you promised."

"You're not going to lose me, Luc, and I need you to make sure of that."

"I hate this," Luc said taking her into his arms and holding her tight, breathing in her scent. Anne could feel his heart beat against her and knew she shared his concerns. Their love making that night was intense and they both fell asleep out of pure exhaustion.

TWENTY-ONE

MORNING CAME TOO soon and the plan was put into action. Anne drove to the pick-up point in the heart of Stanley Park, Vancouver. She nervously climbed out of her Shelby and paced up and down, knowing that a few vampires were watching her closely enough. It was not long when she recognized Vamp Six, also known as Roy, coming toward her. She froze; the look on his face was pure revenge. She stood her ground as he came right up to her, his eyes black with anger and looking down at her. "Not going to run, bitch," he hissed, showing his teeth.

"No, I'm not going to make your day — not today anyway," she smiled back at him; this was just making him angrier. He displayed his anger with a growl and grabbed her arm with such power it would have snapped but she felt it bruise instead.

"Don't make a spectacle of yourself; all I have to do is scream and I'm sure people will come to my rescue and I'm sure Raymond will not be happy." Anne winced through the pain in her arm. If it weren't for the vamp blood she took that morning, her arm would have surely broke.

He pulled her with him toward a black panel van, throwing her in the back. She found two other vampires she had not seen before. He climbed in, backed the van up and then took off. Anne, not seeing where they were going, hoped for the best.

It was a long ride; the van rode into a darkened area, either a tunnel or a building, she was not sure, being completely disorientated.

DALE PILOTED THE black, Bell 430 helicopter with Roman, Luc, Mia, and Michael hovering above the tunnel the van disappeared into. The one grey vehicle following the van reappeared on the other side of the tunnel but the van didn't, which meant it was still inside.

Luc panicked. "Get them back in there; the van is still in that tunnel and they need to find it," Luc shouted into his microphone.

"Luc, calm down; they can't go anywhere but out," Roman commented.

"I don't think so. I think Luc's right — someone needs to get in there. This doesn't feel right," Michael replied. "Land this thing, Dale. I want to go in by foot and have group three join me."

Dale found a spot and hovered at 100 feet or so from the ground as they weren't allowed to land without permission. Michael jumped out landing perfectly on his feet.

"Shit, I wish I could do that," Luc thought out loud.

"Yes, well I wish I was still human," Mia replied.

"Wow, this is not the time guys," Roman said.

BACK IN THE VAN, Anne found them stop while still in the dark. The two vampires sitting on either side of her grabbed her and escorted her out of the side door of the van into a door in the wall that led them into a tunnel.

The hallway was lit up by bulbs that hung from the ceiling every hundred meters or so. Anne counted them as she passed, taking note of what direction they turned and how many lights they passed just in case she needed to get out again, until they came to where Raymond was located. He was standing in the center of a large room with concrete walls and floor. It smelled damp and felt cold. Anne could not understand why anyone would build such a place, but here she was, scared that she wouldn't be found, but trusting Luc and his persistence in finding her no matter what, no matter how long. With that thought, she was confident and her confidence showed, which was a mistake. Raymond noticed it. So he made plans to intercept her rescue crew, meeting their surprise with his own.

"Well, well, welcome to my grotto, Miss Patterson, but we're not getting too comfortable. As soon as we take care of your backup coming our way, we will be moving on," Raymond advised. "What backup?" Anne lied trying to make him believe there was no one following them.

"You forget I was part of Sir Robert's council for many years and I know how Florence works," Raymond snickered. "I wasn't turned yesterday." Walking to one of the monitors on a nearby table, he turned it for Anne to see the action.

As Michael and four others came into the hallway, she saw Raymond's men attack them with swords. Michael worked through two men on his own. Their heads flew off their shoulders with ease. Anne felt her breakfast wanting to come up. She swallowed hard to keep herself from getting sick. The fight was still on when Raymond grabbed her and took her out of the room.

They were followed by Vamp One, aka Adrian, and Roy making their way through various tunnels up a horizontal ladder that went on forever until they reached a trapdoor that led onto a helicopter pad high up the mountain. It was covered in clouds so she couldn't see what was around her. Now she really was in trouble, but she still had a couple of aces up her sleeve that she hoped still worked. They climbed into the helicopter as the pilot waiting for them started the engine. While the rotor blades were getting their speed, Raymond told Anne to take off all her clothing and put a jumper suit on. She hesitated, which prompted a clean backhanded slap across her face. Preventing any more abuse, she decided to do what she was told. Raymond smiled as she undressed, making her feel very uncomfortable. She decided not to look at anyone as she got into her polyester jump suit. Roy grabbed her clothing and shoes and threw them out the door, just as they were airborne.

JUST AS MICHAEL and group one got up to the helicopter pad from the trap door in the mountain, Dale arrived with Sir Roberts' helicopter and crew on board, landing where Raymond departed fifteen minutes before. Michael climbed into the chopper and gave Luc Anne's clothing, which contained a tracking device in one of her shoes. He looked at Roman knowing they were screwed. Florence radioed through to Dale and the rest of the teams to regroup at a designated location and wait for further instructions.

"We're wasting time here," Luc stressed his concerns to everyone listening but no one said anything back to him. Luc put his head in his hands leaning onto his knees with his elbows, shaking with anger. He wanted to kill something, anything with his bare hands. Once they landed, he was the first to jump out. He headed for the nearest tree, and hit it with his fist, breaking two of his fingers. In pain, he gripped his hand with the other and landed on his knees, screaming at the top of his lungs. His hand started to heal, which was just as painful as breaking it. Tears ran down his face as Roman got to him, trying to help his friend up. He didn't like seeing him in so much pain, physically or emotionally.

"Luc, we'll find her; we just need them to be stationary to do so." Roman tried to explain their next move, but Luc took a swing at him. Roman ducked just before Luc's fist would've connected his jaw. Roman slipped around and grabbed Luc's arms. "Listen to me, and trust me — we've not lost her yet."

"How? Haven't we got the only tracking device to find her in there?" Luc shouted, pointing toward the helicopter.

"No, that's not the only tracking device, Luc," Roman acknowledged.

"What?" Luc calmed down enough for Roman to release him.

"It's something only Anne, Florence, Ian and I know about, and I'm going to keep it that way until Florence says it's okay to let you know what it is. You've got to trust me on this, Luc, as your friend. On Anne's life, we will get her back. I won't lie to you, Luc; please, do you trust me?" Roman looked over at his friend. Luc just nodded and followed Roman to one of two large truck-trailers standing in the parking lot they landed in. On top of one of the trailers was a large satellite dish and inside they found a mini-command center, fully equipped. Florence was sitting in front of a couple of monitors, with the rest of group two doing their thing at various command posts in the trailer. The only sound was a beeping sound coming from where Florence was sitting. Looking over at Roman and Luc, she noticed something had transpired between them and with a raised brow, Roman told her Luc just had an incident with a tree.

ANNE FELT HER heart sink deeper the further they flew away from the one she loved. In addition, she felt colder the closer they came to the Rocky Mountains. They finally circled a small lake and landed in a clearing of trees close to a large cabin. They seemed to be very high up in the mountains as there was snow on the ground although it was the middle of July. Anne was man-handled into the cabin and thrown into one of the bedrooms. She found the room very cold, dark and furnished with only a bed. She climbed into it, shaking with fear and cold. She threw the covers over her head and taking her hands, she covered her ears trying not to hear things going on around her. She was scared and alone!

TWENTY-TWO

ANNE WOKE UP being dragged by two vampires into another dark room that was virtually empty except for a familiar table she had been strapped to before, a tripod with a video camera on top of it and three large lights that weren't switched on yet. It looked like a movie set. Anne started to panic when they started to strap her down to the table, which was horizontal. The vampires strapped her arms down starting just under her armpits, then above her elbows and then on her wrists; the straps had a few links to them so she was able to move her arms up from the table slightly. There were straps over her forehead, around her chest just under her breasts, and above her knees and ankles. They were really laying it on thick this time, making sure she would not move an inch. Then she understood why as the table started to tilt up vertically; the straps held her in place as gravity pulled her down. The lights were then switched on, which also provided warmth, but she could not see beyond them and wondered who else was in the room with her. With all the movement around, strapping her down, she didn't realize they stripped the polyester jumper suit off her and all she had on was her bra and panties.

🦉

BACK AT THE TRAILER, Florence received a call from Sir Robert telling her to go to a Web site. As she punched in the Web address and password he provided, the site appeared on the screen: an image of Anne strapped to a metal table that tilted at about a ninety-five degree angle. She had her eyes closed because of the bright lights shining on her; she was pale, scared and vulnerable. Luc started to shake. "No, what the hell are they doing displaying her like that?" he shouted.

"Raymond is starting a world-wide bidding war amongst the covens," Florence advised.

"What!" Luc was now pacing like a caged lion.

Florence was now getting the next stage of the rescue in place. She paged, "Dale take team three with you and follow the co-ordinates of this signal I'm sending you. Once you reach the vicinity, radio in for further instructions."

"Yes, ma'am," Dale replied over the speaker.

"We're sending out a team now to locate her; it won't be long," Florence reassured him.

"I want to be out there to kill this son of a bitch. I want my hands around his neck," Luc said through his gritted teeth.

"Roman, could your team get the Black Hawk ready for Luc?" Florence asked, and then turned to face Luc. "I understand, but I need you to talk to Anne first," Florence replied.

"How do I talk to her?" Luc asked confused.

"We have surgically implanted a tracker and she has a state-of-the-art communications device in her ear. So she will be able to hear us. But you need to prevent her from talking back to us, otherwise she will give herself away and Raymond won't be gentle about removing that tracker. She needs to find another way to do that without causing suspicion," Florence explained.

Luc looked over to Roman, realizing that was what he was trying to explain earlier.

"Luc, here, use this microphone. You'll need to talk to her gently without alarming her," Florence handed him the microphone.

Watching the monitors closely, Luc took a deep breath and spoke into the microphone. "Anne? Darling, it's me Luc; don't move. Raymond must not know you can hear me, so keep still," Luc said softly.

On the monitor, Anne was exactly as she was a few minutes ago. Luc pressed the mute button. "How do we know she can hear me?" Luc asked.

"We don't. We may need her to give a signal of some kind," Florence replied.

"Great." Luc released the mute button. "Anne, move your right hand's fingers if you can hear me," Luc asked looking at the monitor. Nothing happened, and then a second later, Anne moved her right hand's fingers as to stretch them out, still not showing any expression on her face, her eyes still closed and her breathing appearing even.

"Good job. I'm coming to get you. Stay strong for me. I'm handing you over to Florence. Love you," Luc whispered, pressing the mute button again.

On the monitor, they could see a tear running down her cheek. Next thing, Raymond appeared on the screen. "Good afternoon, gentlemen. I invited you all to join me in my little auction. The highest bidder will win the Feeder. So Sir Robert, if you are smart, bid high and you'll get your little Annie back." He laughed.

"For those that don't believe me when I say she is unique, I'm willing to give you a little demonstration," Raymond said. Turning, he walked toward Anne. He took her hand, turning it palm up, brought it toward his mouth and he bit into her, feeding from her. Anne's eyes opened wide and she screamed. She squirmed trying to release herself.

Luc went ice cold and just stood there; it happened so quickly, he didn't expect this. Roman grabbed Luc supporting him before he either broke something or fell to his knees. Roman was not taking any chances in the confined space of the trailer.

"Roman, get him out of here," Florence demanded. "Is the Hawk ready for takeoff? Find her, this is getting dangerous," Florence shouted.

Roman, holding Luc, nodded and carried Luc out of the trailer.

ANNE GRITTED HER teeth. She vowed when Mia attacked her to never go through this again, but fate was not on her side. Anne looked over at Raymond sucking the blood from her wrist; he looked back at her with a sneer in his eyes. She stared at him until he stopped; he licked her wrist to seal the puncture wounds and with the back of his sleeve, wiped the blood off his mouth. Smiling at her, he then turned around addressing the camera again. "Roy, you have the honors. I'm sure you would like to take revenge on her for slitting your throat," Raymond said with the cruelest of grins. Anne could not believe what she was hearing; then Florence started to talk to her.

"Anne, stay calm. Luc is on his way. Stay calm, my child. Breathe, Anne, breathe," Florence repeated until she saw Anne's chest move.

Anne did what Florence was telling her but her heart was racing. "God, no! Please, Raymond. Stop this, please?" Anne begged.

Roy walked up to Anne and hissed at her. Anne could feel him vibrate with anticipation in what he was about to do. He took his fingers and traced the artery in her neck that ran from her ear down to her collar bone and up again. Holding her chin up, he took his tongue and felt her pulse in her throat. He whispered in her ear, "Bitch" before he bit down into her. Anne didn't make a sound this time; she just concentrated on Florence's voice in her head telling her to stay calm and breathe and that Luc was coming to get her. Anne kept concentrating on Florence until the blood being drained from her made her weak and finally rendered her unconscious.

TWENTY-THREE

ROMAN PULLED LUC out of the trailer to the Black Hawk helicopter that was standing on a flatbed trailer just next to the trailer that housed the command center. "You need to get to her, don't you?" Roman asked Luc. He just nodded. "Then let's go." Luc got into the pilot seat, a seat he thought he would never be in again. It was war — his war. This time he was going to rescue someone he loved and kill the one that put her in danger.

Joined by Michael and Mia in the back seat, Roman joined Luc in the front with the coordinates as to where Anne was. Luc prepared the Hawk for takeoff and headed toward the Rocky Mountains. On Luc's takeoff, they heard Dale announce that they were a few miles away from the target and needed further instructions. As Florence was busy talking to Anne, the team leader for team two advised they land a safe distance from the location and proceed with caution by foot. "Roger that," Dale confirmed. It took forever to get up to where Anne was located. The beeping of the tracking signal was getting stronger, which made Luc's heart pound faster, as if the two beats were in rhythm.

As they were getting closer to where Dale had landed the Bell 430 helicopter, they heard that they arrived at the cabin where Anne was held and were given permission to proceed and take no prisoners. Secretly, Luc hoped he would be the one to kill Raymond himself but he would rather have Anne safe with Raymond dead than have them wait for him to do the job. Being human, he would not get to the cabin fast enough, even with vamp blood running through his veins.

The first team entered the cabin and surprised many of Raymond's men. They then advised the team leader and Luc that Raymond and his two goons learned of their surprise attack and had made it to their helicopter and took off. Luc changed his focus; he dropped Mia and Michael off at the cabin and took flight pursuing Raymond's AH-6J "Little Bird" helicopter. He wanted those three vamps dead. It didn't take long for Luc and Roman to catch up to the smaller helicopter but being smaller, it was also very agile. It was able to sway around peaks and trees, getting Luc to use his skills rather than speed. They swooped down into ravines and up and over cliffs, only just missing the odd treetop or two. Luc could not get a clear enough shot to take down the "Bird" yet, but he was a patient man. Under these situations, he had to be. Then he spotted two military helicopters on the horizon before he heard them radioing Luc, warning him that he was in restricted airspace. Luc advised them that he was in pursuit of the "Bird" that contained three felons, but apparently they had received permission to be in this airspace and Luc had not. Luc had to either stand down or be shot down. Roman advised Luc to do the former. Against his will, he turned around and headed back to the cabin to find Anne.

As Luc and Roman landed the Hawk and ran toward the cabin, Luc saw Michael carry Anne out in a blanket. Luc first thought she was unconscious again but was surprised to see her move her head to face him as he approached them. Michael handed her over to Luc with a smile, confirming that she was all right. "Luc?" Anne put an arm around his neck as he took her; she buried her face into his neck, feeling his warmth.

"You're safe now and you're never ever going to do this again," Luc warned.

"Oh, shut up and kiss me," Anne said weakly. He did, first gently then became greedier as if he couldn't get enough of her.

Roman cleared his throat. "Will you two excuse me but we need to get back for debriefing," Roman advised.

Luc looked up and found Roman, Mia, and Michael smiling at them. "We need to get back," Roman repeated.

Florence advised teams one and three to stay behind, collect data from the cabin and clean up the mess, while the rest of them made their way back to the Manor.

As the Hawk landed, Sir Robert, Meghan, Ian, and Florence were waiting for them. Luc helped Anne out of the helicopter, still wearing her underwear and a blanket. Meghan came running up to Anne, wrapping her arms around her so tightly she could hardly breathe. "I thought you would be a goner this time for sure," Meghan said.

"Well, gee, thanks for the vote of confidence," Anne replied weakly.

"Meghan, we need to get Anne to the medical center before she falls over," Ian interrupted. While Ian and Meghan went with Anne to the medical center, the rest went to the command center for debriefing.

"This whole episode does not sit right with me. Raymond knew we would close in on him as soon as he went online. Either he's very ignorant or he's playing us," Roman stressed his opinion to the team.

"He also must have planned his escape ahead of time to be able to get into restricted airspace and have backup to chase us off," Luc added.

"Let's run this down. I'm sure he's responsible for the various missing person reports that hit the lower mainland these last few months, which increased these last couple of weeks. They're all young men between the ages of twenty-five and thirty-five, with the exception of Mia," Florence added.

"But as a rogue, she was left loose to fend for herself and cause havoc," Roman said.

"Attacking Anne was a twist of fate and an additional benefit on our side. Raymond didn't count on her being another Feeder, nor did he count on Mia being able to be an asset to us either," Luc stated.

"Then he let Michael fend for himself. He could've been very useful to Raymond, going on Michael's background." Roman noted.

"But remember, Anne's flask was at his cabin. Someone would have put it there for him," Luc reminded them.

"Well, there are more questions than answers here, it seems," Sir Robert observed. "What I want to know is, why did he involve my little Meghan?" he asked.

"Well, Sir, she became very handy. She was able to give him firsthand information, on Anne, our operations and you, Sir," Florence replied.

"I personally think he is after your power and your coven in Canada," Luc added.

"But he is going about it all the wrong way. Why involve Anne in this and not you, too?" Roman looked at Luc.

"I think he underestimated Anne," Luc stated.

"Yeah, she turned out to be tougher than you, eh?" Roman teased.

"Okay, before you two decide to take this conversation to another level, I think we should list all the questions and start getting some answers," Florence interrupted the two *boys*. "I'm concerned about Anne; she has been through a lot since we found her on the side of the road. I'm not sure how much more she is willing to take before she throws in the towel," Florence remarked.

Luc didn't think about it until Florence mentioned it. Throughout his life as a Feeder, this last couple of months has been hell. He couldn't imagine how he would manage being all new to this.

"I should take her up to the cabin for a bit," Luc said, thinking out loud.

"You may want to ask her what she wants to do," Florence advised knowing how Anne reacted to her when she did things without consulting her first.

MEGHAN HAD TO take a walk to clear her head of everything that had happened these last few days. Thinking back to the first day she met Anne, she knew they would become close friends and loved her dearly. Now Meghan betrayed her friendship and trust because of a man that showed interest in her, seduced her and used her. *How could she be so naïve and foolish.* Meghan's mind was racing in all directions on how stupid she was and how badly she hurt the people and vampires she loved. Kicking the sand as she walked, she noticed a man sitting on the edge of one of the mooring docks. He was a large man with very short red hair, wearing jeans and no shirt. The red hair was thick on his chest. As she came closer, she could see it was one of the newly turned vampires. She had not been introduced to him yet as he came and went so often that she only saw him in passing. Everyone had been kept busy, because of her stupidity, helping Raymond, putting everyone — especially Anne — in danger. As she walked onto the jetty, he turned to face her. Meghan noticed he didn't look too well. He had been sitting in the sun and his skin looked like it was blistering and drying out.

"What the hell are you doing out in the sun like that. Don't you know it's not doing you any good?" Meghan ran up to him, surprised to find him like this.

"Go away, lady," Michael said weakly.

"Why are you doing this to yourself?" Meghan asked as she bent down next to him. He looked like he was in pain; he was handsome and strong but obviously very stupid.

"It's an experiment," was all he said before he started to slump over, dangerously close to falling into the water.

"Wow, there," Meghan said as she pushed him back onto his back. As he stared up at her, she noticed his vampire eyes were a transparent gold going red, which experience told her he needed nourishment and fast.

"Do you have nourishment with you?" Meghan asked hopefully, knowing if he didn't, she was in danger.

Michael pointed weakly to the cooler that was next to him. Meghan stepped over him and opened the cooler to find two flasks of blood. She opened one, turned and lifted his head up for him to drink from it. As he drank from the flask greedily, he looked up into her beautiful chocolate brown eyes. Meghan looked back into his eyes and noticed they started to solidify but his skin needed to get out of the sun.

"You need to get into the shade. Can you get up?" Meghan asked.

"Yes, thank you," Michael replied turning over weakly onto his hand and knees, finding Meghan trying to help him up. He took her small hand in his and looked up to her, noticing how small she was.

"Lean on me a little. There's a little cave in the cliffs to the right of us," Meghan pointed out.

"Great, vampire going to his cave," Michael said with a smile as he lifted himself up with a little help of Meghan.

"What the hell are you thinking?" She pulled at his arm with all her might. "You could have killed yourself," she said grabbing the cooler. "Or was that your intention?" she asked worryingly as she tucked herself under one of his arms and started toward the cave.

"No, that was not my intention, believe me. It was just an experiment that didn't go the way I planned."

"No shit," Meghan said sarcastically, as they made their way over the beach toward the cliffs. *What was this guy thinking? Shit, he's big and God, he's handsome.* Meghan's mind was racing.

"Thanks for coming to my rescue," Michael said interrupting Meghan's thoughts, as they got to the cave, which was cool and moist. "This is perfect," Michael said.

Meghan pushed his heavy arm off her shoulder. Michael fell onto the sand and Meghan sat down on a rock closest to him, panting. As she was trying to get her breath back, Michael looked up at this beautiful young girl dressed in Goth black. "I'm Michael O'Sullivan; pleased to meet you," he stretched out his hand.

"Meghan McKay," she said taking his hand in hers. Michael pulled her down next to him.

"What're you doing?" she said, landing on her back in the sand next to him.

"I don't know," Michael replied leaning over her, looking at her round beautiful face down to her soft lips with a metal ring pierced through one of them. *What a pity that she had to interfere with such beauty,* he thought.

"You're smelling me," Meghan said, recognizing the look in his eyes. She has been around vampires too long — she knew what they looked like when they wanted to seduce and feed. "Don't you dare. I have the cooler with the other flask for you if you need more nourishment."

"Thanks again," Michael said as he sat up. He reached over to the cooler and took out the second flask and drank it down within two gulps.

Meghan got up. "What stupid experiment were you conducting

on yourself?" she asked.

"How long I can stand the heat of the sun before I pass out."

"So how long was it?"

"Less than an hour."

"And if you had passed out and fell into the water, who would have fished you out and gave you the nourishment?"

"You got me there."

"So you admit it was a very stupid experiment, wasn't it?"

"Admitted."

"I don't suppose you'll tell me why you didn't think this one through?"

"No, but it did help me meet you," Michael smiled.

"Now that is the dumbest come-on line I've ever heard."

"I wasn't coming on to you."

"What are you doing then?"

"You got me again." Michael started to laugh. "I think I have sunstroke."

"No shit," Meghan said standing up and walking out of the cave.

"Hold on, wait for me," Michael shouted as he took out a shirt and sunglasses from the cooler's side pocket. He then put them on and ran toward Meghan. Catching up to her, he took her hand in his. "So why dress up like you're going to a funeral?" Michael asked as he looked her over.

"It's called Goth," Meghan explained.

"Okay, may I say something?"

"Shoot."

"It doesn't suit you. I think you would look stunning in softer colors," Michael said looking down at her.

"Really?"

"Yes, really."

"Are you always so presumptuous?"

"No, just with you."

"Oh my God, you're really full of yourself, aren't you?"

"I'm honest to those I like and care about."

"Why should you care about me? We just met."

"I like you and the fact you cared enough about me to save me from certain death is big in my book," Michael smiled.

"Well, I think we will get on well then, now that we've established we like and care for each other," Meghan grinned.

WHEN LUC MET up with Anne later that day, they decided to go for a walk down on the beach. Luc wanted some quality and quiet time with her before the "farewell and thank you" dinner Sir Robert planned for all the Councilors and their families before they returned to their homes. Holding hands, they walked barefooted on the sand along the water's edge.

Luc did decide to ask Anne what she wanted to do. It surprised her, but she appreciated it, and answered his question as honestly as possible.

"Well, I would love to get my *normal* life back, which I know will not be possible. I have fallen in love with you and the family and cannot imagine my life without any of them or you. Especially you, Luc. I'm not going to give you up for anything Sire Raymond Pitout throws my way. Besides, I still need my blood drained, more so now than before because of what has happened these last few months. My body is over-stimulated and therefore it needs to be drained more often."

"When did Ian realize this?" Luc asked surprised to hear this bit of news.

"Well, Ian has this theory. He suspects the reason I'm recovering faster is because my body is over-generating blood due to being drained so many times these last few weeks. He also suspects it to ease off again," Anne explained.

"So how many times do you need this to be done?"

"Ian wants to keep me regular." She giggled, thinking about how it sounds. "He wants me to feed every two weeks," Anne continued.

"What, every two weeks? You can't be serious, Anne; that's way too much," Luc interrupted.

"Luc, calm down. He won't drain me as much as he does when we do our monthly." She tried to clarify it. "Ian explained it to me this way; we have five liters of blood in our bodies, right? So when we feed once a month, they take three liters of our blood, but now that I feed bi-weekly, he will only take two liters per feed. That way I keep more each time and there's less risk of my heart being unable to manage with too much blood pumping through it."

"You do realize they gain a liter a month by doing this," Luc advised.

"Well, then it's a win-win situation."

"So will you need to come to the Manor every two weeks?"

"No, Ian will be setting up a room at *Safe Haven* for me."

"Safe Haven?" Luc asked, looking at Anne.

"Yes, that's what I'm calling the house now, because that's what it is to me."

"You do have an interesting way of putting things and that's one of the things I love about you." Luc picked her up and swung her around; she grabbed him around his neck and laughed. She felt safe with him; this is what she loved about him and what made it even more special was being loved back.

As he put her down, they noticed another couple on the beach not too far away but enough just to make out their silhouettes due to the angle of the sun. "Is that not Michael and Mia?" Anne asked.

"No, she's too short to be Mia; that's Meghan." Luc squinted against the sun.

"Oh, Ooooh," Anne said in surprise.

"No, don't interfere with them now; you can ask her all about it when she gets you ready for dinner," Luc warned.

"Will Meghan still do that for me now that we're an item," Anne wondered.

"Why not? Your situation has not changed at the Manor," Luc advised.

"I suppose you're right; it just feels like everything has changed since you let me into your life."

"Oh. How so?" Luc asked.

"I feel like I'm whole, complete in a way; does that make any sense?" Anne looked up at Luc. He smiled knowing exactly what she meant.

TWENTY-FOUR

MAKING THEIR WAY back to the Manor, Anne kept on looking back to see if she could see Michael and Meghan, but after a while, she gave up as Luc kept on reminding her to stay out of it.

Getting to her room, she ran her own bath and putting on the jets, stepped into it and soaked. Anne got out when she started to prune and realized Meghan still had not made her appearance. So wrapping a towel around her, Anne decided to call Meghan's room to see if she was there. It took two rings and Meghan answered a bit out of breath. "I just got in. I'll be right there, Anne. Sorry," Meghan sang.

"I'm just making sure you're all right. I wanted some company, but you get ready and then come over, all right," Anne said politely, not letting on she was dying to find out what was going on with her and Michael.

About forty five minutes later, Meghan walked into the room. Anne dropped her favorite pendent that she wanted to wear as her accessory that evening. Meghan's appearance had completely changed. Instead of her *Goth black,* she was wearing a soft lavender silk dress that had a little bodice covering her shoulders and breasts, with low-heel sandals. Anne didn't realize how beautiful she was under all the black. Meghan didn't have her black make-up on nor all the piercing metal she wore in her nose, eyebrow, and lip and wherever else they were lodged.

"I need help," Meghan said as she walked in smiling at Anne's reaction.

"Could you send Meghan in? I don't know who you are," Anne teased.

"Ha, ha, very funny, but seriously, I need help with my make-up and nails."

"What's going on — why the sudden change in appearance?" Anne asked suspiciously.

"New month, new direction," Meghan replied.

"And a new man, perhaps?" Anne could not help herself. She was just bursting to find out. Now this drastic change of appearance certainly pushed her over the edge to ask.

"Maybe," Meghan teased.

"It's Michael, isn't it?"

"How?"

"Luc and I were taking a walk on the beach this afternoon and saw Michael but we weren't sure if it was you he was with."

"I kind of bumped into him. I decided to take a walk on the beach. I needed to clear my head with all the crap that has been going on these days and there he was, sitting on the pier. So I introduced myself; we started chatting about all sorts of things," Meghan said, crossing her fingers behind her back not telling Anne the complete truth of what happened.

"You do know he's a vampire?"

"Yes, of course I know he's a vampire and I also found out he's Mia's twin brother; you know they're not identical twins?"

"Yes, Meghan, I know that, but don't get too serious," Anne warned.

"We just talked, Anne, besides, once bitten twice shy." Meghan laughed.

"Good." Anne smiled.

"So are you going to help me here or not?" she said, changing the subject.

"Yes — sure — what do you need?" Anne made her way to the bathroom.

"Pastels colors — all I have is black," Meghan followed.

It took them twenty minutes to change Meghan from Goth to Princess. They painted Meghan's toes and while they dried, Anne did her make-up.

"Remember, less is more," Anne said turning Meghan so she could see the end result reflected in the mirror.

"Oh fu—"

"No! You don't use that language now, remember?" Anne interrupted.

"Anne, could you take me shopping in Vancouver tomorrow? I need a new wardrobe."

"I don't know what Florence has planned but we can ask. I don't see why not."

It had been two hours since Luc left Anne at her door to get ready for dinner. It felt like forever. When finally she walked in, in a pink silk dress that cupped her breasts and hugged her hourglass body then flowed down to the floor, he couldn't wait to get it off her again. But what came in next, he was not prepared for.

"Ladies and gentlemen, may I introduce the new Meghan McKay," Anne said, stepping aside as Meghan walked in. Everyone gasped.

"Oh, my little Meg is back." Sir Robert beamed as he walked over to Meghan to give her a big hug and a kiss on her forehead. This was the first time Anne had seen affection coming from the head Councilor.

Anne walked over to Luc and slid her arms around his waist. He put down his drink and slid his hand over her hip to her butt then up her back to her shoulder. The material felt soft under his hand and he realized there weren't any undergarments under her dress. He looked down at Anne with a lifted brow.

"Shh, our secret," she whispered.

"God, you have no idea what you're doing to me," he whispered in her ear seductively.

"I had no choice; silk shows up every little thing," she shivered at his touch.

Meghan came up to them with a large smile on her face. "Florence said it would be all right to go shopping tomorrow. She and Mia will be coming with us so we'll make it an all girls shopping day. It's going to be so much fun."

"That's great," Anne said, feeling Meghan's excitement.

As Meghan was discussing what she needed and planned to buy, Luc excused himself and came back with a cocktail for Anne.

After dinner, everyone went to the den and Anne made it over to her favorite corner of the balcony to watch the moon dance on the waves. This time, Luc stood behind her with his arms around her waist. She leaned against him to feel his warmth. "I want you," he whispered in her ear.

Anne could feel him harden as he said it. "Now too soon?" she asked. Holding her closer to him, she could feel him tense. "Let's go," he said as he took her hand and led her out of the den to his room. The door wasn't even closed yet when he was on her, his mouth was devouring hers as if this was his last kiss. Anne started to giggle; she didn't realize how nervous she was until he took hold of her. Luc stopped and looked at her. "What?"

"Nothing, just nervous," Anne replied. "I just need a bit of air, if you don't mind."

"Sure," Luc said and took her hand and led her to his balcony. Anne leaned against the wrought iron railing. Luc leaned against her again, running his hand over her hips and up to her breasts while he nibbled her ear. Anne moaned at the pleasure of it and leaned into him, feeling his hard body against her back. She put one hand up to his neck, grabbing his hair and wrapped the other behind them, pulling him closer to her. He turned her around, kissed her and took her hands to undo his pants and cup him. Feeling his hardness in her hands surprisingly aroused her even more. Luc started to lift up her dress slowly, then pulled it over her head. With all the imagination he had earlier, it didn't come close to the real thing. Anne had nothing under the dress except her skin that was as smooth as the silk dress itself. Feeling her under his hands, he wanted more all the while Anne was taking off his shirt and pulled down his pants, kissing and tasting him. Luc then turned her around again; he reached down between her legs with his fingers, stroking her softness. The moment he touched her, she jumped with pleasure. She moved her butt against him and found his hardness against her. She held the railing and dropping her back, aimed her butt toward Luc's erection, driving him crazy. "Take me, Luc," Anne whispered. Slowly he slid into her; she was hot and wet, ready for him. Anne gasped as he filled her, his erection hitting deep inside her core, which shot pure pleasure up her spine. Her legs weakened. Luc, taking her hips in his large hands, held her up to him and slowly rocked himself inside of her. With every thrust hitting that secret spot, she could feel herself climb higher and higher until it spilled over the edge. She gripped the railing, her knuckles turning white, as she cried out in gratification. As she convulsed, Luc found himself getting harder. He held her tighter and with a hard deep thrust, sending shockwaves down the shafts of his erection, he climaxed, filling her up. Once he got his breath back, he picked her up and took her to his bed. Too hot to climb under the covers, they lay on top of the quilt in each other's arms and finding peace, they fell asleep.

TWENTY-FIVE

MORNING CAME TOO soon and Anne had to get ready to meet Meghan, Mia, and Florence at the docks at nine o'clock. They took a boat to the mainland and once there, they found a vehicle that Sir Robert had arranged for them to use as needed. Anne offered to drive the BMW M6 Cabriolet, loving to feel the 500 hp it had to offer. Florence had to warn her about her speed several times before they got to Yale Town, which was one of Vancouver's trendy and upscale districts, home to some of the city's top fashion and design houses as well as cutting edge restaurants and bars. They shopped till they dropped; everyone nearly bought new wardrobes before Meghan finally finished her shopping list and some. They then decided to go for lunch at one of the restaurants with an outdoor patio that had a casual yet chic atmosphere. Florence and Mia kept them company as they ate; everyone was in good spirits and enjoyed each other's company. Anne noticed Florence looked a little uneasy, hoping it wasn't that she, too, was hungry and didn't bring any nourishment with her.

"What's up?" Anne asked Florence.

"Nothing."

"Florence, I know something's up. If you need nourishment, we can go back to the car and get some."

"No, please. No, it's not that; it may be worse." Florence took the menu and pretended she was reading it, lifting her eyes at something behind Anne every now and again.

Meghan, sitting across from Anne, looked up at what was behind her and also started to look concerned. Anne went for her bag under her chair and while doing so, looked at Mia, but she didn't seem to understand the situation either. So Anne took out her compact and making believe she was fixing her lipstick, looked behind her through the mirror. "What am I looking for?" Anne asked while tilting the mirror around and saw various people in different stages of eating their lunches.

"There are two men sitting at about five o'clock, if Meghan was noon," Florence explained. "They have been following us since we started shopping, at a distance at first, but now they're getting bolder and too close for comfort."

Anne saw two men both dressed in black — what's new? — sitting a few tables behind her, with two untouched beers on their table: One had long slightly wavy blond hair, dark eyes, with a harsh face and a scar under his left eye, the other had his back to her but had light mousy brown hair cropped into a military style cut. "Who are they?" Anne asked.

"Two of the Celtic Militia," Florence answered.

"Militia? – army, right?" Anne asked. Florence nodded.

"From the Irish Coven — what I can't figure out is why," Florence asked herself out loud.

"What do you suggest we do?" Mia asked before Anne had a chance to.

"We need to ease ourselves back to the car and get the hell out of here, as far away from those guys as possible," Florence suggested.

Anne noted the seriousness and nervous tone Florence had, which unnerved Anne. Meghan was as white as a sheet and didn't say a word; she signaled the waiter and indicated she wanted the bill. Once the bill arrived and was paid for, they all picked up their parcels and packages and briskly made their way through the crowds to the parking lot and their vehicle. Anne once again climbed into the driver's side; this time Florence didn't stop Anne from speeding, and they headed for the Lions Gate Bridge. Turning onto Stanley Park Causeway Road, Anne noticed a black Jaguar XKR swerving around vehicles to get closer to them, but was unable to appreciate the look of the car; she knew this was neither the time nor the place. She geared down to get more out of the BMW as she maneuvered around slower traffic to get distance between them, before she hit the Highway toward Horseshoe Bay. "Florence you may have to phone the marina and let them know we need the boat ready for departure, as we may be in a bit of a hurry; they're on my tail."

"Shit!" Florence said as she looked behind them. "Where?" Florence asked.

"Black Jag, two cars back; they should try to overtake that minivan any moment," Anne replied and her words weren't cold when the Jaguar overtook a Dodge Minivan swerving out of on-coming traffic.

"Can you lose them?" Florence asked.

Anne smiled. "Love to, but no guarantees. We're hitting the highway soon, so I may get distance," Anne replied. The BMW may be large but it has power if you use it correctly and Anne knew how to use engine power to her advantage.

As soon as Anne hit the highway, she had ten kilometers to get enough distance between the Irish and them before she had to turn off toward Sewell's Marina. They would then know where they were going for sure.

Swerving in and out of traffic, Anne made it look so easy, as she reached speeds between one hundred fifty to two hundred kilometers per hour. Meghan clenched her fist so hard, she would have nail dents in her hands for weeks.

Florence and Mia seemed to look relaxed but who could tell? Vampires didn't carry emotions on their sleeves like humans do. Anne was getting her adrenalin rush again and was in her element all the way. *Enjoying herself a bit too much,* Meghan thought. Mia sat next to Meghan turning her head to look behind them every now and again and noticing Meghan not looking too well. She reached over to take one of her clenched hands into her own. She smiled, reassuring her, which she knew wouldn't help. Being human, she remembered, wasn't easy when it came to fear. In a way, she missed that feeling, having her heart race and adrenalin making her sweat slightly. Florence was on the cell phone to the Marina asking them to have their boat prepared for departure, which took some persuasion, but Florence's calm bribing manner got them what they needed. Anne got at least ten car distances from the Jag, which was not all that good but was still working on it as she turned off onto Keith Road then left onto Bay Street. Sliding the car into Sewell's Marina's parking lot, Meghan was out before the car was turned off to get her stuff out of the trunk, not all the enemies of the world would prevent her from her purchases. Florence and Mia helped and ran with vamp speed with their packages toward the boat, Meghan and Anne a close second. They were in the boat taking off when they noticed the Jag pull into the parking area.

"Do you think they will find a boat and follow?" Meghan asked panicking.

"No, I made sure Stan wouldn't let anyone depart the marina for the next hour."

"How did you do that?" Anne asked.

"Money speaks volumes," Florence smiled.

When they got to Sir Roberts' Private Island, they moored the boat and carried their packages up to the Manor. Feeling a little relieved at being back, their spirits were up and cheerful again. The men sitting in the living room when they arrived wouldn't have thought anything was amiss until Florence briefly gave them a rundown of their day, ending with the chase and evading two of the Irish army's best men.

"Great, now we have the Irish wanting our Feeders," Roman said.

"How do you know they want Luc and Anne?" Mia asked.

"Thank Raymond and his world-wide display on the internet for that. I'm sure it's not only the Celtics that will want our Feeders now, but everyone else that was given the password and was able to bid for Anne," Roman replied.

"Oh my, I'm sure Raymond did this on purpose; he knew that this would happen," Anne said angrily.

Florence called the three security heads to the control center for a meeting to advise them of what transpired that day. It was a good thing Florence insisted that the security personnel stay behind for a couple of days longer to tie up some loose ends and organize a hunt for Raymond and his new family before they, too, left the Manor.

"How can you be sure that was their intention to take Anne? Trust me when I say this, I know these men and if they wanted Anne, they would have her by now," the Halifax team leader said.

"Maybe we should contact the Celtic Council and find out what they want," the Calgary leader advised.

The rest of them thought that would be risky but a good idea, so Florence sent an e-mail requesting a conference and asked why they sent two of their best men out to Vancouver. The reply was a minute later, requesting that the conference between the two Councilors be concluded in an hour's time.

Sir Robert and the teams sat in the command center's board room and waited to be linked. Finally a big, red haired Irish man appeared on the large monitor mounted on the wall.

210 ANITA E. VILJOEN

"Good evening, gentlemen and ladies," he bellowed.

"Good evening, Sir Gregory," Sir Robert announced.

"So you bumped into my finest, did ye?"

"Yes and we want to know why," Sir Robert asked.

"Well, it's like this — we're a little curious," Sir Gregory replied.

"Curious about what?"

"Your Feeders, Sir Robert, your Feeders."

"What about them?"

"You have two active ones now, don't you Sir Robert?"

"Yes, so?"

"Planning to obtain anymore?"

"If possible, yes. Why?" Sir Robert said, getting a little anxious.

"Well, we need to know how you're planning on doing this," Sir Gregory replied with a little grin on his face. "As you know, we have one of our own and through the centuries there has always just been one or at maximum, two overlapping."

"We had the same situation," Sir Robert acknowledged.

"Until now."

"Yes, until now. What's your point or concern, Sir Gregory?"

"Sire Raymond Pitout and his little auction — I paid top Euro for your little Annie as he named her."

"Anne was not Sire Raymond Pitout's to auction off in the first place, Sir Gregory. She is under contract with me and there will be no negotiations for her."

"I was afraid you would say that. I'll be in contact with you again. I need to consult with our elders," Sir Gregory said, then nodded and the signal was disconnected.

"Shit, I wonder how many covens paid for Anne, not getting a return on their investment," Luc wondered aloud.

The room fell silent.

TWENTY-SIX

THE TEAM DECIDED to keep on alert. As far as the Celtics were concerned, Sir Robert talked to Sir Gregory and persuaded him to personally hold off what they were planning and help them find Raymond and his lair of vampires to get their revenge and steer them away from Sir Robert's Council. Sir Gregory said he would hold off and would do his best from his side to find out more about Sire Raymond Pitout, as he came from France centuries ago and history always has a way of repeating itself, so they may get an idea of what Raymond may be up to. They found the Celtics weren't really a threat; they only wanted what they paid for, which led them to help Sir Robert's teams.

LUC TOOK MICHAEL and Roman up to the cabin in the Rocky Mountains again to backtrack and trace Raymond's movements before, during, and after Anne's and his abductions. The Calgary and Halifax teams went up to Yellowknife where Raymond lived and had his original family of twelve.

☾◌☽

FLORENCE KEPT TABS on the media for any further developments of the missing young men country-wide and followed up
with the other team leaders with their investigations.

☾◌☽

ANNE AND IAN had to get back to work as they had patients to
see. Mia joined Anne in her scheduled appointments and routines
for safety sake; it also kept Luc happy. Mia followed Anne down
the cancer care ward of the RM Hospital early that morning; she
knew now where Anne was going as they had been there before.
When they got to Mr. Thompson's room, Mia said she would sit
at the nurse's station and wait for her unless she wanted her closer.
Anne felt safe at the hospital now and needed to talk to Mr.
Thompson in private anyway.

Anne knocked and entered Mr. Thompson's room to find him
reading a book.

"Anne, so what happened? Your bodyguard didn't like the idea
of you skipping off on her like that. I'm glad to see everything
went well." Mr. Thompson smiled.

"Thanks for helping me out the other day; it was a bit intense
and a lot happened," Anne said and filled Mr. Thompson in as to
what happened right up to the day before they came back to
Maple Ridge.

"Well now you know not to underestimate the enemy, Anne.
You could have lost your life, but I'm glad Luc insisted that Mia
be here to protect you."

"You know Luc?" Anne asked surprised.

"Of course I do. I taught him everything he has to know about
being a Feeder," Mr. Thompson winked.

"Could you tell me about how you met him and what he was
like back then?" Anne asked.

"Well, to give you a little background: Luc served under the 82nd Airborne Division of the U.S. Air Force. He and others in his division were sent out to drop a squadron of Parachute Infantry, as part of the invasion of Normandy. It was known as Operation Neptune, an airborne assault phase of the *Overlord Plan*; you can find it in the history books, you know? Anyway, Luc was intercepted by a German fighter plane and shot down. He bailed out of the plane just in time, but landed in a wooded area, nearly breaking his damn neck. Thank goodness a patrol of French infantry found him dangling from a tree. They cut him down and got him to the closest Army hospital they could find and it happened to be where Ian and I were stationed at the time."

"You were stationed with Ian in France?"

"Yes, the whole family was in France during World War II to help out. Sir Robert didn't join the armed forces but infiltrated the German network and supplied the Americans and English with vital information."

"He was a spy?"

"Yes," Mr. Thompson replied. "Getting back to Luc, Ian got Luc nursed back to health and in doing so realized what he was and took him under his wing, so to speak. Slowly, Ian explained what the family was and what I was and how to become a Feeder. Ian helped him physically and mentally getting back on his feet. Luc and I became good friends and when the war finally ended, we all came back to Canada."

"When did you become a Feeder, Mr. Thompson?"

"Oh, my. I became a Feeder at the age of sixteen and stopped using vamp blood at the age of sixty."

"So how many years have you been drinking vampire blood?"

"About 388 years, give or take a few, not sure. I came over to Canada with Sir Robert McKay as his Feeder back in 1621."

"Wasn't that the same time Dr. Anderson and Florence came over, too?"

"Yes," Mr. Thompson said, not elaborating.

"Did you know them when you were on the ship?"

"I met them on the ship, yes."

"Mr. Thompson, who turned them? I know it happened on that ship because Ian told me that when I first met them, but I didn't asked them then."

"Sir Robert turned them."

"Why?"

"They were dying and Sir Robert took pity on them. He saw their potential in starting his family here in Canada. They have been together ever since."

"And you provided them with blood."

"Yes."

Anne was busy massaging Mr. Thompson's hands while she sat next to him in silence for a bit, processing everything they just discussed.

"Mr. Thompson, you stopped drinking vamp blood at the age of sixty. Why?"

"I lived my life, Anne; everything should come to an end sooner or later. I wanted it to be fully human, not thinking that in the twenty years without vamp blood, I would get cancer. But that's the hand I was dealt so I'm playing the game till the end," Mr. Thompson said without a hint of sadness. He looked content.

"Mr. Thompson, you're not worried about dying alone?"

"Alone — I'm not alone, Anne. I still have family," he said, surprised at the question.

"Then why do you want to die in hospital and not at the Manor?"

"Sir Robert had already asked me to go over to the Manor. I declined."

"Why? They have a medical center there to take care of you should you need extra care, but at least you will be with all of us."

"Are you offering this for you or for me?"

"I guess it's for me. I would like to be with a family that loves me when I die," Anne said.

"I suppose to be close to others does help, but I can't bear others feeling sorry for me," Mr. Thompson said.

"I understand but we feel sorry for you now anyway." Anne smiled.

"As strange as that sounds, you may be right," Mr. Thompson laughed.

"Please consider it?"

"I will."

"I'll give you till tomorrow. When I come back, I would like to know."

"You're certainly giving me a lot of time," Mr. Thompson said sarcastically.

"There's no better time than the present. Besides, I would love for you to accompany me for one of my biweekly feedings. I will need to do it at the Manor; Dr. Anderson has been quite busy lately so the house has not been set up for it yet. I also may have more questions for you."

"Oh, really, have you not sifted through my brain enough already?"

"No," said Anne smiling as she was making her way out. Mia saw Anne leave the room with a smile on her face. Standing up and starting to walk toward Anne, her cell phone rang; it was Florence asking her to go past her apartment. Mia was wise enough not to ask why, so she agreed and clipped her phone back onto her belt. "So how did it go?" Mia asked Anne as she came up to her. "Great, I got so much information from him," Anne replied. "Who just called?" she asked.

"It was Florence. She wants us to go past my apartment."

"Oh, when last have you been there?"

"Not since I was turned."

"Really?" Anne asked surprised.

Mia just shrugged and gave Anne her address. They made their way to Mia's apartment in silence. Mia was a bit apprehensive about going back to the last place she was human. She left everything behind the night she went out to meet her girl friends at the bar. As far as they were concerned, she was missing or dead.

When they arrived, Florence was already there waiting for them. Anne was pleased to be able to support Mia in this tough transition, but it needed to be seen to and many questions needed to be answered. Mia let them all into her apartment. It looked exactly the way she left it a couple of months before. She noticed her answering machine's light flickering and automatically walked over to listen to the messages. There were a few from her girl friends asking her to phone them as soon as she got this message, a couple from her manager at the restaurant she waitressed, first concerned, then saying she was fired, another from various fashion houses asking her to model for them.

Mia looked over to Florence with tears in her eyes. Anne didn't know vampires could feel emotions let alone cry, but it was evident they did. Florence walked over to Mia and put a hand on her shoulder. "We need you to close this door of your life, Mia."

"How do I do this?" she sobbed.

"Firstly, you need to call your friends and co-workers to let them know that you are all right as far as they're concerned. It's up to you if you want to keep in contact with them, though," Florence explained. "I will help you move out of here, so we need to know what you want to keep and what you like to part with. As you know, you are part of our family now, so you can either move into our home or find another apartment where no one knows you. It will be safer keeping your identity of what you are a secret," Florence advised.

Anne walked over to Mia and seeing how upset she was, took her hand in hers. "I'll help you get through this if you want me to," Anne said.

"I'll appreciate your support, Anne, but I need to take care of this myself."

"I'll leave the SUV. I'll go with Anne," Florence said giving Mia the keys.

"You call as soon as you need me for anything." Anne squeezed her hand, and then left with Florence.

TWENTY-SEVEN

MIA CLOSED THE door behind them, giving Anne a reassuring smile. The first thing she did was call her friends and co-workers, advising them she was *alive* and well. It was harder than she expected; if she died, she would be going straight to hell the lies she was telling. She also had to phone a detective at the Maple Ridge RCMP, Missing Persons Department, advising him she was not missing any longer, which proved to be the hardest to do. She had to go down to the Police Headquarters to confirm her identity and give a statement as to what happened. Again, she had to lie; she advised them that she went off with Raymond Pitout, found out it didn't work out between them and when she came back, she found that her friends reported her missing. Mia found herself at the Police Headquarters for hours; finally, when she was allowed to leave, she went back to her apartment to pack a few personal items into boxes left by Florence. It was past midnight when Mia came home to *Safe Haven* with a SUV full of boxes containing her clothing and personal items. As Mia walked into the house with a couple of boxes, Florence came out of her office to see how she was and helped her unload the rest of her things. Anne woke up hearing Mia's voice downstairs. As Anne came out of her room, she saw her standing with Florence in the foyer.

"You're back," Anne said excitedly, coming down the stairs tying her robe's belt around her waist.

"Yes, sorry it took so long. I didn't realize the cops were involved. A couple of my friends reported me missing, so I had to clear that mess up. I never lied so much in my life," Mia explained.

"I'm sorry you had to go through that," Florence sympathized. "It was much easier to be turned in the sixteenth century than it is now. Thank goodness you and Michael don't have close family; it could have been harder," Florence said.

"I need some nourishment," Mia stated.

"Certainly, there's some in the kitchen. I took some out to warm up earlier for Ian, so it should be the perfect temperature now," Florence explained going back to the study.

"Thanks, Florence," Mia said heading toward the kitchen; Anne followed her to make a cup of tea and catch up on Mia's day.

While boiling the water, Anne noticed Mia was deep in thought as she sat at the kitchen table drinking her nourishment.

"What's up, Mia?" Anne asked concerned.

"I don't know if I can do this for the rest of eternity, Anne," Mia said with sadness in her eyes.

"I'm sure it can be difficult right now as it's all new to you, but I'm sure it gets better in time. Maybe you should talk to Roman about this; he has such a beautiful way of explaining things," Anne noted.

"Yes, that he does, but he makes me nervous," Mia said.

"Nervous?" Anne stopped pouring the water in her cup. "Why does he make you nervous?"

"You can keep this a secret if I tell you, right?" Mia asked nervously.

"Right," Anne frowned.

"I like him."

"Like him?" Anne looked puzzled. "I like him, too, but I don't get nervous," Anne said.

"Yes, but I *really* like him. Heart rate rising, palm sweating, adrenalin pumping — if I could feel those things — like him," Mia tried to explain.

"Oh, you *like* him," Anne finally got it. It must have been the hour they were having this conversation, because she was sure she would have understood Mia sooner if she had more sleep. "So what are you going to do about it?" she asked.

"I'm not going to do anything about it until I know for certain he feels the same way. Right now, I think he's scared of me," Mia said.

"Scared of you?" Anne asked.

"Every time I'm near him, my electrical current shoots up and I'm sure he can sense the buzz of energy from me, so he stays far away."

"Well, I don't blame him; you shocked him twice," Anne laughed.

"Yeah, I just wish I could control it though," Mia replied unhappily.

"Maybe you can with practice."

"Maybe. I'll ask Florence to help me with that because she seems to be very interested in my *ability.*" Mia said then looked up toward the door. "Ian's home."

"How do you know that?"

"I hear his car coming up the driveway."

"Mia, may I ask you some questions about the differences you experience between being human and being a vampire?"

"Sure, I don't think there are rules against that, especially coming from a Feeder," Mia said smiling but Anne noticed it didn't quite get to her eyes. "Finish making your tea and we'll go up to your room," Mia advised.

Anne did that, while Mia finished her nourishment, rinsed out her cup and laid it upside down on the drying rack, and then poured a cup of nourishment for Ian. Cup in hand, Anne and Mia left the kitchen just as Ian came in the front door greeted by Florence with a long exclusive kiss. Anne stood dead still, admiring how long Florence and Ian have been together still so intimate and in love. As they turned to face them, Anne could feel herself blush. "Good morning, Dr. Anderson," Anne said noting the time.

"What are you still doing up?" Ian asked.

"I'm chatting with Mia but on my way back up to bed," Anne explained feeling like a little girl again.

"You need your rest. I noticed how hard you have been working again," Ian said.

Anne smiled and walked over to Ian and gave him a peck on the cheek. She loved him dearly as he reminded her so much of her father. Ian held her by the shoulders. "Stop calling me Dr. Anderson, will you? I'm Ian," he smiled.

"Ian," Anne confirmed.

Mia came over with his nourishment and handed it to him. Taking his hands off Anne, he took the cup. "Thanks, Mia. Oh and Anne, Mr. Thompson said *yes* to your and Sir Robert's invitation."

Taking Florence around her waist with his free hand, they left to go to their room, which was on the opposite side of the house from where Anne's and Mia's rooms were. Anne noticed all the boxes were missing from the hallway. "Where're your boxes?"

"In my room. Come on, it's late and Ian's right; you need your rest," Mia said as she started up the stairs. In the room, Anne and Mia were lying on Anne's bed getting comfortable.

"So what's the difference?" Anne asked taking a sip of her tea.

"Where do you want to start?"

"Well, let me explain what happens to me when I take vamp

blood and you confirm or explain it," Anne suggested.

"All right." Mia shifted on her side to face Anne.

"Light — it's more intense. It's as if I can see the colors in it."

"Well, light hurts my eyes. That's why we wear sunglasses during the day and that's why the house lights are dim. Sun also drains my energy if I'm in it too long," Mia explained.

"Wow, I noticed the lights and the sunglasses but I thought it was because it looked cool," Anne laughed. "What do you see at night, then?" she asked.

"The night is not dark; it's like dusk all the time. I also see thermal images of things, so it's easy to identify them," Mia explained.

"Explain thermal images."

"A thermal image is seeing the heat a living thing projects; the darker the image, the colder it is and the lighter it is, the hotter it is."

"What about your hearing?" Anne asked.

"I can hear sounds humans can't, just like I can hear your heartbeat clearly right now, but my hearing can be controlled so that loud noises can't hurt me."

"What about other senses?"

"To give you a rundown of how I feel physically and emotionally, it's like being high all the time. I don't feel physical pain but I can get emotionally hurt. I feel the air physically move around me and sense the temperature change when someone warm, or should I say human, enters a room. I'm very strong and more powerful than you can imagine. I don't get tired at all physically at night but need to rest, mostly during the day when the sun is out; like I said before the sunlight drains me."

"Oh, so that's why when it's cloudy you seem to be fine moving around with me but when it's sunny you don't come out at all," Anne said now understanding the reason.

"Well, there you are. Anything else?" Mia asked.

"I don't mean to pry but don't go through what I did with Luc. It took a long time to convince him that we are meant to be together. Roman does not have issues like Luc has, so get Roman to understand the way you feel about him. It's easier on the heart — believe me," Anne said quietly, taking her last gulp of tea and putting the empty cup onto the night stand.

"I think it's time for you to get some sleep," Mia said, noting it was close to three in the morning already. Giving Anne's hand a squeeze, she made her way to the door. "Good night, Anne," Mia said and left.

"Good night, Mia, and thanks." Anne settled down under the covers and fell asleep almost immediately.

Mia made her way back to her room to find all the boxes she packed earlier stacked in one corner of the room. She started to unpack her clothing into the walk-in closet that was in between the bedroom and bathroom. It didn't take as long as packing them as she didn't know what she would like to keep and what she didn't. She unpacked all her personal mementos and laid them on the floor to take another look at before she put them into the shelving units and drawers in her room. There were photos of her and Michael in uniform, before he left for Afghanistan, and older photos of their parents and past pets, little trinkets Michael brought back from his overseas visits, various books, albums, CDs, her stereo system, TV and alarm clock, which she was sure she would never use again, but which had memories attached to them and made her feel more human. It then struck her how she missed being human. It meant giving up a lot of things she loved, like eating her favorite meals, clubbing with her friends, and meeting different guys. She felt lonely and miserable. She had feelings that she couldn't explain going through her right now so she decided to take a cold shower. The sun was breaking through the windows already when she decided to climb into the shower and wash her hair. Being cold blooded now, she found it pleasant that the shower be cool. She just wanted to feel the water hit her body and freshen up, then go to bed and rest a little before she accompanied Anne to work. But she kept feeling the urge deep inside of her she never felt before; it was not like being hungry and needing nourishment but this was an urge for a man. Mia laughed at herself for feeling this way. Was it because she and Anne spoke about Roman and her feelings for him that had been hidden and were surfacing that made her feel this way? Also, perhaps knowing Roman, Michael, and Luc should be coming back today got her wound up. Mia didn't know what to make of it and decided to ask Florence.

Getting dressed, she went down to find Florence back in her office.

Knocking on the door, Mia said "Sorry to bother you, Florence."

"No bother. What's up, Mia?" Florence asked. As she turned around to look at Mia, she could tell what was wrong.

"I'm not quite sure how to explain this but I feel—"

"I know exactly what it is," Florence interrupted and got up to take Mia by the hand and walked her back to her room.

"No matter what, you do not come out of your room — for your own safety and the ones in this house," Florence said sternly.

"But what's going on with me?" Mia asked.

"You're going through your hormonal stage right now. I'm sorry I can't help you through this, but I can tell you that you need to work on controlling it and the desire working its way through you, Mia," Florence said despondently.

"I never had the feeling before. How do I satisfy it?" Mia asked in a panic.

"I may be able to send Christopher and Calvin up to help you, but that's up to you, and please don't kill them," Florence smiled at Mia.

"What? Why should I do that?" Mia really started to worry.

"Mia, like I said, you'll need to work this out yourself." With that, Florence left the room and closed the door behind her, finding Anne walking out of her bedroom ready for the day.

"Off to work, I see," Florence said.

"Yes, is Mia ready yet?" Anne asked.

"No, she won't be joining you today," Florence said sternly.

"Oh, why not?" Anne knew by Florence's tone not to ask but it was out before she could stop herself. "Sorry, Florence, you don't need to explain."

"Good, have a good day then," Florence said walking back to her office.

Anne walked past Mia's room trying to listen for her but thought it wise to leave things as is and went to work without her.

TWENTY-EIGHT

ANNE HAD A long day at work so she was exhausted when she came back to Safe Haven. As she walked in, she heard furniture breaking, shouting and screaming and all of a sudden one of Florence's vampires, number three, aka Calvin, came flying over the balcony shirtless, landing in front of her. Anne screamed in surprise and fear. Number three got up shaking his head and walked down to the basement. "What the hell is going on here?" Anne shouted.

"Anne, I'm in here," Florence called out from the den, reading the daily newspaper.

"What's going on here?" Anne repeated her question, hearing more furniture being thrown around upstairs. It was coming from Mia's room.

"Oh, it's Mia going through her hormonal stage right now," Florence replied, not taking heed to the noise or swearing.

"I didn't know vampires got PMS," Anne said in amazement.

"We don't physically but we do go through the hormonal ups and downs. But Mia is not PMS-ing; she's ovulating, which according to Ian is worse. She will kill to be satisfied, and so far although no one has died yet, by the sound of it, she has not been satisfied," Florence giggled.

"Oh my God, you can't be serious," Anne said.

"Anne, let me ask you something. How many female vampires have you come across since you've been with us?" Florence asked.

"Hmm, two: you and Mia. Oh yes, a few in the councilors' families," Anne replied, hoping it was not a trick question.

"Yes, you are correct and how many men?"

"Oh gee, a hell of a lot. I would say one hundred and forty give or take a couple," Anne replied trying to be accurate. "But why?" she asked.

"Good question. The answer is simple. We're dangerous," Florence replied followed by another smash of furniture. "There are covens made up of just women and they are the strongest covens in the world. Vampires don't mess with female vampires if they value their lives," Florence smiled.

Just then Roman came in and had the same reaction Anne had — well not exactly the same — he didn't scream or have a body nearly drop on him. As he made his way up the stairs to investigate, Florence came out of the den calling after him. "Roman, I wouldn't go in there if I were you," Florence advised.

"She's wrecking the place," he said on his way to her bedroom.

As he reached the door, he could hear her swearing and tearing something; he entered quietly. He found pieces of furniture in bits and pieces, curtains pulled off rails, bedding lay around and pillows torn with feathers all over. Mia had her back to him tearing a pillow, kneeling naked on the bed. He approached and grabbed her from the back, pinning her arms to her sides, lifting her off the bed with her feet four inches off the ground.

"Stop it, Mia, stop it; calm the hell down," he repeated. Mia wrenched and kicked, trying to get out of his hold. "Let go of me, you bully," Mia shouted, letting go enough electrical charge to have him drop her. She hardly touched the floor when Roman grabbed her by the throat and pushed her against one of her bedroom walls. Mia had another surge of anger go through her; she thought if she was human, she would be gasping for air right now. Roman had her lifted off the floor with one hand. He felt the shock run through him, but this time he held on, the tingle surprisingly aroused him. "Will you calm down?" he said gritting his teeth as he fought against the electrical surges going through him one after another.

Tears started trickling down Mia's cheek; she closed her eyes trying to calm herself. She opened them again when she felt his breath on her face; he smelled like lavender, which surprisingly soothed her. The shock waves ceased so Roman released her slowly back down to the floor but didn't let her go. He started nibbling her lower lip then teased her with his tongue. She opened her lips and let him in; he tasted as good as he smelled. She could not get enough of him. She hungrily allowed him to take her where she wanted to be hours ago. She tore off his shirt and started unbuttoning his jeans. *God, he looked good in jeans*, she thought, arousing her even more. She couldn't wait — she had to have him now. Taking her hands in his, Roman slowed her down. He kissed her down her neck, down to her breasts. One at a time, he licked and teased each one till they peaked with desire. "I want you now," she pleaded.

"Calm down," he said seductively, knowing he was driving her crazy. He made his way down her stomach and then found the soft spot between her legs. She shuddered with pleasure. While he was down there with his tongue teasing her, he took off his boots. Just before she came, he stopped. "No!" she cried. He stood up again, taking her hands to help him undo his jeans; stepping out of them, he lifted her up and kissed her, making their way to the bed.

Taking his erection into her hands, she gasped at the size. Roman smiled. "If you're not able to handle me, you need to back off me now, otherwise you'll be in *big* trouble," Roman mocked.

"You want to bet," Mia replied shifting under him and kissing him. "Take me now," Mia begged. "Are you sure?" Roman asked. Looking into her eyes, he saw something in them he didn't understand. As they held each other, Mia surrendered to him fully and felt overwhelmed with emotions she didn't expect. Neither of them understood what they felt and saw in each other, but one thing was for certain: they both needed sexual release very soon.

"Yes!" Mia replied and opened herself to him. She slowly guided him in. The charge was overwhelming as she came. Shaking violently, she felt herself bite down into something. At the same time she came, hardly entering her, he felt her bite into him sending a shock wave of sexual ecstasy down his spine. By the second thrust of his hips, he exploded into her, filling her up.

They lay there for a while not moving, letting the orgasms dissipate, just to find them starting up again. Roman was still in her when she felt him swell with arousal. He kissed and nibbled her neck while his fingers teased her breasts. She moved her hips to take him in even deeper than before, not thinking it possible. Roman closed his eyes, feeling the burn of desire run up the shafts of his erection as he was riding her for the second time. This time she could feel him pulsate as he reached another orgasm. The largeness of him touched places in her she didn't think existed. The second time she came, she held him tightly and wrapped her legs around his hips, feeling every muscle contract with desire. They lay quietly in each other's arms, saying nothing, just feeling each other's desires and fulfilling them. It took a couple of hours for her head to clear when she sat up leaning on one elbow to look at him. It was then she saw the blood. "Oh no, what happened?" she gasped.

Roman was lying with his eyes closed and didn't realize what she had seen. "What?" he said and jumped up.

"You were bleeding," she cried.

"I know. You bit me earlier this evening." Roman sighed with relief and lay back down, taking her into his arms.

"When, why? I couldn't have possibly done that?" she asked frantically.

"Don't worry, vampires do it to each other in heat of passion all the time," Roman explained.

"But you didn't bite me," she noticed.

"No, that would have sent you over the edge."

"I was over the edge many times tonight. How much further over the edge could a bite take you?"

"You'll be surprised but you're not ready for that yet."

"Why do you always challenge me?" she started to get angry.

"I'm not challenging you; I'm just being considerate."

"Take me there?" Mia asked.

"Maybe later," Roman teased.

"No now!" she climbed on top of him taking his hands in hers and lifting them above his head. Leaning over him, she put her neck to his mouth and feeling him going hard against her stomach, she lifted herself up and guided him into her again. Roman had never come so many times in one night before. He also never had a lover able to take him so far in before either. As Mia rode him, he could feel her tense like she did before she came, which would be a perfect time to bite into her. Taking his arms out from under hers, he held her head exposing her throat and he put the other arm around her body to stabilize her. As he bit down into her, she gasped and her eyes widened with surprise. Her whole body jolted and vibrated, and she thought she was going to die with pleasure, if that was at all possible. She let out a loud cry as she came; it took her far over the normal level of ecstasy. She fell down on top of him with pure exhaustion, which she hadn't felt since she became a vampire. Roman laughed at her. "You see, you're not ready for it yet," he whispered in her ear.

"Hmm, you're right," was all she could manage to say.

∞

A FEW DOORS down, Anne and Luc were lying in each other's arms. Hearing Mia and Roman most of the night was really a challenge to stay focused on what they tried to achieve. "You think they are finally done?" Anne asked mockingly. Luc's chest vibrated with a laugh. "I certainly hope so."

Propping herself up on one elbow looking down on Luc, she said "Do you think we can achieve what they did if we drink more vamp blood?"

"We achieve quite a lot with the amount running through our veins already; do you really want to see where it takes us if we had more? How much more intense can it get without being dangerous?" Luc said in a worried tone.

"I suppose you're right; it's intense already and really satisfying," Anne smiled down at him.

"Come here," Luc took her around her waist and laid her on him.

"Oh my, Mr. Hastings, you surprise me." Anne giggled, feeling his hardness against her stomach.

"Miss Patterson, before I surprise you even more, I need to ask you something." Luc looked nervous all of a sudden.

"Shoot," Anne said smiling.

"Will you marry me?" Luc asked.

"What?" Anne asked, lifting her head up a little more to focus on Luc's face.

"Will you marry me?" Luc repeated the question.

Tears started to roll down Anne's face with the overwhelming joy she felt. Anne took Luc's face between her hands and started kissing him. "Yes," she said as she kissed him all over his face.

"What did you say?" Luc asked teasingly between her kisses.

Lifting her head up again and looking into his eyes, "I said yes."

"I was hoping that was what you said," Luc said as he lifted her up and glided himself into her. Anne gasped with the thrill of him in her and the happiness running through her. She held him tight, never to let him go, as he took her to her favorite place and filled her up.

Luc moved her into his arms again and leaned over to the side table drawer and took out a little black box. Anne's eyes widened as she saw what he had in his hand. "You didn't think I wouldn't make it official, did you?"

"You planned this?" Anne asked, surprised.

"Yes, I did. When we dropped Michael off at the Manor, I asked Sir Robert if I could ask you to marry me. Being under contract with him, I had to find out if it was all right," Luc explained.

Anne smiled at him, understanding perfectly. She took the black velvet box he offered her. As she opened it, she found a large emerald surrounded by six diamonds. She gasped with delight.

"It goes with your eyes," Luc said.

"Oh Luc, it's beautiful," Anne said as she had him put it onto her ring finger. "It fits perfectly; thank you, Luc, thank you so much," she said starting to cry again.

"It's my pleasure, my love," Luc said and held her tight against him feeling her wet face against his.

Anne could not wait to tell everyone about her engagement to Luc and show off her new ring, but they decided to wait until they were all together at the Manor on the weekend.

TWENTY-NINE

AFTER LUC'S MEETING with Sir Robert, which apparently went off well by the look of them, Luc and Roman went back to the mainland with the Black Hawk leaving Michael behind on request. It was late evening and he thought he may find Meghan in the den with Sir Robert as it was nearly her supper time and as tradition, they always met for drinks first before she had her meal. Michael walked into his favorite room to find Meghan sitting at the bar chatting to Sir Robert who was in his favorite chair next to one of the patio doors that led out to the balcony. The door was open, letting in the sea breeze and the gold and red sun rays that touched Meghan's skin, making it glow against her pitch black hair. It took his breath away to see her like that. She was in a soft yellow sundress that insinuated her womanhood and made her look like a Greek goddess.

"Well good evening, Michael," Sir Robert greeted Michael seeing him standing at the doorway staring at Meghan.

Clearing his dry throat, Michael greeted them back politely.

Meghan jumped off her bar stool and walked over to Michael.

"What're you doing here?" she asked excitedly.

"I can always leave," Michael teased.

"Don't be silly, young man. Come join us, have a glass of whiskey with me," said Sir Robert not catching Michael's taunt.

"Thank you, Sir Robert." Michael bowed and took a seat next to him while Meghan poured him a glass of scotch whiskey.

"So what made you stay at the Manor?" Sir Robert asked.

"Well Sir, firstly, Meghan, and secondly, we did our assignment so until we regroup and receive new orders, I asked Florence for some R and R," Michael said smiling at Meghan.

"So you're here to court Meghan, eh?" Sir Robert asked surprised.

"With your permission, of course, Sir," Michael replied.

"Well this is a surprise. You do know she's human?" Sir Robert asked.

"Yes of course, Sir," Michael shocked at the statement took his eyes off Meghan and looked over to Sir Robert.

"And she will stay human until she turns thirty or I decide otherwise. No harm will come to her mentally or physically, do I make myself clear?" Sir Robert asked sternly.

"Sir Robert, really?" Meghan chipped in.

"Do I make myself clear?" Sir Robert repeated.

"Yes, Sir! I wouldn't dream of turning her or harming her in any way, Sir," Michael replied. "I respect her and you too much for that, Sir," he added.

"Good," Sir Robert warned.

Meghan was called to supper and after she dined with her two favorite vampires joining her at the table with their nourishments, Sir Robert retired to his office to take care of some important business. She suggested to Michael they take a walk in the gardens, to be out of ear and eye surveillance that was scattered all over the Manor.

"So you came to court me?" Meghan teased.

"Yes and have my life threatened," Michael replied.

"Oh, that was just a warning. You haven't seen Sir Robert angry or threatening; it isn't pretty."

"I'm sure it isn't."

"I've never been courted before," Meghan said, feeling a little nervous about actually dating someone and not just winging it.

"Never?" Michael stopped at a garden bench and took a seat.

"No, never," Meghan said sitting next to him, but making sure she didn't touch him. Michael noticed her effort with the way she crossed her arms as they walked making sure he didn't take her hand.

"Meghan, am I making you nervous?" Michael asked.

"No, not at all," she lied and deliberately looked away from him.

"Meghan, look at me and say that again."

Meghan's heart started to race and she felt her cheeks flush. "All right, a bit, yes," she said still not looking at him.

Michael leaned over and took her chin in his hand and moved her head over to face him. "Why? Is it because of what I am?" Michael asked.

"Not because you're a vampire — it's because I'm attracted to the man you are," Meghan whispered.

"Well, thank you for your honesty but I think you should be nervous at both," Michael said and got up to put some space between them.

"Michael, stop, don't walk away from me," Meghan said, upset. "If you're going to walk away because of my honesty on how I feel about you, I will lie to keep you near me," Meghan murmured.

"I'm not walking away from you because you told me you're attracted to me, Meghan. I'm putting some space between us because of what I'm capable of doing to you. God, you have no clue, do you?"

"Yes I do. You smell my blood and hear my heart race. You're newly turned, so I can imagine what it must be like. It's like having a plate of fresh delicious cookies put in front of me and being asked not to eat them."

Michael laughed. "Yes, you're a very large batch of fresh double chocolate cookies."

"Double chocolate. Mmm, now you are talking," Meghan teased and got up from the bench and walked over to him. "Michael, I trust you," she said taking her hands to touch his face. He closed his eyes as she held his face and brought it down slowly to her. She lifted herself onto her tiptoes and kissed him lightly on his lips. As he felt her warmth, he felt a surge of pleasure he had not experienced before run through him. He opened his eyes and took her around her waist, lifting her up. She giggled. "You trust me?" he asked.

"Yes."

Holding her up in one arm, he grabbed her hair in his hand and brought her head down to meet his lips again, but this time he kissed her with so much passion, they both were at each other's mercy. Meghan felt his tongue in her mouth exploring, tasting, as she explored and tasted back. She felt like her heart was going to explode. She held him tightly against her and felt him harden.

The next thing she felt was being dropped. Michael let her go and fled as fast as he could to get away from her before he did her any harm.

The one minute she was being kissed, the next she was on the slate stone walkway, panting, dizzy and confused. She had no feeling in her legs so she lay there for a while getting her breath back. "Wow that was intense," she smiled to herself.

Finally, she got up and dusted herself off and made her way back to her room where she took a shower to freshen up before bed — still smiling.

🌀

THE NEXT MORNING, she needed to talk seriously to Michael on how they were going to make this relationship work and she was determined as ever to make this work. She never felt this way with anyone, ever.

🌀

BY FRIDAY, ANNE had made arrangements to get Mr. Thompson ready for his stay at the Manor. Ian helped Anne get the medical supplies together and was surprised she had convinced Mr. Thompson to go — not as surprised and excited as Sir Robert was, to finally have his old Feeder and friend back spending his last days with him.

That afternoon, Ian and Anne got Mr. Thompson settled into the ambulance and accompanied him to the helicopter that would get him to the island. They arranged a medical helicopter to accommodate the stretcher and monitoring systems as Mr. Thompson got weaker over the few weeks and Ian didn't want unnecessary stress put on him. While Ian and Anne accompanied Mr. Thompson, the rest — including Roman and Mia finally coming out of their room — flew with Dale in the Bell helicopter.

As they flew toward and around the one tower of the Manor, Mr. Thompson's heart monitor beeping started to race. Ian looked over at Mr. Thompson and smiled. "Are you nervous or excited?" Ian joked.

"Both," Mr. Thomson smiled weakly.

As they landed, Anne noticed everyone waiting for them. Florence and a couple of her men were standing with Sir Robert on one side, on the other were Roman, Mia, Luc, and Michael towering behind Meghan with his hands on her shoulders. Anne was the first to climb out, followed by Ian; she walked toward Luc while a couple of Florence's men helped get Mr. Thompson out of the side door of the helicopter. Once Mr. Thompson was pushed past the rotor blades, Sir Robert moved over to his side and took his hand.

"Thomas, my friend, welcome. I am so glad you decided to come," Sir Robert said with a weak smile on his lips and tears in his eyes.

Mr. Thompson covered Sir Robert's hand with his other and squeezed it. "Thanks to Anne and thank you for having me, my friend," Mr. Thompson smiled back. Everyone was a bit emotional as the two longtime friends were reunited. Ian made certain Mr. Thompson was allocated a suite close to the medical center, should an emergency arise, Florence settled him in and made sure he rested before the evening's festivities, as there was a lot of celebrating to do that night.

LATER THAT AFTERNOON, Ian called for Anne to prepare her for her biweekly feeding. Anne was getting better with the needle now and didn't need to be put to sleep while Ian inserted it. This time, she dragged Meghan to join her in the hour it took to complete the feeding. Hooked up and blood tapping, Anne had the chance to catch up on Meghan's weeks. Today, Meghan was wearing a soft summer dress. It had a cream background with pastel colored flowers all over it, and it made her look young and cool. It reminded Anne of a laundry detergent advertisement.

"So how are things progressing with you and Michael?" Anne asked slyly.

"Whatever do you mean?" Meghan said in an aristocratic manor and then started to laugh when Anne's eyebrows lifted in surprise. "I'm in love, Anne: L-O-V-E," Meghan spelled out, her face glowing and her eyes wide.

"Already, huh? So what's it like for you to be in love?" Anne asked.

"Like you said, it's hard to explain. I have never felt like this before. It's hard and easy — it's a high and it's a low — it's agonizing and wonderful — all at the same time." Meghan replied as she twirled and giggled.

"Mmm, that sounds about right," Anne said weakly.

"I never thought I would ever feel like this, Anne. It's absolutely wonderful but there is only one problem," Meghan sat down next to Anne on the bed.

"What's — that," Anne said, finding it difficult to concentrate.

"Sir Robert won't approve of this. I'm in love with a vampire and a newly turned vampire that's also scared of loving me fully," Meghan said sadly.

"Mmm – Meghan, sorry but something's not quite right," Anne stammered.

"I know. I don't know how to go about convincing the two of them I'm serious about this and I'm going to make it work," Meghan said not noticing Anne getting paler. Only when Anne got sick, partly over her beautiful summer dress, did she realize Anne was ill. "Oh my goodness — Ian!" Meghan shouted.

"Something's — not quite right," Anne said again. "Stop this," she said weakly.

As Ian walked in, Anne was heaving again but this time nothing came out. Meghan had run to the sink to rinse the part of the dress that Anne got sick over and then went back to her side with a wet facecloth. Ian disconnected the IV and found her blood pressure dipped dangerously low. "Anne, stay with me." Ian was concerned. He noticed the blood they tapped was just over half of what they set out to take. Then he saw blood seeping through the sheets. Ian lifted the bedding finding blood coming from under her. Anne looked down and gasped. "Meghan, do you mind if I could have a word with Dr – um — Ian for a minute?" Anne asked.

"Sure," Meghan said as she left the room wiping her dress off as she walked.

"I had menstrual cramps this morning, so I guess I'm menstruating. I've always been irregular and very heavy in blood loss," Anne said weakly, trying not to get sick again.

"That may be the answer," Ian said. "Let's hold off with the feeding till your menstruation is over, then try again in two weeks time."

"All right," Anne said hesitantly.

"What else is bothering you, Anne?" Ian noticed the look she had when she wanted to say something else.

"Well, I'm giving you a heads up; Luc and I are engaged and wanting to be married soon. I'm concerned about having children."

"Why should you be concerned about having children?"

"If I react like this having my period, will I be able to stay pregnant?" Anne asked nervously.

"Oh, Anne, why do you think you won't stay pregnant?" Ian asked confused sitting on the side of her bed and taking her hand.

"My mother couldn't keep her babies; she lost many before and after me. I was their miracle baby, so it worries me," Anne said nervously feeling tears run down her cheek.

"What happened to your mother doesn't mean it will happen to you," Ian explained.

"How can we be sure of that?" Anne asked.

"I'll contact a specialist and have him run some tests for you, if you like," Ian suggested.

"Thanks. I'll appreciate that, but I want you to keep it between us till I know what the results are," Anne said.

"Anne, I'm not sure. Luc wouldn't like to be kept in the dark about this. Think about it seriously. I won't let anyone know but I do advise you to tell Luc."

"I understand."

"In the meantime, I want you to take some vamp blood to see if it helps with the cramps and the blood flow," Ian said as he left the room to obtain some.

THAT EVENING, AFTER a nice warm shower and getting into one of Sir Robert's beautiful gowns, Anne stood at the full-length mirror in her room looking at herself. She chose an emerald green dress with thin straps that came over her shoulders. The skirt flowed to her knees looking cool and elegant. She put her favorite pendent on again and her engagement ring that went with the dress and her eyes. Everything looked in place as she looked at her reflection looking back at her, Anne put her hand on her stomach wondering how it would feel to be pregnant with Luc's baby, and she smiled at the thought then turned toward the door. As she went to open it, Luc knocked; it startled her. Opening the door, they smiled to each other. "Ready, soon-to-be Mrs. Hastings?" Luc asked.

"Yes, Mr. Hastings, as ready as I'll ever be," Anne replied.

As they came to the stairs, Meghan came out of her room in a beautiful cream and yellow chiffon dress; she looked absolutely stunning. Luc opened his elbow for her to put her arm through. "Will you be so kind to accompany us to the ball, my lady?" Luc teased.

"It would be my honor, Lord Hastings. Good evening, Lady Anne," Meghan said as they walked down the stairs to the den were everyone was waiting excitedly. Walking into the room, Anne saw Mr. Thomson sitting in an easy chair next to Sir Robert near an open window. Florence and Ian were sitting at the bar with Mia and Roman, chatting and laughing. Michael left the bar and came toward Meghan; he took her hand from Luc and accompanied her back to the bar, seated next to Mia. Mia, in turn, handed Luc his whiskey, Anne asked for water as they approached the bar.

Sir Robert stood up and clapped his hands, getting everyone's attention.

"Before the evening starts, I would like to make two announcements. Firstly, I would like to welcome my oldest and dearest friend back to the Manor and hope he stays with us till his sorrowful end. Cheers to you my friend." Sir Robert lifted up his glass and everyone saluted Mr. Thompson. "Secondly, I'm proud to announce the engagement of my two other Feeders as they have decided to get married sometime this summer, I hope sooner than later as I'm sure Thomas would love to be in attendance," Sir Robert said slyly.

"No pressure there," Mr. Thompson said smiling. "Congratulations."

Everyone lifted up their glasses and congratulated Luc and Anne, and then one by one came over to them to admire the ring on Anne's finger. They kissed, hugged and slapped — especially Luc — on the back.

After supper, Florence, Meghan, Mia, and Anne sat around a small coffee table and started making plans for the wedding and reception. Meghan had run to get a pen and paper pad from Sir Robert's office to make notes. Everyone had wine in hand and was in good spirits, but Anne, drinking water that whole evening, was a bit out of sorts. Meghan and Mia were the only ones who noticed but said nothing. They decided they would go to New Westminster to shop for a bride's dress that following Monday. They then decided the date for the big day would be in August, just a few weeks away. Anne came up with the date as it was Mr. Thompson's birthday on the eighth of August and what a perfect date to remember for the rest of their lives. They chatted and made lists upon lists till late that night. Luc retired for the night, but Anne, high on vamp blood and excitement, wanted company so she decided to stay with Meghan for the night. They chatted till the early hours of the morning when Meghan fell asleep and Anne lay next to her, imagining her dress, and then got up to watch the sun rise.

THIRTY

"MEGHAN, I HAVEN'T been a vampire long so I don't know what my capabilities are. They are intense. I don't want to hurt or kill you in the heat of the moment," Michael said.

"Then turn me so you don't have to worry about it," Meghan suggested.

"No, Sir Robert will turn you; for me to do it just to satisfy a need right now is wrong."

"You heard him. Sir Robert only wants to turn me at the age of thirty; he thinks I'm still too young."

"Then you will wait till then."

"Michael, that's seven years away. I can't bear to be without you that long. Can't we just try one step at a time? I've done it with a vampire before and I'm still alive," Meghan said with regret.

"Like I said, I'm new at this. I don't have the experience Raymond had," Michael said sadly.

Michael stepped away from her and turned to the library window. Meghan started to cry.

"Meghan, Meghan, wake up — you're dreaming," Anne said and sat down on the bed next to Meghan and laid her hand on her shoulder. "Meghan, are you all right? You were dreaming."

"What, Wh—?" Meghan said, confused.

"You were crying in your sleep," Anne said.

"Oh, Anne," Meghan sat up to hold Anne and started to cry again.

"What is it Meghan? What's upsetting you?" Anne asked.

"It's Michael — everyone thinks I'm too young to make my own decisions and I do love him. I love Michael so much it hurts, but he doesn't want me the same way," Meghan sobbed. "Don't get me wrong, he loves me, too, but he's too scared to make love to me. He's concerned about turning or killing me in the heat of it all."

"I understand why. It's very different with a vampire; it's more intense than it is for a human. Michael is newly turned so he —"

"I know that — don't you think I know that?" Meghan shouted, jumping out of bed and putting on her robe.

"It's just I want to be turned now to be with him, but Sir Robert won't do it until I'm thirty. I can't wait that long without having him, Anne. I'm burning for him," Meghan said and sat back down on the bed next to Anne.

Anne put her arm around her. "Do you really want to become a vampire, Meghan? It will mean you will have to die, become un- dead; you'll not be alive to enjoy what life has to offer. I want you to talk to Mia and get her point of view being a female vampire, being recently turned and just having had sex for the first time as a vampire," Anne said.

"What, Mia, with whom?" Meghan asked surprised.

"Roman, but you see they're both vampires so it's not dangerous. Although what I heard *did* sound rather dangerous," Anne laughed. "Then, once you've done that, maybe you and Michael should talk to Sir Robert and state your case; maybe he'll change his mind," Anne said not liking the idea of Meghan being in between life and death and never having an end.

"All right, I'll talk to Mia after breakfast," Meghan said getting up to wash up and dress. Anne left to do the same.

Anne did not eat much for breakfast, which concerned Luc and Meghan. "I'm fine; it's just a bit too early for me to eat. I'll have something a little later," Anne promised. "Come on, Meghan, we have an appointment to talk to Mia this morning, remember?" Anne said, changing the subject.

"Yes, I know. I'm right behind you," Meghan said in better spirits.

They asked Mia to meet them in the Library; they found her sitting and waiting for them at the end of a large oak table, paging through a book.

"Morning, Mia," Meghan said pulling out a chair on her right and sitting down, and Anne taking a seat to her left.

"Morning ladies. So what's this all about?" Mia asked.

"Well, Meghan has fallen in love with your brother, Michael, and has decided to become a vampire," Anne said frankly.

"You don't beat around the bush, do you?" Meghan added.

"Wait a second here; let me get this straight. You're in love with Michael?" Mia asked shocked with the news.

"Yes," Meghan replied.

"And you want to be turned?" Mia asked concerned.

"Yes," Meghan replied again.

"Dumb choice — not for falling in love," Mia put her hand on Meghan's, "but wanting to become a vampire."

"Why do you say becoming a vampire is a dumb choice?" Meghan asked.

"Good question," Anne added.

"Anne, do you agree with this?" Mia asked surprised.

"No! That's why I advised Meghan to talk to you, having been recently turned," Anne said.

"What's wrong in being turned? You have eternity with Roman, don't you?" Meghan asked realizing too late that was the wrong thing to say as she felt a shock go through her hand.

"Ouch" Meghan yelled and jumped up out of her seat.

"Oh goodness, sorry, Meghan. I need to control that," Mia said getting up from her seat, too.

"Ladies, please, let's not get excited here over the men in our lives right now. We'll discuss that later," Anne suggested. "Mia, will you please sit and explain why it's not a good idea to be turned, just to have sex."

"It's not just because I want sex!" Meghan yelled, still agitated.

"Well, then explain why," Anne asked.

"It's because I love Michael and I want to be with him forever. I don't want to get old and die and leave him alone for the rest of eternity," Meghan said sadly.

"What does Michael say about this?" Mia asked.

"I haven't discussed this with him yet," Meghan said.

"Well, that's your first mistake," Mia said. "You'll need to find out how he feels about you and the rest of eternity thing."

"Sit, Meghan. Let Mia explain what it is like to be a vampire first," Anne advised.

As Meghan sat down again, Mia put both of her hands on the table and took in a breath she didn't need. "I'll start with being turned. The night my girlfriends and I went to a bar to celebrate an upcoming photo shoot that would put my name on the map, we were approached by this man who, as you know now, was Raymond. He was mysterious looking, dressed in black jeans, a black T-shirt and a baseball cap that he wore just over his brow, so it was difficult to actually see his face. We were quite drunk at that stage, so as the night went on, I decided to accept a ride home with him. I didn't make it to his car as we started to make out in the alley next to the bar. That's where he bit me. In the heat of passion, it aroused me but as my blood was leaving my body, I could feel myself drift into death. Fear set in and there was nothing I could do to stop him from killing me. I was helpless and scared. I must have passed out because the next thing I remember was him kneeling over me and seeing drops of dark blood running into my mouth from his wrist. I grabbed his wrist, drinking it hungrily, needing more; he let me drink from him. As I swallowed, I could feel it go down and as it hit my stomach, a lot of things started to happen all at once. As his blood was absorbed by my body, replacing the blood he took from me, I felt my warmth leave me. He then pushed me off him and grinned as he walked away leaving me alone in the alley. I was cold as ice and the pain of turning into something monstrous was excruciating. My body twisted and turned, tying to get away from the pain. My senses heightened. I couldn't adjust fast enough. My skin burned, feeling the air run across it. My eyes burned with the little light coming from the street. My ears screamed with pain from the sounds of people, music and cars. I could even hear the rats in the bins gnawing on garbage. My head felt like it was going to explode, my body ached, but the worst of all was the hunger. I needed to be satisfied urgently. Not knowing what I needed, I grabbed food out of the garbage bins. That didn't help so I grabbed a couple of rats and tore into them. Realizing their blood satisfied me the most, I hunted like a wild animal for anything with four legs. Thank goodness I didn't go for humans, because there was a large supply all around me. I ran into the wooded area that morning as the sun was coming out and it burned my eyes and skin. I found a hollow under a large tree and crept into it; that was where I stayed and slept that day, just to wake up to hunger again. I ran through the trails finding the odd rabbit, stray cat or dog that night. I again slept in a hollow somewhere that day. Finally, by the fifth night, I ran into Anne. When she got out of her car to inspect her flat tire, I could feel the warmth of her, and see the blood flow through her veins. She was scared and angry so instinct was turning on all my senses to hunt her."

Looking over to Anne, she saw tears roll down her face. "I'm sorry, Anne."

"Never mind, we already put that aside; carry on," Anne sniffed.

"As I bit into Anne, I felt her blood absorb into me. I found myself getting stronger, energized, and most of all, being satisfied and full. It was the best feeling I had since that bad ordeal a few nights prior. Once I found myself feeling whole again, I realized Anne didn't die like the other creatures I fed on. I then heard a vehicle coming and panicked, so I threw Anne to one side and ran back into the woods. I climbed a tree and watched when Luc and Roman came to rescue her. It was raining hard so I was wet but not cold. I never felt cold since I was turned. They took Anne away in their car. Being overcome by my new-found life source, I decided to follow them. I ran parallel to the roads all the way to *Safe Haven* where I hid for a while then found Anne getting into a shower. I watched her through the bathroom window — until you saw me," Mia smiled at her. "I had to leave as I sensed Roman was after me, so I ran into the river and swam quite a distance, then backtracked to Anne's vehicle and got her address from her purse, which she left in her car, and then waited for her to come back to her apartment. Jen was downstairs in the office and it took all my willpower not to go down there to feed on her. Finally, Anne arrived and I knew I had to have her help me. Later, she brought in Roman and I knew I was safe at last. Roman explained what a vampire was like, explained the sights, sounds, the feelings and most recently, I found out being a woman vampire is the most powerful thing. Vampire men are afraid of us; we are powerful and, hell, we can be moody and very sexual."

Anne started to laugh. "That's absolutely true."

"Apart from giving you a rundown on my turning, let me add that it's a soulless, empty and monstrous way to live. You can view it positively by seeing it as immortal, forever, don't have to eat, will never get fat, feeling like you're on a high all the time without the side effects. Negatively, as a woman, you feel unfulfilled, won't ever taste the food you love, or feel warmth, the sunlight hurts your eyes, skin and drains you. The worst for me is I'm a living dead thing with no soul, with no choice in having a child and no closure to life."

They all sat for a while looking at each other, with tears running down their cheeks.

"Wow," was all Meghan could say.

"So?" Anne asked, feeling chilled.

"I have been living with vampires most of my life. Sir Robert raised me since I was eight, when my parents died. I knew nothing about what it felt like, as I never thought of asking. It always looked glamorous, powerful and well, like you said, I only saw the positive things you mentioned. Not once did I think about the negative side of things. Why do you feel so negative about being a vampire, Mia? You also mentioned you feel unfulfilled. I thought you and Roman were together. Don't you want to be with him forever?"

"He did fulfill me sexually but I need more than that. I have a feeling deep inside that I can't explain that still needs to heal. I suppose it's the anger, regret and hatred I feel because I was turned so abruptly and left to fend for myself. That may not be that way for you."

"All right, let me ask you this, then. I want you to answer me honestly. *If* you had fallen in love with Roman first and had a choice in being turned to be with him, knowing how he makes you feel forever, would you?"

"Yes," Mia replied.

"Shit, Mia, I'm trying to steer her away from becoming a vampire. Now you've gone and done a three sixty on me."

"Sorry, Anne, but Meghan used the 'if' word – hypothetically. But it *isn't* like that for me. I still feel negative about it; let's make that clear."

"The 'if' question answered what I needed to make up my mind about turning, though," Meghan smiled.

"Oh for goodness sake," Anne threw up her hands. "Mia, do you think she should become a vampire?"

"No, life is a beautiful thing to have. Before you make up your mind, I want you to talk to Michael first and secondly, you need to think very seriously about your future as a human, what you'll be giving up."

"Fine, he's probably waiting for me," Meghan said as she got up to leave.

"You get back here and give us an update on that talk," Mia said as Meghan disappeared out the door.

THIRTY-ONE

MICHAEL HAD BEEN thinking about Meghan and fulfilling their needs; he ached for her. It had been a couple of years since he had a woman. She felt like a girl, a young innocent girl, but he knew she wasn't innocent. Meghan told him about Raymond and others before him when she needed to satisfy herself; she used many, just like he did when he was younger. Now that he was thirty-two and had been deployed to Afghanistan twice, he knew more than just doing things without thinking them through first. Strategizing, planning, it all led to success in more ways than one, including the sun experiment, he smiled to himself.

The day started out sunny but as the morning progressed, the clouds came in, making it pleasant for him to sit outside on the garden bench and wait for her. He heard Meghan before he saw her; it sounded like her meeting with Mia and Anne went well as her spirits were high. Michael sighed knowing he would have to either dampen that spirit or even have to hurt her by telling her he didn't want to turn her into a vampire.

"Hi," Meghan greeted him as she saw him.

"Hi, how did it go?" Michael asked, knowing the answer.

"Okay I suppose, but before I tell you what I decided to do, I want to know how you feel about being a vampire."

"It has its moments. Some days when I'm on the hunt for Raymond, the asshole that did this to me and my sister, I'm glad I have the strength to be able to kill him with my bare hands. Then other days, when I'm with you and need to be gentle and knowing how fragile you are, I wish I was human."

"So if you don't have to handle me as fragile anymore, won't it make it easier?"

"I like having you fragile," Michael said as he took her by the hand and pulled her into his lap.

"Don't change the subject."

"I'm not. I'm showing you how I can handle something fragile." Michael started nibbling her ear. "Stop it," Meghan giggled.

"Come, let's go for our walk down to the cave," Michael said standing up and putting Meghan down. She watched him closely as they walked in silence down to the cave she took him to the first day they met.

As they got there, Meghan noticed a blanket lying on the sand and a picnic basket waiting for them. "You planned this?"

"Yes ma'am," Michael said leading her to the blanket and sitting down next to her. He leaned over to the basket, took out two glasses, and poured some orange juice in one for her and some "L" blood for him. Before he gave her the glass, he bit into his wrist and added a couple of drops of his blood into her glass.

Meghan's eyes widened and she gasped as he did so. "What're you doing?"

"You'll see. I have a source that told me this will help you," Michael explained.

"I've never drunk vampire blood before; it's strictly forbidden. Sir Robert won't be happy about this."

"I don't think he is happy about you courting me either, nor will he be happy about the idea you have in your head being turned before it's time," Michael handed her the glass. "Now drink up, before the blood ferments."

Meghan closed her eyes and pinched her nose thinking it would taste awful but surprisingly it tasted like orange juice. She drank it down fast before it went even frothier; the acid of the orange didn't mix well with the vampire blood.

Michael, finishing his drink, took both glasses and put them back into the hamper. Taking Meghan into his arms, he lay her down beneath him. Making sure not to put his weight on her, he had one knee between her legs and the other on the outside, hip to hip. Looking down at her, he saw her doe-brown eyes change into a golden brown. She smiled at him as she closed her eyes to feel the changes taking place. "This is unbelievable," Meghan sighed. "I didn't know it felt so, so . . ." Meghan opened her eyes again. "Wow, you're gorgeous."

Michael laughed. "Now that's a new description of my features I never heard before."

Meghan lifted her head and kissed him deeply, holding him tight, and making sure he did not leap out of her arms again. She stirred beneath him as he kissed her back. Michael could feel her heartbeat against his chest and the strength of her grip she had on him. He stopped and looked at her. "You sure you want to do this?" he asked.

"Yes." Meghan smiled, noticing the look in his eyes. "You're smelling me again. This time if you do nip me, make sure you follow through." Meghan noticed this statement unsettled him a bit.

"I'm not planning on nipping or biting you, Meghan," Michael said sternly.

"Sorry. I didn't mean to say that; it just slipped out." Kissing him again, she felt him relax a little as her kisses moved from his lips to his jaw up to his ear and down his neck. He kissed and nibbled her back as his hand slipped under her dress over her stomach toward her breasts. She moaned as his cold hand sent tiny shock waves down her spine to her toes. She then grabbed hold of his T-shirt and tugged it off while he did the same with her dress. Sitting up, she started untying his belt and his jeans while he unclipped her bra; with all the tugging and pulling, they soon settled back down onto the blanket in each other's arms, naked. She felt warm against his skin and he felt cool against hers.

Michael could not get enough of touching her skin, feeling the warmth and softness of it under his hands. He kissed and tasted as he touched, noticing goose bumps where he had been. Meghan moaned and twisted under his touch. She was burning up. She needed him to touch her where it mattered most but it seemed he was avoiding that area. So she took one of his hands and led it down between her legs where she was ripe and ready for him. Keeping her hand over his, she pushed her middle finger with his under hers into her, finding it warm and moist. She gasped as they both slid into her and pushed her hips against their hands. She felt his cool finger, with her warm one, touch and rub against her till she came. Keeping his finger in her, he could feel her pulsate with pleasure. As she thought it was over, he replaced his finger with his erection. She gasped with the rhythm and fullness of him in her. She found herself climbing toward another peak. Meghan felt Michael go stiff and he lifted himself off her by straightening his arms so that just their hips joined. She watched as his fangs lengthened, his eyes darkened and he hissed. She noticed the concentration in his face, keeping his mouth as far away from her as possible. His thrusts went deeper and harder into her, his rhythm increased until she reached the peak and plummeted into another blissful climax. Michael let out a growl from the back of his throat as he threw back his head. He reached his goal and shuddered with the pleasure of it.

As his orgasm passed, Michael opened his eyes and looked

down and saw Meghan looking back at him with tears in her eyes. "Are you all right?" he asked concerned.

Meghan nodded as the tears ran down the side of her face.

"Did I hurt you?" She shook her head. "You're not convincing me." As he wanted to lift himself off her, she held on to him with her legs, shaking her head again, asking him not to move off her. She took hold of his neck bringing him down to her. Still not able to say anything, she held Michael close to her listening to him sniff her neck. With a sigh, she drifted off to sleep with Michael still in her. A while later, she heard her name in the distance, getting louder.

"Meghan, wake up; please, my love, wake up," Michael whispered in her ear.

"No — I'm not dreaming this time, am I?" she asked, not opening her eyes as she felt Michael hardening inside of her.

"No, you're not dreaming. I need you to wake up and let go of me. You may be in danger holding me down like this. I need nourishment. Making love to you took a lot out of me and I'm getting a bit voracious." Michael didn't sound like himself so Meghan opened her eyes. She found him staring down at her inches from her face, with those dark vampire eyes that could attack her at any moment. She let go of her arms that were around his neck but not her legs; she liked the way he felt in her. "Please, Meghan, let go," he growled.

She leaned over a little and grabbed the hamper, opened it and gave him the flask that held Luc's blood. He grabbed it from her and swallowed what was left in it. "Shit, it's not enough." He started to panic.

"Michael, here, take some from me," Meghan offered her wrist.

"No, don't do this. Let go of my hips, Meghan, before I hurt you."

"Michael, calm down. Your blood is helping me so my blood can help you. Besides, you don't need too much — trust yourself."

"Meghan, don't let me do this," Michael begged.

"Trust me, Michael."

"Stop me," said Michael surrendering to the hunger and bit down into Meghan's wrist. As he drank from her, he could feel her warmth inside of him. She tasted so good he didn't want to stop until he heard her saying his name. He calmed down and focused.

"Michael — Michael!" Meghan called.

He pulled her wrist away from his mouth and licked the wound clean and kissed it.

"There, you see — you can do it."

"Meghan that was a very stupid thing for me to do. It could have gone horribly wrong," Michael said angrily this time. Without warning, he lifted himself up from her. "Get dressed. We are going back to the Manor."

"Michael I—"

"Don't say another word — get dressed," he interrupted.

"Michael, please don't do this," Meghan's tears rolled over her checks as she watched him put on his jeans and T-shirt. He grabbed her dress and underwear and threw them at her. "Get dressed," he growled.

"I'm sorry, Michael."

"Sorry won't bring you back from the dead if I accidently kill you," he said and left.

Meghan sat staring at the spot where she last saw him; the anger in his face was unforgettable. Her heart ached. The pain ran from her chest down to her fingers. She slowly got dressed and packed up. The hamper suddenly felt heavy as she picked it up. *What had she done? Her stubbornness and selfishness may have lost him. Will he ever forgive her for this?*

Leaving the hamper in the cave, she walked up to the Manor and asked Sir Robert's assistant if she could have a word with him. She was shown to his office where she sat and waited for him.

As he entered, Sir Robert could sense something had transpired and it upset him to see his granddaughter in pain. Her eyes were swollen from crying and her face pale. He came over to her and lifted her head up with his finger. "So what brought this on?" he asked, not too politely.

"I'm in love and I don't know what to do about it," Meghan said softly.

"In love with whom," said Sir Robert, not sure if she was still seeing Michael.

"I love Michael and I want to be with him for eternity. Can you help me?" Meghan begged.

"Do you know what you are asking, Meghan?" Sir Robert asked.

"Yes, I do."

"You fall in love a lot so how do you know this is the one, Meghan?"

"I don't fall in love with everyone I go out with, Grand Master, and you know it," Meghan replied sarcastically. Meghan always used *Grand Master* when she was very angry with him.

"What about Raymond a few months ago?"

"I was not in love with him. He charmed me into believing he was everything to me. He seduced me and I'm trying to get over that and I wish you would, too."

Meghan started to cry and thought her request was getting to be a hurtful argument she didn't want. "Well, if you're not prepared to do this, I will ask Michael to," she bluffed, knowing Michael wouldn't dare.

"He wouldn't do that, Meghan; he is a military man and they respect their superior's orders," Sir Robert replied.

"I wouldn't disrespect you either, but I love this man with my soul, Grandpa."

"Grandpa?" Sir Robert asked with astonishment and pride. She actually called him Grandpa, something he secretly wanted to hear for such a long time.

"Sorry, Sir Robert, that just slipped out."

"That's quite all right, Meg, but that's part of the reason right there. You're the only one in my bloodline that's left. If I turn you now, it stops forever," Sir Robert explained with sadness in his eyes.

"Oh my, Sir Robert, you wanted me to fall in love with a human so that I can have children?"

"Yes."

"How do I fall in love with a human when I live on an island filled with vampires?"

"Well, I hoped it was going to happen when you attend university in the fall or would have happened while you were at school or college," Sir Robert replied.

"Well, I'm sorry it didn't," Meghan said looking as if all her wind had been knocked out of her. "Is that the only reason you won't turn me now?" Meghan asked

"Yes."

"Well then, we're in a bind because I don't want someone else's baby. I want Michael's, but he's a vampire, so that will never be." Meghan put her head in her hands.

"Even if you could have his child or any other man's child, I don't think it's time."

"Why not?" Meghan whispered.

"You're too young," Sir Robert said.

"Ah, I'm twenty-three; I'm not all that young. Many of my school friends are married with children already, so what makes me any different?" Meghan asked.

"You're my grandchild and I want to make absolutely sure you're ready for this," Sir Robert replied.

"How ready do I have to be if all I know is how much I love Michael and want his child and want to be with him forever?"

"Well, Meg, you just created a problem right there."

"What?"

"You're going to have a human child and want to raise it as a vampire," Sir Robert explained. "How old does the child have to be before I turn you?" he asked.

"Oh my, this is getting worse by the minute," Meghan said sitting up in her chair again. "Can't we take it one step at a time? I need to think," Meghan said as she got up.

"Good, now that's mature of you; I give you twenty-four hours for a solution," Sir Robert said as he sat back down in his chair with his elbows on the rests and his fingertips touching.

"What, why this is all hypothetical anyway. Michael and I can't have children, so there's nothing to solve this."

"What would you say if there is a way you can have Michael's child?"

"Meghan's head jerked up looking at Sir Robert. "Don't say something like that and not mean it."

"You know me. I never say something unless I mean it." Sir Robert looked back at Meghan.

"Grandpa, please."

"According to Michael's military records, he had an option to bank some of his semen."

"Did he take that option?" Meghan asked hopefully.

"He did and may be able to make a couple of withdrawals for artificial insemination."

"Great, but why tell me this if you know it will lead nowhere?" Meghan said sarcastically.

"I can't solve all your problems, Meghan. That is how you learn and grow up."

"You have a solution to this, then."

"Yes, but I want to hear one coming from you by tomorrow evening when you come back from your shopping for Anne's dress."

"Oh yes, that's tomorrow; goodness, I need to find her." Meghan ran out of the office.

Just as she left the office, Meghan stopped, turned around and went back in; "Sorry, Grandpa, am I dismissed?"

"Yes, Meg," Sir Robert laughed, shaking his head.

THIRTY-TWO

THAT EVENING, MEGHAN phoned Anne's room, telling her she couldn't make it to help her get ready for the evening. Anne didn't mind Meghan not being there as she was capable of doing everything herself, but she did miss her company. She wore a short black cocktail dress for the evening. Before she knocked at Luc's door, she tried Meghan's but there was no answer. She hoped that Meghan had already gone down for cocktails. As Luc and Anne walked into the den, she noticed Meghan was not there either. They greeted Sir Robert and Mr. Thompson, followed by Florence and Ian, and then made their way to the bar where Roman, Mia and Michael were sitting. "Where's Meghan?" Anne asked.

"I thought she was coming down with you, like always," Mia replied.

Anne looked over at Michael; he just shrugged. "Don't give me that; she was with you last, as far as I know," Anne said.

"She was with me this morning but I left her on the beach and haven't seen her since."

"Did you leave her upset?" Anne guessed.

"Yes, we did have a few words."

"Great, she is the most vulnerable person on this island and you leave her on the beach upset. How upset?" Anne asked getting angry.

"Look, Anne, we had a fight, a little disagreement — that's all," Michael said getting defensive.

"No, that's not all. She was prepared to turn into a vampire because of you, for goodness sake. She is head over heels in love with you and would do anything to be with you Michael. How upset was she?"

"Shit!" Michael slammed his drink down so hard the crystal glass broke into a thousand pieces.

"What's going on over there?" Sir Robert bellowed from his chair.

"Have you seen Meghan this afternoon by any chance, Sir Robert?" Anne asked.

"Yes, she came to see me rather upset, but she left not much better I'm afraid. I didn't solve her problem for her. I told her she needed to do that herself. I also gave her till tomorrow night to do so," Sir Robert said thoughtfully.

"What? Why? God, doesn't anybody care about her feelings? She's young and foolish. I need to find her," Anne ran out before Luc could stop her.

Running after her, Luc was overtaken by Mia. "Let me handle this, Luc. You go back. Sir Robert won't like it if too many of us are not there for cocktails."

"All right, keep me posted," Luc said and turned back to the den.

Mia caught up to Anne at the stairway leading up to their bedrooms. "Meghan didn't answer her door earlier; maybe she is in there ignoring my knocking," Anne said.

"She's not there."

"How do you know?" Anne asked, stunned.

Mia touched her nose; "Maybe we should start at Sir Robert's office and work our way to where her freshest scent takes me."

"Great, lead the way."

Heading back down the stairs, they made their way to the office then out to the garden over the helipad toward the stables. When they got there, Anne asked one of the stable hands if he had seen Meghan. "She had taken her horse for a ride this evening, miss."

"Do you know which way she went?"

"Yes, she went on the back trail toward the docks, miss."

"How far is that?"

"Quite a way, you may need a horse to catch up; she didn't leave all that long ago."

"Then we'll do that, please," Anne said.

"Just saddle one for Miss Anne here. I'm faster running. Besides, I make horses nervous," Mia said.

"Is it not the other way around?" Anne teased. "You go ahead, I'll catch up."

"Okay." Mia dashed off.

"Shit, that's quick; a horse can't even run that fast," Anne said in amazement.

"Excuse me, miss, this is Pegasus."

Anne looked up at a beautiful, fourteen-hand, pure white stallion. "Oh goodness, thank you — sorry — I didn't ask your name."

"It's Samuel, miss," he said, handing the reins over to her.

"Thanks, Samuel, help me up, will you?" Anne asked politely, tucking her dress up as she mounted the horse. As she got on, she hardly put any pressure to the stallion's sides when he took off like a bullet. Anne hadn't felt such power between her legs for a long time. The adrenaline shot through her veins as Pegasus raced across the meadows into the wooded trail. As she entered the woods, she slowed him down into a canter. It took her at least fifteen minutes before she came to a clearing again and found Meghan and Mia sitting on the grass and her horse grazing behind them.

"Hey, look what the horse brought in," Mia smiled.

"So all looks well, no blood and guts," Anne smiled back with relief to see Meghan in good spirits.

"You had us worried there, kiddo," Anne teased.

"Hey, I'm just a few years younger than you, kiddo," Meghan teased back.

Anne climbed down and walked up to Meghan and gave her a very tight hug. "Don't do this to me. I told you when you need to talk you can always trust me to do so. You had me very worried there for a very long minute," Anne scolded.

"Sorry Mom, but there is nothing to worry about. I had a little scare this morning but I'm fine now. I have quite a bit of thinking to do so I decided to come up here to my favorite spot. At night you can see Seattle's lights from here."

"Don't you go changing the subject. What did Sir Robert and Michael say to you that scared you?" Anne asked.

"Well firstly, neither one of them is willing to turn me, not yet anyway. Secondly, as you know, I'm the only relative Sir Robert has left and if I don't produce any offspring, his bloodline stops with me."

"But Michael should be sterile since he became a vampire," Mia said.

"Right but I received a bit of news that he apparently banked some sperm before he left for Afghanistan," Meghan explained.

"No way," Mia said surprised.

"Way!" Meghan acknowledged. "The only reason I think Michael did that was he, too, thought he was the only male left in your bloodline and decided to bank his sperm just in case something happened to him."

"So what solution do you have to this problem, then?" Anne asked.

"I decided, should Michael still want me, I'll stick to being a human until I have children, and take vamp blood to age slowly until such time I decide to be turned," Meghan explained.

"As simple as that?" Anne asked.

"Yes, as simple as that," Meghan replied

"Nothing is as simple as that," Mia said looking for a loophole.

"Why not?" said Meghan.

"You said 'should Michael still want you.' Why doesn't he?" Mia asked.

"I did a very foolish thing this morning," Meghan said and proceeded to tell them what she had done.

"He fed on you? Where?" Anne asked.

"I made him," Meghan said as she took off a large bracelet covering the healing puncture marks. "I realize now how stupid it was for me to do that. I was selfish and careless. I already beat myself up about it so don't bother making me feel bad. I'm already beyond feeling bad. I'm heartbroken," Meghan sniffed back a sob.

"You certainly did a lot of growing up today," Anne said.

"I guess I have," Meghan agreed.

"Well that's that." Mia slapped her thighs as she got up. "We need to get back to the Manor, let Michael know you're safe and sound."

"Why would he think otherwise?"

"I overreacted a little about not knowing where you were," Anne explained.

"But I think the shock therapy did Michael some good," Mia giggled. "I'll meet you back at the stables."

Meghan and Anne collected the horses and trotted back to the stables. They could see Mia was talking to Michael as they approached. Meghan's heart skipped a beat when she saw him.

"Great, now I'm going to get it."

Riding up to them, Meghan was already putting her defenses up by not looking at him. Anne noticed Meghan tense up as she dismounted and handed the reins to Samuel.

"May I have a word in private," Michael asked Meghan as she stepped around her horse.

"Sure, let's take a walk along the cliffs back to the Manor; that way if I can't take it anymore, I'll just jump," Meghan said sarcastically.

"Meghan you have already given us all a scare."

"No, Michael, I haven't. You all overreacted; all I did was go for a horse ride."

"You missed supper, which is very unlike you."

"I told Ian and Florence where I was. Did you bother asking them?"

"No and they didn't bother telling us either," Michael said, finding this whole situation ridiculous.

"Michael, we need some time to get to know each other a bit more, don't you agree?"

"What? Are you the same Meghan that tricked me into feeding from her this morning?" Michael looked down at her.

"I didn't trick you but I was careless; I admit that," Meghan said.

"I'm still angry with you about that."

"Fine, I don't blame you for being so, but will you forgive me if I ask for it?" Meghan stopped and looked up at him.

"Yes," he replied.

"I'm sorry, Michael, please forgive me for acting like a childish fool," Meghan said as she looked down in regret. Michael lifted her head and kissed her gently on her forehead. "I forgive you." They walked hand in hand until they got to their favorite garden bench. Michael sat down and patted the seat next to him for Meghan to sit. Meghan sat and leaned her head against his shoulder. "Meghan?" Michael whispered.

"Mmm," Meghan replied.

"How much do you love me?"

"More than life itself."

"I thought so," he said, putting his arm around her.

"How much do you love me?" Meghan asked.

"More than eternity," he said, kissing the top of her head.

"I thought you would say that," Meghan smiled.

"You better have something to eat and get some rest; you have a big shopping day tomorrow."

THIRTY-THREE

🦉

"WAKEY, WAKEY, RISE and shine," Meghan said, waking Anne up with a cup of coffee.

"Look who's so chipper this morning," Anne moaned.

"Well, it's your day; how are you feeling?" Meghan asked as she put her cup down.

"Fine," Anne said sitting up. "Why?"

"Mia mentioned she smelled blood on you and suspects you're having your period and secondly, you're not sharing Luc's bed these last few days," Meghan replied.

"I didn't know you guys decided to become detectives," Anne said sarcastically.

"We're just concerned about you, Anne, just like you were last night."

"Touché," Anne smiled.

"Yeah, well get up and we'll meet you downstairs."

Forty minutes later, Anne joined Florence, Mia, and Meghan. They took the same boat over to the mainland as they did when they went shopping for Mia and the same BMW was waiting for them, all gassed up and ready to take them to Columbia Street in New Westminster to start their hunt for the perfect dress. By noon, they still had not found the one. Anne was apologizing every time she saw Meghan roll up her eyes as if to say, "Here we go again."

"I don't seem to find anything I really could say is *the one*," Anne said in dismay. They had already been through New West and into Downtown Vancouver from cheap to top of the range, from consignment to designers. Anne recognized all the designers names from the dresses that hung in her wardrobe at the Manor, so to top these designer gowns with a wedding dress that outdid those and that went with her personality was hard.

"Maybe you're not in the mood for this today," Meghan said.

"No, it's not that. I always wanted to wear something antique but not retro or over the top Victorian, something that has sentimental value to it," Anne explained.

"I think I know what you're looking for but let's have something to eat first and look around some more for bridesmaid dresses and wedding accessories. We still have a long list to complete before we head back," Florence advised.

Anne and Meghan grabbed a sandwich and water while on the run between one bridal shop and the next. They had quite a bit accomplished and had a few packages in hand to prove it. Walking down the street heading back to the car, Anne stopped in her tracks and went ice cold. "What is it?" Florence asked.

"It can't be," Anne said shaking her head.

"What's wrong?" Florence asked again.

"Look," Anne said. All three women looked in the direction to where Anne had indicated. Standing under a large tree looking right back at them was Adrian, Florence's ex-security vampire now working for Sire Raymond Pitout. "If there's one, where's the other?" Florence said and started to look around.

"There," Mia indicated with a nod toward Roy standing a few meters behind them. "Do you think there are more of them?" Mia asked.

"I don't know and don't want to find out. If we make a move to threaten them in any way, we may find out, so keep calm," Florence said knowing these men's capabilities. "Anne, press your distress button we gave you, without making it too obvious."

"Sure." Anne, finding the remote in her purse, activated it. "Done," Anne said satisfied. "I really hoped this was all over with," she said nervously.

"It won't be over until we catch and kill that bastard," Mia said through her teeth.

"Do you think they want Anne?" Meghan asked Florence.

"Possibly, let's go and find out," Florence answered.

"Are you crazy?" Meghan said, grabbing Florence by the arm before Anne could react.

"No, I don't think they will chance doing anything in public," Florence said. Leading the way with Mia taking the back, they started to walk toward Adrian. He didn't move and seemed to be waiting for them. As they approached, Florence said, "Why am I not surprised to see you again?"

"I was hoping not this soon," Adrian replied.

"To what do we owe this pleasure?"

"Trust me, there is no pleasure in this arranged meeting, Florence," Roy said from behind them. Florence and Mia just looked back at him but Anne and Meghan jumped with fright not expecting him there.

"Shall we take it somewhere more private?" Adrian suggested.

"I don't think so, safety in numbers," Florence answered.

"What about taking a seat over in the park — do you think you could manage that?" Adrian asked sarcastically.

Florence looked over to where he suggested then looked at Mia and nodded. "That may do."

As Florence, Anne and Meghan took a seat at one side of the picnic table, Adrian and Rob sat on the other side, while Mia stood directly behind Anne.

"You have been very busy trying to make Sire Raymond's movements difficult," Adrian began.

"I was hoping to, apart from capturing and bringing him in for judgment," Florence said.

"Which will lead to certain death," Adrian stated.

"Correct, he has broken many laws," Florence replied.

"What will you say if I tell you that not all Covens are in agreement to that?"

"Every Coven has its own laws, Adrian; we all know that, but he has broken our most sacred one."

"We can sit here all day discussing what laws he has broken but he has a proposition for you so he sent us to pass it on," Adrian smiled.

"So what does he propose?"

"He has left the country and he will stay out of the country and not pursue Sir Robert's council and its members, if they leave him alone and send your hunters back to where they came from."

"So he left the country. Is Canada getting too hot for him to handle?" Florence laughed.

"Ha, no, he has found other interests in Europe or was that Africa," Adrian replied with a shrug.

"I don't think so, but as to his proposal, it is not for me to decide."

"Then find out. I have to give him an answer in an hour."

"Or what?"

"He will make Sir Robert's council and its members suffer the consequences," Adrian advised.

"It will be hell on earth," Roy warned.

"May I?" Florence asked as she took out her cell phone.

Adrian nodded.

Florence then dialed the Manor and asked to speak to Sir Robert.

As Sir Robert answered, all he said was they were on their way and not to agree to anything.

∞

LUC AND ROMAN WERE looking over some sketches of what the council room needs to look like for the wedding. They were thinking of using it as the chapel.

"I don't know if this is going to work."

"Why not? It has everything. You have an altar, pews and a double door entry."

"It also has a lot of negative energy in here. This is where vamps are sentenced to death for Christ's sake – No I don't think Anne and I would like to make our marriage vows in here."

"Then—" Roman was just about to say "where" when Luc's emergency pager went off.

"Shit no, not again," Luc and Roman ran to the command center to get their locations. All four signals indicated that they were still together in a park in downtown Vancouver.

"Dale, contact the Air Traffic Control Center and ask permission to land the Bell helicopter in that park," Roman asked.

"Yes, sir. Do you need me to fly, sir?"

"No thanks, Luc will take it from here. Oh! Contact Michael and have him meet us at the helicopter."

"Yes, sir."

Not long after Roman and Luc got into the helicopter, started it and warmed it up, Michael appeared with their duffel bag containing their kit consisting of their swords, guns, extra silver bullets and their protective gear.

"Let's go," he shouted as he got in and settled into his seat and put his earphones on when they got permission to land.

☮

"YES, SIR," WAS all Florence said and snapped the phone shut. "I'm afraid we will not be agreeing to his proposal and that means we will still be nipping at his heels until he is brought in for sentencing. Which leaves me with the decision; do I take the two of you in now or later. What do you think, Mia?"

That was Mia's cue to attack; it happened nice and quick. As Florence jumped over the table and staked Rob from behind, Mia touched Adrian with so much voltage that he tumbled over and landed on his back. As he hit the dirt, Mia was already on him with a stake in the heart.

They propped them both up into their seats so fast that passersby would not have known what had happened a few seconds before. Anne had her hand over her mouth preventing herself from screaming, while Meghan sat looking very stunned and not able to say a word.

☮

FIFTEEN MINUTES LATER, the helicopter landed in a clearing, three hundred meters from where they sat, bringing in a lot of attention from the public. The three men stepped out and walked toward them in a triangle, Roman leading the way. They were all in black, the wind of the rotor blades blew Roman's long black hair over his face, which he ignored. He was focused in getting to them and so were Luc and Michael, their faces stern and ready for a fight. Their long black coats covered up the long swords they were carrying.

As they approached Mia, Meghan and Anne thought the same thing but it was Meghan who said: "God, they look gorgeous." All the ladies started to laugh as Meghan started to run toward Michael and jump into his arms hugging him with her arms and legs. He looked stunned for a minute but then embraced her, spun her around with a smile of relief, sealing it with a warm kiss. Anne at the same moment ran up to Luc. He grabbed her around the waist and kissed her.

Mia, standing next to Florence, smiled at them relieved that the men finally arrived.

"What's so funny?" Roman asked as he approached looking at Mia.

"Love," Mia replied taking her gaze from her friends over to him, looking directly into his eyes for a second; this unnerved him. Breaking their gaze, he looked over to the two traitors pinned in their seats having no fight left in them, which disappointed him as he turned and walked toward them.

Florence felt the tension between Mia and Roman, wondering why. They bonded to each other a few days ago, and once vampires bond to each other it's committed. Florence made a point to find out after this matter at hand was taken care of.

Luc and Michael joined Roman and Florence getting the two traitors to the helicopter followed by Mia, Meghan, and Anne. Taking their seats, they made their way back to the Manor, securing the two traitors in lockup.

THIRTY-FOUR

☙❧

THAT EVENING, AS soon as Florence left Sir Robert's office, giving him a briefing of what happened that day and their decision to hold off with the trial of the traitors till after the wedding, she went to the control center where she had her office and sent for Mia to join her there. As soon as Mia walked into the room, Florence asked her to close the door behind her and take a seat across from her. Mia noticed the deck was neat and particular with everything in place just like Florence's personality.

"You're probably wondering why I asked you in to see me," Florence said.

"Yes, to be honest I was," Mia said sitting on the edge of her seat not quite relaxing into it.

"It's personal, so do you want me to carry on?" Florence asked noticing Mia's uneasiness. Taking a pen off the desk and twirling it between her fingers Florence studied Mia.

"Sure, what's on your mind?" Mia asked cautiously.

"Roman," Florence said and waited to see Mia's reaction.

"Roman?" Mia asked.

"Yes, you and Roman."

"What about us?"

"What's going on with the two of you?"

"Nothing," Mia said suspiciously

"Nothing?" Florence asked, surprised. Knowing Roman over one hundred years, she knew there was something going on between them. She knew Roman was not the one to instigate it and therefore thought it best to talk to Mia.

"Yes, nothing is going on," Mia said hoping that one day there would be but not until she is comfortable in what she has become. She still hated the fact that she needed blood to survive and made sure no one watches her feed.

"So there's nothing going on with the two of you. No commitment or anything?" Putting the pen back down on the desk and leaning a bit forward.

"No!" Mia started to feel very uncomfortable now, desperately wanting to leave.

"Mia, I don't understand. The two of you were intimate, shared your blood and you have no feelings toward him?" Florence looked baffled.

Mia smiled and now understood what Florence was trying to find out. "Florence, I was in need for someone to take the edge off and he did it — nothing more." Mia lied because she did have feelings toward him deeper than what she wanted to admit but that fact she would keep to herself for now.

"Are you serious?" Florence said astonished and disappointed.

"Quite honestly, Florence, I think he's scared of commitment and my electrical charge. I don't think he's ready for me or me him."

"Have you asked him how he feels?"

"Are you kidding me? He's a man and men don't talk about their feelings."

"What about the blood contract?"

"The what?" Mia frowned at Florence.

"As you know, blood is important to a vampire. It's a source of life; if their blood is exchanged they are committed to each other."

"Now that Roman didn't explain to me," Mia felt her anger building and her electrical charge rise.

"Blood makes and breaks deals; it seals contracts."

"Well, there will be blood to break this deal, don't you worry about that. Just wait till I get my hands on him," Mia replied vibrating with anger, getting up from her chair and heading for the door.

"Now Mia, that's not the reaction I was hoping to get from you," Florence said standing up from behind her desk.

"What kind of reaction were you expecting, Florence?" Mia yelled.

"Understanding."

"Understanding of what? Are you kidding me?" Mia shouted and opened the door and walked out.

Florence running to the door, called after her. "Mia, talk to him; he has been alone for a long time and he needs someone like you."

WITH SWORDS OUT, Luc and Roman were dueling in the gym, releasing aggression built up by not being able to fight the traitors earlier that afternoon. Roman had the upper hand by chopping away at Luc's sword sending him in retreat a few steps before Luc turned the tables on Roman and slid in some new techniques Florence taught him. "Ah, that was a sly move," Roman jumped out of the way of the blade, which barely missed him. Sparks bounced off the steel as the swords hit each other. They were concentrating on the task at hand when Mia stormed into the room straight toward Roman. She aimed a shocking punch into his guts, sending him flying through the air, landing in a stack of pool chairs.

Luc stood there in shock for a while and then wiped the beaded sweat from his forehead with the back of his arm. "I think that's my cue to leave," Luc said, holstering his sword that hung from his belt and left the room.

"What the hell has gotten into you?" Roman asked as he untangled himself from the chairs and dusted himself off.

Mia was so angry, she buzzed with unused energy; she just stood there glaring at him trying to find the words. "We committed?" she finally hissed out her question. "Committed to what?" Roman asked, not quite understanding what she was going on about.

"To each other," Mia replied, now talking through her grinding teeth.

"Hmm," Roman was not prepared for this. He didn't think she would find out about what they did that night would mean more than just sex and love bites. He also didn't realize "hmm" was not the answer she was looking for and she slammed into him again but this time, she held on to him, pumping pure angry voltage through him. He was in excruciating pain that made him weak as he fell onto his knees, looking up into her eyes, begging her to stop. She noticed his pleading eyes and let go of him. He fell onto his stomach and winced with pain. Feeling no strength in his arms and legs, he lay there for a while. Slowly, his ability to move returned. Pushing himself up onto his hands and knees, he got up. "Shit, what the hell is wrong with you?" he shouted. Mia stepped a couple of steps back away from him still shaking.

"Explain to me why you didn't mention what exchanging blood means to vampires while they're intimate with each other?" Mia said slowly with anger.

"Mia, just give me a fuckin' second to get my bearings," Roman yelled back so that he could choose the right words.

"A second is over, explain now," she shouted as she took a step toward him again. This time, he had his guard up and as she wanted to hit him again, he grabbed her arm and twisted it up her back; the current from her vibrated through him so he pushed her away from him. "Mia, please don't do this. Just give me some time to give you the correct answer for you to understand why I did what I did," Roman said.

"Fine," Mia replied and paced up and down waiting for him to explain.

"All right, I admit I should have explained it to you. You bit me without knowing what you did, being in heat, but I should not have bitten you back. You surprised me; you did something to me that I can't explain. I've never felt like that before in my human or vampire life and it scared the hell out of me," Roman explained walking up to her, hoping she had calmed down enough to listen to him.

"You never felt like what?" Mia stopped pacing and looked into his eyes.

"I felt like I'm feeling now."

"Damn it, Roman! Tell me. How am I supposed to know how you feel when you can't tell me?" she said, starting to feel rather frustrated.

"I feel like ..." Roman flew into her, taking her mouth with his and kissed her with such passion and force, it knocked her senseless so no energy could expel from her. His passion was like a block to her electrical current; it numbed her. His hands were all over her; she could not keep up.

"Stop, Roman," Mia pleaded between his kisses.

"Don't," she pushed and turned away from him, shaking her head not believing what just transpired. "We have a problem, Roman."

"What is it?"

"I don't think I can do this."

"Do what? I'm not asking you to do anything," Roman walked up behind her and held her shoulders.

"I have so much anger inside of me, Roman, I can't control it. You just felt how bad it can be. If I didn't care for you, it could have been worse. I don't know what I could have done. I must find a way to control the anger and the charge I expel because of it. It sucks being a vampire," Mia smiled a little.

"Mia, Florence and I will help you get through it."

"I'm sorry, Roman, I cannot commit to you until I have," Mia turned and put her head on his chest.

"I understand," Roman said and took her into his arms and held her close to him. "It took me a long time to get used to the idea myself, but in time and with support from this family, you will get through it."

Roman didn't recall how it felt to be tuned but when he came to understand what he had become, he thought of himself as a monster. Florence, Ian and Sir Robert helped him transform and supported him in everything. It took him a long time to get used to the idea and the new way to survive but he was never angry. The only way for her to get past this anger is to resolve the problem by using her energy to destroy the threat.

THIRTY-FIVE

∞

BY MID WEEK, Ian took Anne and Meghan to a fertility clinic where Dr. John Mitchell had his practice He did fertility tests on both women and advised Ian that Michael's sperm arrived at his clinic safely from the military hospital where it was stored. With Meghan, they started a course of injections to increase her egg supply and explained that she may need to return ten days after her next period. With Anne they took blood samples to check her estrogen and progesterone levels, and took a scan of her uterus, womb and ovaries to check if she had any blockages or growths. The tests came back negative so she should not have any concerns about becoming pregnant naturally and keeping the baby.

As they returned to the Manor, Anne explained to Luc that she went with Ian and Meghan for moral support, keeping her concerns to herself. They were to be married at the end of that week and she felt that not finding a dress was more of a concern.

☺☺

THAT EVENING, THE Manor celebrated Meghan and Michael's engagement. They explained they would hold off on their marriage date but did decide to conceive a child first, as time was of the essence and marriage could wait until things settled down. Florence had Michael on different assignments after Anne and Luc's wedding, especially with the new threat that Sire Raymond Pitout held against their family. Once the council of families arrived for the wedding, they could stay a little longer to meet and decide the fate of the traitors.

Anne and Luc decided to go up to Luc's cabin for their honeymoon for a couple of days. That way they weren't too far should anything happen.

After drinks and supper, Florence joined the ladies at the bar and asked them to join her in Anne's room. As they opened her door, they saw a large dress bag on her bed.

"What's that?" Anne asked, surprised.

"Open it and take a look and tell me what you think." Florence smiled at her.

Anne ran over excitedly and unzipped the bag to find something made of old white lace and silk. Gently she pulled the rest of the bag off and out fell an antique white lace wedding gown. Everyone gasped with the delicateness and detail of it. "I can't, Florence, this is too fragile to wear," Anne noted.

"Nonsense. Try it on and see if you like it," Florence replied.

Slowly, Mia and Meghan took the dress from Anne and she undressed. They then slowly draped the wedding dress over her. It felt like soft rose petals against her skin and fit her like a glove. The lace covered her head like a veil but was part of the dress. Like a cape, it was attached to the shoulders, opening at the neck and draping over her breasts. It hugged her hips before it flowed out and down her legs to the floor, leaving it longer at the back so that it trailed as she walked. Anne looked up to find everyone staring in shock at her and tears in their eyes. Walking up to the full-length mirror, she saw what everyone was wide-eyed about. It was extravagant.

"So what do you think?" Florence asked, her voice sounded a little chocked.

"Oh, Florence, it's — it's beyond words right now, but this *is* the one," Anne replied.

"Sorry it took a couple of days to give it to you but I had to get it altered to fit."

"But Florence, I couldn't, I mean —"

"Yes you could. You're the closest to what I have as a daughter and besides Ian told me what you asked of him. He is so proud; you have no idea what this means to us," Florence said as she came over and embraced Anne lovingly.

"Thank you," they said jointly.

Reluctantly, they took the dress off her and stored it back in its bag and hung it in Anne's closet.

"What about Meghan?" Anne asked.

"Ah, Meghan, when you set a date, Sir Robert has a dress for you to try on, too," Florence replied.

"I do? He does?" Meghan asked, surprised.

"Yes, it belonged to his wife, Gabriella," Florence said.

"Sir Robert was married — when?" Anne asked in surprise.

"She was Sir Robert's true love and the last one he married," Florence replied.

"Now you have me interested," Mia said.

"Well, ladies, get comfortable and let me tell you a little about Sir Robert. I won't go into too much detail otherwise we'll be here for a century or more." She waited for everyone to settle down.

"Sir Robert de Sable, now known as Sir Robert McKay, was one of the knights of King Richard I (also known as the Lionheart) that fought in the third crusade. Later, he was made Grand Master of the Templers for a short while when he supposedly died suddenly but that was when he was turned. Where and why this took place I don't know as this happened back in 1193.

"He returned to Scotland within the year because the scorching heat of the desert was not made for vampires. He buried himself under the sand during the day and came out to hunt at night. He made Scotland his home for a few centuries, watching over his children's-children's-children and so on. He married numerous times until he met Gabriella Pitout in Paris, France, a sixteen-year-old daughter of a French nobleman."

"Pitout — what a coincidence," Mia said with a chill running down her spine.

"It's not but I'll get to that in a bit," Florence replied. "So to carry on, Sir Robert took her back to Scotland were they lived happily for twenty odd years when she fell very ill. Sir Robert was away on business of state when he heard of the news she was sick but when he returned she had already died so it was too late to turn her. Gabriella's father sent his son Raymond to her funeral and that was when Sir Robert met him. At that time Raymond found out what Sir Robert really was. Raymond was not a vampire then and it was not until after the World War II when Sir Robert and his family returned to Canada — to this Manor in fact — that Raymond Pitout knocked on his door. Imagine Sir Robert's surprise to not only find Raymond a vampire but that he found Sir Robert after all these years. I've found out from our Celtic friends that after his sister's death, Raymond made it his life mission to take revenge on Sir Robert for not turning her and giving her eternal life like he has. So this mission to destroy Sir Robert is what we are dealing with now. Vengeance can be a horrible thing," Florence explained.

"Why did Sir Robert come to Canada?" Anne asked getting a little more comfortable next to Meghan.

"He was following his bloodline, which in 1621 decided to

settle in a new Scottish colony called Nova Scotia, which means New Scotland, where he stayed for a bit. There he met Thomas Thompson, a young sailor and fisherman, who became a very close friend, and by accident he found out he was a Feeder. They went back to Scotland together to sell most of Sir Robert's possessions and castles as he wanted to start a new life in Canada close to his relatives. On their way back in 1659, on a ship destined for Montreal, Quebec, they met a young couple: a doctor and his wife from London, Dr. Ian and Florence Anderson." Florence smiled, remembering the trip. "We fell seriously ill, so Sir Robert gave us an option, which we took. Sir Robert turned us and started his family of vampires in Canada. We stayed in Montreal till 1689 when the first inter-colonial war in Quebec started. Sir Robert and his new vampire family moved with the fur traders down the St. Lawrence River where we found a young orphaned Iroquois boy. We named him Roman. He was turned later when he was attacked by a bear and nearly killed. In 1846, we ended up in Vancouver and built this Manor. We volunteered in World War I and World War II, where, as you know, Luc joined the family as their second Feeder. Over the centuries, many vampires joined Sir Robert's family and a Council was formed. That's it for tonight, ladies. Tomorrow is decorations and setup for the wedding so you need your rest," Florence stated abruptly, as she stood up, gave Meghan and Anne a good night peck on the cheek and escorted Mia out with her.

As Meghan left directly behind Florence and Mia, Anne was left sitting on her bed alone in her room. She started going through her notebook of things she still had to do and get. With satisfaction, she scratched off the wedding dress as an item to purchase. She then turned to the phone next to her bed and dialed Luc's room number. Within a couple of rings, he answered sleepily.

"Oh sorry, darling, I didn't realize the time. I just wanted to say goodnight."

"It's all right. I'm glad you called. We haven't been together for a bit and I miss you. Is everything all right?" Luc asked, concerned as he noted she had not been herself lately. Although he blamed it on the stresses of the wedding planning, he still decided to ask.

"Yes, now that I found my dress, I feel much better. I'm a bit concerned about Mr. Thompson, though," Anne replied.

"Why?"

"I visited him this afternoon and he looked very weak, I hope he makes it for our wedding," Anne replied.

"I spoke to Doc and he said he is stronger willed than he looks," Luc replied trying to give Anne some hope.

"Oh, okay," Anne was not convinced.

"Anne, he will be fine. Don't concern yourself over him tonight; get some sleep," Luc said.

"You are right. I can't do anything about it anyway. I miss you, too, by the way."

"I'm next door, you know. You can always come join me," Luc teased.

"No. I'll be sharing your bed for the rest of my life in just over forty-eight hours, so you will have to be patient," Anne smiled.

"It will be the longest forty-eight hours to date."

"I know what you mean. Good night, Luc."

"Good night, Anne."

She put down the phone, smiling at herself, feeling content and serene, a feeling that had been absent these last few months.

THIRTY-SIX

THAT SATURDAY, FORTY-eight hours later, Anne woke up excited to start the day knowing she would be Mrs. Hastings by the end of it. Getting up, she made a call to Meghan's room to check if she was awake first before she started washing up for breakfast. As the phone rang, she looked out the window finding the sky cloudy but it didn't look like rain — the perfect vampire outdoor wedding day she smiled. There was no answer. Putting down the handset, she shrugged making her way to the bathroom. The phone rang, startling Anne. Laughing at herself, she answered it. "Good morning," she said cheerfully.

"Good morning, future Mrs. Hastings. How are you feeling this morning?" Meghan asked hoarsely.

"I just phoned your room and had no answer. Where are you?" Anne asked.

"Bathroom, I missed your call by a second. Do you want to join me for breakfast down by the pool this morning?" Meghan asked, dismissing Anne's question.

"Sure, see you in about half an hour."

"Great."

Twenty minutes later, Anne walked out onto the pool deck to find Meghan having a cup of weak, black tea waiting for Anne. "Good morning," she said cheerfully.

"Where is everyone else this morning? The place looks and sounds deserted," Anne said, disappointed not seeing Luc joining them for breakfast.

"Everyone is on some kind of wedding mission this morning," Meghan smiled.

"What kind of mission are you on?"

"The Maid of Honor kind of mission and that is to keep you away from everyone else this morning," Meghan answered, taking a bite out of a slice of dry toast. "Speaking of which, you are expecting a special guest from the mainland in half an hour so eat up," Meghan pointed to Anne's plate.

"Special guest — who?" Anne asked as she started on her eggs.

Meghan shook her head and smiled at her, taking a sip of her tea. They finished their breakfast and were relaxing with their second cup when Dale's helicopter flew over them, saluting them as he did so.

"Here's your special guest," Meghan got up excitedly. "Come on."

Anne looked at Meghan, taking her last sip of her coffee and wondering who it could be. Getting up and following her to the helipad, she watched as Dale got out and opened the back passenger door for what looked like Jen, her receptionist.

"Oh my goodness," Anne ran up toward her. "What a surprise."

"Do you really think I would miss this special day?" Jen asked, giving her boss and friend a tight squeeze, while two other passengers Anne didn't recognized got out. Anne gazed over to Meghan to see if she knew who they were.

"Ah, Louis, Margret thanks for coming. This is Anne the bride and Jen one of the bridesmaids, the other one will join us soon."

Louis and Margret shook Anne's and Jen's hands without saying a word. Jen looked over at Anne lifting her brow and Anne replied shrugging her shoulders "Come along, let me show you to the room we will be using," Meghan said smugly. Everyone followed her, with Dale carrying their bags. Once they arrived at Anne's room, Louis and Margret opened the luggage Dale dropped off, taking out hair accessories, make up and various paraphernalia needed to prepare Anne for the wedding. While the helicopters flew overhead delivering more vampire guests, Anne was soaked, washed, brushed and polished for three hours before she couldn't take it any longer. Mia arrived with her bouquet of cream-and-white roses tied with a satin lavender ribbon. Mia found Anne sitting in front of the full-length mirror in her long, white silk robe having her hair and make-up done by Louis and Margret in silence. "Oh my God, you look great," Mia said as she walked over to Anne giving her a kiss on her cheek.

"Thanks. Help me," Anne whispered and winked. "The bouquet turned out beautiful. Thanks again for suggesting roses, Mia."

"Come on, Mia, it's time you got ready. Otherwise you'll make us late," Meghan said as she hopped, trying to get her other shoe on without sitting down.

"Well, I'll have better balance for one thing," Mia teased.

"Meghan, stand up. Let me see the dress." Anne stood up as this was the first time she saw it on her. It was a cream chiffon gown with a portrait shirred neckline, a charmeuse gathered waistband with silver to grey to lavender appliqué detailing. It had a full-length A-line skirt with side ruffles, a lavender sash and the back had introverted pleats. The bridesmaids had the same but the appliqué was silver to grey only. They all wore lavender shoes and accessories. Turning around to show Anne the flow of the skirt, Meghan stopped and looked very pale all of a sudden. "Excuse me, I think I have the wedding jitters," she said and dashed for the bathroom. This was the second time Meghan got sick. Anne followed her to hold back her hair and dress.

"Are you all right?" Anne looked at her a little worried. Meghan was still vomiting a little. After a while, Anne handed her a glass of water to rinse her mouth out. "I must be more nervous about this wedding than what I thought," she smiled weakly.

Anne turned to Mia now standing at the door. "Get Ian to bring Meghan something to settle her stomach, please, Mia?" Anne asked.

"Sure," Mia replied taking Meghan to Anne's bed to lie down.

Jen walked into the bathroom and looked at Mia and then at Anne suspiciously. "Anne, may I have a word?" Jen whispered.

"Certainly, what is it?" Anne asked seeing Jen's frowning and knew that look of concern.

"I didn't know you knew Mia well enough to ask her to be your bridesmaid," Jen said.

"Well, in fact, I know her very well. You know Roman, the guy that escorted me to pick up some more clothing a couple of months ago?"

"Oh God, yes, he was gorgeous," she said, remembering him as if it were yesterday.

"Well, they're together," Anne explained.

"So he's off the market, then?" she asked, looking very disappointed.

"Yes, I'm afraid so," Anne said relieved, hoping that was all Jen was concerned about. Just as she was prepared to leave, Jen took her arm.

"Another thing," Jen murmured. "What's up with everyone?"

"What do you mean?" Anne felt anxious.

"They act a little weird. I can't put my finger on it but something's not quite right."

"There is nothing weird going on, Jen. I should know; I've been with them long enough. I need to get ready," Anne said and returned to the bedroom hoping Jen didn't put her investigating hat on. She would be in for a very large surprise if she did.

As Jen wanted to interrogate Anne some more, a butler came in with some sandwiches, tea and *supplements*. He laid the trays down on the desk for the ladies. Half starved herself but not forgetting her manners, Jen poured Anne a cup of tea and filled her plate with a few sandwiches before she helped herself to the same, forgetting all about her concerns.

THIRTY-SEVEN

LESS THAN FOUR hours later, Anne walked through the garden down a flagstone path with Dr. Ian Anderson at her side. Jen and Mia, her two bridesmaids, and Meghan, her Maid of Honor, walked ahead of her, making their way toward the gazebo chapel especially built for the day. Luc stood off to the side a little, waiting with Roman and Michael at his side. Sir Robert McKay stood looking down on them all from the platform under the gazebo, all looking very handsome in their tuxedos. Passing rows upon rows of vampire guests whom Anne had gotten to know over the last few months felt a little overwhelming and she was slightly sad not having a family of her own to see her getting married to the man she loved with all her heart and soul.

Luc stopped breathing as he saw Anne coming down the path. Roman had to lean over and remind him to take a breath. His heart raced and his palms started to sweat. This was it; the woman he loved will be with him from now on. Shaking his head, he couldn't believe how stubborn he was not letting her into his heart and life sooner. He watched her make her way closer to him. Anne noticed Mr. Thompson sitting next to Florence in his wheelchair as Ian led her near them; she stopped and kissed him on the cheek just before Ian handed her over to Luc. Tears ran uncontrollably down her face as Luc took her hand from Ian; she was happy to have waterproof mascara on, otherwise she would look like a raccoon by now. Luc took out his handkerchief and handed it to her to wipe her face. She smiled to thank him.

Sir Robert started the ceremony and announced his welcome to everyone, read through the vows and then finally announced Anne and Luc as husband and wife. When Luc took Anne by her waist and kissed her lovingly on the lips, she realized everything was over. She didn't remember saying, "I do." Everything was a blur. "We're married, it's over?" Anne asked Luc confused.

"Yes," he laughed.

"Did I say everything correctly?"

"Yes, Anne, you said everything on cue — are you all right?" Luc said still holding her close, looking a little concerned.

"Yes, yes, I'm fine. It just all happened so quickly," Anne said looking at her finger to find the wedding band on her ring finger and then hearing clapping and cheering. Then the music started. "Come on, Mrs. Hastings, let's party." Taking her hand in his, he led her to the ballroom where everyone threw white rose petals and lavender streamers as they entered. The large ballroom was decorated in white and lavender, with twinkle lights and silk; no expense was held back in decorating and accessorizing. They danced their first dance, cut the cake; threw the bouquet, which Mia surprisingly caught and nearly threw it again until Meghan stopped her. Jen mingled, danced, ate, drank and danced some more with various unknown vampire men under the watchful eye of Meghan until she advised her it was time to leave. Jen came over to Anne and Luc, wishing them all the best and left escorted by Dale to fly her back to the mainland. With relief that Jen was safely on her way home, Anne danced some more until she was about to drop dead out of pure exhaustion. It was three o'clock in the morning when she and Luc decided it was enough and made their way up to his room, undressed and falling into bed, hardly touching the pillows, fell fast asleep.

Anne, regrettably, started to waken; she could feel the headache before she opened her eyes. As she did, she found Luc leaning on one elbow watching her. "Good morning."

"No, hmmmm, no it's not," Anne moaned and turned on her side to face him closing her eyes again. "Just a little longer," she begged.

"We need to get to the cabin by this afternoon. Otherwise we won't have our wedding night, which we already missed out on last night."

Anne's eyes flung open. "Oh my, you're right. We didn't — Oh sorry, Luc, I passed out as I hit the pillow. I was so tired."

"Don't worry about it. I did the same thing; it's not as if we haven't made love before."

"Yes, but that was our wedding night," Anne said disappointedly.

"We'll make up for it tonight, then. I promise."

"What about now," Anne said moving closer to him.

"Well, if you're up to it," Luc teased.

"Why wouldn't I be?" Anne looked at Luc to see surprise in his face. "Sorry, that came out a bit bitchy, didn't it?" she said, not knowing why she felt so moody.

"Quite, are you okay?" Luc asked concerned. "I first thought it was due to the wedding jitters but you're still not yourself. Talk to me, Anne." Luc took her into his arms and held her tightly as she started to cry.

"I'm so sorry, Luc. This is all so overwhelming. I realized when I walked down the aisle yesterday, I had no family to share our special day. I never thought I could feel so lonely with so many people around me. This is so selfish because you didn't have anyone either, not really," she sobbed.

"Oh, Anne, my beautiful Anne," Luc took her face in his hands. "Look at me." Kissing her wet eyes "You are my family now like I'm yours, till we decide it's time to enlarge it." Anne started to cry even harder then. "God, Anne, don't do this. I can't fix this and you're scaring me." Luc held her again even tighter. "What do you want me to do to make you feel better? Talk to me." Luc rocked her, finding tears of his own. "Please," he begged.

Anne knew she had to tell him about her fears of starting a family but she needed to find the words between her tears. She moved to focus on his face, noticing tears in his eyes. "Oh Luc, I'm so sorry," she leaned in and kissed him lightly on the lips. "I have such fear about having children. I'm scared I will be like my mother who had a lot of difficulty in keeping her babies full term. They called me their little miracle – they named me Anne, which in Hebrew means Grace, as it was by the Grace of God that I was born. I don't want to go through that, Luc. I want to give you children as it's important to me but —"

"Shh — that's enough," Luc interrupted. "We'll talk to the Doc and see if there's a test to find out if that's the case."

"I already did." Anne looked away from his shocked look, knowing she should've told him sooner as Ian suggested. "It was foolish of me not to tell you this sooner but I didn't want you to go through this."

"And?" was all Luc could say.

"And I'm not my mother. All the tests came back negative. I'm more than capable of keeping our babies full term. And that's why I didn't want to tell you, but I'm still concerned about it."

"Anne, I want you to promise me something." Luc sat up and looked down at her. "I want you to promise me that you will never *ever* keep anything from me again. Even if it's the smallest thing that concerns or worries you, I want you to tell me about it, share it — understand?" Luc looked sternly at her.

"I promise," Anne whispered.

"Okay, then. Now, come here." Luc leaned down and kissed her lips and moved over her, but as he started to nibble her lips, the phone rang startling them both. Sighing Luc rolled off Anne and leaned over to answer it. "Morning," Luc said sounding irritated.

"Morning, Luc, sorry to wake you but I need to let you know that Mr. Thompson has taken a turn for the worse and he's asking for you and Anne. We're in the medical center," Florence said despondently.

"Oh God, no, we'll be there right away," Luc said and put the phone down looking over at Anne. She noticed Luc's face and felt a chill going down her spine. "What is it?"

"It's Mr. Thompson."

"Oh Luc, no," Anne cried and jumped out of the bed, getting into the first thing she got her hands on to wear. He followed Anne out of the room, still pulling a T-shirt over his head and they ran down the hall holding each other's hands. When they got to the medical center, they found everyone there. Not saying a word, they walked into the ward where Mr. Thompson lay. The heart monitor beeped slowly and he had on an oxygen mask, which he tried to take off as he saw them approach him. Sir Robert was sitting on the opposite side, holding his hand and removed the mask for him to talk. "Anne — Luc."

"Shh, Mr. Thompson, keep your strength; we're here," Anne said as she took his other hand with her free one. "No, I need to say thank you, for being here, for my friend," Mr. Thompson said softly looking over to Sir Robert and smiled. "I told you Luc will finally find someone special; being another Feeder was a bonus. God was good."

"Yes, he was," Sir Robert agreed and took Luc's hand. They made a circle holding each other's hands. Mr. Thompson closed his eyes. "Yes, good," he said smiling as his heart monitor made its final bleep. The Feeders and Sir Robert stayed, looking down at

Mr. Thompson for a while, not quite believing it was over. Tears rolled down their cheeks. "Goodbye, my friend," Sir Robert finally said getting up and he kissed Mr. Thompson on the forehead and then left the room. Ian switched off the heart monitor's bleep; it was silent. Anne kissed Mr. Thompson's hand that she was holding and felt the heat of his hand leave him. Luc took Anne into his arms, holding her head against his chest. Looking over at Mr. Thompson, thinking what a long life he had, Luc hoped he would go the same way someday. With family and friends around to say their final farewells, knowing you're loved is a peaceful way to die.

THIRTY-EIGHT

THE DAY OF THE funeral was a wet one, as if the heavens were crying, too. Anne and Luc stood under their umbrella watching Christopher, Brad, Calvin, Dale, Michael and Roman lift up the coffin onto their shoulders and start walking toward the graveyard. Anne didn't expect to find one on an island of vampires but there were a few gravestones surrounded by a stone wall and iron gates. The cemetery was located behind the stables, high on a cliff overlooking the sea. Behind the six carrying Mr. Thompson was Sir Robert looking very solemn holding Meghan's hand, followed by Ian, Florence and Mia. Anne and Luc fell in behind them with the council of families following in order of Calgary, Ottawa and Halifax.

The procession was a long one, the walk slow and peaceful as the rain gently fell and the tears rolled down most faces.

Mr. Thompson was laid to rest in silence as they filled the grave with earth. Anne said a little prayer as Sir Robert took up his bagpipes and played "Amazing Grace."

Anne looked up to see Meghan suddenly take off running

toward the Manor. "Stay. I'll go and see to her," Anne said squeezing Luc's hand.

Anne ran after her, catching up as Meghan made it to the main floor washroom, getting sick again. Knocking at the door, Anne asked, "Meghan, are you all right?" concerned after hearing Meghan heaving.

"No," Meghan answered.

"Can I come in?" Anne asked as she opened the door slowly, finding Meghan kneeling over the toilet. "Oh, Anne, what is going on with me? I can't keep anything in anymore," Meghan sobbed.

"Did you tell Ian about this?"

"No. I hoped by today everything would be back to normal, but it has been quite a rollercoaster ride these last couple of days so maybe once everything settles down I'll be better," Meghan said feeling heat rush through her body.

"Let me help you back to your room, so you can get some rest," Anne suggested. Helping Meghan up, Anne noticed her skin felt cold and clammy. Meghan felt weak, very nauseous and light-headed. As she got to her room, Anne helped her into bed, taking off her black tailored pants, jacket, and shoes, and she draped her quilt over her damp body. Anne then got a cool damp cloth from the bathroom and placed it over Meghan's forehead. Anne pulled up a chair next to the bed and sat next to her, taking her clammy hand in hers. "You should rest, Meghan. Maybe you'll feel better once you wake up," Anne whispered.

"Stay with me, please, Anne?" Meghan begged.

"Sure, rest," Anne said watching Meghan sigh, turn onto her side and close her eyes.

Ian, Michael and Luc came into the room as Meghan fell asleep. Anne stood up indicating with her finger on her lips to keep quiet. They all proceeded back into the hallway and closed the door for Meghan not to be disturbed.

"What happened?" Ian asked.

"She's been getting sick since yesterday and can't seem to keep anything she eats and drinks in," Anne informed them.

"I treated her for pre-wedding jitters," Ian acknowledged.

"That's what I thought it was, too, but it seems to be getting worse. It could be all the turmoil today but she's tough. I think it's more than that," Anne said.

"Maybe it's something she ate or a stomach bug of some sort," Luc suggested.

"Maybe. A blood test will confirm if it's a viral or a bacterial infection," Ian said walking into Luc's room picking up the phone and asking one of his assistants to bring a few vacuum tubes to take Meghan's blood.

A few minutes later, Ian and Anne were back in Meghan's room. As Ian took her blood, she moaned in her sleep. Anne held her hand and sat next to her bed again. She watched Meghan as the rhythm of her breathing made Anne doze off.

Anne heard her name in the distance. As she woke, she lifted her head off her arms with Meghan's hand still in hers. It was Luc whispering her name. "Anne, wake up. Ian wants us in Sir Robert's Office."

"What?" Anne asked sleepily. "Is she still sleeping?" Anne looked over at Meghan still sleeping peacefully.

"Yes, Ian gave her a sedative so she'll sleep for a few more hours; come on," Luc lifted her up, leading her to the bathroom to splash water over her face to wake up.

Walking into the office, which always made Anne feel a bit anxious, she found everyone there. Ian and Florence were sitting directly across from Sir Robert with his desk between them. Roman and Mia sat on the far side. Michael was next to Florence, so Luc and Anne took the two seats next to him.

"Good. Now that we all here, Ian, please tell us what's so important and why?" Sir Robert said, sounding a little annoyed.

"I'm sorry to do this but I have made a very unfortunate

discovery and I needed to let you all know," Ian explained.

"Well, what is it?" Sir Robert asked irritated.

Ian shifted uneasily in his chair. "Sir Robert, what I'm about to tell you is nothing either short of a miracle or misfortune and it may shock you either way. So I won't delay by saying Meghan is pregnant," Ian said closing his eyes.

"What?" Sir Robert choked and stood up. Everyone else gasped at the news. Michael stood up, too.

"What? I thought her appointment with Dr. Mitchell was not till next week," Michael asked.

"It is," Ian confirmed.

"Then who the hell has she been with besides me?" Michael asked looking down at Anne sitting beside him. "The only time she wasn't with me was when she was with you."

"Well, I didn't get her pregnant, if that's what you're implying," Anne replied.

"Don't be ridiculous. I didn't suggest you made her pregnant. I'm asking if you knew who she may have been with," Michael yelled.

"No one, she has been with no one. How could you imply she was unfaithful to you – how dare you? She loves you," Anne yelled back.

"Stop!" Sir Robert hit his fist on the table. "Ian, is it possible to find out?"

"Yes, but only once the baby is born. To find out now, the only way is to ask Meghan," Ian explained.

"Then do that now," Sir Robert roared.

"Yes, sir," Ian said, tapping Anne on the shoulder to have her join him.

As Ian and Anne walked into Meghan's room, they found her still asleep. Ian walked over and leaned over her. "Meghan, wake up," Ian said putting his hand on her shoulder giving her a gentle shake. "Meghan, girl, wake up."

Meghan moaned and rolled onto her back, opening her eyes with difficulty. "What is it?" Meghan asked.

"I need to ask you something and I need you to be honest," Ian said.

"Okay," Meghan replied confused. Anne got onto the bed and crawled over to Meghan's side taking her hand again.

Meghan looked over at Anne seeing anxiety in her face. "What's going on?" Meghan sat up and leaned against her headboard.

"I will know if you're lying, you do know that?" Ian stated.

"Yes, what's going on?" Meghan asked looking very nervous.

"Have you had sex with anybody in the last month?" Ian asked.

Meghan's eyes widened, her heart raced and she felt she wanted to get sick again, but there was nothing left in her stomach; she started to heave.

"Meghan, take a deep breath and calm down. It's not a difficult question."

"Yes it is. If Sir Robert finds out I've taken vamp blood to have sex with Michael, I don't know what he will do to him," Meghan said, then gasped and put her hand over her mouth.

"He knows and he's blaming Michael. Shit, I need to save him." Meghan wanted to jump out of bed, but Ian pushed her down again. "Meghan, the inquiry is not whether you took vamp blood or not," Ian explained.

"Then what is it about?" Meghan asked, a little relieved.

"I'm asking if you had sex with a human," Ian asked.

"No, who said I had sex with a human and why should I if I love Michael? You're confusing me." Meghan looked at Ian then Anne.

"Meghan, you're pregnant."

"Huh?" Meghan said, stunned. Her mouth dropped and she looked at Anne, then back at Ian, and then started laughing. "You were joking — with a smile she looked into Ian's serious face — right?" Meghan asked for clarification.

"No," Ian said looking down at her. Meghan started to tremble.

"You're serious? How the hell can I become pregnant with a vampire? They're supposed to be sterile, for goodness sake." Meghan started to rock herself. "How is this possible?"

"Meghan, it's not possible. That is why you need to tell me if you've had sex with a human this last month," Ian asked again.

"No, I haven't. I haven't left this island and when I did, I was with the girls. God, I don't believe this." Getting out of bed, Meghan started pacing. "Who else knows about this?"

"Everyone is waiting for you down in Sir Robert's office," Anne said quietly.

"What?" Meghan fell on her knees. "Michael—" she said and started to heave again. Anne got to her as quickly as she could and knelt next to her. "Ian, can you be wrong about this?" Meghan said, looking up at him.

Ian bent down putting his hand on Meghan's back. "I did the test four times and it came back positive every time. There's no doubt."

"Ian, can you give Meghan something safe to stop her getting sick?" Anne asked.

"Yes, but she needs to eat and drink first."

"I need to know how this happened to me. This can only be Michael's — you have to believe me," Meghan cried.

Anne looked up at Ian. "What do we do now?"

"I don't know. I need to do some inquiries, research, tests and whatever it takes to explain this. I promise, Meghan, I will find out how this happened," Ian said.

"Ian, do you believe me?" Meghan asked.

"I believe that you believe this is Michael's baby and I will do all that I can to support that claim, unless I prove otherwise." Ian got up and went to the door. "I'll get the kitchen to bring up some dry toast and black tea. I'll be back later with something to help you," Ian said and walked out.

"God help me. Anne what do I do now?" Meghan asked holding herself.

"I really don't know, Meghan. This is quite a situation to be in," Anne said, feeling tears rolling down her own cheeks. "All I know is that I will be here supporting you all the way, making sure you stay strong and healthy to keep this baby full term." Understanding Anne's concerns, Meghan turned to hug her. "Thanks."

Walking back into Sir Robert's office, Ian found everyone still waiting for him.

"Well, what did you find out?" Sir Robert asked as Ian walked in.

"Meghan was as surprised as we were about being pregnant. She claims she didn't have sex with anyone other than Michael, so believes the baby is his. I promised her I would find out if this is at all possible so I'm going to do just that. Florence, I will need your help in this," Ian said as he looked at her. She nodded in acknowledgement.

"Do you believe Meghan was telling the truth?" Sir Robert asked.

"Yes, she was telling the truth, but—" Ian stalled.

"What?" Sir Robert asked.

"She believes she is telling the truth but there could be other means involved in getting her pregnant without her knowing or remembering it."

"Are you saying someone could have drugged and raped her?" Michael asked.

"Yes, that is a possibility," Ian confirmed.

"Oh God, no." Michael got up and started to walk out. It felt as if someone paralyzed him by staking him in the heart again.

"Michael!" Ian called after him. "I suggest you stay away from Meghan till I have some answers."

"Yes, sir," Michael acknowledged.

Florence turned to Roman. "Keep an eye," she said.

Roman got up and followed Michael to their quarters.

THIRTY-NINE

IAN RETURNED TO his office in the medical center and phoned a friend and vampire doctor in Germany who might have some answers. "Good evening, Herr Doktor Gries, it's Doctor Ian Anderson."

"Gutenabend mein Freund, wie geht es Ihnen?" Dr. Gries greeted his friend in surprise.

"What can I do for an old colleague?" he asked with a slight German accent.

"I have a situation here and have a question that needs urgent answers," Ian replied stressed.

"It sounds as if you're quite desperate?" Dr. Gries, asked.

"I have a human that may be pregnant," Ian started to explain.

Dr. Gries started to laugh. "Yes, humans do become pregnant from time to time," Dr. Gries teased.

"We suspect the father of the baby is a vampire," Ian said ignoring Dr. Gries' comment.

"Ah, so this is where it gets interesting. Yes, I've heard of a few cases where this has happened in the past — some good, others bad," Dr. Gries explained.

"Could you share those with me to present to our council?" Ian asked.

"Certainly. Firstly, how long ago was the vampire turned that impregnated the woman?"

"He was turned in July, so that's just over a month now."

"How far along do you suspect the woman to be?"

"A week or so."

"It's possible for this to happen, however it depends on how much his sperm has mutated with vampire influences that is the concern. The sperm went into a dormant state when the human was turned, due to the body cooling down. While they are in this state, they can mutate as they absorb the vampire's new molecule structures. The older the vamp becomes, they start to degrade and then die. So the child the woman is carrying can be either fully human, or part-human, part-vampire, or the worst it can become is a vampire best described as a demon. These need to be destroyed," Dr. Gries described.

"How many have delivered healthy children and how many of them had to be destroyed?"

"If you're looking for percentages, it's a 10 percent chance the child will be fully human and 30 percent chance the child will be a hybrid. The balance has been destroyed."

"So the chances are not great. Who do you know that successfully had a human child and who had hybrids?"

"I'll have to look that up and e-mail the report to you. In the meantime, you should give the mother human or vampire blood as supplements, whatever she desires. That way she will keep the food she eats in, otherwise she may starve to death. If the child is hybrid or otherwise, she may require both and crave raw meat."

"Thank you for your help, Herr Doktor," Ian said.

"It's always a pleasure; keep in touch and let me know how it works out."

"Yes, will do, good night," Ian put the phone down and sat

looking at the phone as he wondered what Sir Robert will decide to do about his great-granddaughter's baby. The chances of the baby being human or hybrid are minimal. Not delaying any longer, he advised Sir Robert about his findings and arranged a council meeting later that night.

All were summoned to attend the council meeting. This time, Ian and Meghan sat in the middle of the council room. Meghan looking very pale and surprisingly kept in the dry toast and tea. Anne didn't know what Ian gave her for not getting sick but it had been hours.

Anne sat with Luc followed by Florence, Mia, Michael, and Roman behind Ian and Meghan now sitting in the middle of the council room. The side door opened and Sir Robert with the three other councilors came in, taking their seats behind the large, solid wood table.

"To order," Sir Robert hit his fist on the table. "Dr. Anderson, please advise the council what has happened and your findings," he requested.

Ian got up and bowed to the council. "Good evening, ladies and gentlemen. The situation we find ourselves in this evening started this morning when I had taken blood from Meghan McKay for testing. For the last two days, she has been experiencing nausea and sickness, not keeping any food down. Having concerns about her health, I did a few tests to rule out any bacterial or viral infections, which came back negative. I then decided to do a pregnancy test, which came back positive. This test I did four times to correctly determine its accuracy. After questioning Meghan McKay, it was determined that she had been sexually active with Michael O'Sullivan this last month. I believe her statement and now have evidence that a newly turned vampire can in fact produce offspring in a certain amount of time before the sperm dies off. However, there are a few complications which will determine keeping this baby or not."

"What? I'm keeping this baby, considering nothing," Meghan shouted as she stood up.

"Sit down, Miss McKay. You have not been addressed," Sir Robert yelled. Michael stood up and went over to Meghan, putting his hands on her shoulders, sitting her down and leaving them there while he stayed behind her. His cold hands sent shivers down her spine and tears in her eyes. Meghan knew she had to fight for this baby no matter what the council decided. She was still human and decided they could not determine her or the baby's fate.

Anne, sitting behind Meghan, could sense her anxiety and knew she would support Meghan, no matter what. Luc looked over at Anne as he felt her hand tighten around his. He was glad they would not have to go through this but being a Feeder, these last few months could also prove to be unpredictable.

"Carry on, Dr. Anderson. What kind of complications?" Sir Robert asked.

"According to the e-mail I received from the International Vampire Council, there have been nine successful pregnancies over the centuries. Twenty became pregnant but didn't carry full term or were terminated before birth. Of the nine births, one was fully human with no complications, three were hybrids, and the rest were vampires with bad results, ending in execution."

"You mentioned hybrids — explain?" Sire Aldridge asked.

"Hybrids are part human, part vampire. Apart from eating human food, they feed on human and vampire blood. All of the children were born boys. We can determine that Meghan's, should she be carrying a hybrid, would be a boy."

"What are the risks involved in keeping a hybrid child?" Sire Wright asked.

"Apparently there are no risks to the families but if provoked or threatened, they do turn vampire, which has been useful in many councils according to the report. One such hybrid is head of their security. He has been known for his ruthlessness as well as his kindness. They are partly mortal so feeding on vampire blood will prolong their lives a lot longer than our Feeders. As hybrids, they age slowing already, but they will eventually die. To date, none have. Hybrids only have been documented since the sixteen century so there could be older cases around."

"So since the sixteenth century, only one human and three hybrids have been documented?" Sire Wright noted.

"That is correct," Ian replied.

"Ian, how long were the pregnancies and childhood?" Sire Coupler asked.

"The pregnancies full-term take an average of thirty-eight weeks after conception, like any human pregnancy. It has been suggested it does this because the fetus is in the human body and adapts to the human cycle. Once born, a hybrid feeds from the mother. It will grow like a human baby but according to the report, once it starts eating solid foods, it will eventually need vampire and human blood to survive and grow properly. That is when aging slows down. All three children started requiring blood at various ages: one at two, one at five and the last one at sixteen."

"Sixty percent of the pregnancies are vampire. What are the risks in this?" Sir Robert asked, concerned.

"According to the report, the vampire fetuses drained the human mothers from the inside, killing them and turning them. This process was a long and slow process with disastrous results. It would claw its way out of the womb when ready to be born. There have been reports these children looked like demons, were hairless, had stone-like skin, their fangs could not retract and they had super vampire strength. They killed and fed on everything and anything they came across. The only way to kill these children was decapitation. Fire and silver had no effect on them," Ian explained and looked down at Meghan; she had her hand over her mouth and was shaking violently. Michael looked stern with

318   ANITA E. VILJOEN

his jaw clenched, wondering how he could have done this to the one he loved.

"How do we determine if the child Miss McKay is carrying is human, hybrid or vampire?" Sir Robert asked.

"It's a bit soon now to determine this but we can do an *ultrasound* by the eighth week," Ian replied.

"If it's vampire, will we be able to terminate the pregnancy without endangering Miss McKay in any way?" Sir Robert asked.

"I don't know, Sir Robert," Ian replied.

"How long do we have to make a decision to keep or terminate the fetus?" Sir Robert asked.

"Within the first trimester — no longer," Ian replied.

"So we have twelve weeks."

"Less. I determined Meghan is just over a week pregnant."

Sir Robert whispered something to Sire Wright sitting on his left and then to Sire Aldridge and Sire Coupler to his right and they all nodded. "We'll reconvene in eight weeks time and we will then determine the baby's fate," Sir Robert announced. "This meeting is concluded, however while we're all present, Florence, have the traitors brought before us."

"Yes, Sir." Florence said as she stood up, bowed and left the council room to summon her security men to accompany the two vampires that defected from Sir Robert's family to the council room.

FORTY

MEGHAN AND IAN got up, giving Florence, Michael, and Mia the seats at the center table. The remaining three security men came in with the two traitors. Their appearance shocked Anne. Their eyes were black and sunken, their skin grey, evidence of not feeding enough. She noticed their eyes weren't red to suggest starvation like Mia's when she fed on her. They were placed kneeling between the councilors and the middle table where Florence now sat. Meghan left the council room looking quite shaken. Anne was going to follow her but Roman stopped her from doing so. Leaning over, he whispered, "Meghan has a reason for leaving — you don't. The council will not approve."

Anne swallowed hard, not liking the idea of what was to happen to these men; she may hate them but didn't want to be a witness to their demise. She grabbed Luc's hand with both of hers for the hope of feeling safe, which she did, but not sheltered from what was to happen.

"To order." Sir Robert hit his fist on the table for the second time.

"Adrian, I present this question to you: what made you desert this council for Sire Raymond Pitout's?" Sir Robert asked.

"Wealth and power, which you refused to provide your loyal subjects, not to mention freedom of will. You're old in your thinking and believe in old traditions. This is the twenty-first century and Sire Pitout provided us the option to control our own destiny," Adrian explained.

"Did Sire Pitout provide you the freedom, the wealth and the power promised to you?" Sir Robert asked.

"Not completely, but we could not settle down long enough to find out."

"Do you honestly think if he let you do what he promised he could control you as part of his family? The answer to that is NO!" Sir Robert bellowed. "Let me tell you why: he is planning to be the one to have the wealth and power not you. He needed you to weaken me. At least he thought he planned it that way but, in fact, he made me stronger by turning Mia and Michael for me. They're much stronger than the two of you will ever be. You deserted this family and our rules are very clear on that. The charges of kidnapping our Feeders, draining them for profit and endangering their lives have also been laid against you," Sir Robert stated.

Roy started laughing. "This is so pathetic. You have no idea what Sire Raymond is planning for this council and to state that Mia and Michael are stronger than we are is as weak as your statement. Your lady Feeder is stronger than any of you, for a human that is. I can imagine how strong she will be as a vampire. She tastes real good fresh, too. You should try her sometime," Roy said licking his lips and eyeing Anne.

"Shut up, you lousy excuse for a vampire," Mia shouted.

"Turning you must have been interesting," Roy mocked.

"That's enough; you have no respect for this council or its members. I lay my sentence of death for you to choose," Sir Robert said.

"I choose my own demise. Well, well, well. You can't give out a sentence without pity, can you? Well then I choose to fight this female to the death. If I win, I walk," Roy glared at Mia.

"I choose the weapon," Mia interrupted.

"Very well," Sir Robert said. "Release the prisoner from his restraints."

As Dale and Christopher took off the silver chains keeping Roy weak, Calvin took Adrian to one side and Florence moved the middle tables out of the way. "This is crazy. Mia is newly turned and has no fighting skills to speak of," Anne whispered to Luc.

"So what weapons do you require, Mia?" Sir Robert asked.

"None — bare hands and fangs," Mia replied.

"A vampire cannot kill another vampire bare-handed," Roy said and laughed.

"You can't — I can," Mia replied clearing Roy's smile off his face.

"We'll see about that," Roy mocked.

Mia stood in the middle of the room and closed her eyes feeling the energy build. Taking advantage of this, Roy grabbed Mia from the back wanting to break her neck, but the voltage going through her sent him flying into the seats on the side of the council room. Before he landed, Mia was on him, taking her hand to his chest, grabbing his shirt and throwing him back to the middle of the room. Roy shook as the current still surged through him. She kicked him in his side as he lay there.

"Now who does not have any fighting skills to speak of," Mia said, smiling as she grabbed his head between her hands. She closed her eyes, sending the highest voltage she could muster through her hands into the vampire. She heard an explosion and only once Anne screamed did she open her eyes to see Roy's head had exploded between her hands, his blood and brains dripping from her fingers. His body lay at her feet, headless with black blood oozing out of his neck. Mia looked over at Adrian now looking back at her in fear. As she was about to walk over to him,

Sir Robert cleared his throat. "Mia, that's enough, thank you. Adrian is being punished; we need him sentient for now," he said in a low voice.

FORTY-ONE

ANNE STAYED BY Meghan's side the full eight weeks. They hardly left Meghan's room, apart from Anne's feeding schedule. Anne ate meals with her, making sure she kept it in; she bathed her, stayed with her as she slept and mostly tried to keep Meghan company and in good health. Ian came in one morning, advising them the sonogram had arrived and it was time to see what the fetus was. Anne accompanied Meghan to the medical center where she changed into a medical gown and lay on one of the medical beds with the equipment and monitors ready to reveal Meghan's baby's destiny. Anne sat on the opposite side of the monitors, holding Meghan's hand when Michael walked in with Ian.

"What is he doing here?" Anne asked as she stood up.

"I asked Ian to have him present; it is his child too," Meghan advised quickly before Anne got too upset. Michael just nodded his head at Anne and stood behind Ian not saying a word. His mind raced with questions and concerns as he looked at Meghan; she'd lost a lot of weight, her skin was pale and eyes sunken. Meghan saw the concern in his eyes and tried to reassure him everything would be fine with a smile but her weak state could not even accomplish that.

Ian walked over to the monitor and switched it on, lifting a sheet over Meghan's legs to the lower part of her abdomen and lifting the medical gown up, revealing her slightly swollen belly; he squirted gel on it. Meghan gasped at the coldness of it, which stunned Michael. "It's just cold," Meghan said to calm him. Michael nodded again.

Ian then took the handheld device from the sonogram and put it onto Meghan's belly, revealing black and white images on the monitor. Finally, Ian found what he was looking for and stopped pressing hard against Meghan to reveal more of his discovery. Ian then turned a dial up and a whooshing sound came out of the speakers. "What's that?" Meghan asked weakly.

"That's your baby's heartbeat," Ian explained with relief.

"Oh God," Meghan cried. Tears now ran freely down her face. Looking over at Anne, she noticed that she had the same reaction. Then looking over at Michael, she noticed him tense up and clench his jaw, his eyes set on the monitor hoping to find a human fetus and not a demon. Understanding his concern, Meghan looked up at Ian. "What is it, angel or demon?" she asked.

Surprised by the way Meghan asked the question, Ian answered, "According to the report, if it has a heartbeat, it could either be human or hybrid but definitely not demon." Ian smiled back at Meghan. "To determine if the baby is human or hybrid will prove difficult at this stage. That can only be determined after it's born. Now it's up to the council."

As Meghan relaxed just a little receiving the good news of her child not being a demon, she noticed Michael was no longer in the room. She sighed and gripped Anne's hand for support in hopes of not losing it. Her baby's life is now in the councilors' hands.

As soon as Meghan was moved back to her own bed, she asked Anne to sit with her till she fell asleep. "Anne, I need you to promise me something," Meghan whispered.

"What is it?"

"I want to keep this baby no matter what the council decides tonight. Even if it's hybrid, I don't care. As long as it's healthy, I'm keeping it — do you understand?" Meghan said squeezing Anne's hand.

"As long as it's healthy, I will support you in keeping it," Anne agreed. "Now rest."

Just as Meghan was settling in, Ian came in with a vile of vamp blood. "What is that for?" Anne asked.

"Meghan needs to take some of this to get her strength back up," Ian explained. "All of this is new to me, Meghan, so I'm working strictly on what the International Vampire Council's report is advising me to do."

Meghan nodded. Taking out a dropper, Ian then administered two drops of vamp blood into Meghan mouth. She felt it absorb into her tongue and into her blood stream. Closing her eyes, she felt it warm her body up, repairing and energizing her as it worked through her. Opening her eyes, she felt hunger for food and no need for rest; she felt wonderful. "Oh, great, this is how I should feel," Meghan said and smiled. "I'm hungry."

Anne started to laugh and felt relieved her friend was back, but she suddenly felt tired and drained. She made sure Meghan ate well and insisted that she take a walk. Meghan noticed Anne not looking all that well and insisted she take a nap and instead had Mia join her for that walk.

ANNE WALKED INTO her room finding Luc sitting at the desk typing on his laptop. Turning around hearing someone walk in, Luc was surprised to see Anne standing in the doorway. His surprise turned to shock to see how worn she looked. Damn, he missed her. Getting up he walked over to where she was standing, swept her off her feet and carried her over to their bed. Laying her down onto the pillow, he bent over her looking into her eyes. Seeing tranquility in them, he knew Meghan would be all right and they can get on with their lives together. Moving over her tired body, he lay down next to her, taking her into his arms and holding her while she slept.

∞

THAT EVENING, THEY were back in the den with everyone dressed up in their formal dress for cocktails. Meghan, celebrating with a virgin margarita, was looking much better but her spirits were not as elated as Anne expected them to be after the decision the council made in keeping the baby.

Anne sat next to Mia at the bar, looking at Meghan with concern. Meghan sat in one of the overstuffed chairs opposite Ian and Florence deep in thought. Luc stood with Roman and Michael on the opposite side of the room, near one of the unused fireplaces. Sir Robert was bellowing in laughter at one of the other councilor's jokes, as they sat in leather settees and chairs to the left of Anne. Sir Robert's laugh startled Meghan from her thoughts; she got up and walked out onto the slate patio, hugging herself as she went. Anne hopped off her bar stool, excused herself from Mia's company, and followed Meghan outside.

"What's the matter? You look a bit down. You should be happy and relieved," Anne asked Meghan putting her hand on her shoulder. Meghan sighed looking over to where the three men stood, and then back to Anne. "It's Michael. I don't think he's accepting this pregnancy or me quite so well."

"Have you spoken to him about it yet?" Anne asked.

"No. I have been avoiding him because he looks so sad, Anne," Meghan sobbed.

"He's probably doing the same thing to you. Maybe the two of you should talk."

"You're right. Could you tell him to meet me at our garden bench? He'll know the one," Meghan said and walked over to the stairs leading to the small rose garden to the right of the den.

As Meghan left, Anne went over to Michael and asked him to meet Meghan at their garden bench. Michael nodded and excused himself. Making his way to the garden, he felt apprehensive. He stopped when he saw Meghan sitting on their bench looking out at the sea. Slowly he made his way over to her. When Meghan noticed him, she stood up to face him. He looked solemn. "You look the way I feel," Meghan said quietly, hanging her head down to her chest. Michael walked over to her and lifted her head with his finger, tilting her head back to look into her eyes. "You look a little better but still very thin," Michael whispered.

"What do you think about all this?" Meghan asked getting to the point.

"I think I was a fool doing this to you. I hate myself for making you go through all the doubt and anxiety alone. I don't want to lose you Meghan."

"Michael, you won't lose me or our child. I'm strong and I had Anne helping me through these last couple of months, but the fact you didn't come near me or find out how I was hurt me more than you can imagine," Meghan said and turned away from him.

"Meghan, that's not true. I did want to be there for you, but Sir Robert told me to stay away from you until we found out what the baby was. I kept up with your progress and was glad that you asked me to the sonogram. But when I saw you and how weak you looked, I hated myself; I hated what has happened to you. I was scared this baby was killing you until I saw you this afternoon walking with Mia. You looked better but I still could not bring myself to talk to you because I thought if *I* couldn't forgive myself how could *you* forgive me," Michael explained as he walked up behind Meghan and put his hands on her shoulders. "Forgive me Meghan."

Turning around, Meghan slid her arms around his waist and leaned in against him. "I forgive you. I love you and want you so much."

"Meghan, please tell me that wanting me is not sex?" Michael asked in surprise.

"Of course it is. I may be pregnant but not dead. I still have needs," Meghan teased.

"Meghan I don't —" Michael panicked and tried to pull Meghan away from him. The vamp blood in Meghan's veins prevented that from happening.

"Don't worry about it. I'm not going to ask you to," Meghan interrupted Michael with a smile. Looking up at him, she saw the concern on his face. "We can't get pregnant again, you know," she teased.

"Meghan," Michael said, as his tone deepened, shaking his head.

"Michael," Meghan said copying his tone.

FORTY-TWO

ANNE AND LUC finally had their honeymoon, not at the cabin as they first planned, but Luc took her to Hawaii where they visited Pearl Harbor. Then they went over to England, Scotland, France, and finally Egypt. Anne loved sharing Luc's and Sir Robert's family history. It was painful but necessary to close that chapter of his life with someone he now loved. Egypt was Anne's destination of choice to unwind and enjoy some of the wonders of the world. By the end of October, they had to come back to the Manor, firstly, to feed because they were overdue and started to feel sluggish. Secondly, Anne wanted to be with Meghan to support her with her pregnancy as she would be twelve weeks along already.

MICHAEL DIDN'T LEAVE Meghan's side until Anne and Luc returned from their honeymoon. Meghan was overjoyed to have her friend back and Michael was relieved. He started to hate her mood swings as he didn't understand them at all. They seemed to be arguing about everything, which was putting more stress on Meghan's emotional rollercoaster.

"Get out," Anne heard Meghan shout as she came up the stairs. Feeling energized after the feeding and toasty from the sun bed, she made her way to the new room she now shared with Luc, to get dressed for the day.

"Fine, I'm going," Michael shouted back, walking out of their room and meeting Anne in the hallway.

"Morning, Anne," Michael greeted her as he made his way down the stairs looking rather agitated. "Morning, Michael, is everything all right?" Anne asked as she smiled back at him.

"Fuck no. Good luck with her today," he said as he made his way down. Anne then decided to check up on Meghan before she got dressed. Walking in, she found Meghan still in bed looking very solemn.

"What's going on? Why are you still in bed?" Anne asked as she approached.

"Oh Anne, I'm so frustrated I can kill Michael, but he's already dead so—," Meghan shrugged, crossing her arms and glared ahead of her.

"Why? What did he do?" Anne started to laugh watching Meghan act like a spoiled child again.

"It's what he won't do."

"And what would that be?"

"A woman has needs, even a pregnant one," Meghan threw back the quilt, got up and went to the bathroom to pee — again.

Anne sitting on the edge of the bed watching Meghan from the bedroom asked, "What needs would that be?" Realizing what she meant, she said, "Never mind." Anne got up, went to her dresser, and took out some clothes for Meghan. "Here, you wash up and get dressed. I'll make a doctor's appointment this morning," Anne advised as she placed her clothes on the bathroom vanity. "I'll meet you in half an hour," Anne said as she left the room to go to hers.

Washed up and ready to go, Anne knocked at Meghan's door to find her ready and in better spirits. They made their way to Ian's office.

Behind his desk working on his computer, he looked up to find Meghan and Anne standing at the doorway.

"So to what do I owe the pleasure of seeing the two of you today?" Glancing at his calendar, he said "We don't have an appointment till the end of next month, unless something's up?" Ian got up and made his way around his desk looking concerned.

"No, nothing to be concerned about," Anne said quickly. "We just had a question about sex during pregnancy."

"A-Anne," Meghan sang, embarrassed, looking down at the floor, cheeks turning red.

"Oh, is that all?" Ian smiled understanding Meghan's embarrassment. "Well take a seat, you two," Ian directing them to the vacant chairs in front of his desk and returned to his own. "What do you want to know?"

"Firstly, is it safe?" Anne asked looking over at Meghan shifting uneasily in her chair.

"Yes, it's safe in the first two trimesters but you need to be a bit more cautious in the third."

"Is it safe for the baby?" Meghan asked.

"Your baby is fully protected by the amniotic sac and the strong muscles of the uterus, which are also sealed by thick mucus at the cervix, which will help guard against infections," Ian explained.

"Secondly, is it safe to have sex with Michael?" Anne asked.

"I don't see why not. They found themselves in this situation without any risk."

"Ah well, that's debatable," Meghan said shyly.

"What do you mean by that, Meghan?" Ian asked leaning forward in his chair.

"Our first and only encounter was a bit — how can I put it?"

Meghan struggled in explaining to Ian what happened between them with Michael ending up feeding off her.

"Intense?" Ian asked.

"Yes, that too, but no," Meghan started to get rather nervous, which made her heart race and body sweat. Anne knew that Michael bit her but didn't know the full extent of the experience and now wondered what Meghan didn't tell her that could be so awkward.

"Meghan, you need to find the words to explain your concern, otherwise I can't help you," Ian said getting edgy.

"Do you want me to leave and talk to Ian alone?" Anne asked.

"No, no, please stay. Just promise me you won't tell Grandpa?" Meghan asked looking at Ian.

"I promise, what we discuss here is between us," Ian assured Meghan. Anne got up to close the door for privacy when she noticed Michael standing in the hallway looking at her as if he saw a ghost. Anne nodded to him and saying nothing, closed the door and took her seat. Taking Meghan's hand, she gave her a little squeeze for reassurance.

"As you know, Michael gave me a little of his blood to be able to be strong enough to handle him. It made it easier but he had to concentrate so hard." Meghan felt tears running down her cheek. "When he transformed, I found it beautiful, erotic, yet the power of it and all the energy he used not to hurt me was commanding. I want him so badly but at the same time I'm terrified, especially now that I'm pregnant," Meghan wept.

"Did he?" Ian asked.

"Did he what?" Meghan asked, confused.

"Did he hurt you?"

"Yes, a little, but the vamp blood took care of it. Then after a while, he needed nourishment and because we ran out, he took some from me."

"What?"

"Just a little. He didn't want to, but I made him do it. He won't let that happen again. He would make sure of that," Meghan said quickly.

"Meghan, no wonder Michael won't come near you," Ian advised. "I'll talk to him."

"You will?" Meghan asked enthusiastically. "For or against us making love?" she then wondered.

"I'll see what he says first but under the circumstances, we are all inexperienced as far as human and vampire relationships go. They normally don't end well," Ian said as he picked up the phone and requested the person on the other end to send Michael to his office.

Three seconds later, there was a knock at the door. Anne got up and opened it to find Michael not looking very happy staring back at her. Clearing her throat, she excused herself and left as Michael took her seat.

THAT EVENING BEFORE dinner, they all filtered into the den for cocktails. Anne sat next to Luc, closest to the now-lit fireplace, joined by Roman and Mia, then Florence and Ian, all making themselves comfortable in the overstuffed wingback chairs. Sir Robert was entertaining the three councilors on the other end of the den when Meghan walked in alone. Anne noticed her first. She got up, excused herself and made her way to her.

"What's wrong?" Anne asked straight away.

"Nothing — everything — and then some," Meghan replied sadly.

"Do you want to talk about it?"

"Yes, after dinner if you have time."

"Certainly," Anne replied, taking her hand and leading her back to where she was sitting.

"Good evening, Meghan. Where's Michael?" Ian asked.

"I don't think he will be joining us this evening," Meghan said solemnly.

"Oh, why not?" Florence asked.

Suddenly Meghan got up and ran out of the room; shocked, Anne got up to follow when Ian stopped her. "Let her go."

"What the hell happened after I left this morning?" Anne asked Ian staring down at him.

"Sit," he replied sternly. Surprised by his tone, Anne sat; everyone looked at each other waiting for an explanation which didn't come.

In silence, they ate dinner. Thereafter, Anne took Mia aside and claimed to the others they were going for a walk in the garden.

"What's going on?" Mia asked, feeling the tension.

"We need to find Meghan," Anne replied.

"I don't think she went out too far; it's dark already. Besides, we can't run around the island with these dresses on," Mia commented, eyeing their designer silk creations.

"You're right," Anne replied. "Meet me here in fifteen minutes."

FORTY-THREE

RETURNING IN JEANS and a sweater, Anne found Mia pacing, holding her raincoat. "Ready?" Anne asked. Mia nodded. "This way," she said. Anne followed, knowing Mia could pick up Meghan's scent as they went along. Running over the wet lawns down to the beach, they got to the docks where they found Meghan sitting at the edge of the illuminated pier, rocking and holding herself.

"Thank God we found you," Anne said with relief. "Meghan, what's going on?"

"Do you know that this is where I met Michael?" Meghan said ignoring Anne's question.

"No, I didn't," Anne said sitting down next to her, dangling her legs over the jetty, Mia doing the same but on the other side of Meghan. They all looked out into the moonless night for a few moments. "It's here where he did that stupid experiment to see how long he can stand being in the sun without protection. It nearly killed him." Meghan smiled at the memory.

"He did what?" Mia asked concerned.

"Yep, his skin was scorched and his body drained, stupid fool. I was foolish enough to fall in love with him there and then. I wonder what happened with once bitten, twice shy. I should have stuck to that." Meghan shook her head and rubbed her belly. "Now this."

"Meghan, what's going on?" Anne asked, taking Meghan's hand in hers.

"It's over," Meghan sighed.

"What's over?" Mia asked.

"Michael and I, our little team," Meghan sighed again. "He's moving out of our room as we speak."

Anne looked over at Mia with surprise on her face. "Oh Meghan, tell us what happened," Anne asked.

"After you left, Ian discussed Michael's fears in having sex with me while pregnant. It turned out he would rather move out and stay away than risk endangering the baby and me."

"Could Ian not give him advice?" Mia asked.

"How? Ian isn't having a sexual relationship with a pregnant human," Meghan said getting up and walking off the dock onto the beach.

"I know for a fact there are other ways of satisfying sexual tension," Mia advised, getting up and following Meghan, with Anne pacing behind them.

"Yeah, well maybe you should let him know what they are," Meghan yelled out of frustration and anger.

"You're such a little drama queen, you know that?" Mia yelled back at her.

"Fuck you," Meghan turned facing Mia.

"No, fuck you," Mia replied.

"Hey, hey, stop that, both of you. Come on, ladies, settle down," Anne shouted angrily. "Mia, back off. Meghan is upset; she doesn't need to be tormented right now."

"Then answer me this: if you love him so much, why didn't you ask him what he wants? Compromise, do something, anything," Mia asked.

"Because he didn't give me the chance to, that's why," Meghan replied. "He stormed out of Ian's office and I haven't seen him since. On my way to supper, Calvin and Brad came up to our room with boxes saying they were to remove his clothes and personal items," Meghan started to cry again.

"Shit, that Irish temper — we both have that, with a good dose of stubbornness. God, I'm sorry, Meghan. He can be such an ass sometimes," Mia said sympathetically and made a note to talk to him about it as soon as she got back.

"Thanks," Meghan replied calming down again, "but I still don't have a solution to this problem. I'm still a horny pregnant woman, now without the man I love more than life itself." Meghan stood there looking back at them, defeated. The sight of Meghan pulled at Anne's heart and sorrow twisted deep in her guts. "Oh, Meghan," Anne whispered. Looking past her, Anne noticed a silhouette of a man walking toward them. Mia seemed to know who it was and started with vamp speed toward him and with her electric current, sent him flying back about a hundred meters. "Oh my God, what's she doing?" Anne said, shocked at the sight. "What?" Meghan then realized something has transpired and slowly turned around to look at what Anne was staring at. Not able to see too much, they made out two silhouettes of even height hovering a few feet off the ground.

"Anne, do you see what I see?" Meghan asked as she started walking toward the hovering duo.

"Meghan, no don't," Anne said, trying to keep Meghan from advancing, but curiosity took over. So instead, she took Meghan's hand and joined her. Slowly, they walked toward Mia, and as they got closer, they recognized Michael clearly in pain as Mia held him by the throat.

"Mia, let him go — now," Anne shouted.

Losing concentration, Mia let go and they both fell back to the ground, lying unconscious in the sand. "Are they dead?" Meghan asked as Anne ran over to check up on them. "Of course they're dead, but I'm not sure if they dead, dead," Anne replied looking over Michael's limp body.

Mia started to laugh. "It will take more than that to kill a vampire. Besides, he's my twin brother. I can't kill him even if I wanted to."

"You still fight like a girl," Michael finally murmured as he slowly gained consciousness.

"Really, now," Mia got up and gave him a hand. "Do you want to go through that again?"

"No, thanks, once was painful enough," Michael said taking her hand to help lift himself up. Looking around, he saw Meghan heading up the stairs toward the Manor.

"Meghan wait; we need to talk," Michael yelled as he ran toward her.

Anne stood staring at Mia, trying to wrap her brain around what just happened. "Michael got the message; I'm sure they'll sort it all out," Mia said bringing Anne back to reality.

Michael caught up to Meghan and fell into pace with her, walking briskly across the lawn in silence. Meghan tried to find the words for all the emotions spinning through her, and then she abruptly stopped. Michael still in pace took two steps before he realized she had stopped. He then turned around to find her staring at him with her big, brown, doe eyes. It staked him; he was paralyzed and unable to say a word. *God what have I done?* he thought, seeing the pain in her face.

"Why?" Meghan then managed to ask as a tear ran down her cheek.

"I'm terrified, I'm a coward and I'm so, so sorry," Michael said falling to his knees. "I know I'm asking for forgiveness a lot lately but please, Meghan, forgive me," he pleaded.

"You hurt me deeply, Michael," Meghan said as she stepped toward him, taking his head and holding it against her. Michael, in turn, wrapped his arms around her waist, holding her tightly. "I'm not sure I can trust you with my heart; it felt as if you ripped it out and stomped on it," Meghan whispered. Michael winced at her words. "Meghan, please don't shut me out. I realize I've made a very big mistake," he pleaded. "This is all very new to me."

Meghan, taking his face in her hands, looked into his eyes and said, "I realize that. I'm as scared as you are, if not more, being human. I need you to promise me that you'll never run off from a problem again. We have to sort it out together, use each other's strengths to get through," Meghan suggested.

"Please forgive me," Michael replied.

"I forgive you, but you will have to earn the trust back."

"That's all I ask for," he said. Getting up and taking her into his arms, he kissed her, slowly and tenderly at first, then as the heat built in them, they hungrily tasted each other.

"Michael don't — don't start something you can't finish," Meghan pleaded between their kisses.

"This is where I start earning your trust back." Michael smiled, bent over to pick her up, and carried her back to the Manor to their room where she discovered he had not packed up his things after all.

FORTY-FOUR

FOUR MONTHS LATER, Florence received word that Sire Raymond Pitout was back in Vancouver and this time they were not letting him slip through their fingers again.

Florence and her team spent hours planning and communicating with other councilors' security teams and a plan was put together meticulously.

Over the weeks of incarceration, Florence convinced Adrian, her once top security man, to return to her team. She couldn't trust him fully so she had Mia shadow him wherever he went. It struck fear into him, believing putting one foot wrong he would be terminated. He finally agreed to help in exchange for his "life."

Florence was to use him to fish out Sire Pitout by putting the word out that Adrian escaped capture and he went underground until such time Sire Pitout contacted him through various channels made available to him.

∞

IN THE MEANTIME, life was growing in Meghan's womb and by the end of the second trimester, Ian thought it would be a good time to check the baby's progress and he brought in the sonogram again. Meghan was lying in the medical examining room with Ian on one side, Anne and Michael on the other. All were a little apprehensive and a little excited to find out how the baby was progressing.

Ian, first checking for the heartbeat, found the whoosh-whoosh sound again, making everyone smile. Then after a squirt of cold gel, Ian took the end of the sonogram and watched the images on the monitor as he moved from side to side of Meghan's large abdomen. "Oh, thank God," he said.

"What is it?" everyone asked together.

"It's a girl, which, according to the report, means the baby must be human. Hybrids born previously have all been boys."

Michael grabbed Anne and gave her a big hug. "Yes, it's a girl." Letting go of Anne and bending down to Meghan, he kissed her all over her face. "She's going to be our little Gem," he said and kissed her deeply. Meghan tried to push him off her, feeling very embarrassed about kissing him in front of everyone. The news of the new baby girl was celebrated that night with the rest of the family and council members.

∞

FINALLY, A MONTH LATER, Adrian sent word that he made contact with Sire Pitout and his coven and a plan was put into action. Adrian met up with Sire Pitout at one of his secret lairs, which was an abandoned warehouse in an industrial area located on the Fraser River.

Once Florence received the location of the warehouse and

confirmation that Sire Pitout was there, she called in Sir Robert's team and her security men for a meeting.

Sir Robert sat to one side listening to Florence as she went through the different strategies involving Roman, Mia, Brad, and Christopher in one team coming in by boat and Michael, Florence, and Dale by air. The ground crew will be Aldridge's four men, Wright's three men, and Coupler's five men; they were to enter the warehouse in various locations.

"Okay, where do I fit in all this?" Luc asked as he realized Florence didn't include him in the plan.

"Luc, you're coordinating the plan from the house. It's not worth risking a Feeder," Florence advised.

"But —"

"Whether you like it or not, it's an order," Florence said sternly, seeing his reaction to her statement. "I need you to run the command center back at the house; take Anne with you."

"Roman, Michael: go down to the armory and organize the team's weapons. Dale, prepare the Black Hawk to get it ready and armed," she ordered.

Returning her attention to Luc, she said, "On your way back to the mainland, you'll need to take the ground crew with you. They can get into the required vehicles from there." Looking at her watch, she said, "Lady and gentlemen, get as much nourishment and rest as possible. I want everyone ready to depart by two o'clock and at the warehouse in their designated positions by five. Dawn is when Sire Pitout is sluggish and with the element of surprise, we'll have him in our custody."

Luc found Anne with Meghan in their room sitting by the fire. They could not sleep with all the activities and excitement in the Manor since they found out Sire Pitout was back in town. "Well, what's the plan?" Anne asked Luc as he entered the room.

"You and I will be back at Safe Haven coordinating the command center. Florence does not want to risk having me involved with the takedown," Luc said with disappointment.

"Well, that takes a load off my shoulders," Anne got up and walked to Luc and put her arms around his waist. "I know you would like the action but we're important to them alive."

"What about Michael?" Meghan asked apprehensively.

"He will be with Florence and Dale in the helicopter; they plan to penetrate the warehouse from the roof a few minutes after the ground crew gets into position," Luc advised.

"Luc, may I join you and Anne at Safe Haven? I need to be able to hear what's going on to keep sane," Meghan asked, rubbing her belly.

"Sure, but I'll run it past Florence first," Luc said as he kissed Anne on the forehead. "If you would excuse me, I need to freshen up," he made his way to the bathroom.

"I should go back to my room; it's late, and we all need our rest before things start getting busy. Give me a ring when it's time to get ready," Meghan said as she got up, gave a quick peck on Anne's cheek, and left the room.

After Luc's quick shower, they had food sent up to the room to eat and made a call to Florence. They were in bed by eleven, wishing for a few hours sleep that didn't come.

◥◉◉◤

AT TWO O CLOCK, Luc was in the Bell 430 with his passengers and Dale was in his Black Hawk with his, making their way over to the mainland. Adrenalin pumped through Luc's veins as he went back to the Manor to pick up the rest of the ground crew, Meghan and Anne. By five o'clock, everyone was in place ready to go. The ground crew was the first to enter the warehouse, made possible by Adrian shutting the alarm down and unlocking the doors. It was still dark but, being vampires, that wasn't an issue and diligence was needed to execute the surprise effectively.

Luc, Anne, and Meghan sat in the command center, listening to the crew's low tone conversations as to where they were and what they saw. Every now and again, they would hear a vampire's sword slash through another, to keep everything as quiet as possible. They carried guns, which would be used once the element of surprise had been compromised, but the swords were the weapon of choice at the moment.

Aldridge's four men were the first to find Sire Raymond Pitout's quarters; they advised the rest. Florence sent Roman's team to join them, knowing Mia would be the best to bring Raymond down without killing him. He was the only one to be brought out of there alive. Wright's three men and Coupler's five found Sire Pitout's army's resting quarters and had their hands full eliminating them as they slept. Some woke sensing their presence and a few fights broke out.

IN THE MEANWHILE, Roman's team arrived at Raymond's quarters, followed by Florence and Michael. They found him resting with a female vampire. As they staked her, she was able to scream, waking the man up to find himself surrounded by Sir Robert McKay's security team. "Good morning," Mia said as she put a couple of volts through him, which rendered the man unconscious. Turning him around onto his back, they found it wasn't Sire Raymond.

"Well, well, well, if it isn't Sir Robert's security team," came a voice from behind drapery dividing the room.

"Shit," Mia said and looked up at Florence. They realized they had been compromised.

⑥⑥

LUC FOUND THE whole plan executed very smoothly until now. He looked over to Anne and Meghan looking back at him with the same fear and surprise he felt. Turning his attention back to the situation at the warehouse, he advised Wright's and Coupler's men to join the rest as soon as possible, as they needed help — they've been ambushed.

⑥⑥

FLORENCE AND HER team found themselves surrounded by two to three dozen men with swords and Sire Raymond standing a little ahead of them in the center of the room. A little over to one side was Adrian with a smirk on his face.

"So you still believe Raymond will give you everything?" Florence aimed her question at Adrian, and then looked over to Raymond. "What did you promise Adrian for his loyalty?"

"Ah, this and that," Raymond smirked. "A little more than what you can offer him," Raymond replied walking up to Adrian with sword in hand tilting it up onto his own shoulder and resting the other hand on Adrian's.

"More than his life?" Florence asked gripping her sword so hard she could feel it bend a little.

"No!" Raymond replied and with vamp speed stepped back and swung his sword toward Adrian, decapitating him. Adrian's body, still holding his sword, fell to the ground hard. As it did so, Raymond's men attacked from all sides, Mia seeking Raymond out, made her way toward him, sending bolts of energy through Raymond's men as she did so. Aldridge's four men, Florence, Roman, and Michael held their own with swords flying left and right, slicing through air and flesh, killing as many men as they could.

JUST AS LUC thought the situation was getting out of hand, he heard Wright's and Coupler's men arrive. Then he heard Mia screaming, sending a charge through Raymond as he put a silver bullet into Michael's chest. Luc tried to slam down the mute button on the control panel, but it was too late: Meghan heard the shot and Mia shouting out Michael's name.

EVERYTHING WAS SILENT in the warehouse. Mia held her brother in her arms as his energy started to leave him. "Florence, what's happening to him?" Mia sobbed. Florence made her way to Mia, putting her hand on her shoulder. "He's dying, Mia. The silver in the bullet is poison and it hit the heart directly; he hasn't a chance. God, I'm so sorry," Florence said.

"Me—gh—an," Michael whispered looking up at Mia.

Roman came over to where they were and picked Michael up. As he did so, he looked into Mia's eyes. Seeing anger and hate in them, he knew what she had to do. Mia followed his gaze to where Raymond lay unconscious. Florence noticed the exchange. "No, Mia, we'll bring him in for judgment and termination rendered by the council, not by you," she said, holding Mia back. "You will have your revenge, I promise you." Florence then lifted Mia up with her and assessed the room. "Roman, take Mia and Michael to the helicopter. I'm on my way with Raymond. The rest of you complete the mission."

"TELL ME HE'S all right." Meghan looked at Luc pleading for a positive answer. "I don't know, Meghan. I heard what you heard;

maybe it was Mia warning Michael to get out of the way," Luc replied looking over at Anne for some help. As the mute was still on, none of them knew what was going on. "Luc, I'll take Meghan out to get something to drink while you find out what's going on," Anne added.

"No! I want to stay," Meghan pleaded.

"Meghan, please, come with me. We're just speculating and this is upsetting you and the baby. Once we have the facts, Luc will let us know what happened. Come now," Anne said as she walked Meghan out the room.

ꙮ

FLORENCE PICKED UP Raymond's unconscious body and joined the rest in the helicopter; the crews below doused the warehouse with various chemicals. Dale airlifted Florence and the team out of harm's way. He then waited for confirmation that everyone on the ground was a safe distance from the warehouse. He shot a missile into the building, destroying it.

ꙮ

ANNE AND MEGHAN were sitting in the kitchen with a cup of tea each when they heard the helicopter land in the back of the property. Running out to meet them, they saw Roman carrying Michael's limp body, followed by Mia and then Florence. Dale took off again with Raymond with instructions to deliver him to Sir Robert's Manor for incarceration and to bring Ian back to the house again.

Meghan's heart sank deep into a bottomless pit when she saw Michael. Roman laid him down on one of the sofas in the sitting room. Meghan noticed his skin turning grey and his eyes, when open, glazed. "What happened?" Meghan asked softly. "He was shot with a silver bullet," Florence replied solemnly, standing behind her and putting her hands on her shoulders. Giving them space, Luc, Anne, and Roman stood at the doorway, quietly watching while Mia sat on the sofa with Michael's head on her lap, Meghan kneeling beside him holding his hand. "Meg—love," Michael stammered.

"Shh, keep your strength. Ian will be here soon," Meghan whispered.

"Meghan, I'm sorry but there's no chance . . ." Florence broke off and walked out of the room.

"What do you mean no chance? For what?" Meghan looked concerned in what Florence was trying to say.

"Meghan, he's dying," Mia wept.

"No! Michael, stay with me." Meghan lifted herself up and held Michael's head up, shaking him a little. "Michael — focus — darling — Michael," Meghan pleaded.

"Promise me, you — stay — human," Michael said and with all the energy he had left, he grabbed Meghan's hand and brought it to his mouth and kissed it.

"I promise. I love you so much; please don't leave me."

"I'll — be with — love you — eternity," Michael gasped.

Meghan felt his grip loosen. His eyes closed. "Michael, no, please — Oh, God." Meghan sobbed and started to shake and cramped up with a surge of pure pain going through her body. Buckling over, she held her belly, which went hard as a rock. Then warm liquid ran down her legs. "O God, no, not now!" Meghan wailed.

"Oh, shit," Anne said and ran over to Meghan. "Her water broke; get her over to the sofa," Anne asked Luc now standing beside them and helped Meghan get to the sofa opposite Michael's. Mia, still holding Michael's head rocking as she cried, was oblivious to what was happening around her. Florence, hearing the tone in the room, ran back to find Meghan in serious pain.

She asked Roman to take care of Mia and Michael while the rest of them got Meghan up to one of the spare bedrooms.

AN HOUR LATER, Ian arrived and found Meghan nearly fully dilated. He determined the shock of Michael's death brought the labor of their baby on faster than normal.

"Meghan, when did you feel the first contraction?" Ian asked when another painful contraction eased.

"When — I heard the gun shot and Mia scream Michael's name." Meghan replied, panting to get air and sitting up a little more to do so.

"That was four hours ago; why didn't you tell me?" Anne asked stunned, patting Meghan's face with a cool wet cloth.

"I thought it was one of those false contracts — shit, here comes another one," Meghan said squeezing Anne's hand. "Focus on me, Meghan, and breathe like we practiced," Anne stated as she took a deep breath held it and let it out. Luc smiled from the bedroom door, watching his wife coaching, wondering when it will be their turn. He then noticed Ian and Florence getting everything ready for the birth: towels, hot water, medical supplies, and instruments. The look of them made him a little nervous. Roman interrupted Luc's intense concentration on the activities in the room when he brought Mia up. "May we come in?" Roman asked at the door getting everyone's attention. "Sure," Ian replied, looking at Meghan as she blew out air; she nodded her head in acknowledgement. Anne patted the side of the bed for Mia to sit next to them and noticed her eyes were red from crying.

Meghan felt pressure build, giving her the urge to push. Taking in a big breath, filling her lungs with air and holding it, she pushed down. "What are you doing?" Anne asked.

"I need to push – shit, the pain," Meghan cried. "I can't do this

— make it stop," she pleaded. "Ian, can we give her something for the pain?" Anne asked, concerned.

"Yes, but not quite yet. I don't have any medication that will help, but a little vamp blood will do the trick. Meghan, we need you to hold out with the pain a little longer," Ian explained.

"Shit no – now, I need help now!" Meghan screamed through another contraction, sweat beading on her forehead and a glare of pain in her eyes. Luc couldn't take it any longer and left the room with Roman close on his tail.

MAKING THEIR WAY to the den, they found the whiskey and poured themselves each a full glass and swallowed it as if it were water. "What a fuckin' day," Roman said as he slammed his empty glass down and refilled it. Another scream coming from the top floor made Luc refill his, too.

AN HOUR LATER, there was an eerie quietness in the house, and then finally, a tiny wail of a newborn infant filled the air.

As Luc and Roman entered the room, they found Meghan holding her baby. "She's perfect; everything is where it should be," she said, looking down at her little girl she and Michael created with sadness, remembering she would never meet her father. Tears ran down her cheeks with joy and sadness as she heard her little Gem start to cry, too. "She may be a little hungry, Meghan," Ian advised. Taking the infant, he wrapped her up in a clean towel and laid a pillow on Meghan's lap, making it easier for her to latch onto Meghan's breast. As soon as she latched on, Meghan felt the milk come in and a tugging sensation in her belly and then a strange sting that surprised her. "Shit, that hurt," Meghan moaned. "I think she bit me."

"What?" Ian asked with concern.

"I think she just bit me; get her off me," Meghan said with panic.

"Meghan, hold on, we can't just rip her off you," Ian replied, looking over at Florence who was now next to him. Anne and Mia sitting on the other side of the bed got up to help, but what could they do? Little Gem was latched and sucking hungrily on Meghan's breast.

"Actually, it feels quite pleasant now," Meghan smiled. "Let her finish, then we'll see what she has done." Meghan felt a feeling of contentment, peace, and joy as her little girl fed from her. As she fell asleep, filled and satisfied, Ian took her and lay her in a padded hamper Florence dug out for the newborn to sleep in. As he did so, Meghan found two tiny puncture marks on one side of her nipple. "She has fangs," Meghan said, startled with the discovery. "My little Gem has fangs." Meghan started to laugh. "She has a little of Michael in her."

After the realization that Gem was a *hybrid* — the first female of their kind — Florence advised Sir Robert of their discovery, which was received with happiness and concern.

FORTY-FIVE

∞

DALE GOT SIRE Raymond Pitout back to the Manor and into the security quarters without incident. However, it didn't take long for the International Vampire Council to find out about his capture and it wanted him expedited to Europe for charges against him there. The Celtics also wanted a piece of him, but Sir Robert McKay and his council refused to comply with these orders. At first, as they felt they took the risks apprehending him and losing one of their own, they felt they had every right to terminate him themselves. However, Sir Robert found the International Vampire Council had more authority over his, so they reluctantly handed him over to them.

∞

MIA FELT A LOT better since she executed Roy and witnessed the destruction of Adrian, but the capture of Sire Raymond Pitout was bittersweet and short-lived. His expedition to the International Vampire Council in Europe was an unexpected turn, so she made sure she would accompany his transfer. She personally handed him over to the IVC and planned to stay there until he was executed.

∞

ROMAN WOULD BE patient with Mia and would wait for eternity for her to become fully his. He secretly loved her but that would be revealed once she was ready to hear it.

∞

LUC AND ANNE would have children eventually; for now, they lived as Feeders for the vampires and made their home in Luc's cabin. Anne closed her office but still volunteered at the hospital and helped Ian out as much as she could. Jen, her friend and colleague, found another job and stayed in contact with Anne.

∞

MEGHAN RAISED HER daughter, feeding her some of her blood and Michael's blood that was stored. He, like always, planned ahead just in case, as he did with his sperm, which Meghan would use eventually, but not for a while yet.

∞

SIR ROBERT MCKAY kept a tight rein on his family and council members. He was a stern man and he learned that many things are not always simple with a lot of surprises on the way. His many-great-grandchild would be one of those surprises and he looked forward to watching her grow. . . .

LaVergne, TN USA
08 October 2010
200002LV00002B/10/P